"No more, please, Wanmdi Hota, no more," Alisha begged as she slipped in and out of consciousness. The green-eyed beauty felt her warrior upon her naked and eager body. His lips were upon her lips, his heart beat against her heart; they were entwined in the arms of love.

Alisha's mind swirled in a peaceful, intoxicating sea as Gray Eagle entered her to skillfully—almost desperately—make love to her. She had no strength to deny him as he fiercely and possessively held her in his strong embrace.

Alisha tossed in a feverish world while Gray Eagle's fiery kisses burned her willing mouth and branded her creamy breasts. And as she gasped with remembered pleasure, she cried out in her sleep, "Oh why, my love, why? Why did you love me—then leave me to die? . . ."

BESTSELLING ROMANCES BY JANELLE TAYLOR

SAVAGE ECSTASY (824, $3.50)

It was like lightning striking, the first time the Indian brave Gray Eagle looked into the eyes of the beautiful young settler Alisha. And from the moment he saw her, he knew that he must possess her—and make her his slave!

DEFIANT ECSTASY (931, $3.50)

When Gray Eagle returned to Fort Pierre's gates with his hundred warriors behind him, Alisha's heart skipped a beat: would Gray Eagle destroy her—or make his destiny her own?

FORBIDDEN ECSTASY (1014, $3.50)

Gray Eagle had promised Alisha his heart forever—nothing could keep him from her. But when Alisha woke to find her red-skinned lover gone, she felt abandoned and alone. Lost between two worlds, desperate and fearful of betrayal, Alisha hungered for the return of her FORBIDDEN ECSTASY.

FORBIDDEN ECSTASY

BY JANELLE TAYLOR

ZEBRA BOOKS
KENSINGTON PUBLISHING CORP.

ZEBRA BOOKS

are published by

KENSINGTON PUBLISHING CORP.
475 Park Avenue South
New York, N.Y. 10016

Printed in the United States of America

For Sheila T. and Sara K., two great friends and proofreaders . . .

Acknowledgement to:

Hiram C. Owen of Sisseton, South Dakota, for all of his help with the Sioux language and helpful facts about the inspiring Sioux nation. Thank you . . .

The Last Farewell

The sun and sand called out to her,
"Betrayal!" they chanted in fiery unison.
He was gone forever more, never to return, to reclaim.
The sun burned his words of defeat into her brain;
Hot, dry winds lashed at her tormented flesh.
They jointly mocked her sufferings,
They chided her naiveté, her folly, her dreams;
Without warning, the time for turning back had come.
Her heart was rent by loss, by needless sacrifice . . .
At last, the sun slowly sank into the earth's golden bosom,
Releasing her from her nightmares and unbearable
   agonies.
The zephyr winds blew softly now,
Releasing her from their stinging cruelty.
It had ended, as suddenly and painfully as it had begun.
Her mind pleaded retreat, but her warring heart rebelled,
Against the torment involved—

                                    in the last farewell . . .

Chapter One

The waiting seemed endless, threatening. It tugged at Alisha's senses like an indistinct yet imminent danger. But she did not know why. She was plagued by two needs: a fierce craving for water and a hunger for Gray Eagle's return. She was uncertain as to which desire loomed foremost in her mind; then she realized the answer was his speedy return, for that would solve all her problems and fears. The heat and glare of the sun were merciless, tormenting. The sun seemed to possess the power to sear both flesh and mind as it intimately caressed the sands with its shimmering fingers.

Still, an eerie presentiment continued; no, it grew heavier and deadlier as time passed by. Alisha shaded her jade-green eyes, now streaked with red from the sun's incessant brightness. She studied the horizon. As her eyes slowly searched the landscape, the only movements she could detect were the vacillating heatwaves between the sun and sand which spun mirages and ghostly chimeras. At that time, Alisha would have been overjoyed to see anyone or anything. The feeling of total aloneness inspired brief moments of insanity . . . or the dread of being in its thrall.

Alisha's thoughts tumbled and changed focus as if trapped in a kaleidoscope. She wondered why Gray Eagle had not returned. He had been gone for nearly two days now. She feared he had been attacked by some enemy tribe, perhaps injured or killed. No, her frenzied mind screamed. She would not even think such impossible thoughts. She must assume that something had delayed his prompt return to her side.

Alisha had already debated the idea of trying to follow his faint trail or to retrace her own path to the Si-Ha Sapa village. She had dismissed both ideas; on the open plains, distance and direction were quickly distorted. She could just as easily wind up in some enemy camp herself or become lost in the vast wasteland. She had no choice but to wait for Gray Eagle or for a messenger from him.

If only he had left her horse behind or some food and water . . . but he had said that he needed her horse to carry their supplies on his return trip. He had also told her that he needed to carry the water skins with him in order to refill them. He had stated he would be back within a few hours, but that had been two days ago. Now, here she sat waiting for him, without food or water or a means of escape.

She laughed softly. Escape . . . there was no longer any need or desire for escape from him. They were married now. He had vowed his love for her. How very intoxicating those words had sounded: "Ni-ye mitawa; waste cedake, Cinstinna." Her heart beat happily as the memories of the past months raced wildly through her thoughts. So very much had changed in only a few short months—and now she possessed everything that she had ever dreamed of. She had Gray Eagle, his love, his acceptance, and unbelievably her own acceptance as the daughter of Chief Black Cloud of the Si-Ha Sapa.

So many events—terrifying, ecstatic, incredible—had led to her acceptance by Gray Eagle and by his people. It seemed as if Fate were charting her new existence. Otherwise, there was no logical explanation for this sudden and exhilarating change in the direction of her destiny. Soon, she and Wanmdi Hota would return to his village, and a whole new and wonderful life would begin for them.

Alisha told herself she should not worry about his safety. She chided herself; was he not heralded as the greatest warrior of all time? Was he not a living legend to both friend and foe? The mere mention of his name, the sight of him, the deadly tone of his voice could drive terror and respect into the heart of any man who might be tempted to oppose him. He had proven his great courage, daring, cunning, and intelligence numerous times. He awed both white men and Indians. No one would dare to resist his intrepid authority. For certain, she knew what it was like to go against his wishes or commands.

Yes, she could remember what it was like. But the time had come for complete forgiving and forgetting. Surely, in time, all the bad memories would vanish completely. When he was at her side, nothing else mattered. He was her life; he was her future. In truth, Alisha loved Gray Eagle more than life itself.

Yes, she unwillingly remembered. . . . Yet, she decided that it was worth the price she had paid, all the pain and suffering, for she had finally won her heart's desire. There had been so many days and nights when she had doubted her very survival; yet, she was alive, well, and happy. There had also been countless times when she had faced his brutality and hatred; yet, she had finally won his love and his acceptance. She had changed greatly in these past months. She had learned so many things about life and love, but she had learned so much more about herself.

She was a woman now, a married woman, and she was deeply in love with her husband. Gray Eagle had taught her love. No longer did it matter that she was white and that he was Indian—at least, it mattered not to them. In fact, it seemed incredulous that the Gray Eagle she had married was the same warrior who had killed her uncle, destroyed her fortress, and ordered the deaths of many whites. It was hard to imagine those same lips which had kissed her so gently and passionately and had spoken such tender words of love to her were the same lips which had ordered her punishment and humiliation so many times in the past. It was as it had been on other occasions, as if there were two men sharing the same powerful body. The Gray Eagle that she knew in private was not the same fierce and deadly warrior that he presented in public. Yet, there was an inseparable intermingling of both men on nearly all occasions.

Even now, Alisha found it difficult to mentally describe him or to understand him completely. For some unknown reason, she had fallen hopelessly in love with him at their very first meeting. Perhaps that meeting had been the real reason for the ensuing warfare between them. He had first met her as his deadly enemy, as a captive of her people. How cruelly they had treated him! But his bravery and virile magnetism had drawn her to him that very first moment their eyes had met and fused.

In spite of the heat, Alisha shivered as she recalled that ominous look which had been in Gray Eagle's stygian eyes as her people had beaten and mocked him. His glance alone should have warned them of the great power he was capable of unleashing. It had gone unnoticed, a tragic error which had cost them all of their lives, all except hers. But then, she had not hated, abused, or taunted him. No, she had sided with him and had helped him at a great personal price. Perhaps it had been predestined for all of the others to die and for her to live. Still, the pain of her losses haunted her. She wondered if she would ever know her full role in the deadly events of

. the last fateful day of her village . . .

She sadly shook her head to clear it of these unwanted reflections. No doubt it was a combination of the heat and her solitude which had brought them to mind. Her eyes eagerly searched the horizon once more, praying he would return and all would be well. She sighed lightly as she hugged her knees to her breasts, the sigh only serving to remind her of her thirst. The dryness of her lips and throat made it difficult to swallow. Never had she been this thirsty in her entire life. Immediately her weary mind challenged her.

Yes, she had. There were two other times she could recall being this thirsty. There was that day not so very long ago when she had endured the long march from her devastated fortress to the Oglala camp, that time when she had feared Gray Eagle the most. And then there was the time when she had foolishly escaped his camp and his tormenting love, the time when he had rescued her. And both times he had saved her life in the midst of danger.

Alisha could not permit herself to closely analyze that day when Gray Eagle's tribe had attacked her people's fortress, destroying everything and everyone in sight. Even though she now knew his motives for such total and violent destruction, she had to force herself to suppress the bitterness and sadness that these unbidden memories renewed. She could understand both sides of this savage war between the white man and the red. To her, both were right; both were wrong.

Her troubled mind asked, will there ever be peace and acceptance between them? Will there ever be a joint settlement in this wondrous land?

She feared not, for the differences between them were too great, the hatred was too deep. Worst of all, she feared that neither side really wanted peace with the other; each only wanted the other banished from this area. She could not deny the fact that her people were the intruders in the New Land. They were the ones who were determined to possess this dreamland at any cost. They could not comprehend that the Indians would never turn their precious lands over to the white man without a bloody fight, a battle in which neither side could win.

Why must people hate and destroy? she thought. Why must they take what is not theirs? I recall all the many reasons why our own wagon train came West. I know my people's motives. I sympathize with them and the troubles they left behind. Yet, it changes nothing; the lands belong to the Indians. Don't they?

Tears came to her eyes, for she knew that others would eventually come here too. They would also ignore all the dangers and warnings just as her own people had done. They would listen to only the colorful tales of this glorious, untamed land where dreams were supposed to become realities. If they only knew the truth . . . those same dreams could easily become bloody nightmares.

There was only one way there could ever be peace; her people would have to learn to accept the Indians as equals. From what she had seen and experienced, it was not so. The whites simply viewed the Indians as wild animals to be killed or to be driven from their hunting grounds. But the Indians were people. They would never submit to such vile treatment. They would strike back in the only way left open to them: war.

It was inevitable that she would once again be caught in the middle of their wars. Perhaps Gray Eagle had been accurate when he had claimed that she was a white girl with an Indian heart. She had lived with his people. She had come to know their ways; she had accepted them as her new people. She realized that there would be no

16

problems if the constant war with her people and his did not exist. But it did. Dread clutched at her tender heart as she envisioned what would happen when more whites came and another bloody, futile battle began. There could be no choice in her loyalty; she was Gray Eagle's wife. She would be viewed as an Indian. How she feared the day when her devotion to him would be tested!

Wanmdi Hota's wife, the pleasant thought seized her and made her smile serenely. This was the fourth day of their marriage, but she had spent only two of those precious days with him. The day of their joining, she had been so consumed with fear and confusion that the hours had passed in a dreamlike trance. But Gray Eagle had understood Alisha's mixed feelings of excitement and dread. He had allowed her to escape the Blackfoot camp, only to follow after her with the truth of his love for her. How beautiful that second day and night had been. For the first time since she had met him, he had spoken to her in English! That moment had been the greatest shock of her entire life. It meant that he had always known and heard what was in her heart, had always understood every word that she had spoken aloud. Later, he had sworn her to secrecy about his knowledge of her tongue. Knowing how valuable this weapon was against the white man, she promised to keep it. She was pleased with this news, for it would be so much easier for him to teach her his own language. He had cautiously warned her that they could only speak her tongue in private.

That first morning when he had overtaken her during her desperate flight from his tormenting love and closeness, they had argued and talked for hours; secrets and desires of both their hearts had been vividly revealed. They were now joined for all time. So many things made sense to her. She could even comprehend what he had

17

done to her in the past and why. Still, a slight resentment remained in her mind against him. So much suffering on her part could have been avoided if he had trusted her sooner. He had recently proven his love and trust by finally revealing his secrets to her. Never again would there be any secrets between them.

With the lie that she was Chief Black Cloud's half-breed daughter accepted among the Sioux, Gray Eagle's honor could be left intact; his high rank could not be challenged or endangered. Only Gray Eagle knew the truth; yet, he had refused to reveal it, to betray her real identity. For only as an Indian maiden could she be accepted as the wife of Wanmdi Hota, son of Running Wolf, and chief of the feared and awesome Sioux. He wanted her as his wife, not as his white captive. His great desire to have her openly outweighed any feelings of guilt and treachery toward his people and his customs.

She had been surprised and shocked when he had informed her that no one, not even his father, must learn of her true identity as a mere white girl. He had also told her of Matu's timely death, that dauntless old woman who had first been her guard; later her friend and helper. It had been Matu's treachery which had given rise to the fabrication of her identity as Princess Shalee, long-lost daughter of Mahpiya Sapa. Perhaps it was a blessing in disguise that Alisha had so closely resembled this missing half-breed daughter. She absently rubbed the akito on her left buttock, mentally envisioning its cresent moon and two, small stars: tattoo symbol of her alleged father, the symbol Matu had carved and stained for all time.

Alisha concluded that such news could mean that only four living people knew the truth about her: Gray Eagle, White Arrow, Powchutu, and herself. It was certain that none of these would ever reveal the truth, for to do so meant dishonor for Gray Eagle and death for her. The pattern had been set; they all had to follow its guidelines.

Alisha mused, what harm could such an innocent lie do? It can only bring safety, happiness, and acceptance for all involved. I love Gray Eagle. I will not lose him, not now. I won his love at a great price, and I will not give it up. Where are you, my love? I need you. . . .

Her mind was flooded with memories of their brief life together. They had endured and overcome so many problems. It was only right that they could be together now. They were in love. All they wanted was to love each other, to be happy. Their differences could not possibly matter as much as their love. Nights of heated passion flickered in her thoughts; days of relaxed contentment in his tepee joined them. Theirs was a love which could survive all time. Oh how she yearned for his return!

Two days before he had set out to hunt and to refill their water skins. He had spoken of a lengthy stay in the nearby mountains, their Oglala honeymoon. This idea had thrilled her racing heart. This way, they could have the time and privacy to come to know each other as they never had before. She had anxiously waited where he had left her, but he had not as yet returned to her side.

The lovely young bride was thirsty, hungry, frightened, and fatigued. She had slept fitfully the night before. The perspiration caused by the extreme heat of the sun and its reflections on the golden sands had robbed her slender body of many of its precious fluids. Without water to replenish those vital fluids, her energy was also slowly evaporating. She could not decide who was in more danger, her or him. Thankfully the sun had begun to sink on the far horizon, warning her of a second night alone. It gradually disappeared, and her spirits vanished with it.

Where are you, Wanmdi Hota? her saddened heart cried out. I could not bear to lose you now, not when I have just found you.

The silence which answered her pleas seemed as a loud, ominous roar in her buzzing ears. She assumed that it was only the eerie solitude and her rising fear which was playing cruel tricks upon her tired senses. At last, there was nothing left of the flaming sun except pink streaks on the distant skyline, streaks shaped like fiery fingers clawing at the expanse of the dark blue sky.

At least she could be grateful for the release from the sun's heat and dazzling glare from the sands. She gently rubbed her tender eyes, knowing that their lack of moisture was not solely to blame on the demanding sun. She decided it was best that Wanmdi Hota had taken her beloved horse with him; Wildfire would only be suffering from the same fierce thirst which she was now enduring.

She massaged her arms to give some slight comfort to the tiny abrasions caused by the stinging sand which had dug into her flesh repeatedly during the past two days. It was uncommon for the wind to be so strong and violent at this time of year. It had reminded her of the Sirocco winds that she had read about—those strong, hot winds which blew across the Sahara Desert and wreaked their destructive will upon the nomads who lived there.

Nervous laughter filled her tight chest as she became aware of how deeply and seriously her panic was affecting her. She had just caught herself thinking of how it seemed that the very elements of sun, sand, and wind were calling out warnings to her, warnings that she did not belong in this untamed frontier. They appeared to be telling her that she was not innately suited to this arid, harsh land and climate.

But the sun had finally vanished, along with its torrid agony. The fierce winds had gradually subsided into gentle, zephyr-like breezes. There was nothing to keep her company now, nothing except the shadows of trees and plants, and the full, silvery-yellow moon climbing above the dark, distant mountains.

Alisha suddenly tensed. She was not alone; wails from several coyotes could be heard clearly in the distance. Hopefully it was true that coyotes did not normally attack and eat humans! She still trembled. Scenes from a similar night not long past washed over her. Strange, she had been awaiting Gray Eagle that night too. She defensively snuggled closer to the small tree in the sparse copse where he had left her.

If only I had some type of weapon, she fearfully and angrily reasoned. Somehow I've made it through two days and one night. Hopefully I can survive this coming one. Please come soon, she silently prayed.

But many hours passed with still no sign of her husband. Fatigue helplessly defeated her battle for awareness. She unknowingly slipped into a deep and dreamless slumber. She did not know when a tanned, muscular man eased down beside her. She did not see the intense way his jet black eyes hungrily roamed over her beautiful face and curvaceous body. She did not hear his ragged respiration as he struggled with the desire to awaken her and to make her his woman. Nor did she know of the cruelty and suffering which he would soon inflict upon her heart, her body, her soul. . . .

Chapter Two

Any type of cruelty toward Alisha was rare in him. It left a bitter taste in his mouth and a gnawing guilt in his mind. He eased down beside her to patiently await her awakening. From his point of view, there was no other way to save her from future harm; there was no other way in which she could ever belong to him. He hoped that in time she would forget these past months she had been in thrall to Gray Eagle. He desperately wanted the memories of this place and all of these people to disappear from her thoughts. But most of all, he yearned for her to purge Gray Eagle from her heart and life. He craved the death of her love for his sworn enemy.

He gazed down at her sleeping face and fiercely vowed, "I will return you safely to your own land across the big waters. I will help you forget all the pain and humiliation you have known here in my land. I will protect you and love you. Never again will you face fear. Never again will you be forced to flee from danger or death. At last there is no more Wanmdi Hota. There is only Alisha and Powchutu. We belong together, my love. Neither the whites nor the Indians want us. We have each other; this is all we need."

The half-breed scout reasoned that these past two days of waiting were necessary in order to convince her of Gray Eagle's supposed betrayal and treachery. Soon she would awaken, and he himself would seal their fates for all time. His keen eyes studied her face once more as

22

rambling thoughts flickered brightly in his mind.

To Powchutu, Alisha was the most beautiful and desirable woman alive. To him, she was far too vulnerable and too trusting, traits that even he would take unfair advantage of very soon. He wondered if his words would break her tender heart. He could not decide if she would readily believe him or call him a liar. But he could not permit her to refuse to leave here with him. If absolutely necessary, he would use gentle force upon her. No matter her reaction, there was no choice now. With the first hint of morning light, they would leave this perilous place forever. Far away from here, they could begin a new and wonderful life together—so Powchutu planned.

He leaned back against the slender tree trunk and lifted his eyes skyward. In a husky tone he softly murmured, "Forgive me, Great Spirit. But I could not allow Gray Eagle to harm my love ever again. I cannot permit him to have the woman I love and need. Twice she has promised to go away with me. I shall hold her to that vow. Now, there is no more Gray Eagle to stop us. He was only a man after all. He died just as any other would. His blood ran just as fast and as red as other men's."

The muscle in Powchutu's jawline twitched with unleashed anger. "The great warrior has finally fallen. They claimed he was indestructible. Yet I have slain him with the ease of a rabbit hunt. Hanke-wasichuns do not count coup," he bitterly added as an afterthought, mentally cursing his mixed bloods. How he wished that he could shout his brave and daring deed louder than the kettle drums could pound.

Gradually Powchutu's mind returned to his confrontation with the warrior, that morning when Gray Eagle had ridden off and left Alisha behind. He allowed his jaundiced mind to drift back in time and to envision the

23

entire matter in vivid retrospect. It had all begun four days before—the night of the wedding—the night when he and Alisha had tried to drug Gray Eagle. Somehow he must have known all their plans. He had cunningly watched them trap themselves in his snare. As planned, Alisha had fled the Blackfoot camp after believing that Gray Eagle had been rendered unconscious by the potion that he had supplied for her. But Powchutu had not followed Alisha in order to join her; Gray Eagle had. Instead, Powchutu himself had been captured and tightly bound by White Arrow, Gray Eagle's best friend and constant companion from youth.

The half-breed recalled how White Arrow had held him prisoner for two long and agonizing days. Only by pretending to believe that Gray Eagle did love and want Alisha, did White Arrow finally release him from his bonds. Powchutu inwardly raged at those bonds which had been imposed by Gray Eagle to prevent him from following after Alisha. To him, it was crystal clear that Gray Eagle had only feigned acceptance of Alisha and of the deception that she was Black Cloud's daughter. Powchutu could not accept this drastic change in Gray Eagle's emotions and actions. His biased mind told him that Gray Eagle had been up to some malicious mischief.

Powchutu earnestly believed that Gray Eagle had no true intention of keeping Alisha at his side as his wife. Powchutu viewed the trek into the open plains as only a means of getting her away from the Blackfoot village as quietly and easily as possible. It looked as the best way to save face before his own people and the neighboring warriors. Powchutu reasoned that Gray Eagle would never permit anyone to learn that he had fought for and married a mere white girl. Such a renowned warrior would certainly never allow a paleface to get away with such a humiliating trick on him. He would surely seal this shameful secret forever with her death, the only sure and permanent silence.

"I am no blind fool," Powchutu growled sullenly. "Does he think he can deceive me as he has her? Could he not see she was innocent of Matu's treachery? Could he not accept the love she freely offered him? As surely as winter comes, he would have killed her and returned to his camp as the grieving husband. Why is my version of this vile deed any different? I have only outsmarted Gray Eagle and saved Alisha's life."

Powchutu had decided to tell Alisha this same story, the one he was certain that Gray Eagle would have used. He knew that it would take a great deal of persuasion, but she would be forced to believe him in the end. How could she doubt him when Gray Eagle had not returned for her? No one, including Alisha, imagined the warrior capable of falling prey to an enemy. Everyone thought him invincible, more than a mortal man.

But Powchutu knew that Gray Eagle was not unconquerable, for he had shot him and left him for dead.

Powchutu closed his eyes and pictured the look of total disbelief upon Gray Eagle's face as he had spoken his claims to Gray Eagle, then shot him. The flintlock pistol had roared loudly, bright sparks had flashed as the ball exploded from the barrel and slammed into that hard, bronze chest. Powchutu reasoned that Gray Eagle had also thought himself incapable of dying, for his last words to him had been, "You not run too far for vengeance of Wanm. . . ." But he had lapsed into unconsciousness before completing his threat of revenge.

Powchutu scoffed venomously, "Dead men walk the ghost trail, not the green forests or the open plains."

Powchutu remembered how Gray Eagle had been

angered at himself for allowing an enemy to sneak up on him. It was the most deadly error a warrior could make. It was clear to Powchutu that Gray Eagle's mind had been on other matters, for his guard had been too low. He assumed that Gray Eagle had been mentally planning Alisha's "accidental" death. For a brief moment, Powchutu had been too frightened to carry out his daring plan to kill him. That burning gaze in Gray Eagle's eyes could strike terror into the heart of the bravest of men; his fierce stare and intrepid aura could immobilize a man. But it had been too late to back down. Cowardice could have cost both his and Alisha's lives.

The truculent warrior had not even pleaded for his life, not that Powchutu would have granted his wish. He had been driven beyond all caution and respect in this, his final battle with his sworn enemy, the man who had reduced the woman he loved to a despised slave.

Powchutu muttered, "He just stared at me in the strangest way when I told him about our plans."

Our plans. . . . Powchutu suppressed a low, pleased laugh. It was amusing for him to think that he had actually convinced Gray Eagle that Alisha had known all about his murder and that she had willingly agreed to it.

"He accepted that ridiculous story about our knowing he could speak English. He thinks we set up that meeting in Matu's tepee where he could overhear us and change our plans to escape. He truly believed you had tricked him," he said, gazing down tenderly at Alisha. "The fool! When I said we wanted him dead so we could escape and marry, he accepted my words. How blind can a man be? Could he not see the love in your eyes for him? Could he not hear it in your sweet voice? He claimed he trusted you, accepted you, loved you. He lied! Where was this love and trust when I spoke such lies to him?"

Once again, Powchutu's thoughts returned to the deadly scene of Gray Eagle's shooting. He mentally relived it as if it was just happening for the first time. While stealthily tracking them, he had sighted Gray Eagle and Alisha speaking near the copse. Rage had filled him at the sight of what he thought were Gray Eagle's deceitful affections and bold attentions toward her. For an instant he had been tempted to shoot him while he was embracing Alisha. He had not dared for fear of hitting her by error. To kill Gray Eagle was one thing, but to do so in front of Alisha was another.

Powchutu had finally decided to attack only if her life appeared in immediate danger. It had been like a sharp knife cutting into his heart to watch her heated responses to another man, even one she loved and married. He had forced himself to observe the fiery actions between them, allowing them to increase his great hatred for Gray Eagle and to strengthen his bold resolve to have Gray Eagle out of her life forever.

At least she was still alive and well. He had feared that he might be too late to rescue her before Gray Eagle could carry out his treachery. He almost wished that Gray Eagle would try to kill her, now that he was here to prevent it. He knew that nothing would be as convincing as a witnessed attempt upon her life. Powchutu wondered just how Gray Eagle would enact her demise. Enlightenment came to him as he watched Gray Eagle mount up and casually ride off with her horse and their meager supplies. It had amazed and infuriated him to realize that Gray Eagle's apparent intention was to leave her alone and defenseless to die. He hastily scanned the direction which Gray Eagle had taken, then turned his line of vision back to Alisha.

Powchutu's brow knit in confusion. He was utterly

perplexed by her obvious calm and her vivid happiness. Of course . . . she must believe that he would soon return for her. He contemplated upon what lies Gray Eagle had told her in order to win her unwitting cooperation in her own death. He waited until she had concealed herself in the trees, knowing that she would be safe for a few hours until he could return. He replaced his field glasses in his saddle bag and headed off in the same direction that Gray Eagle had previously taken.

Powchutu sneered at Gray Eagle's confidence and satisfaction. To him, Gray Eagle appeared so consumed with satanic pleasure that it had dulled his hunter's instincts; not once had he detected Powchutu's dogging presence. He had trailed him for miles to a narrow stream where he had halted to refill two water skins. Powchutu fumed as he watched the warrior take the time to fetch water while Alisha had been left without a drop. Once more, Powchutu's rage was unbounded. Gray Eagle had selected one of the most brutal deaths that a person could endure—dehydration. He had seen death as a result of the lack of water. It was agonizing; it was slow. This savage murder seemed beyond even the cruelty of Gray Eagle.

Powchutu's gaze was transfixed on past reality. As Gray Eagle knelt to refill the water skins, he smiled in tranquility. Powchutu gritted his teeth as he soundlessly eased up behind him. To the naked eye, Gray Eagle was so confident in his prowess and invincibility that he had left his weapons on his horse.

Powchutu smiled in wintry cynicism. How very fortunate for me, and how very stupid of you, he thought. Your smile will soon be gone, my despised foe.

He leveled his flintlock pistol on Gray Eagle, for once grateful that he had traded for this nearly useless weapon of the white man. Although the Indians respected the power of this unfamiliar weapon, they no longer feared it as great magic.

Powchutu theorized that the white man did not realize that the average warrior could fire at least six arrows while he was loading and priming this sluggish weapon. He wondered if they were too blind or too ignorant to realize that they did not stand a chance against arrows, knives, and lances which were used with deadly accuracy and speed. He speculated that one day a white man would make a gun which could shoot more than once or could be loaded with more speed. If so, then the Indians' defense would be unequal to the white man's. No matter; he only needed one shot at this close range.

"Wanmdi Hota!" he shouted angrily.

Gray Eagle dropped the water skin, rose, and whirled to face his enemy, all with the grace and speed of a giant, golden puma preparing for defense against a hungry predator. His proud stance and fearless expression revealed only contempt for his attacker. He haughtily leveled stygian eyes on Powchutu's gun. Slowly he raised his stoical gaze to stare into the eyes of his challenger.

His intrepid aura heightened Powchutu's tension. He laughed to try to conceal it. "Your spirits sleep this day, Wanmdi Hota," he taunted. "You have allowed an enemy to overtake you. At last we have come face to face for a final battle. You will pardon me if I keep the advantage," he sneered.

At Gray Eagle's continued cool stare and infuriating silence, Powchutu lied, "I need not speak in your tongue. Your dark secret has been known to me for a long time, as with Alisha."

Still no reaction came from the powerful warrior. Powchutu was urged to greater boldness. "You are a fool,

29

Wanmdi Hota, for you easily fell into our trap for you. Your pride and hatred have blinded you to the truth. Alisha does not love you; she loves me. Your vengeance will never allow us to escape from here. We cunningly allowed you to set a snare for your own defeat. That day at the fort when you stole her from my side, we planned our revenge right beneath your very nose. We were to leave the fort that very same day; we were to be married. But you had to come for her, to show your great courage and daring by forcing her to be returned to you for more torture. When the soldiers at the fort would not offer her their protection and help, she had no choice but to return to you and to your cruelty. The cowards cared only for their own lives and skins. I was glad when you massacred them all. They deserved to die, just as you do. She, too, is proud and brave. She did not plead with them to help her, for she knew they would not. There was but one way to insure our safety and that of our unborn child; she was forced to pretend love and respect for you. If you are as cunning and intelligent as they claim, then surely you did not believe she could ever love a man such as you!"

Powchutu noted the visible tensing in Gray Eagle's body. He watched the dangerous narrowing of his foe's eyes. He felt that burning coldness touch his very soul. He fully recognized the courage and power that this man possessed. He curiously watched him as suspicion and doubt began to gradually edge their way into Gray Eagle's mind and heart. Although Gray Eagle was praised for his unreadable expressions, there were many emotions clearly visible in his face at that very moment. Powchutu was filled with malevolent pleasure.

Powchutu was not only a good guesser, but he was also a bold and daring liar. Knowing both Gray Eagle and Alisha, he artfully led Gray Eagle to believe that he had totally misjudged Alisha and her affections. All of Powchutu's claims sounded logical. Stone by stone, Powchutu maliciously dismantled Gray Eagle's wall of trust in Alisha, and he uprooted the very foundation of his acceptance of her.

"Does a woman love a man who beats and shames her?" he shouted at Alisha's love. "Does she turn to the same man who has killed her people, destroyed her life and happiness? Does she love a man who has cruelly lashed her before his people only because she sought freedom from him? Can she love a man who steals her from safety and from the man she truly loves? Can she love a man who raped her and who forced her to endure his touch when it is another's that she wants? In her place, would you love her?" he acidly challenged.

Powchutu shifted from one foot to the other as he raged at Gray Eagle. "Did you know that each time you took her on your mat she closed her eyes and pretended you were me? I will kill you for making her endure such shame." He flung his cutting words at Gray Eagle's heart like razor-sharp daggers. "You have no guilt or honor. You know no mercy or kindness. You are not fit to live beneath the eyes of the Great Spirit. All you have is your bloody pride! Pride painted red with the blood of your enemies and your wife. You do not deserve to spend one night with her."

Gray Eagle still remained silent and motionless as Powchutu leveled his charges. "Do you know how I felt when I begged her to endure your touch just to save her life and that of our child's? I was forced to put aside my pride and to become helpless in your desire to have her at any cost. I was forced to watch you take her and ride away. I was as powerless as a snared rabbit! She trusted me, but I could not save her from you. That day at the

31

fort, she pleaded with me not to send her back to you. She asked me to kill her rather than send her away from my side. I held her in my arms and urged her to see there was no other way to resist your power. Your generous heart spared me as her friend and protector. Now I have come to reclaim her. She is mine, Wanmdi Hota, mine! Could you not see the love in her eyes for me? Did you not feel it when she told me goodbye that last day at the fort? Recall that day, Wanmdi Hota, and you will have your answers. You sat there waiting for her to come to you, but she was stalling for more time with me.

"Even now you leave her alone to die, without protection or water. You do not deserve to live. The Great Spirit will not protect the life of one who kills without honor and mercy. But she will not die, for I will save her. I will love and protect her."

Still, Gray Eagle remained alert and silent. Powchutu glared at him, challenging him to deny his claims. When Gray Eagle refused to be baited, Powchutu continued, "Even after all you have done to her, she does not wish to kill you to insure our escape. But she knows you will never permit her to leave here alive. She is pure and gentle. You have done much to harm her."

Powchutu laughed harshly and said, "I have a parting gift for you from Alisha. She said she no longer needs the protection of Shalee."

As he spoke, he tossed a white headband to Gray Eagle: the gift from Black Cloud to his married daughter. Powchutu smiled at his cunning idea. Gray Eagle seized the headband and crushed it tightly in his powerful grip, never realizing that it had not just come from the warm brow of his wife.

Powchutu sensed that he was actually getting through to the great warrior. He was filled with a heady sense of power and confidence. He arrogantly stated, "We were to marry but you took her away from me. My honor cannot permit such cruelty to the woman I love, the woman who will soon bear my child. I will have her back this very day. She has learned your vile secret, that you speak her tongue. She knows you have always heard her words, but ignored them. Your own deceit and treachery has made our trap possible. The talk you overheard in Matu's tepee was a trick. We hoped you would follow after her in my place, just as you did. Then we would have you out here alone and helpless. But I did not foresee your plans with White Arrow to hold me captive. Alisha feared you had killed me. She was planning to keep pretending to be your loving and dutiful wife; she was going to let you think our child was yours. Now, it will not be necessary. I convinced White Arrow of my trust in you. I told him I was returning to Grota's camp. There is no one to help you now, great warrior of the Sioux. You will be gone forever from these lands, just as we will. Alisha will no longer fear the discovery of her deceit. She will no longer feel any fear or shame. If I could not join her, she prayed that you would somehow accept a half-breed child if you believed that it was your own son. Yet knowing how you despised and scorned me because I am a half-breed, she feared you might not accept your own child."

Each time that Powchutu purposely mentioned the child, Gray Eagle's jawline would grow taut, and his hands would clench into tight fists. Dangerous flames would spark and glow brightly in his stygian eyes, then quickly disappear as he sought to control his unleashed emotions. For the first time, he finally spoke, "You will not escape Wanmdi Hota vengeance. She never belong to you, nor to no other man," he vowed icily, his eyes as cold and forbidding as his voice.

Fear coursed in Powchutu's veins at the ominous tone in Gray Eagle's threat. "Dead men cannot seek revenge!" he shouted at him to settle his jittery nerves.

Gray Eagle's dauntless manner taunted him. "I not die easy or quick, Hanke-wasichu. She mine forever," came his too calm argument. "She mine. Never let go. Never."

Gray Eagle had touched a raw nerve by calling Powchutu a half-breed. Returning the insult, Powchutu yelled at him, "You bloody savage! I will be the one at her side this very night. It is my son she carries within her body. I know all you have done to her. You will die for it, you arrogant tyrant!" His body shook with the force of his uncontrollable rage.

"You blind to truth, Scout. Her love words reached my ears many times in tepee. She belong to Wanmdi Hota. You lie to self. She is mine."

Carried away with his unbridled anger, Powchutu did not realize that Gray Eagle had not mentioned the child, nor had he claimed any love for Alisha. He was aware of the fact that he had not denied any of his previous charges against him. He assumed this to mean that he had no defense, that he was indeed guilty of all those accusations.

"You lie, savage! She was trapped by you. Only false words and feigned actions could protect her. She endured it all for me. She could not tell you about our love, nor about our child. You would have killed them both. She left the fort knowing I would come for her when the time was right. What would you know about love or honor! When Brave Bear came to your camp, she feared you had sold her to him; she feared I would not be able to find her in his camp. I laughed as you begged me to go to the Blackfoot camp and talk with her. I would never have told her of your desire to marry her. I would not tell her of your deceitful offer of acceptance and kindness. I knew you lied. It was almost too easy to reclaim her there," he boasted loudly.

He pointed his finger at Gray Eagle and stated emphatically, "You said I was to tell her that she was Black Cloud's daughter Shalee. You said to tell her you had not sold her that morning in your tepee, that they had demanded her return to her father. You said you wanted to marry her. You said to tell her you would never harm her ever again. I told her none of these lies! When we went to Black Cloud's tepee to talk, I told her you spoke English. She could not believe your hatred and cruelty were so deep and strong. The decision was made then; we planned our escape right under the chief's ears and he never knew it. Why do you think she was so terrified by your challenge to Brave Bear for her hand? I will tell you. She feared you might win and reclaim her. Her tender heart could not accept the death of a kind man like Brave Bear as payment for your revenge and for her freedom. We sought to disarm you with her open show of love and respect for you. It worked, for you accepted it all. You were fooled by the white girl you now seek to destroy." His chest vibrated with sarcastic laughter.

"You lie, Scout. She not know I speak her tongue. I tell Alisha one moon past. I spoke truth to her. You pay for trouble. Alisha not go. She wife," he replied, apparently confused by the meanings of many of the English words and by the speed in which Powchutu flung them at him.

"We suspected you could understand her tongue. Too many times you knew things she spoke about. She is no fool. In the Blackfoot camp I answered her remaining doubts. She knows your secret. She knows how you used it against her. We spoke only those words we wished you to overhear. When you learned the truth that she was not Shalee, you dared not dishonor yourself by revealing how a young white girl and a half-breed, a hanke-wasichu," he sneered in livid rage, "had deceived the great Wanmdi Hota. We suspected you would bide your time until her death could be a secret. She was not tricked by all your false words of love. She knows how much you hate her, for you have shown her many times before."

For an instant, it appeared as if Gray Eagle would deny these words, but he had only stiffened and remained silent. His expression said that he was carefully reviewing Powchutu's words. But Powchutu did not want that; it might reveal his own lies. He wanted to savor the most revenge he could before killing Gray Eagle. He wanted him to suffer just as she had done. Nothing could be worse than to be betrayed, deceived, and dishonored. He reasoned that surely Gray Eagle must be feeling all of these emotions. Such feelings made him a deadly foe. He quickly decided that it was time to end this fatal charade.

"She waits for my return where you left her to die this morning. Soon we will be far away. Before five moons have crossed the sky, we will be joined; she has promised me this. Our son will be born before the snows leave the sacred mountains in the spring. We will be free and happy. Your feet will walk the ghost trail before the sun leaves the sky this very day. She is mine for all time. There is no way you can stop us."

"You lie, hanke-wasichu!" he shouted, his great anger vividly showing for the first time. He moved forward as if to attack Powchutu, for a moment forgetting the pistol in his grasp.

Powchutu panicked and fired instantly, the ball striking Gray Eagle's broad chest. He staggered backwards a few steps at the stunning impact at such a close range. His hand swiftly covered the wound near his heart. His handsome face revealed total disbelief, as if he never truly believed that the scout was going to murder him in cold blood.

His expression of shock and pain was quickly concealed. He looked determined to hide his angry humiliation at being bested by an enemy and to conceal the burning pain in his heart. Bright red blood oozed between his bronze fingers and flowed down his muscled chest. It was at that moment when Powchutu saw the white headband clasped tightly against the wound. Inexplicable chills ran over his entire body. In horror he watched the fluffy white feather become saturated with Gray Eagle's blood. It would have been an evil sign if the headband had truly come from her brow. He was thankful that it had not . . .

To disguise his rising fear, Powchutu shouted, "Go to the Great Spirit if he will accept you! I return to my wife and child."

Gray Eagle's knees grew weak and gradually buckled beneath his weight. He slowly sank to the ground to a painful kneeling position. His ebony eyes burned with fury as he vowed, "Your bloods will join on my knife, Scout. I swear to you and the Great Spirit Wakantanka. Wicasta wanzi tohni icu kte sni," he nearly whispered as his strength swiftly waned, unable to make his claim in English.

Powchutu scoffed at his vain words. He countered with Gray Eagle's same vow, "It is I who will allow no man to take her from me, not even the indomitable Gray Eagle himself. You can venge no one, not even yourself! Mother Earth will drink your blood before this day has passed. Never will you set eyes upon Alisha again, not as long as I live and breathe; this I swear to you and the Great Spirit!"

Gray Eagle stunned Powchutu by not singing the death chant with his last energy and breath, as if he still believed that he would not die. "You not run too far for vengeance of Wanm. . . ." He fell forward and did not move or speak again.

Powchutu felt frozen to the spot where he stood. It was done; the mighty warrior was shot. Alisha was free; she was now his. Somehow this final victory did not taste as sweet as it should have. Some hidden place within his heart hungered to mourn the fall of this great warrior. In some other time, friendship could have been theirs. Never had Powchutu felt such respect for any man, nor such fear of one. He was tempted to sing the death chant for him, but quickly realized how absurd that action would be. He stared at the man lying upon the dying grasses. It was difficult to slay a great legend, then just calmly ride away and leave his noble body for the wolves. Yet, Powchutu could not force himself to go near him or to touch him.

Instead, he hurried to his horse. Without a single backward glance, he mounted up and rode back toward the place where Alisha was hidden, waiting for a husband who would never return.

Gray Eagle called upon every ounce of strength and courage which he possessed. If he passed out in this secluded area, he knew his chance for survival was slim. He desperately invoked the Great Spirit's help and love. He was in top shape physically; his stamina was matchless. Yet, his life's blood and energy were quickly flowing from his powerful body.

38

He painfully pushed himself from the green earth, staring down at the wet, crimson grass. He was losing too much blood too swiftly. He pressed his hand to the wound to staunch the heavy flow. His mind swirled dangerously. He vainly attempted to ignore the searing pain which made breathing difficult. Sweat beaded upon his face at his exertions.

For the first time in his life, Gray Eagle thought about death. It had always been some vague threat upon the distant horizon. Now, it was all too real. Surely the Great Spirit would not permit him to die in this humiliating fashion. He would force himself to live for the day when he could avenge himself upon that treacherous scout and his own traitorous wife.

His wife . . . why had Alisha done this terrible thing? How could he have been so wrong about her, so swayed by her lies and deceits? He had denied his pride many times in her favor. He had loved her and married her. Why had she betrayed him, a warrior noted for his prowess, the son of a chief? Her crimes were unforgivable! She would pay dearly for them.

Gray Eagle's vision blurred and a ringing came to his ears. He summoned his waning strength to call for his loyal horse Chula. The mottled appaloosa instantly obeyed his beloved master. He came to stand over him, confused by his owner's behavior. He lowered his head and sniffed at Gray Eagle's body, sensing some danger.

Gray Eagle seized his dangling reins and hoarsely commanded Chula to help him up. The horse pulled back its head, accepting the weighty strain upon his bit. The exertion was too much for the weakened warrior. His knees trembled and gave way, sending Gray Eagle back to the hard ground with a wracking thud. He groaned in agony; once more his vision blackened for a moment.

His hands were red and sticky. The smell of blood filled Chula with tension. He pranced nervously. He realized something was terribly wrong with his master. He waited for another command.

"Help me, Wakantanka," Gray Eagle prayed. "I cannot walk the Ghost Trail with my blood upon Powchutu's hands. Grant me the strength to return to my camp. Wanmdi Hota calls upon you."

As he fiercely struggled to retain his senses, he called upon thoughts of Alisha to infuse him with determination. The scout had spoken truthfully about many things. He was guilty of such evil deeds against her. But she had vowed love and forgiveness. He had trusted her. "Betrayal!" kept echoing within his groggy brain.

"I loved you as I have never loved another!" Gray Eagle thought he shouted but the words were a mere whisper. "I cannot allow you to dishonor me in this cruel way. You are my heart. I will slay you for tricking me. How dare you take another man into your body! You are mine. You will never bear his child!"

All this time Alisha had been plotting her escape and his own death! She had actually traded Wanmdi Hota for a miserable half-breed scout! What a cunning whore she had become. She had been so pure and fragile many months ago. Her love had become more important to him than his own life. She had cast a spell over him which he was powerless to break.

His heart raged at the thought of her with another man. He was Wanmdi Hota, son of Chief Running Wolf of the intrepid Sioux. How dare any woman, especially a white one, rob him of his life! He had been a fool to love her. He had been blinded by desire and love for her. How could she not love and desire him in return? How could she feign such fiery passion?

He stared at the bloody headband within his tight grasp. She had cunningly used his love and the identity of Shalee to carry out her revenge. "No, my beautiful wife, you will never enjoy freedom or your lover. I will kill you first."

As he perilously hovered on the edge of death, the warrior spoke to Chula, instructing him to lie down upon the grass. With his last trace of strength, he pulled himself across the animal's broad back and tied the reins around his wrists. He ordered Chula to rise, gritting his teeth as burning pains shot through his wounded body with each movement.

Once standing, he commanded, "Home, Chula . . ." These words were familiar to the great beast, and he slowly headed in the direction of the Oglala camp, a journey which would require two days' riding at this snailish pace which prevented his master's limp body from falling off.

As Chula began his first steps, Gray Eagle knew his time was running out. For the first time, he felt weakness within his body. Never had he experienced such helplessness. Dreams of Alisha flickered before him as he slipped into a world of black nothingness . . .

Powchutu cautiously weaved his way between boulders, clumps of cacti, slender cottonwoods, and prickly thickets of dying tumbleweed. He halted well away from Alisha's hiding place. He retrieved his field glasses and sat down to guard her. He had been very careful not to stir up any dust which might alert her to his presence. All he could do now was to sit, watch, and wait.

His decision had been made; he would linger for a day or two before going to her aid. Solitude and worry would

41

have Powchutu's desired effect upon her. He would allow her spirits to sink and her doubts to climb. She would be more susceptible to his startling news when she was plagued by fear, suspicion, and weariness. He was positive that it would be days before anyone discovered Gray Eagle's absence. With Powchutu nearby, Alisha would be safe. Even the Great Spirit seemed to aid his cause by sending down light sandstorms which would soon conceal his trail.

This last thought brought another caution to mind. He prudently hid his lethal weapon by digging a deep hole and burying it near the boulder where he hid. He smoothed the sand back into place, then put several rocks of varying sizes on top of the site. If he and his love were somehow captured, there would be no telltale weapon in their possession. Just in case of some unforeseen emergency, he carefully checked out his knife and bow. Finding his new bowstring taut and his bow supple, he then checked out his quiver of arrows. Deciding that all his weapons were in perfect order, he relaxed and smiled triumphantly.

For two days, Powchutu agonized over Alisha's unmistakable sufferings. He wanted nothing more than to rush to her side, give her water, and hold her in his arms. But all would be ruined if he did. She would never agree to return the first day or the second one. She would require some proof of time in order to accept the lies he would utter. Facts would speak louder than any words he could say: Gray Eagle would not return; but Powchutu had come to seek her out and to rescue her.

He hardened his heart to her torment; he blinded his eyes to her needs. Each time she covered her face against the stinging sands, he wished that she had his bandanna to protect her lovely face. Each time that she stood up and eagerly searched the horizon for a sight of Gray Eagle, he made certain there was no warning flash of light from his field glasses. Knowing of her modesty, he would look away whenever she relieved herself. Time and time again he mentally pleaded for her forgiveness and understanding.

He waited until the night of the second day since Gray Eagle's disappearance, then secretly went to her side while she slept. His worried gaze tenderly scanned her pale features as he mentally rehearsed his upcoming talk with her. So much depended upon her immediate acceptance of his story. He would allow her only enough sleep to ward off some of her great fatigue for their long journey, yet not enough to make her wits sharp and clear.

"If I could so easily convince Gray Eagle of your supposed treachery, my love, then surely I can convince you of his. He had nothing to base your guilt upon, yet he actually believed me!"

Powchutu would not admit the fact that it had been his cunning deception that had swayed Gray Eagle. Only Alisha's white wedding headband had convinced him of Powchutu's words. Gray Eagle would never know that the headband now soaked with blood was almost identical to Alisha's, the gift from her Indian father, his gift of love to his new-found daughter.

Certain incidents now returned to haunt Powchutu's peace of mind. He wondered if he had only imagined that there had been another emotion revealed in the warrior's eyes for only a brief moment, an emotion other than shock, pain, and anger. He reasoned that it could not have been physical pain, not before the shot. His look of fury had been easy to read; that other one had not. It was so very mysterious. . . .

Powchutu now had the time to doubt his own wisdom

43

in forcing Alisha to suffer alone. He should have taken a lesson from the warrior himself; he should have boldly ridden up to her that same day and taken her captive until they were far away from this place. In time, he could have convinced her that his daring actions were for her own good. She might have cried and argued with him in the very beginning, but in the end she would have had to accept her separate fate.

Dawn would soon arrive. With its light, they would have to flee as fast and as far as possible. There would be no stopping the bloodbath which would surely follow the discovery of the murder of Wanmdi Hota. Powchutu shuddered to think what the torture could be like for him and Alisha. If it came to capture, he vowed that he would pretend that he had slain Gray Eagle and had forcefully captured Alisha for his own woman. First, they would have to prove his guilt; second, hers. Regarded as Shalee, she would naturally be returned to the Blackfoot camp to some sort of happiness and safety. In any case, Gray Eagle was out of her life forever.

The shrill cry of a hawk flying in circles above them returned him to full reality. He stood up and studied the horizon in each direction, much as Alisha had done for the past two days. Seeing no sign of dust clouds which would signal approaching riders, he assumed that they were still safe. The sun had not completely shown her brilliant face as yet, but it was getting brighter by the minute. It was time to awaken Alisha and to begin their journey toward their new destinies.

He kneeled down beside her sleeping form. He breathed deeply several times as he summoned his courage to carry out the final phase of his plan. He moistened his lips and sighed. Ever so lightly he touched her pinkened cheek with the back of his hand. For what

44

seemed an eternity to him, he hungrily devoured her fine features. He hesitated to awaken her, anticipating the effects his words would have on her.

Yet, he knew that he must press forward without further delay. For some unknown reason, he whispered softly to her in Oglala, "Kokipa ikopa, Cinstinna. I am here, my love. Wake up, Alisha. Alisha . . ." He gently shook her shoulder . . .

Chapter Three

Alisha stirred, trying to focus her sleepy eyes on his features. Confusion was evident in her emerald gaze. In her groggy state of mind, she had briefly mistaken him for Gray Eagle. As her vision and senses gradually cleared, she tried to make some sense out of this curious situation. Why was Powchutu, her dearest friend, instead of her new husband at her side? Adding to her puzzlement was the fact that he was speaking in Sioux.

Although it was difficult to speak, many questions began to painfully spill forth from her parched lips, "What are you . . . doing here? Did Gray . . . Eagle send you to . . . fetch me home? Where is he . . . Powchutu? He has not re . . . returned for days. Did something happen to . . ."

Powchutu silenced her with a gentle finger upon her dry lips. He cursed himself for her needless sufferings. He should have realized that she did not have the stamina of a warrior. "Here, drink some water first. Then I will tell you everything you need to know." As he spoke, he handed her the water skin and smiled warmly.

She drank greedily as she sated her thirst, her eyes never leaving his unfathomable face. She speculated that something must be terribly wrong, and he was stalling the bad news. With trembling hands she slowly lowered the water bag and passed it back to him. Anxious lights glimmered in her entrancing eyes; a ghost of a wary smile played at her lips.

"Powchutu, what's wrong?" she asked, almost too softly to be heard. "I can see it in your eyes, old friend. I've won the battle between Gray Eagle and me. You need not worry about me anymore. The war is finally over; we're married."

He stood up and turned his back to her. He sighed deeply. Then he faced her once more. His intense expression and reluctance to speak warned her that Powchutu bore ill tidings.

"Is he . . ." she began and hesitated. She could not finish such an unspeakable question. Her eyes mutely pleaded with the man who was as close to her as a real brother to tell her his dreaded news.

"Alisha . . ." Powchutu also stammered and halted, searching for the right words, words which would pain her, yet convince her of his story.

He began anew, "How do I tell you such news?" He was finding it harder to trick her than he had imagined. To plan a deception was easy, but to face her while carrying it out was nearly impossible. It had been the same with his plan for Gray Eagle. To plot his murder was simple; but to actually gun him down had been one of the most difficult things Powchutu had ever done in his entire life. Yet, it was too late to turn back now.

"Please, Powchutu," she entreated in growing fear and mounting anxiety. "Tell me what? Is he . . . did some enemy . . . I cannot even utter such thoughts. Tell me," she shouted, panic clawing at her.

"It's over, Alisha," he stated simply, increasing her confusion. He lowered his eyes to conceal the guilt in them.

She observed her friend for a few moments, trying to deduce his meaning. She did not know if he was referring to something about her or him. She was grateful that he had not spoken her worst fear aloud: Gray Eagle is dead. Her brow knit in puzzlement. She pressed, "What is over?"

His dark eyes fused with her worry-filled ones. In an emotionless tone he stated, "You and Gray Eagle. He returned to his village two days ago. He will not return for you." He waited for his callous words to filter into Alisha's dazed mind.

Bewilderment suffused her. "I don't follow you. He went back for supplies. But he should have returned to me by now. Is something wrong in his camp? Why didn't he send someone to get me? He knows I have no food or water."

"You did not hear me, Alisha," Powchutu explained. "He is not planning to ever come back for you. Neither will he be sending anyone to get you. He has already told his tribe that Shalee is dead. He told them you two were attacked by some renegade warriors. He claimed you were killed and that he has buried you out here. Buried you where only he knows the place. I hoped and prayed that he was lying. I guessed he had either killed you or just left you out here to die. Knowing his cruelty and desire for great torment, I felt he had deserted you where no one could find you. This is the season for the last buffalo hunt before winter. He knows it is unlikely that anyone would be around here. He forgot I was the one who drew the map for you to follow. I could guess about where you would be camped."

As he was relating his false tale, Alisha's face went stark white. She began to tremble like an elm leaf in a strong breeze. She shook her head from side to side, silently shouting no . . . no . . . no. . . .

"I swear he will not return for you, today or any other day. Chela will soon take your place in his tepee as was

48

planned before he captured you. Even now she comforts him in his fake sorrow."

Like a violent whirlpool, her entire life with Gray Eagle rushed around and around in Alisha's mind. It was true that their loving truce was new and fragile, but he had vowed his love of her and acceptance of her color. After all that had happened between them just recently, she could not accept such inconceivable news. In her pain, she turned on her friend and lashed out at him. "No! You are mistaken. He loves me! He will come back for me. You'll see. I will wait here for him. He has already chosen me over Chela," she yelled in a jealous rage.

"How many more days will you wait for him, Alisha?" Powchutu retorted, desperate to keep his plan from failing. "How many nights alone will it take to prove my words to you? I would give anything I possess if I did not have to be the one to bring you this news. There is no one else to save you. There is no one else who loves you as I do. You have no food, no water, no horse, and no weapon. Does this not seem strange to you? It has been two days since he left. How long can you survive out here this way? How long before an enemy warrior might find you and capture you? What then, Alisha?"

His train of thought was clear to her. His challenges hit home, deeply and painfully. Her eyes burned from the lack of needful tears; her throat ached with dry sobs. Yet her body lacked the moisture to aid her need for tearful release. Her breathing was ragged and shallow, bringing new discomfort to her throat and chest.

"It cannot be true," she sadly murmured. "He would not leave me here to die. He loves me. I know he loves me."

"I wish it were not true, my love, but it is. He now sits in his tepee, eating and drinking while you go without food and water. He can ride where he pleases, while you are stranded here in danger. He has weapons to fight off his many enemies, while you have nothing to protect your life and honor," he patiently reasoned. Powchutu knew that he was like a brother to her, her dearest friend. She trusted him. He had been the sole source of her comfort, safety, and friendship many times in the past. She would eventually accept his lies.

"How do you know these things?" she suspiciously inquired, pain gnawing at her broken heart.

"I could not follow after you from Black Cloud's village because he told White Arrow to hold me captive there," he began in a tone that he would use if speaking to a small, hurt child.

But Alisha hastily interrupted him, "He told me these things. He wanted to come after me himself. He said there were many things I should know. He speaks English. He said he loves me and wants me. He will keep the secret of Shalee so I can be his wife."

"Alisha!" he shouted at her with impatience, but not for the reason she suspected. "Listen to yourself. What else could he tell you to make you willing to linger behind while he leaves you to die? He knows you love him. He was only taunting you with the offer of his love in return. What better revenge than to let you taste the love that you would soon be denied, the love you would pay any price to obtain? Think, Alisha! For as long as you have known him, has he ever given you a single hint of this love he vowed for you? Has he ever given you any reason to trust him so completely? My God, Alisha, have you forgotten all he has done to you? He killed your people. He kidnapped you, raped you, beat you, and abused you mentally and physically. He left you out here to die! He is a savage."

She angrily turned away from him, placing her hands over her ears to close out his sharp words. In the beginning all those things were true, but no longer. They had been enemies; now they were lovers. It was impossible for a man to hate a woman, then make such passionate and tender love to her as he had done only a few days ago. There were justifiable reasons for all he had done to her. But things were different now; Gray Eagle had proven this to her by revealing his love and his great secret.

Powchutu seized her by the shoulders and whirled her back around to face him. He grabbed both of her hands and pulled them away from her ears, imprisoning them within his powerful grasp. "You cannot hide from the truth! He only seeks to save his reputation. You know the importance he places upon his honor and position. The death of Shalee can protect his name; the marriage to a cunning white girl cannot."

"No! No! No!" she shouted emphatically. "It isn't like that. He told me why he kept the truth from me. He had to make certain that I loved him, that he could trust me completely. He loves me, Powchutu. Why are you doing this to me? He loves me," she argued in vain.

Powchutu sighed heavily, releasing her hands. He knew then that it was going to require more of Alisha's pain and more of his own lies to free her heart from Gray Eagle's strong hold. He relentlessly set out to do just that. "I know he can speak English. I have known for a long time. That day at the fort when he came to demand your return I guessed his secret. He made the mistake of reacting to something I muttered in English. When he came to Grota's camp to seek my help with you, he confirmed my suspicions. I asked him why he needed me to speak for him. He said you would not believe anything he might say to you because you would feel betrayed, angry, and hurt. I should have told you, but I could not. I knew the pain such news would bring to your heart. If I told you he had always heard your pleas and words of love, but chose to remain silent and stern, you would suffer greatly. I saw no need for you to ever know this treacherous secret since we planned to leave here forever. I did not count on his cunning attack upon those plans."

"You knew his secret and you did not tell me?" Alisha had a glimmer of doubt about her friend.

"I'm sorry, Alisha, but I knew how deeply it would hurt you. If you will recall, I did warn you several times not to speak openly before him. He threatened to kill me if I told you the truth. I was afraid you would go to him as soon as I told you. I could not risk your life or mine. Please understand and forgive me," he urged her in true sincerity, yet feigned remorse.

Her expression told him that she did not know what to think or say. Powchutu took advantage of her weakened state. He asked, "Do you remember how Gray Eagle treated you just before his challenge with Brave Bear? If a man viewed such pain and need in the woman he supposedly loved, would he not speak some words of love and comfort to her? How could he remain silent when it might have been his last chance to confess his love? Could a man go to his grave without once uttering those words? He could not, Alisha. I am a man; I know."

"He explained all these actions to me, Powchutu." She rebuffed his logic.

"Did he, Alisha? Or did he simply tell you what you wanted and needed to hear? Think back over your life with him. Was his cruelty only in public or were there times when he punished you in private when no one except the two of you could see and know? If he truly loved you all this time, then wouldn't his hatred only be present before others?"

Powchutu already knew the answers to these questions. He knew the answers would be in his favor, but not because they were true. He knew because she had revealed such things during her delirium at the fort or had innocently dropped hints during talks with him. Knowing of Gray Eagle's customs and his personal ways, he knew the truth, but denied it to her. Ready to end this agonizing battle, he asked the ultimate question, "If he loves you, then why are you dying here in the desert while he is back in his camp with Chela at his side?"

Bitter anger and fear flooded her at the possible truth of his words. She screamed, "Then I will go to his camp! I will know the whole truth from him! I will show his people that he lies! If you speak the truth, he will be dishonored. He will pay for his lies and betrayal!"

"To what end, Alisha? To both our deaths, for I could not allow you to return to him alone. I love you, Alisha. I cannot bear to see you hurt again. I beg you; let me take you far away from here. Forget him; he is danger and death for you. Surely you have become aware of the great differences between you? How long could you survive as the willing captive of a warrior such as he? How long could you be his slave, waiting upon him, wondering when his next attempt upon your life would come? Tell me, Alisha, is this how you wish to spend the rest of your life? You are white; he is Indian."

"Swear to me you speak the truth. Swear to me that he will not return here for me," she desperately asked.

Powchutu met her steady gaze and answered so honestly that she could not doubt his words any longer. "He will never return here for you, Alisha; this I swear

53

upon my life and my honor. I cannot change reality. I cannot ease your pain. But he is lost to you forever. I swear these things to you. Have you any reason to doubt my honesty or my love for you?" he asked.

Alisha was deathly silent. Powchutu's ruse had worked.

Suddenly, an agonized scream torn from Alisha's very heart and soul seared his innermost conscience. How he wished that Gray Eagle could ride up that very moment to comfort the savage wounds which he had just inflicted upon her! In his wildest imagination, he had not considered it would be this terrible for her to bear. The depth of her love for the slain warrior was emblazoned upon his mind for all time. His fierce resolve was temporarily weakened, but he could not call back the sands of time.

Great Spirit, forgive me, he mentally prayed, for I did not know the love they shared could be real. Help me to find some way to ease this pain I have given to her. I would give my own life to have the one of Gray Eagle back again. . . .

The heat of the sun beating down upon his back reminded him of his deeds, warning him of the need for expediency. He approached the tree where Alisha was standing with her forehead against its smooth bark. She had cried until there were no more tears. Her shoulders drooped from the heavy burden Powchutu had just placed upon them. There was an aching emptiness within her. Once more she had been brutally scarred by her forbidden love and her defiant heart.

He touched her arm and called her name. She did not reply. "We must go, Alisha. He might return to make certain you are . . ."

"Don't say it!" she shouted at him in a strange voice that he did not recognize. In a solemn tone she remarked,

"He has won this final battle between us, for I am as good as dead."

Powchutu roughly seized her by the shoulders and shook her soundly. "I won't let you give up or die, Alisha. There is still hope for you. He will not win this time. We will flee this evil place and find happiness and safety somewhere else." His one hope lay in replacing her sadness with anger and determination. He needed to convince her that her survival would thwart Gray Eagle's hatred.

She looked past caring or listening. She said hollowly, "What does it matter now, Powchutu? Where can I go from here? It will only be as it was at Fort Pierre. They will scorn me and despise me. They will taunt me and torment me. I cannot live through such shame and contempt again. I do not belong with the white man any longer; they have already proven this to me. To them, I am white trash, the ex-squaw of the most feared and most hated warrior to ever live. To them, I am soiled beyond redemption."

"Where we will go, no one will know the truth about either of us. No one will learn of your life with him. They will not know I am a half-breed scout. We can make a fresh start there. We'll be free. We'll be happy and safe, Alisha. I promise you these things," he vowed earnestly.

She gazed out across the plains, wondering if her true fate lay in that obscure direction. It seemed as if the sun and sand were calling out to her, urging her to follow this new destiny outlined by her friend. In her mind, the elements themselves cried out, "Betrayal!" as if in fiery unison. Clearly Gray Eagle was gone; their love was voided. He had withdrawn it forevermore, never to embrace her in love again. The blazing sun burned its message of defeat into her troubled mind; it mocked her love and her suffering. It chided her folly, her naiveté, and her rosy dreams. She felt as if all the rays of dazzling sunlight were concentrated into a single beam, piercing her defenseless heart and mind, enflaming and destroying all the good things there had been between them, leaving only the sooty ashes of a once precious love.

As Alisha looked aimlessly in all directions, she refused to think about this treacherous news. She felt as barren and deserted as the vast wasteland before her blurred vision. The one question which kept intruding into her stunned mind was, why? Without any warning, the time for turning back had come. Her heart was rent by this loss, this needless sacrifice, this cruel betrayal. It had ended between them just as suddenly, mysteriously, and painfully as it had begun that day long ago in her fortress. Her mind pleaded for respite; her warring heart rebelled, even knowing that it was over.

She stared at the cerulean sky, accusing the Fates of coercing her into saying her final, heart-rending farewell to this savage land and to her one and only love. In ever-increasing anguish, she realized just how much torment was involved in saying a last farewell. Still, she knew that it must somehow be done.

If she refused to leave here, then so would Powchutu. With all she had lost, she could not be responsible for his death. If Gray Eagle did not love her or want her, there was no way she could change his mind or his heart. To taste the forbidden fruits of Gray Eagle's total love and acceptance and then to have them cruelly snatched from her seemed an agony too great to bear. But bear it she must, if only for her friend Powchutu. Now, he was all she had left.

She raised her puffy, red-streaked eyes to meet his

concerned ones. She smiled faintly. "How can I argue with such logic and truth? If not for you, I would have died here, and no one would have known or cared. I owe you my life and gratitude once more."

She lifted her graceful hand and lovingly caressed his tanned cheek. "When I was brought to Fort Pierre after that so-called rescue by Jeffery and his troop, you were the only one who helped me and comforted me. You were the only one who understood me, who didn't judge me stained for life. No one sincerely accepted me for myself or even gave me an honest chance, except you. You were the only one I could talk to freely and openly. Then when you came to Black Cloud's village to explain matters to me, it was just the same as before. You have risked your life to help me. I think perhaps the real Alisha has only been known and seen by you. Everyone else tries to force me to be someone else, but not you. There is no way to repay you for all you have done for me; no words can express my appreciation and my affection. If Gray Eagle does not love me or want me, then I cannot remain here within the reach of his hatred and cruelty."

She placed her small hand upon his thudding heart and reluctantly acquiesced. "Wherever you say to go, I will come with you."

Powchutu beamed with happiness. In an emotion-filled tone he declared, "I will lead you to freedom, love, and safety. No one will ever hurt you again. If I could change things for you, I would gladly do so. I cannot. It is too late."

Unaware of the reason for his regret and sadness, Alisha smiled weakly and said, "You have done more for me than anyone has. What more could I ask for in a friend? We must hurry before he seeks more revenge upon us."

The half-breed led her to the horses not far away and helped her to mount. He prodded his horse into an easy gait; she obediently followed. Before the sun had topped the distant mountain peaks, they were on their way to a new life, a life that had been paid for with great suffering and traitorous bloodshed.

Chapter Four

Those first days along the trail passed in a blur of speed and anguish for Alisha. The changing scenery rushed swiftly past her vision, as swiftly as if she were trapped inside a runaway carriage which was hurtling toward oblivion. Much of the terrain was dangerous and arduous. They tried to cover at least twenty to thirty miles each day. But the unpredictable weather and treacherous footing would frequently halt their progress.

Powchutu told Alisha that it was about the first of November, for she had lost count of time many months ago when she had been captured by Gray Eagle. Only the dying landscape reminded her of the approaching winter, something that she never wanted to survive out in the open again. She could still recall that bitter, demanding one on her way West. Luckily the temperatures had dipped no lower than fifty degrees so far, and "Jack Frost" had yet to make his first appearance.

Powchutu hoped that they could reach Fort St. Louis before the snows set in for the season. He informed her that if they continued their present pace, they would reach their destination before December. Somehow Alisha could not imagine keeping the same grueling pace for that many weeks. As it was, they travelled most of the night and much of the day. Powchutu claimed that such a plan of action would lessen their chances of capture or discovery, for most Indians would not hunt or travel at night.

59

Avoiding as much daylight travel as possible and by using the river as a guide, he hoped to establish a good lead on anyone who might follow after them. Most of the time, they journeyed along the banks of the Missouri River, clinging closely to its eroded edges. They would occasionally ride for miles and miles in the shallows; other times, they would continually criss-cross the wide fords to conceal their trail. They would cautiously avoid the soft, mushy areas which could leave a track that even a child could follow.

Sometimes travel was slower than usual when he would demand that they walk the horses over large rock beds or travel over a high bluff. He used every trick of the trail that he knew in order to make their tracks obscure. He was always very alert and cunning. He was quick to avoid the camps of the Brule and Crow situated along the riverbanks.

Even in her frequent unmindful state, Alisha still realized that she lacked the cunning, courage, stamina, and skill to make such a trip by herself. It made her aware of her vulnerability and helplessness as a woman. She bitterly admitted to herself that she could not have succeeded in her last attempt to escape from Gray Eagle's village and his loving torment.

Although the journey was exceedingly difficult for her, she desperately needed this demanding pace to drive her into a state of total fatigue, insuring her of dreamless sleep when they stopped for breaks. As they rode along in necessary silence, she would force her thoughts on any subject that she could call forth; she was determined not to think about Gray Eagle or the life that she was leaving behind. Perhaps it had been helpful that her first days had passed in a state of shock and fatigue. Later, she tried to block out all reminders of her painful sojourn in her husband's domain.

When the pain did occasionally break through her tight rein, Powchutu would comfort her. Along the way, they grew closer and closer. He could not help but believe that he would eventually win her heart. She, in turn, could only hope and pray that one day this terrible pain and emptiness would leave her.

One day as they rested in a tree-lined canyon, she sighed and said to Powchutu, "If only Gray Eagle had betrayed me in person, then I would find it easier to deal with the loss of his love. It was so unlike him to be such a coward. I wonder why he did not wish to see the effect of his cruel joke. Do you suppose he ever went back to make certain that I was dead?" She murmured in a melancholy voice, not really expecting an answer.

Powchutu hid his look of guilt from her misty eyes. Her pensive mood bothered him. It told him that she was still thinking about the warrior too often. He quelled his feeling of resentment and replied in an emotionless tone, "Does it really matter now, Alisha? The deed is done. We cannot change things now. You should not continue to dwell upon these unanswerable questions; they only serve to refresh the pain. We must think of our safety and our new life. Gray Eagle is dead to you; accept this." He struggled to stifle his bitter jealousy of his enemy and reached out to caress Alisha's face.

"It is far easier to say than to do, my friend," Alisha replied, looking directly into Powchutu's eyes. "Have you never loved or needed someone so much that it hurts deeply not to have him? Have you ever been betrayed and deceived in the way that I was? I can tell you; it hurts far less to have your heart cut from your body with a dull knife. I want to forget him; I need to forget him. Yet, it is not that simple. God, how I wish it were!"

"In time you will cease to even remember his name or how he looked," Alisha's friend reassured her. "But this can happen only if you permit it. As long as you continue to call him to mind and to ponder upon his past deeds, you will never be able to forget him," he impatiently advised her.

She met his unreadable gaze. "I do try to keep him off my mind, Powchutu. But I cannot control my dreams. Neither can I halt the times he sneaks into my unwary thoughts like some deadly thief in the dark of night. If there was only some magic potion which could destroy all those remembrances, then I would readily drink it this very minute," she declared earnestly.

"In time, Alisha, you will forget."

"Time? Are you so certain that it is the all-powerful anodyne that it is claimed to be?" she remarked in a slightly sarcastic voice. Angry lights danced brightly in her green eyes.

"Get some rest, Alisha. You're too tired to be reasonable or cheerful," he teased her, hoping to wipe off that tight, feigned smile from her soft lips. Succeeding, they both slept for a few hours.

In the beginning, they had headed due east; now, they were slightly slanting toward the south. Powchutu told her that they could follow the Missouri River all the way into St. Louis. Staying close to the riverbank allowed them many gains: water, food, protection, and direction. By the end of the second week, they were both accustomed to the strenuous travelling. Their bodies lost their stiffness and soreness, making progress swifter and easier.

Powchutu gradually increased his alert as they came nearer to the territories of the Santee and the Yankton, a member of the Seven Council Fires of the Sioux. He was extra careful about concealing his and Alisha's trail. Their pace was naturally slowed by this added caution and care. About halfway through the Sioux lands, he spied a half-destroyed Conestoga wagon. He hastily motioned Alisha back into the concealing thickets so that he could check out this strange matter.

"Stay here and don't make a sound," he whispered in her ear. "Strange to find one single wagon out here alone . . . I wonder why the Indians didn't burn it. Could be some kind of trap. Still, we need to pass this way or lose too much time. If anything goes wrong, stay hidden until . . ."

Shock registered upon her pale face. Her eyes grew wide and alarmed. She interrupted him, "You mean there could be some hidden danger out there? Don't go! We'll wait right here until dark, then sneak past it. Please," she desperately entreated him.

He smiled with pleasure at the sight of her concern for his safety. "I want to check inside the wagon. Could be something there we can use later."

"Not if it's dangerous for you," she argued adamantly.

"I'll be just fine, Alisha. Don't worry about me. I promise to be very careful. I didn't mean to frighten you this much. I was only warning you to stay hidden, just in case of an unexpected emergency." He smiled warmly at her.

"Powchutu," she began, still not satisfied with his decision.

He leaned forward and silenced her with a light kiss upon her lips. He then assured her, "I'll be right back."

Alisha fearfully watched him move from tree to tree until it was necessary to enter the open to approach the covered wagon. She held her breath in frightened anticipation. Powchutu circled the wagon, curiously peering inside at different openings in the torn canvas covering. Suddenly he jumped up on the back end and disappeared inside.

Time seemed to cease as she frantically awaited his return. At last he glanced out and looked all around. Deciding it was clear and safe, he leaped down to the tawny grass and headed back in her direction. Without waiting for him to reach her hiding place, she ran out to meet him halfway. Her slender arms encircled his narrow waist, and she hugged him fiercely. Tears of relief streamed down her flushed cheeks.

"You stayed inside too long!" she wept.

Laughing merrily, he scooped her up in his powerful arms and swung her around several times. He dropped down onto the withering, golden grasses with her on his lap. Without regard for their dangerous surroundings, they both began to laugh and to playfully scuffle. They were like two, small children just dismissed from school for the carefree summer. For the first time since their escape, they completely relaxed their guard—and their platonic relationship. They simply revelled in their freedom and in their touch.

The sunset was intoxicating with its intermingled blues, pinks, grays, whites, and golds. Although the landscape was relenting to the demands of the imminent winter, it was doing so with majestic beauty. It shouted its message of the beauty of life-in-death. The evening birds had already begun their musical serenades to each other and to Mother Nature. Cicadas and tree frogs soon joined the abandoned merriment, creating a serene mood and romantic setting.

As Powchutu rolled Alisha to her back and pinned her hands to the ground, his loving gaze locked with her teasing eyes. At the sight of her overwhelming beauty and artlessness, his jovial laughter instantly faded; his dark eyes probed hers for a hint of promise.

Unable to restrain himself, he vowed in a husky voice, "I love you, Alisha. Marry me when we reach St. Louis."

Reading strong love and open desire in his gaze, Alisha became quiet and thoughtful. Then, astonished, she inquired innocently, "You mean you love me?"

Comprehending the real meaning of her question, he smiled and replied, "With all my heart and soul, my love. I have loved you since that first day I saw you in Dr. Philsey's quarters at Fort Pierre. But until now, I have had no right or chance to speak of my love for you. Each day that passes, I come to love you more and more. We are so much alike, you and I. We belong together, Alisha," he said ardently. "I can love you more than any other man ever could. Will you marry me, Alisha?"

"How can I? I am already married to Gray Eagle," she stated with guileless simplicity, feeling just as legally and morally bound to him as if they had been married in a church of her own faith instead of in an Indian village under the starry skies by the ceremonial chief.

"Only under Indian law, not by the white man's. He has no legal claim over you, nor any right to have you," he informed her, trying not to allow his disappointment to show. His dream of her response was entirely different from the disappointing reality.

Enlightenment filled her eyes, for she had not considered any of these facts before now. Slowly considering them, it still changed nothing to her. "Even so, I feel married to him in the eyes of God and in the laws of my own heart and conscience. There was a joining ceremony, much like any wedding. The vows were spoken between us; promises were made. 'Til death, and I am still alive."

Desperately trying to conceal the impact of her words upon him, Powchutu feigned pensive thought. What he really wanted to do was to shake her and to shout that Gray Eagle was dead, freeing her from her stubborn belief that she was somehow, in some mysterious manner, still bound to him. Of course he could not, not without telling her the whole truth of his past deeds.

Near exasperation, he cunningly attacked his dilemma in another way, "The life of a fierce warrior is dangerous, Alisha. For all we know, he could be dead right now. If not, then anytime in the near future. You will never know when his death might free you. As for those vows and promises you two exchanged in the Blackfoot camp, he has broken them first. He has already proven they mean nothing to him. The joining ceremony was only a farce, a cruel trick. Do not believe yourself bound to such a man. Do you plan to spend your life feeling obligated to a man who left you to die, left you only two days after marrying you and declaring his love for you? That fact alone frees you from any vow you made to him." Powchutu argued his case passionately. "I would never betray you or desert you. I would love you more than life itself. Give me the chance to prove my love for you. Gray Eagle was unworthy of you and your love. I have freed you from his trap; you owe him nothing. Can't you see this, Alisha?"

He had chosen a terrible argument. Thoughts of Gray Eagle's death brought deep pain and fear to Alisha. Even knowing what the warrior had done to her, knowing that it was absurd to still love and want him, and knowing that she owed him nothing still did not change things in her heart. She knew that Powchutu was right, but why did the truth have to continue slicing her heart into small and jagged pieces?

She could find no words to adequately explain how she could still love her proven enemy, her own husband. She knew that she would feel like an adultress if she consented to marry another man, even one as kind and important to her as Powchutu. How could she explain things that she did not even understand? How could she interpret the mysterious, strong bond she felt toward her past lover?

In truth, she feared that she would fall into Gray Eagle's arms right that very moment if he should happen to walk up to her. If he but once kissed her in that breath-stopping, soul-trembling way of his, she would forgive him anything. Becoming aware of the potent hold that he still had on her, she shuddered in despair. She fiercely chided her uncontrollable, traitorous mind and body; yet, she knew that she could not honestly deny this obsessive domination. She did not have to speak, for her brooding silence spoke for her.

Powchutu struggled to dispel the rage and bitterness that he was feeling toward her, himself, and Gray Eagle. He was only half successful. The sharp edge to his commands and the iciness of his glare revealed more to her than he intended. He hastily got up and headed back to the wagon. He brusquely stated, "I was right. There are some things in the wagon we can use later. I'll get them. You go back to the horses and wait for me."

She hurriedly jumped up and rushed after him, calling his name in near panic, "Powchutu! Wait! I didn't mean to . . ."

He whirled around to face her, his handsome features unreadable. "Forget it, Alisha. It looks as if my timing is still wrong. We'd best get out of here and pronto. It'll be dark soon. We shouldn't be out here in the open like this anyway. Stupid on my part." With those biting words, he turned and moved forward a few more long strides.

She ran and blocked his advancing path. She looked up into his inscrutable face, searching his eyes for understanding, silently pleading for forgiveness for her unintentional cruelty. All the help he had ever given her rushed to mind, and she said, "How can I forget it? I've obviously hurt you very deeply. I'm truly sorry. It's just that . . ." She halted as she searched for the right words to expose her heart and soul to him in order to make him understand her rejection of him.

At her hesitation, he filled in, "That you still love a man who has done all in his power to destroy you! That you cannot accept me as a substitute for the infamous, glorious Wanmdi Hota! Or perhaps that no man can ever fill his place in your heart. How can you choose hate over love, Alisha?"

Tears brimmed in her emerald eyes at his cutting tone and furious expression. His sharp words clawed mercilessly at her already bruised emotions. With trembling chin and quivering lips, she sadly replied, "No, Powchutu, that is not what I was going to tell you. I was trying to find the right words to express my feelings. Revealing innermost thoughts and feelings to another person, even one as close and dear as you are to me, is like stripping naked in broad daylight. I was simply surprised by what you told me. I did not know what to say in return. I have never realized that you love me in this way. You've never told me before. You've always behaved as my brother. To suddenly hear that you love me as a woman and that you want to marry me, I was stunned. It took a while for this news to settle in."

Several teardrops escaped the corner of her eye and slowly traced a narrow path down one ashen cheek. She quickly brushed it away, as if it had somehow offended her. "As for your other words, they're all true. I know better than anyone what Gray Eagle has done to me; you don't have to remind me. I also know everything that you've done for me. If not for you, I wouldn't care if I lived or died. You were the one who gave me the strength and courage to move on with my life. But love doesn't die that quickly or easily. Just because someone says it is over it doesn't simply vanish like the fog in the morning. I loved him, Powchutu, really loved him. God only knows why! If I could erase all these remaining feelings and all the pain that goes with them, then I would. But how can I? You said in time I would forget him. I need this time to conquer his hold over me. Please understand. Be patient with me just a little longer."

Powchutu realized that he had pushed her too fast. He admitted that she was correct. His anger melted at the sight of her sad, lovely face pleading with him. She did need more time, time she would spend with him. He would move more slowly and cautiously where she was concerned. He had all the time in the world, and she was surely worth courting. His taut body relaxed; his expression became warm and gentle.

"I promise you I will never mention this again until you say the time is right. When you no longer carry any love for him in your heart, then I will marry you that very day. Purge him from your heart, Alisha, as he was purged from your life. You must not live in the shadow of an evil love." He stroked one tear away from Alisha's smooth cheek.

"I know you're right, Powchutu. I will honestly try. Perhaps one day you will become my new sunlight," she teased him as the serious mood between them dissipated into a warm truce.

Matters were settled between them for the present, and

they went to the abandoned wagon and searched its remaining contents. All food and other staples had been previously hauled away. Yet, there were a few things which might be useful to them later: clothing, medicine, and a small amount of money which had been hidden beneath one of the bottom boards.

"Why would they leave these things behind, Powchutu?" she curiously inquired.

"The red man has no use for such garments or for the white man's money. Evidently it was not known what the medicine was," he replied.

Alisha laughed at her mistakes. "Of course," she agreed, holding a paisley print dress up to her shoulders. She giggled and remarked merrily, "If I eat all my vegetables and meat at dinner time, I just might fit into this lovely dress by winter."

Powchutu joined in on her obvious attempt at cheerfulness until the hoot of a nearby owl claimed his full attention. He shifted uneasily and studied the nearby lengthening shadows. "Let's get out of here, Alisha. We've stayed too long as it is."

They quickly gathered anything which seemed usable. They returned to their horses and led them away. In need of alert and silence, they did not speak for the rest of the long night. By the time they found an adequate place to hide and to rest for part of the day, they were both exhausted. He handed her the water bag and some food from his possessions. Later, he unrolled both their sleeping mats and told her to get some sleep. She obeyed him immediately. As weary as he was, his keen senses remained alert even during his light slumber.

Alisha was overjoyed when Powchutu finally announced that they were out of the Yankton territory. He grinned as he added that they were now entering the joint lands of the Pawnee, Winnebago, and the Omaha: all friendly to the white man, especially to the French. Alisha proudly remarked to him that she could speak French fluently, if it was ever called for.

Powchutu seemed confident that they could trade their two horses for a canoe at the Omaha village, which was only a few more days from where they were. He felt that they could make faster time in a canoe. He studied the skies each morning, noting the color changes which were signs of the coming snows. He also hoped they could trade for some warmer blankets and fur wraps. The days had already grown shorter and cooler, with the temperatures reaching down into the forties during the night. He prayed that it would not be necessary to tell her how low they were getting on supplies.

That very night, they suffered the coldness and dampness of the season's first frost. It did not take long for their worn moccasins to become soaked and chill their feet, making walking difficult when the horses were too weary to carry them. That next morning, Powchutu pressed Alisha onward as soon as she had rested for only a few hours. She sensed his urgency against the weather. He warned her that a delay could find the rivers iced over and continued travel impossible, or at best, treacherous.

Comprehending the danger of being caught out in the open during a blinding snow storm, Alisha forced herself to keep up with the swift and demanding pace that Powchutu was setting. She did not tell him about the pains within her lower stomach, nor of the extreme drowsiness which plagued her each day, nor of the nausea that she was now experiencing nearly every day. Knowing how he felt about her, she knew that he would halt his progress to allow her more time to rest. Her naive conclusions were that perhaps the constant riding was making her ill, or the excessive pace was overly fatiguing her, or that the tardiness of her monthly was causing those annoying pains.

When they finally reached the Omaha village, she was greatly tempted to tell her friend about her problems. Seeing the apprehension upon his face, she did not. She reasoned that canoe travel would help her overcome these troubles. If she could only reach St. Louis, then she could see the doctor there. She would not burden Powchutu with this added worry unless it was completely unavoidable. Alisha suffered in silence.

It only required a short time for Powchutu to trade their horses for a few supplies, extra blankets, and a bark canoe. It was fortunate for them that the Omaha hunters needed horses. Also, the Omaha were generous by nature to people who seemed in great distress or who had fallen upon hard times. Luckily, they traded frequently with other white men and assorted trappers. Knowing they could bargain with other white men for gold coins, the Omaha even accepted the money which the couple had discovered hidden in the deserted wagon. The canoe was gradually loaded by two friendly braves and a cheerful Powchutu.

As they bartered and labored, Alisha was busily studying the Omaha village. This village, with its earth-covered or bark lodges which were larger than buffalo skin tepees, was unlike any camp that she had seen before. The grounds were cleared and cleaned. There were several large campfires which seemed to be shared for cooking by more than one family. A genial atmosphere was present in this village.

She alertly noted many racks where hides had been

stretched and attached for cleaning and curing. Even though it was chilly, barefoot and scantily clad children played near the lodges in small groups. The working women would only occasionally glance up from their chores to study the two new visitors. Their casual attitudes told her that visitors were a common sight here.

Powchutu had previously explained the Omaha economy to her. It was based mainly on hunting and on trading the corn and vegetables which they cultivated. He had also eased her apprehensions with the pleasant news of Indians' friendship with the white man and of their animosity with the Sioux. Still, Alisha remained within arm's reach of Powchutu during their entire visit at the village.

After a short rest, with food supplied by the chief himself, the sojourners were on their way once more. Several of the friendlier braves offered suggestions of safe places to rest, ways to avoid ice blocks around the edges of the river, and where to find other tribes who could give them supplies and food. They thanked the Omaha for their kindness and climbed into the laden canoe.

Powchutu was slightly amused by the numerous offers which he had received for his woman. He jovially remarked that he just might consider one of them if she failed to obey his commands. Laughing in open happiness, he lifted the paddles, and their journey continued.

Trying to conceal her discomfort behind humor, Alisha said in an unruffled tone, "If the price had been higher, my dear master, no doubt you would have accepted one of them. Thankfully I am necessary to you; I mean with my French tongue and all."

Her tone gradually became serious as she modestly inquired, "Do you think we can find some secret place to camp tonight? I think I would trade my soul for a bath.

73

I've never felt so nasty in all my life. Even a small bath would be sheer heaven."

"You talk as if you haven't had one for weeks," he teased her lightly, recalling how fussy she was about cleanliness. "Seems the first time I met you, you were taking a bath."

Her eyes widened with indignation. She retorted, "I was not. I was already finished. Besides, we might not have met if I hadn't ordered that bath in order to meet the illustrious Lieutenant Jeffery Gordon." Not wishing to call to mind those terrible days at Fort Pierre, Alisha quickly changed the subject. "Other than a sponge-off here and there, I honestly haven't bathed. Just imagine when we get to St. Louis and we can soak in a hot tub filled with lots of bubbles and a splash of perfume," she tempted him in a flirtatious tone.

"Together or separately?" he replied roguishly. He threw back his head and chuckled in amusement at her expression.

She blushed a light pink and lowered her long lashes demurely. Gathering her daring, she playfully asserted, "Have you no shame or manners, young man? I mean, to wickedly suggest something so personal as mutual bathing." Her saucy laughter gave way to unsuppressed giggles.

"If I know the laws of white slavery, Little One, then I could command you to be at my side at all times. Could I not, my beautiful slave?" he challenged.

Her enchanting eyes lifted to meet his amused ones. She lowered her silvery voice to a seductive whisper and murmured, "I tell you what. . . ." An uncontrollable cry of pain escaped her colorless lips. She involuntarily clutched at her lower abdomen as she struggled to restrain her labored breathing.

Powchutu instantly lowered his paddle and called out, "What's wrong, Alisha? You're white as snow."

When the sharp pain ceased, she replied in a shaky tone, "Probably something I ate at the Omaha camp." She lied, knowing that the discomfort was getting worse. She had hoped that she could hold out until they made camp for the night, for their new travel plans called for movement in the daytime and rest at night.

They were too far downriver from the Omaha camp to turn back against the swift currents. Yet, they were also two more days' journey from the next friendly village. Powchutu worriedly scanned her ashen face and the pain revealed in her eyes. It was obvious that she was not telling the truth. He could sense that she did not want to worry him or to halt their progress.

"The truth, Alisha!" he demanded sternly, his tone almost angry. "How long have you been ill?"

She tried to dispel her guilty expression before his very vision. It failed to trick him. "I will be just fine in a little while. Let's make as much distance as possible before dark. Remember; winter's coming?"

Her ruse to divert his thoughts failed.

"How long?" he repeated.

Alisha nervously nibbled at her lower lip and sighed lightly, as if she were trying to decide upon a cunning answer. As she did so, the boat headed for the nearest shore. She glanced up at their rapid change of direction. She noted his intention.

"We can't stop now. It's too early in the day. We must make better time before dark." Her arguments fell upon deaf ears.

Powchutu landed the boat and tied one end to the nearest tree trunk. He gently shoved the canoe around until he could easily reach her and lift her out. She argued that it was unnecessary to carry her like a baby. He ignored her claims and walked over to a large tree, placing her on the ground near its base. Without a word, he returned to the canoe for blankets, food and water. He was distressed to discover that their medicine pouch had either been lost or stolen back in the Omaha camp. He came back to her side and knelt down to check her over.

"Where is the pain, Alisha?" he asked firmly as he handed her the water skin. After she had sipped some of the water, he covered her with a blanket. His jet eyes bored into her jade ones, demanding the truth.

She flushed a deep crimson and hastily looked away from his close scrutiny. In rising embarrassment she stammered, "It's . . . personal."

"Pain isn't personal, Alisha! Tell me!" he almost shouted in exasperation, mistaking the reason for her reluctance to tell him what she considered the problem.

She angrily met his glare and stated matter-of-factly, "It has to do with a woman's monthly problems! Satisfied, nosey?"

He studied her ashen face as well as her last words. "Do you always become this ill every month?" he curiously inquired as if he were her doctor.

Her eyes flew open wide in astonishment. She flushed an even deeper red at his boldness. Reading the great concern in his eyes, realizing that he was only trying to help her, she gradually calmed down. She remarked modestly, "No, I don't."

"Is this the first time? Any other problems?" he pressed, somehow suspecting that she was still hiding something from him. Alertly noting the frightened and ashamed look which flickered across her features, he knew that he was correct.

"Please, Powchutu," she entreated him. "This is most

embarrassing. It's private. From what I've seen, such pain isn't uncommon in some women. I'm certain it will be gone in a day or so. Can't we just continue on down-river? I can't hurt any less in the canoe than lying here," she reasoned.

"You can be more comfortable here. What other problems are you having?" he asked, utterly ignoring her claims of privacy and modesty. "We're not leaving until you tell me everything. Everything, Alisha," he stressed.

Observing his fierce determination, she sighed heavily and petulantly. She reluctantly complied with his orders to confess. "All right, you win. For the last few days I've been having dull pains about here." She pointed to her pelvic area as she continued, "They come and go, mostly dull, sometimes sharp like earlier. I've had some nausea during the early morning hours, but it's probably from the continual movement of riding. Sort of like mal-de-mer," she suggested. At his confused look, she clarified, "Seasickness. Many people become ill from constant motion."

"Besides the nausea and pains, what else?"

She caught the subtle change in his expression and tone of voice, but did not understand the reason. "What do you mean, what else? That's enough, isn't it?"

He glared her down, forcing her to give in to his command. "I have been extremely sleepy and tired. We have been travelling fast and hard these past weeks. That's all, Slave driver! End of confession. End of talk. Now, let's get moving before we have to spend the entire winter right here."

"Not so fast. One last question," he stated in a curious tone. "When was the last time you had your . . . monthly?" he inquired, using her word for the lack of a better one. She would never know how much he dreaded

77

her answer, nor how much anguish it would require in order to relate his growing suspicions.

She gaped at him in stunned silence for a long time, wondering why he would ask such a brash question. "What does that have to do with anything?" she naively exclaimed.

He met her guileless gaze and carefully replied in a slow and even tone so as to not overly frighten her. "Late monthlies, morning nausea, sleepiness, tension, and discomfort in that area of a woman's body usually mean only one thing, Alisha."

She pondered his words for a short time, recalling that it had been many weeks since her last cycle. She could be mistaken, for she had no way of keeping track of time. Within moments, the truth abruptly came to her: her last cycle had come before her rescue and trip to Fort Pierre. Her befuddled brain argued against that possibility, for her tormenting sojourn at Fort Pierre had been sometime back in August. This was mid-November; that would add up to many months of missed cycles. She instinctively knew that this was unnatural.

Powchutu was keenly studying her changing reactions as she was slowly reasoning out her puzzlement. She kept going over the list of symptoms and analyzing them. The truth struck her like a thunderbolt out of a clear blue sky. She gradually whitened as the numerous facts added up to his same conclusion: pregnancy. With this new fact to add to the list, she hurriedly analyzed her problem once more; there could be no error or miscalculation.

She looked up to find him intently watching her. "You already know, don't you?" was all she had to say.

"You're carrying Gray Eagle's child," he spoke her fears aloud. "Do you know how far along you are? Any guess at all?" His voice was low and even, concealing the impact of this startling news upon him.

His eyes glued to her face; his ears became fully alert. In his heart he knew that she would never be free of Gray Eagle now. She would always have his child to remind her of him.

It was a cruel twist of fate. Suddenly another fact hit him: Gray Eagle was alive within his child. It was possible that the Great Spirit had planned things this way; perhaps he was allowing Gray Eagle to make some payment for his past evil deeds. His dead spirit could make amends for his past crimes; his son could make a newer and better man than he was.

Many times it was believed by the Indians that the Great Spirit sent a dead warrior back to earth in another form in order to earn his place in the heavens or to pay for past deeds of cowardice and cruelty. Powchutu's heart lightened greatly as he viewed this event as forgiveness of his own crime. As he saw it, he had not completely destroyed the great warrior, for he still lived in his unborn child. His guilt vanished; his spirits soared.

Another truth came to him. His heart quivered with new excitement and hope. Alisha would surely need a husband's name for her child and for their protection. It was almost like a blessing in disguise. Seeing this complication as a new advantage to his own cause, he smiled cheerfully.

"Why are you smiling? What am I going to do now? I know nothing about babies. Should I return to Gray Eagle and beg him to accept me for our child's sake? Surely this will change his mind about revenge toward me?" Their child sparked hope in Alisha's heart.

"You cannot ever return to him!" Powchutu shouted before thinking clearly. He promptly regained control over himself and his wayward tongue. His wits were hastily assessing his new problem. A cunning idea came to him.

"Gray Eagle would never accept your word that the child is his, even if he dared to claim a half-breed child as his own. Do you honestly think he would allow a half-breed son to lead the mighty Sioux? You have seen how he despised me for my mixed bloods. He viewed me as lower than the white man. You would only endanger your life and the life of your child. In his rage, he might slay you before you could explain your incredible return to him. Consider this: how would he view a son with green eyes and auburn hair? He would be unable to prove his position as father. He would always be suspicious and doubtful of you." Powchutu warmed to the description and elaborated. "Far worse, Alisha, suppose the child favors your parents. How would you then convince him that the strange child is truly his?" he cruelly challenged, hoping to turn her thoughts from dreams of a return to the Sioux camp.

"But the child is his!" she protested. "Surely Gray Eagle considered such an event since he forced me to sleep with him every night!" Powchutu winced. Alisha continued, "Besides, why would I return to his cruelty if I were lying about the child? If he knows anything at all about pregnancy, the mere timing of the child's conception and birth would reveal the truth to him. I was carrying this child before I was taken to Fort Pierre. How can I simply leave here without even telling him the truth, without giving him a chance to either claim the child or to deny him?"

"He would not believe you, Alisha." Powchutu struggled to extinguish her hope. "No doubt he would claim it as one of the soldier's at the fort, or perhaps as Brave Bear's, or even as mine. How do you think he will feel if you returned to him after fleeing with another man? He would be forced to slay you to hide the truth of his earlier deed. You must think of the child, Alisha, your child."

Before she could reason further with him, he added, "Remember all the women and children from your fortress? Do they still live? Do not over-estimate his happy reaction to the news about a child of his own," he ominously warned. "He has not desired a son of his own before now. He has never married Chela or another. Why should he want a suspicious half-breed as his first son? Should he feel any more love or respect for his child than he does for its mother, his wife?"

Alisha flinched at his cutting words, yet did not deny them. It was clear that she could not return with assured safety. It was also clear that she was very distressed and frightened by this unforeseen event.

Powchutu calculated that he would allow her the time to adjust to her new predicament, then offer her marriage to him as the only solution. He walked around for a time, allowing her to deal with her warring emotions.

Alisha wondered if this news would have made any difference in Gray Eagle's decision to kill her. Could any man deny his own child, or even think to kill it? She fully recognized the real problem: he would not believe that the child was his. His hatred and cold bitterness against her and her people would not permit such a belief. So many unrelated thoughts bombarded her weary mind at once: penniless, orphaned, and pregnant—even worse, unmarried in the eyes of the white man.

While going over her scanty options, she knew that she could not marry Powchutu now, for it did not seem right to saddle him with the child of a man that he hated deeply. There was another fact to consider: Gray Eagle would always be there between them in the form of his child, preventing forgetfulness and joy. It was as if Gray Eagle had insidiously found a way to remain in her life and heart forever. She angrily cursed his violent intrusion into her life that day long ago. How could she ever be free of him now?

She fretted about the new burden that she might become to Powchutu. It had been difficult enough before now, but with her ill and pregnant . . . "I promise I'll try not to be very much trouble for you, Powchutu," she said. "I'm sorry about this complication. I swear to you that I did not know about it. I didn't even suspect the truth. How can any woman be so naive and stupid?" she said in despair.

Powchutu tenderly brushed away her tears. He smiled and said, "Do not worry, my love, for I will love and protect both of you. You cannot be blamed for this event. Things will work out just fine; wait and see. But for now, you must rest and eat well. It is not good to have such pains at this early time," he said in a tone of sincere worry.

She was utterly perplexed by his tranquil mood and encouraging words. "You aren't angry with me? You'll take care of us anyway? Gray Eagle's child, too?"

He caught the unmistakable softness of the words, "his child." "Of course I will, Alisha. From this day forward, it is only your child. I will guard its life as I will your own. There is no problem I cannot fix or take care of," he proudly boasted.

She smiled at him and hugged him tightly. "What would I ever do without you, Powchutu?" she uttered in open relief.

"Rest, love. We will press on tomorrow if you are better. If not, we'll remain here for a few days. We need to make St. Louis before winter if we can. But there's nothing for you to worry about. I will be at your side from now on. Nothing will ever harm you again."

After a light meal, Alisha slept fitfully throughout the cool night. As for Powchutu, he carefully watched over her every movement. He was grateful for the added warmth of the extra blankets from the Omaha traders, for this night was much chillier than any other had been. He could only hope and pray that Alisha would be well enough to continue their journey by morning. He could almost smell winter in the air; he could certainly read her clear messages upon the face of Mother Earth.

He allowed Alisha to sleep until she awoke on her own. She gently chided him for doing so, knowing how many of their daylight hours upon the river had been sacrificed for her well-being. He grinned and played the dauntless hero before her, revelling in her gratitude and affection. She giggled and shook her head in mock exasperation; she playfully accused him of spoiling her too much.

After a light breakfast, Powchutu packed their possessions back into the canoe. He insisted upon carrying her to the boat and gently placing her inside. She settled herself as comfortably as possible, then smiled warmly at him. He returned it, then winked at her. He agilely climbed into the other end of the canoe, and their trek resumed once more.

As she lay slightly reclining in the canoe, Alisha feigned light slumber so that she could do some serious thinking. The night before, the mere thought of pregnancy had terrified her. But now that she had been given some time to adjust to this incredible truth, she was strangely relieved and ecstatically happy. In an unexplainable way, she was not totally losing her love, for she was carrying a vital part of him within her slim body. She, Alisha Williams, would give birth to the first-born son of the legendary warrior Gray Eagle. It was only just that she should be granted some reward for all her past sufferings and sacrifices. What could better replace a lost love than his own child, an inseparable part of them both?

Alisha finally decided that this news did not really upset her at all. She admitted that she wanted this baby very much. She was certain that it would be hard to raise a child alone, but she would have Powchutu to help her. At that thought, she began to fret over how she would deal with his declaration of love and offer of marriage. Frankly she did not know what to say or to do. She decided that she had enough things to occupy her mind without looking for more. She would allow time and necessity to reveal what course of action she would take where he was concerned.

The fact that she slightly resented any man taking Gray Eagle's place as husband and father bothered her deeply. For certain, she could not permit this to happen until she was completely over him. The idea of a wifely submission to him or to any other man caused her blood to run cold. Yet, all she had to do to warm her very soul was to envision Gray Eagle's smile, or to recall his passionate lovemaking, or to call to mind his husky voice whispering into her eager ear, or to picture his handsome face with those captivating eyes, or to bring to mind how it felt to touch him and to lie near him at night. He was such an all-consuming man. He was completely intoxicating. If not for the baby, she would now be in body-wracking tears. Her heart ached for her lost love; yet, it gradually mellowed with the joy of impending motherhood.

Alisha silently thanked God for giving her a new reason to live and to love. Next to Gray Eagle, this was the best gift she could ever receive. She stirred just enough for Powchutu to realize that she was only resting, not sleeping. He began to entertain her with several songs that he had learned as a child. Her mind blanked out all her past worries and her present concerns. She lost herself to his mellow voice and sunny songs.

After many hours upon the river, Powchutu decided to halt for a rest and to allow her to stretch her cramped legs. He headed the craft toward the nearest shore. Upon landing, he jumped out and tied up the canoe. He once again helped her out and carried her to a nearby section of dried grasses. This time, she permitted his gentle aid without a word. In fact, she liked the pampering that he was giving her. As she rested, he returned to the canoe to fetch water and food for their late afternoon meal.

As they shared dried fruits and corn cakes, they chatted and laughed about nonsensical matters. It was soon obvious that Powchutu was taking longer than necessary to eat and to rest; she knew that this was solely for her own benefit. She finally told him that the pains had lessened to a dull ache, but that she did feel much better today. Although she was telling the truth, he looked skeptical and overly concerned.

"You worry about me far too much," she gently scolded him, her eyes simultaneously smiling her gratitude for his abundant help and kindness.

"And how much is too much?" he teased playfully.

"You know what I mean. It isn't necessary to coddle me the entire way to St. Louis. We're wasting a lot of time. I assure you that I've survived far worse times and conditions."

"But not while you were pregnant," he argued.

She laughed in open amusement. "Now who's the naive one? If memory serves me correctly, you said I must be at least three months along. That would mean that I have gone through many things in this delicate condition. Would it not, my friend?" she teased him in return, gaiety dancing in her forest-green eyes.

"I tell you what, Miss Williams. If by the time we . . ." He abruptly halted, cutting off the rest of his statement. He came to instant alert, eyes and ears strained for another warning of what he feared to be true. His entire body was tense and taut, his face impassive, his eyes pensive. He hardly breathed as he called on all his instinctive and learned senses to help him in this dark moment of peril.

Chapter Five

At the first tell-tale scent of what could only be white trappers, Powchutu silently signaled Alisha to be still. His complete concentration was on the danger at hand.

A raspy voice yelled out, "Drop it, Injun! Ya don't wants us to hurt yore woman, duz ya?"

At Powchutu's dauntless refusal to drop his knife or to lay aside his loaded bow, another voice called out, "Ya both dead if'n ya don't do it fast, Injun."

Alisha's panicked gaze sought out the location of the second man's voice. It was clear that he was between them and the river; it was also evident that they were trapped between at least two crude men. "The gurl goes first," he warned the hesitant Powchutu once more.

Powchutu's fathomless gaze read her anxious one. He was furious with himself for placing her in this dangerous position. It was too late to berate himself for moving so far from the water. At the time, it had seemed a good idea; one that would shield Alisha from the cold draft blowing across the river's choppy surface. He had recently promised her that she would always be safe at his side. How could she ever trust his promise of protection again? Powchutu was filled with wordless fury.

As he saw things, he had two choices: obey the trappers' command, or kill Alisha before they could harm her. For certain, he did not trust either of these unseen men. Even if Alisha had not been pregnant, he knew that she could not withstand an attack by two, rough men. His mind was working fast. Enlightenment suddenly flooded his black eyes. He winked at Alisha.

He boldly called out in excellent English, "I am not an Indian. My wife and I are from Fort Pierre, up north a ways. It was burned out by the Sioux a while back. We're heading downriver to St. Louis. We're only dressed like Indians to get through this territory safely."

He waited for his words to have some favorable effect upon their attackers. There was total silence for a short time. Then, the two men began to consult with each other across their heads.

"What'cha think, Buck?" the first man called out.

"I say the red bastard is lying through his Injun teeth! I heard 'bout that Fort Perr. Wadn't no survivors. Injuns kilt everbody. I say we cut out his lying tongue," came the second man's opinion.

Alisha cringed in terror, for she knew too well what such men did to Indian maidens. In desperation she shouted to him, "He is not lying! We are from Fort Pierre. We escaped the Sioux who attacked there. I swear it," she frantically added.

"How 'bout that! They both speak Enlush. Where'ju lern our tongue, gurl? Yore man teach'cha? She'd be worth some easy cash to Old Frenchy," he slurred.

"We are not Indians!" she angrily shouted, knowing they did not want to accept the truth. "Look for yourself," she recklessly challenged them. "I have green eyes and auburn hair. You know Indians do not."

The second man did not permit her even this small victory. "Ya cud both be half-breeds. Anybody knows half-breeds er just as dangerous as reglar Injuns. 'Sides, a man'ud be a fool to let ya git away," he threatened her with an evil laugh and sneer.

As Powchutu was trying to think of some safe way out

of this precarious situation, he allowed Alisha to divert
the men's attention with her questions. He was furious
with himself for allowing these two ruffians to overtake him. A thought flitted through him: now he knew
how Gray Eagle must have felt when he had allowed
Powchutu to surprise him at the river. The similarities
between these two dangerous situations did not sit well
with him; it hovered like some evil omen.

The course of action was decided for him; one of the
trappers fired a musket shot, striking him in the upper
left arm. Although he had not winced or cried out, blood
flowed down his tanned arm like water rushing over a
cascade. He prepared himself for their coming attack,
guessing that they were about to rush them. As the first
man raced from the dense cover of the nearby bushes, he
tensed for a battle. But before they could tangle, the
second man had his knife blade at Alisha's throat.
Powchutu instantly assumed a crouched, alert position.

"Drop it, Injun, or yore woman's dead!" he snarled
out between clenched, rotting teeth. The stench of his
body and clothing was enough to make her want to retch.
One hand held the broad skinning knife near her throat,
while the other one held a large mass of her hair in a
painful grasp. At Powchutu's reluctance to obey his last
command, he angrily twisted her hair and jerked it
roughly, snapping her head backwards.

A loud scream was torn from her lips, and Alisha unexpectedly struggled to wriggle away from his tight grip.
The man muttered a curse and moved to kick her in the
buttocks as a warning. Ignoring the stinging pain on her
scalp, Alisha managed to turn her body around to attack
his knees and to try to make him fall. But the kick was
already in rapid motion. She was forcefully struck in the
lower abdomen instead of her derrière.

Lights danced ominously before her blurred vision; nausea swept over her, and she swallowed rapidly to control it. Excruciating agony in the depth of her womanhood threatened to envelop her in darkness. A loud humming sound filled her ears. Her face was ashen, making her large green eyes appear like two emerald stones on a white background. She helplessly doubled over in overwhelming torment, clutching protectively at her stomach. Moans of steadily increasing pain escaped from her colorless lips.

The brute simply assumed that her pain was caused from the blow that he had inflicted upon her. Accustomed to fighting with men, mainly Indians, he did not realize how forceful and damaging his swift blow had been. Irritated by what he thought a ruse, he roughly grabbed her two upper arms and yanked her to her feet. He shook her violently, hoping to terrify her into total obedience. His relentless, cruel actions only served to increase Alisha's suffering. He cursed her and began to shake her even more convulsively.

Alisha was completely unaware of Powchutu's strained voice yelling at the man that she was pregnant. He warned the man whom he was fighting with what would happen to both of them if she were injured. But the malevolent man only laughed at him and taunted him with what he would do to Alisha once Powchutu was dead.

Infuriated, Powchutu tried to free his knife from his attacker's grip. But tragically, Powchutu was making time-consuming mistakes in his strategy; his urgency to be done with this man was taking its toll on his strength. He had helplessly watched the effect of the other man's impact upon Alisha's slender body. He was in a near frenzy to get free and go to her aid. He was not using his skill and power to the best of his ability. He would frequently risk a glance in Alisha's direction, inadvertently permitting the other man to prolong the deadly struggle between them. They danced in a duel of death. Powchutu's face suddenly filled with unyielding determination to have this matter settled quickly and favorably.

Feeling a sticky wetness between her legs, Alisha feared what might be taking place within her weakened body. Dauntless strength came from sheer desperation, desperation to protect this last link with the man she still loved. She resolved that she would not lose this baby, not even if she had to kill to insure its safety. She fearlessly increased her struggles with the trapper whose intentions were to ravish her. She slapped at him, and she clawed at his scarred face with broken nails which left tiny rivulets of blood.

During their struggle, he succeeded in throwing Alisha to the hard ground. He instantly flung himself upon her seductively positioned form. He grasped her head between his large hands. In lecherous delight, he stared at her. Aware of her entrancing beauty for the first time, he wantonly and coarsely hunched his swollen manhood against her. His lewd, hungry grin warned her of his intentions. His gaping look of lust was as clear as the sky above her.

Alisha tried to close her ears to the indecent remarks which were flowing from his drooling lips. He ripped at her bodice; he yanked at her hem. He was nearly beside himself with uncontrollable desire. He was like a rutting beast who was governed by undeniable, animalistic lust. His crazed eyes told her that there would be no stopping his defilement now, nothing short of his death.

She wildly resisted his brute strength while nearly fainting from severe cramps. She knew the danger to her

91

life and to that of her unborn child from this man's intended violation. She prayed that she would have the energy to delay him until Powchutu was free to help her. If Powchutu lost his battle with the other man, she knew that she was as good as dead.

The trapper grasped her proud, trembling chin. Before she could react, he brought his mouth down upon hers.

Alisha never knew what stopped her from gagging into his mouth. Her small hands beat at his muscled back and clawed at his leather jerkin. His squat, thickset body was unmovable. His scraggly beard chafed her delicate skin, and his fingers dug into the tender flesh of her chin. As his odious mouth savagely ravished hers, her right hand somehow touched his knife sheath at his flabby waist. Her quavering fingers automatically closed around the thick handle of his skinning knife. She cautiously eased it from its holder and slowly brought her hand upwards; her sole intent was to halt his brutal attack upon her by cutting his face.

Just as her hand was neck high, he glanced up and called out to his friend, "Better hurry, Jeremy. She's a real looker. Lot'a fire in'er. She'll warm our beds fur a long time. You kin have yores just as soon as I git mine."

"Be right there," came a breathy reply. "This Injun's dead," he confidently added.

Hearing their threat, Alisha fearfully screamed, "No-o-o," in a wailing tone. As the lone word escaped her lips, the knife came up and sliced the trapper's throat.

Blood spurted from the open wound like a raging geyser, splattering over her face and chest. Frothy bubbles eased from the gaping red line. For a brief moment he stared at her in utter disbelief, then in painful reality. But before he could retaliate, he fell across her: dead.

In rising panic Alisha shoved his limp, heavy body off hers. Dazed and frightened, she slowly sat up. Waves of dizziness and agony swept over her entire body. She stared at the bloody form beside her; her glazed eyes passed to her own bloody hands and chest. She did not have the wits to react to the outraged shout beside her as the other trapper knocked Powchutu aside and made a dash for her.

His yell was as piercing and menacing as the war cry of an Indian warrior. Before Powchutu could recover his balance, the trapper had buried his dagger deep into Alisha's left shoulder. In her state of shock and terror, she did not even feel this new pain. All she felt was the endless agony which was threatening to rip her apart. Her last conscious memory was the lurid sight of someone else's blood upon her two shaking hands. As she helplessly sank to the ground, Powchutu gave the Sioux war cry and charged the man like one insane with bloodlust.

This time, the battle between them was brief and deadly. Thinking Alisha slain, his rage knew no limits. In less than five minutes, both men lay dead in their own blood. Powchutu rushed to where Alisha lay on the blood-soaked earth, ashen and motionless. His joy was boundless as he quickly discovered that she was still alive.

As easily as possible, he carefully withdrew the dagger from her shoulder. He cursed the lack of medical supplies once again. Blood poured from her jagged wound, saturating her dress and matting her long hair. While he nervously considered what to do for her, he placed his open palm against the wound to staunch as much blood as possible. Without any medicine, all he could do was to bandage the wound and pray for her life.

As his frantic eyes darted about, they alighted on the

93

streaks of blood on Alisha's legs. As gently as he could, he rolled her to her side and looked beneath her. The back of her doe-skin dress was drenched in bright red blood. He realized the worst of his fears. Alisha was miscarrying.

For once, he was totally ignorant of what to do for her. The woman he loved more than life itself was rapidly bleeding to death in his arms, and he was helplessly unskilled to help her. He let out a loud groan of anguish, then vowed in anger, "Damn you, you bloody bastards! I could kill you both again."

Another white man eased into the small clearing just to the right of Powchutu's back. His senses dulled by his great pain and worry, Powchutu was unaware of his presence. The stranger's keen blue eyes promptly took in the evil sights before him, their unmistakable meaning very clear to him. Distressed by such senseless hatred and murder, he swore aloud. "My God, what happened here? Is she hurt badly?" he inquired, more so to let the man holding Alisha tightly in his arms know that he was no threat to either of them.

Powchutu was instantly on his feet, his stained knife in his hand, ready to do battle with this newly arrived enemy. The other man propped his bow and quiver of arrows against a tree, then slowly lifted his hands upwards to indicate a truce. They faced each other, each sizing up the other.

Powchutu sarcastically asked, "These your friends?"

"Nope. But I do know who they are: Jeremy Brown and Buck Conners. Bad lot. Been a lot of trouble in these parts lately. Sooner or later, I knew they'd get something like this."

Powchutu's keen gaze hastily assessed this new-comer's manner. He seemed cautious; yet, not the slightest bit threatening. He was dressed in the typical trapper's attire: fringed buckskins and high-topped moccasins.

His full, dark hair rested just above his broad shoulders. He appeared rugged and powerful and had weathered, tanned skin. The creases around his mouth and near the corners of his eyes showed that he smiled and laughed a great deal.

This towering stranger patiently permitted Powchutu's close scrutiny. In the final analysis, it was his clear, honest eyes and kindly manner which dismissed Powchutu's suspicion of him. The stranger said with obvious sincerity, "Sorry I didn't arrive sooner. The odds might've saved your woman's life. Your wife?"

Powchutu risked a quick glance at Alisha. The anguish in his eyes told the stranger a great deal about his emotions. Without thinking, he shook his head no. "Sister?" came the next obvious question. As Powchutu replied negatively again, the man asked if she still lived.

Powchutu defensively stated, "If you value your life, get away from here. She's hurt bad. I need to tend her, not mix words with a stranger. Not one with friends like those two," he snapped, nodding his head in the direction of their bodies.

"Like I said before, they weren't friends of mine. I have a cabin not too far from here. You're welcome to use it. I got medicine and bandages there. Either take my word for it and let me help you with her, or I'll be on my way. Fact is, she's bleeding pretty bad. I'd say you need some skilled help with her." Sincere concern could be easily detected in his drawl.

The aura around this particular white man told Powchutu that he could be trusted. Powchutu said, "You're right. The name's Powchutu. I was the scout at Fort Pierre until the Sioux wiped it out a while back. We were heading downriver to St. Louis when these two men bushwhacked us. My medicine bag was stolen back at the Omaha camp when we stopped there for supplies." Powchutu did his talking as he was tending to Alisha, hoping to halt the steady flow of blood until he could get her to this generous man's cabin.

"Name's Joe Kenny. I've done lots of scouting for wagon trains heading out this way. Gave it up after my last run. Too much trouble and too little reward," he remarked, followed by a somber laugh. "From now on, it's strictly trapping and hunting for me. Who is the girl with you?" he inquired as he leaned over to assist Powchutu.

Taking in the first full view of her face, he inhaled loudly and sharply. "Alisha Williams!" he exclaimed in disbelief. "Sakes alive! What's she doing here like this?"

Chapter Six

Powchutu turned a suspicious gaze to Joe's shocked face. Coming back to full alert, he curiously questioned, "You know Alisha?"

"Sure I do. I scouted for her uncle's wagon train about a year or so ago. We were good friends. Never met a better woman in my life. She's dressed like an Indian. You, too. What happened to her? What's she doing here with you?"

"Later. She's been stabbed in the shoulder, and she's also miscarrying. One of the men tried to rape her; they struggled while I was fighting with that other man. She killed him. Hell, I don't know anything about female matters. She's bleeding to death, and I can't even help her," he snapped at his own incompetence and frustration. "I promised her I wouldn't ever let anyone hurt her again. Some help I turned out to be . . ."

"Let me take care of her. I've had lots of practice with babies and female troubles. In my travels, I've done just about every kind of medicine and doctoring that's possible. Even cut off a man's leg one time. Bit by a rattler. Gangrene set in. Surprised the hell outta me when he finally pulled through, almost good as new," Joe modestly confessed as he worked on the unconscious Alisha.

He chatted, trying to calm Powchutu. "I've even had lessons from several Indian medicine men: shamans, they call themselves. Smart men, you know? I can't stop the bleeding out here," he finally confessed. "We'll have to get her back to my cabin and work on her there. I'll carry her. You bring my weapons and any of your gear you don't want stolen by stray braves."

Without asking for Powchutu's agreement, Joe took over the situation. He wrapped Alisha in the blanket which Powchutu handed to him. He lifted her light frame in his strong arms, then gave the scout the directions to his cabin. As Powchutu anxiously gathered their belongings, Joe headed off into the trees to their right.

He abruptly halted and called back over his shoulder, "Best shove these two bodies into the river, Powchutu. Wouldn't do to attract a pack of wolves during the night."

After a brisk ten-minute walk, Joe shoved open the door to his cabin and walked inside. He gently lay the lovely woman down upon his narrow bunk bed. He turned to gather what supplies and medicines he would need in order to try and save her life. It was evident that she had lost a great deal of blood and that she was growing weaker by the minute. For the first time in his life, Joe felt incompetent and afraid.

He came back to stand beside the bed, gazing down at Alisha's pale face. "Often wondered what happened to you, my beautiful lady," he murmured to himself. "Thought I'd drop in on you and your people later in the spring. What a waste . . . If I told your people once, I told them a hundred times to settle near the Omaha or Pawnee. No, they had'ta challenge the mighty Sioux for their lands. Fools! I warned them over and over. They should'a listened to me. I bet they're all dead or captured by now. Else you wouldn't be here with a half-breed scout from a burned-out fort. I wonder just what you mean to him . . . that look on his face tells me you're mighty special to him . . . but what about you, pretty lady? Is he special to you, I wonder?"

He lovingly caressed her cheek. He sadly muttered, "The trouble is, it's women and children who suffer the most. Stubborn men deserve their fates; innocents like you do not. Can't imagine how you got away from them. That scout has a lot of explaining to do."

As he carefully placed his knife inside Alisha's bodice and his hand on her neckline, Powchutu came inside the doorway. He instantly halted in fear and in shock. He finally managed to shout, "What are you doing, Kenny? I'll kill you if you harm her!" He rushed forward to attack Joe.

Joe flashed him an irritated glare. "I can't hardly tend her wounds when they're covered up, can I? The easiest thing to do is to cut off her dress. Any unnecessary movements will cause more bleeding. She's already lost too much blood as it is. Alisha is perfectly safe with me, Scout. We're old friends," he acidly reminded him.

Watching the warning glare become an apprehensive stare, Joe curiously inquired, "What is Alisha to you, Scout? How'd you two get away from the Indians? Anybody else alive back there?"

As he talked, he carefully cut away Alisha's torn and soiled dress. In case she might need this dress later, he was painstaking in removing it; he cut it straight down the front, then across both shoulder seams. Very gently he lifted her slender body and told Powchutu to pull it from beneath her. Seeing how much she was hemorrhaging from her female parts, he glanced up at the scout and stated clearly, "You're right, Powchutu. She's definitely lost her baby. I best halt the bleeding as soon as possible or we might lose her. Your child?"

Powchutu had turned away, unable to look upon her

bloody body in his guilt-riddled frame of mind. "No," he admitted without even realizing that he was answering Joe's question. "It was Gray Eagle's. It's all my fault. I should never have helped her escape from him. Will she die, Joe? All I wanted to do was to protect her from his cruelty and hatred, just to get her back to her own people where she belongs. It wasn't right for her to be his captive slave, for him to treat her so savagely. She should be free and happy," he absently murmured in a solemn tone.

Joe was staring at him in stunned disbelief. "Did you say the child was Gray Eagle's, the Sioux warrior? Son of Chief Running Wolf?"

Powchutu's onyx eyes met Joe's startled blue ones. His bitter opinion of Gray Eagle was evident in his cold eyes and frigid tone. He was blaming Gray Eagle for her illness, for it was his fault that she was in a position to be attacked by those two trappers. The only guilt that Powchutu placed upon his own shoulders was the burden of not protecting her against further harm. He had permitted someone to harm her while she was in his keeping . . .

"That's right, Kenny. He attacked their fortress, killed all her people, and captured her. She's been with him most of the time since midsummer."

Astonished at this incredible news, Joe argued, "But he has never taken a white female captive before, not that I've heard about. God, he hates the whites! Why Alisha? Why didn't he let one of his warriors have her? Gray Eagle and Alisha?"

"There has never been a woman like Alisha," Powchutu said solemnly. "You should know that. Even the indomitable Gray Eagle could not resist her. She was his woman until a few weeks ago. I helped her to escape from him," he proudly boasted.

"Are you saying Gray Eagle loved her?" The tone of his question was so strange that Powchutu's curious gaze devoured his unreadable expression.

"Look at her back. There you have your answer," he retorted in anger.

Joe inhaled sharply at the sight of the healed lash marks. His hand went out instinctively to touch the ghostly scars upon Alisha's ivory skin. He moved his hand over them, mentally determining their age. His mind was in a violent maelstrom; his thoughts ran one way and then another. He appeared more deeply shocked and angered by this new fact than by the news that Gray Eagle had enslaved Alisha.

Before he could speak, Powchutu fumed, "Yes! He did that to her. That, and far worse things. From the first time he took her captive, he has treated her this brutal way. Three times she tried to escape from him. Each time he refused to let her go. Whatever it took to get his way, he did it and took her back to his tepee. He was worse than an animal."

"It's clear there's a lot to tell. Later. Right now, we've got to stop this bleeding. About the only way I know how is to pack her with clean strips of cloth. First, we'll need to boil it with some medicine. You put the water on, and I'll get the strips ready. You can dress her shoulder wound while I take care of her other problem."

For the first time, Joe noticed the still bleeding wound on Powchutu's upper arm. He grabbed a clean strip of cloth and secured it around his hard bicep. "That'll halt the bleeding. Looks like a flesh wound. I'll tend it later. Best we try to save her life first."

After the water came to a rapid boil, Joe dropped a measured amount of yellow powder into the pot; he then placed long strips of white cloth into the same pot. While

101

they were boiling together, Joe took some of the warm water and proceeded to bathe Alisha.

As he gently removed the drying blood and dirt, he took great pains to ignore her curvaceous body. As fiercely as he tried to concentrate upon her condition, her enticing figure succeeded in reminding him of how long he had been without a woman and of how frequently his thoughts had been upon this very female. Right about then, he was so confused by the events of this unnatural day that he was not sure what he felt or what he thought.

When she was clean, Powchutu set to tending the knife wound upon Alisha's shoulder. Joe moved between her spread legs and began to carefully insert the sterilized, medicated strips of cloth into her vagina, just as he had once seen a doctor do in a similar case. He recalled that the doctor told him that the tight packing should halt the hemorrhaging and force clotting. He knew that the packing should be left in place for three days, then very cautiously moistened and withdrawn. He worked slowly and gently, pushing the strips into place with the butt of a hunting knife. Already aware of the fact that he did not have any forceps, he decided that he would worry later about the personal way the strips must be removed.

Powchutu finished long before Joe did. As he continued his work, Joe explained what he was doing and why. Powchutu thanked him for his help and for his much-needed knowledge and skill. Joe smiled as he accepted Powchutu's gratitude. After completing his task, he told Powchutu they would have to wait until much later to learn if Alisha would require any laudanum for her pain. Joe thought it best not to administer it to her until she roused. That way, they could discover if she had some other injury that they had overlooked. It would also let them know of her real condition. All they could do now was to wait and to watch.

Joe cleared away the medical supplies, wash basin, and used cloths. He covered Alisha with a light blanket, then turned to the scout. He cleaned and dressed Powchutu's injury. After placing salve upon the lacerated flesh, he rebound it snugly. His keen gaze recognized the intense way the scout was staring at the unconscious Alisha.

As Powchutu had done previously, Joe covertly sized up this strange man who had mysteriously appeared with the white woman. Joe's piercing gaze glanced over the powerfully built man before him. Beneath his leather weskit, Joe could see strong, hard muscles which flexed and rippled with his agile movements. His long, firm legs which gave height to his towering frame were encased in buckskin leggings and high-topped moccasins. His skin was bronze; his piercing eyes were midnight black. The square angles of his face made him appear a handsome, yet sardonic looking, man.

His daring, strength, and courage had been proven in the bloody clearing. His concern and affection for Alisha were undisguised. His manner was reserved, somewhat secretive and defensive. Joe came to realize that, depending upon how the scout was dressed and how he behaved, he could pass for either a white man or an Indian: a fortunate trait in these parts. Joe was baffled by this man who appeared open, honest, and sincere; yet, Joe sensed mystery and guile. He was alarmed by something which he could not place his finger on—and he was determined to know all about the half-breed.

As they sat drinking coffee and talking, the subject was Alisha and her recent past. Powchutu informed Joe of her capture and of her life in Gray Eagle's camp. He went on to explain about her attempted escape and the beating

Gray Eagle gave her for it. He sullenly related the events of her rescue by the cavalry from the fort. He angrily disclosed their vile treatment of her until her recapture by Gray Eagle.

Joe was astonished by the daring of Gray Eagle; it was incredible to think that he would simply ride up to the fort gates and demand the return of his white captive. He was also shocked and angered by the soldiers' cowardice in complying with the demand to release Alisha or die. Naturally he was further surprised to learn of Alisha's acceptance among the Indians as Shalee, the daughter of ˙Black Cloud of the notorious Blackfoot tribe. But Powchutu promptly told Joe that even this event had not spared the girl from the cruelty of Gray Eagle. It seemed impossible for her to be free of him. Joe could not comprehend why the infamous warrior would go to such lengths to possess a woman that he so obviously disliked. He gradually concluded that there was more to this strange behavior than the scout was telling.

He listened closely and intently as Powchutu blurted out the same terrible lie that he had told Alisha. The scout did not dare tell anyone the real truth. He was even uncertain as to why he was confessing so much to this total stranger. He decided that it had to do with her past friendship with this man.

Joe had no choice but to accept the words of Alisha's liberator. The scars upon her body declared Gray Eagle's brutality. Joe readily saw that Powchutu was in love with Alisha and that he had risked his own life to rescue her. He could also discern what her present condition was doing to him. Reading all these emotions in the scout's eyes, he concluded that this man was suffering as much as she was. Yet, there was some niggling, intangible detail about Powchutu which gnawed at the edge of his keen mind. There was something vaguely familiar about him. It was strange, for they had never met before.

Putting aside this weird sensation, Joe asked, "Why would the warrior marry her, then try to kill her? The facts don't seem to add up right to me. . . ."

Once more, Powchutu related his side of the truth. He shrewdly inquired, "You told me you led her people out here. That means you knew her pretty well, right? Can't you imagine how she might react to such cruelty? She's generous, tender-hearted, and peace-loving. She would go for a truce, right? She hoped this marriage would be that truce. She did everything he demanded. It was never enough for him. He didn't want her, but he wouldn't allow any other man to have her. He seemed to enjoy hurting her. He didn't want her to be happy with the people at the fort, so he came after her. He wouldn't let her marry Brave Bear. He wouldn't let her leave with me, not unless . . . unless I helped her run away from him. Our lives won't be worth anything if he catches up with us."

The astute Joe caught the change in the half-breed's voice, but could not explain it. Powchutu went on with his narrative, "That day when I found her on the plains, he had just ridden off and left her without food or water. He came riding into his camp with a sad look on his face. Said she had been killed by some enemy warriors. He didn't fool me. I knew he was lying. I searched and searched for her until I found her. I prayed he hadn't killed her yet. Even though it had been two days since he left her there, she could not believe he would do such a thing without some just cause. But, I tell you, his only cause was hatred for the white man. She has never understood this kind of blind hatred and senseless killing. Gray Eagle chose her to bear his hatred of the white man, to endure torture and punishment."

Joe deemed it best not to tell this angry, bitter man that he had met the notorious Gray Eagle on several occasions, but not in a very long time. He did not tell the scout that he was probably the only white man who had escaped the wrath of the most feared Indian in history. Yet, knowing the great warrior as he did helped to convince him of Powchutu's deceptive tale.

In his wildest imagination, Joe could not picture the truculent warrior capturing a white female and holding her prisoner in his tepee. The fact that he later married her was utterly incomprehensible and incongruous. To think of Alisha as the slave-wife of Wanmdi Hota was too farfetched to accept. That is, unless Gray Eagle had some secret, satanic plan in which he wanted to use her in a particular way. He wondered if the scout had already determined the real motives: hatred and pride.

For certain, Gray Eagle was a very proud man, perhaps too proud and too protective. Joe had always respected his courage, superior skill, cunning, power, and magnetism. He was a man to be greatly feared and wisely obeyed; yet, he commanded respect and affection. He was as well-known for his generosity as he was for his avowed hatred of the intruding white man.

Joe admitted to himself that Gray Eagle was the main reason that no more whites had come this far west to settle. It was this unconquerable warrior himself who had taught Joe the reality of the war between their two races. Once, they had fought off a band of renegade warriors, only to discover later who had been the other man behind that next boulder.

Both men being intelligent and reputable, they quickly acknowledged the prowess and value of the other. They mutually exchanged a new-found truce and friendship.

They had camped on that same spot for three days, sharing stories and adventures, gaining a new respect and insight into the other's thoughts and ways, and building a bond of trust and affection. Afterwards, they had occasionally run into each other along the trails. More than once Gray Eagle had spared his life or had ordered it spared. Joe was not a man who easily forgot friendship or help. It was gradually becoming clear to Joe that the warrior whom he had known, befriended, and admired was not this same man who had tried to destroy someone as precious and as beautiful as Alisha Williams.

Knowing Alisha from the past only increased his anger toward Gray Eagle and these acts of violence. Punishment of male enemies was one thing; putting innocent females to the lash was quite another. Totally baffled by this news, Joe could only assume that something had radically changed in Gray Eagle. He was temporarily saddened by the loss of such a great man. This feeling of betrayal gradually lessened and was replaced by bitterness and anger.

If Joe had doubted Powchutu's statements at first, it was not for very long. Within two days, Alisha was running a high fever and was now delirious. Joe winced in anguish as he empathized with Alisha as she revealed the choppy tales of brutality and hatred which she had endured. His heart went out to this gentle, loving creature who had won his calloused heart on their way out West. He could recall the many times when she had freely offered her help, even her food and water ration, to others who were less fortunate than she. He could remember how she had personally doctored the sick and how she had assumed the chores of anyone too weak to do them. She had done this all without grumbling, without wanting any thanks, without any extra benefits, or without regard to her own safety.

Joe had been quick to notice that she was a special kind of woman, the kind who did not come along very often. In some ways, she had too many good qualities, for people were constantly taking advantage of her. If not, then they jealously found ways to make her suffer for her beauty and gentle nature. It infuriated Joe to see such a rare blossom treated so badly. He could only reluctantly imagine the terrors that she must have endured since he had last seen her: penniless, vulnerable, abused, and alone.

As the days crawled by, Joe and Powchutu took turns bathing Alisha's hot, moist brow with cool, wet cloths. They constantly forced liquids down her dry throat. They caught rabbits and netted turtles to make nourishing soup for her. On the third day, Joe removed the vaginal packing with great care and some difficulty. Both men were ecstatic to learn that the dangerous hemorrhaging had ceased.

An infection had inflamed the knife wound on Alisha's shoulder. It had grown puffy and an angry red; the surrounding area began to fill up with pus. On the fourth day, Joe announced to the scout that he was going to open the infected wound, drain it, pour medicine into it, and then sear it shut with the heated blade of his knife. Seeing no other choice, he allowed Joe to do as he had suggested.

Even in her continued state of unconsciousness, Powchutu had to hold her down when Joe opened the festered injury and when he later cauterized it with the white-hot blade of his knife. As Powchutu held her down, Alisha twisted and groaned in agony. Her delicate cheekbones raged a bright red against the whiteness of her flawless complexion.

As Joe held the torrid blade against her skin, she cried

out in defiance. The two men's eyes met and locked in mutual understanding and sympathy, for it was to Gray Eagle that she spoke. They assumed that she was dreaming of past tortures and was pleading for release.

Many times Alisha called Gray Eagle's name. Over and over the tragedy of their lost and treacherous love spilled from her lips. As Joe tended the lovely woman, he heard her tell of horrors that caused him to wince in anguish and disbelief. Frequently he turned his face away, knowing he should not be overhearing the intimate details of their nights and days together; yet, he could not leave her side when she was so ill.

Ensnared in a feverish world, Alisha returned to those days of happiness and blissful nights of love. Gray Eagle was holding her fiercely and possessively within his strong embrace. He was trailing fiery kisses over her willing mouth and creamy breasts. Her mind swirled in a peaceful, intoxicating sea as he entered her body to skill-fully—almost desperately—make love to her. He had always known how to strip away her will and reason, even on the first night he had taken her.

Alisha envisioned him lying upon her naked and eager body. She felt his sensual mouth upon hers. She sensed the power, prowess, and masculinity which exuded from her invincible, magnetic warrior. His lovemaking was all-consuming, lovemaking she could not deny. His hands and lips carried her to the heights of passion and fulfillment.

Many times Gray Eagle had skillfully driven Alisha to the point of mindless frenzy in her insatiable need for him. In the beginning, she had lacked the knowledge or experience to resist him; later, she had lacked the will-power and desire to do so. She had loved him from that first moment their eyes had touched as bitter enemies.

But love and desire had quickly dispelled their hatred and hostility. They had shared a love which was overpowering and complete.

In her delirium, Alisha could hear him speaking huskily and tenderly, revealing his love and need for her. Countless days and nights of shared passion returned to comfort and to haunt her. One particular day flashed vividly before her hazy senses. It was the day after their marriage in the Blackfoot camp when Gray Eagle had come after her to confess the secrets of his heart. Her confused mind floated back to that monumental moment in time.

She smiled as she watched the virile warrior repeat his joining vows in English for her to hear and know how much he loved and wanted her. Laughing gayly, she softly and lovingly repeated her vows to him. They had finally surmounted all of the problems between them; for a time, they shared only love and passion.

She heard his tender words, "I will love you always. I will never forsake you in life or in death. I will always protect you, even with my own life. Waste cedake means I love you, Little One," he had translated the beautiful words which she had longed to hear for many months.

As she murmured in her illness, that day became real to her. Gray Eagle's mouth closed over hers in a tender kiss as they slowly sank to the ground, oblivious to all but each other and their need for shared love. Love was so rich, deep, and full when it was shared and returned, Alisha sighed to herself. They lay in the warm sunlight, kissing deeply and hungrily.

They were entwined in the arms of love. His kisses along her throat burned like the desert sun. He whispered words of love and endearment to her, sparking her response to him. Her blood raced wildly through her veins. It pounded instinctively in demand for fulfillment.

Alisha's hands caressed his hard back with light, tender touches and then hard, passionate caresses. She pulled him even closer and tighter to her, inspiring him to bolder moves. He nibbled at her lips and ears with light bites and sweet kisses. He explored every inch and recess of her mouth and body, as she did his. He teased and tantalized her again and again with lips and hands. She moaned in desire and pleasure, begging for more.

Her head rolled from side to side as he nibbled and caressed her breasts swollen with hunger and passion. She discovered the intoxicating thrill and joy of touching him and bringing him the same joys he gave to her, all without shame or modesty.

With each stroke, Alisha's body craved more and more of him. He was around her and within her; he was her life and breath. Higher and higher they climbed on the spiral of love and passion. She clung to him taking and giving all of the love she had felt and suppressed for him. They touched, kissed, and caressed, conquering the many months of heartache, denial, and suffering with love and happiness.

The beautiful delusion swirled as Alisha listened to Gray Eagle's last words, "Life is meant to be shared with the one you love. I should not have waited so long to see and feel this love between us. My pride and honor dulls in the face of such love and beauty."

"I love you, Wanmdi Hota," she cried out to her phantom lover. "I need you, my love . . ."

As she slipped in and out of consciousness, she pleaded, "No more . . . please, Wanmdi Hota, no more . . ." She cried desperately, "Kill me now . . . just let me die . . ." But the most perplexing and repetitious question was, "Why, my love, if only I knew why?"

And as he listened, Joe wondered what unknown despair plagued her feverish mind so deeply.

Joe decided it was best to give the suffering girl a small dose of laudanum for her pain. Afterwards, she was in a deep state of unconsciousness. Her restlessness ceased. She did not speak again in her sleep. For three more days, they cared for her and watched over her. It was more than a week after the attack by the trappers when Alisha gradually regained her senses.

Finally, Alisha's darkened eyelids fluttered open. With great difficulty, she blinked several times. Her mind in a cloudy whirlpool, she could not comprehend where she was or why she was in pain. A deep-toned masculine voice spoke to her from a distance; his fuzzy features leaned over her face. She tried to focus on them, finally succeeding. Her confused thoughts gave way to doubts as to whom she was seeing before her hazy vision.

"Joe?" she forced the inquiry from her dried lips.

He smiled in open relief and nodded. "One and the same, Miss Alisha. How are you feeling today? You gave us quite a scare, young lady," he chided her gently.

Alisha could not recall what had happened. She murmured, "Have I been ill? Is my uncle very worried about me? Go and tell him I am much better. Have I delayed our journey for very long?"

Before Joe could correct her, Powchutu stepped into her line of vision. Her eyes met his, calling on her hazy memory to place his handsome and familiar face. Her thoughts began to immediately clear. The rapid changes in her expressions told both men that her brief confusion was dissipating.

Tears came into her eyes. She touched her lower abdomen. "The baby? Did I . . ." was all she could manage to get out. The pain in her emerald eyes tore at

Joe's heart and ravaged Powchutu's gut. There was no protection from the truth.

"I'm terribly sorry, Miss Alisha. We did all we could to save it. The bleeding's stopped. We had a problem with some infection in your shoulder. You've been out cold for over a week." Joe's tone was gentle and sympathetic; his blue eyes were filled with concern and affection.

More tears eased down her flushed cheeks, cheeks like two red roses against a snow-white cloud. Her attention had ceased after his first two sentences. Joe had never seen such anguish as was now revealed in her green eyes. He wished that he could somehow destroy it. He could not; no one could.

Her gaze suddenly grew hard and cold; her eyes glowed like frosty chips of ice. A tight, harsh voice stated, "I killed him, didn't I? The one who . . . kicked me, the one who murdered my child? He's dead, isn't he?"

Joe nodded, but did not speak aloud. There was a strange, unnatural dullness in her eyes and voice. She looked down at her outstretched, opened palms. She stared at them in a curious way. In an emotionless voice she asked, "Why did you wash his blood off my hands? He deserved to die. I wish I could kill him again."

Slowly her eyelids closed and she sank back into her world of merciful blackness. Later, she would not even recall these statements. Within moments, she was breathing evenly. The two men glanced at each other. Without a word, they walked outside. Not wanting her to accidentally overhear their conversation, they stepped away from the cabin to a nearby tree.

Powchutu spoke up first. "How long before I can take her on to St. Louis? The best thing for her now is to get her out of this bloody wilderness and back to her own kind. All of this will be even harder on her than anything else she's endured so far. To kill a man and to lose her child. . . . She loved Gray Eagle," he unwittingly admitted. "God knows why, but she really loved him. She wanted this child because it was his, a last reminder of her love for him. Now, she's lost everything, Joe."

"It'll take time for her to heal completely," Joe said, "in mind and in body. Can't rush these things, Powchutu. She needs to rest for at least four or five weeks, maybe more. You're both welcome to stay here for as long as necessary, for the whole winter if need be. I could use the company and the help. How about it?" he entreated with hidden selfish motives.

"Thanks, Joe, but no way. We're still too close to the Sioux territory to my liking. I intend to get her away from here just as soon as she can safely travel. It wouldn't do for him to find her again, especially not after losing his child. He doesn't give up anything that belongs to him. If only he had loved her half as much as I do . . ."

"You planning to marry her in St. Louis?" Joe curiously inquired.

"If I can convince her that she isn't truly married to him. She believes those Indian vows she took with him are binding. I've tried to tell her they aren't legal under the white man's laws. In time she'll have to forget him and the hell he's put her through. I can only hope and pray it will be with my help and love."

Joe was completely befuddled by this incredible news. For the life of him, he could not decide what he thought or how he felt. All he was certain of was that the girl who lay seriously ill inside his cabin was very special to him, very special indeed.

He tried to force the thoughts of what she must have endured in these past months from his mind. He could too easily recall the bright, gentle, charming girl who had

114

been the source of his pleasure and happiness along their journey out here last year. Not only was she very beautiful, but she was also the kind of woman every man wanted. She was the ideal wife, sister, lover, and daughter.

"Tell me something, Powchutu; how do you know she loves Gray Eagle? I mean, after all he did to her, it seems impossible."

Powchutu visibly winced at the question. He sighed heavily, then ventured, "Alisha never understood the hatred between the Indians and the white man. When those men at Alisha's camp captured Gray Eagle and beat him simply because he was an Indian, she seemed helplessly drawn to him. She made the fatal mistake of seeing Gray Eagle as a man. Call it pity, guilt, or kindness. For all I know, it could have been a fascination with his courage and strength or his good looks. She was young, naive, and vulnerable. She was susceptible to a man such as he. You're probably aware of how women feel about such men. They can't resist them. And Gray Eagle took advantage of Alisha's innocence. He turned her own emotions against her." Powchutu sighed. "If I had been there, this would never have happened. I have no doubts she would have loved me if she had met me first."

Joe raised his eyebrows imperceptibly. "But that still doesn't account for her love for him after she learned the truth about him. When she saw what he was like, how could she not hate him in return?" Joe argued with the scout's illogical reasoning.

Powchutu sighed in exasperation, shaking his head in disbelief. "Surely you've seen this kind of deceit before, Joe. It happens a lot of the time with female captives. After the warrior first captured Alisha, he was gentle and kind to her, but only in private. He held her very life within his grasp. He gave her everything she needed to survive. She was with him day and night for months. From what I could glean from her, he was not brutal when he took her. Best I could learn, he must have been very gentle and skilled. An innocent like Alisha wouldn't be able to resist such magic," he reluctantly confessed to Joe. "She was frightened and confused. She didn't know if she would even be alive the next day. Living on the edge of death and fear seems to influence the female mind in some strange way. They begin to cling to the person who controls their survival. In Alisha's case, I think Gray Eagle intentionally tricked her into loving him. Later, when he quit his pretense, she was already in love with him. Like she told me, love doesn't die easily or quickly. He seems to have some mysterious and powerful hold over her, and I intend to destroy it for all time."

He turned and looked Joe square in the face and stated, "He convinced her he came to the fort to get her back and he married her because he loved her. He said he had always loved her since that first day. Wouldn't you say her treatment says differently?"

Joe rubbed the scratchy, two days' stubble on his unshaven face. He seriously pondered Powchutu's words for a long time, then declared honestly, "Sounds strange to me. So much of it doesn't make any sense at all, not from what I've heard about him. If all he wanted to do was punish the soldiers at the fort for the attack on his camp, it seems like any female captive would have served his purpose for shaming them. Fact, why not demand several women for peace? Why Alisha? I don't understand why he spared her life in the first place, not since she was one of the people who humiliated him. From what I know, he prizes that honor and pride of his above everything else. Why keep her in his tepee for so long if he hates whites? You said he personally tended her wounds after that lashing for trying to escape from him?"

Powchutu gritted his teeth in open irritation. His eyes narrowed and hardened at Joe's persistence in this matter. "Only to make her well enough to suffer more punishment! He couldn't stand the idea that a mere white girl had saved his life at her fortress. He was determined to show her what a powerful man he was! Knowing her like you do, wouldn't you agree his idea of forcing Fort Pierre to turn her over to him was a good trick on them? He didn't know how they treated her while she was there. All he wanted was revenge on all of them, including her. What better revenge than demanding the return of the white girl they had just rescued from his camp, and send her back to more cruelty? Imagine being forced to sacrifice a beauty like her."

"But why keep her alive for so long, especially since she seemed to be so much trouble for him? He must have known she loved him. Her obedience must have counted for something. She seems brave, intelligent, and generous; qualities Gray Eagle is known to respect and to reward." Joe stunned Powchutu with his following question, "Are you positive he didn't love her, didn't at least want her badly?"

In suppressed fear and in livid rage, Powchutu nearly shouted at him, "You tell me, Kenny! Would he ride off and leave her to die if he wanted her? Would he return to his tribe and tell them she was already dead and buried?"

"There could be some misunderstanding here, Powchutu. You said he fought a challenge to the death for her with Brave Bear. If he knew the truth about her, then why battle another great warrior just to marry her? Why not let him have her, or why not expose her deceit?" he pressed, seeking clarity of this disturbing mystery.

"I've told you before, Joe. At the time of the fight, he didn't know she wasn't Shalee. At least he couldn't prove she was or she wasn't. Still, he wasn't about to let her get away from him. He discovered the truth the day of the wedding. Knowing about that damned pride of his, he wouldn't dare let them find out he had risked his life and his honor for a tricky white girl. He went through with the joining ceremony, then planned a way to be rid of her without any damage to his pride. If you could have seen her or heard her that day when I finally found where he had left her—left her without food or water—then you would know how much I hate him!" he stormed in rising fury.

Powchutu's voice abruptly became soft and sorrowful, surprising Joe. His jet eyes were misty and full of pain. His broad shoulders slightly slumped, as if he had suddenly been handed the entire collection of burdens for the world and ordered to carry them. His voice was void of nearly all emotion when he finally spoke.

"It's all my fault, all of this. At first I told her—no, pleaded with her—to obey him in every way. I hoped he would be merciful and kinder to her. I was a bloody fool, Kenny. He didn't give a damn if she was good or bad, just as long as she was around to torment. I even tried to teach her everything I knew about him and his people. I thought such knowledge might help her in some way. She gave and gave, and he took and took and took. Do you have any idea how I felt when I begged her to do anything he commanded? I couldn't think about how much I loved her; all I could do was try to make her captivity easier to bear. It tore my heart to send her back to him again. But I had no other choice, Joe. You can see that, can't you? I was only one man against thousands of

Indians and all those soldiers. I could kill'em all for what they've done to her. Of all people, she never deserved any of this."

Another confession escaped his lips. "The only way I could help her was to free her from his hold. So, I helped her escape. That was another mistake. It nearly got her killed. For what? She still loves him even now," he admitted as if his heart was breaking.

Powchutu leaned against the tree and put his hand to his forehead. He spoke in grief. "Who knows, maybe the child she was carrying would have made some difference in his feelings toward her. Hell! We didn't even know she was pregnant until just before the attack. No doubt she'll hate me for this accident. Maybe I should place her in your care and leave tonight. You saw the way she looked at me a while ago. She didn't even speak to me." He laughed sadly and sarcastically exclaimed, "Funny, she didn't even know I loved her until after we began this bloody trip to freedom. I never told her before. I thought Gray Eagle was finally out of her life, then along came his child. Now, they're both gone, and she'll blame me."

"Why didn't you take her back to him when you learned about the child she was carrying?" was Joe's obvious question.

Powchutu laughed cynically. "Do you think for one minute he would believe this child was his? Do you think he would simply take back his runaway wife? What could he tell his people about her miraculous rebirth? Even if he had waited until the birth of the child, what if the child had been born with green eyes and auburn hair? The doubt of his fatherhood would have inflamed him further against her. You keep forgetting one very important fact, Joe: he has already tried to kill her two times before. Why

119

should a half-breed child of suspicious birth make any difference to him?"

"What did Alisha say about returning to him?"

"Just what you're thinking. But she realized it was too late. She knew the trip back would be dangerous and futile. She was having problems before those men attacked us. Fact is, that was why we were camped there, to give her some time to rest. I suppose I pushed her too fast and too hard in her condition. But I swear I didn't know she was pregnant. She was afraid he might even kill her before she could tell him why she had returned."

"After you found her that day, you said she wanted to go to his village and confront him with the truth?" Joe asked.

"Yes, but I wouldn't let her. If she dared to shame him by revealing his evil deed, he would have found some way to get around the truth and his guilt. They saw her as Shalee, the daughter of Black Cloud. She couldn't speak his tongue, not much of it anyway. She wouldn't know what he was telling them. He could claim dishonor in her running away with me. He could say he was too hurt and too ashamed to tell them the truth. Who can say what lies he would have told had she returned! When I told her I would go East with her, she decided not to return. She knows how he hated me. He would have killed us both. She was more afraid for my life than for her own."

Powchutu shifted restlessly as guilt gnawed at his heart. "When she learned the truth about him, she was like a wounded doe. God, I hope I never see her like that again. She really believed he loved her, that she had won his heart at last. That lie hurt her far more than his lashing did. We've got to help her, Joe. She'll have to face her loss. It'll be hard for her. She'll need us."

"You mean if she'll let us help her, don't you? Alisha is a proud woman, just as proud as Gray Eagle. If you left her here while she is still so ill, how would she feel?"

"Probably think I had betrayed her and deserted her just like he did. But if I thought my leaving was best for her, I would go this very night. She's the only woman I've ever wanted, Joe. I would do anything for her."

Joe was studying him very closely and carefully. For some reason, he felt that Powchutu was telling the truth, that he was actually willing to give Alisha up if that was really what she needed. It was even tempting for Joe to advise Powchutu to leave. After all, he loved Alisha, too. He could easily imagine what life with her would be like during a long, cold, and lonely winter. He realized that it was too selfish to encourage the scout to leave. Knowing that Alisha might need this special friend, he could not.

"If it helps any, Powchutu, I must agree with what you did for her. It just shocked me to hear that Gray Eagle had captured her and held her for so long. Just isn't like the warrior I've heard so much about. Guess you and Alisha know him better than most whites. Alisha's suffered too much as it is, Powchutu. I think it would hurt her more if you left her now. The only thing that matters is her health and happiness. We'll do whatever is best for her, agreed?"

"Fine," Powchutu replied absently, his dark eyes scanning the direction to the river. "Think she'll be well enough to travel before the snows hit?"

Speculating upon the reason for the scout's anxiety and unexpected question, Joe asked, "Do you think he might come after her?"

"Don't know. Once the truth of her escape is known, no telling what might happen." His handsome features

121

were lined with worry. But it was not Gray Eagle's revenge that he feared; it was the furious band of blood-thirsty Sioux warriors which would be headed by Gray Eagle's loyal friend White Arrow.

"What do you plan to do in St. Louis this winter? Got any money or friends there?" Joe asked.

"As soon as I get Alisha settled in some kind of safe and warm quarters, I'll find something to do until spring. All we'll need is food and shelter. I have a little money we found in an old, burned-out wagon along the trail here. It'll last for a while. Don't worry. I promise to take good care of her."

Joe wondered if he should tell Powchutu about the money which Alisha's uncle had placed in safekeeping with Hiram Bigsley, the banker-of-sorts for this growing area. Uncle Thad had feared the loss of all his wealth from either a storm or from robbers. He had wisely entrusted a large portion of it to Hiram Bigsley of Bigs-ley's Mercantile and Trust Company in St. Louis. Joe decided that he would save this news for Alisha, hoping it would somehow solve some of her fears and troubles.

"You could stay on here for the winter. I could use the help and the company. I'd be willing to split the profits from our trapping right down the middle," he generously offered the scout. "By springtime, Alisha will be strong and healthy again. We could all head down to St. Louis together to sell our furs and hides. We would all have plenty of money by then."

"I wish we could stay here, Joe. She could use the time and solitude. But I don't dare risk those Sioux catching up with us. I dread to think they might track us here and harm you after we leave. I did all I could to conceal our trail. I shiver to think what Gray Eagle might do to her if he learns she's escaped his final vengeance. She'd never survive another lashing," he shrewdly stated to gain Joe's approval and sympathy.

Disappointed, Joe offered, "If you do change your mind, the invitation still stands. I'd better get back inside and check on our girl." He turned and walked back into the cabin with the scout's gaze boring into his back.

Chapter Seven

Joe and Powchutu ate a light meal of johnny cakes and fish stew later that evening. They had hoped that Alisha would wake up and join them. She had not. She was very weak and pale; she was physically and emotionally drained. These past weeks had been agonizing for her. All she needed for the present was sleep, warm food, and plenty of rest. Her shoulder wound was showing signs of improvement, as were her other injuries. Soon she could join them for meals and light talk.

Unable to sleep that night, Powchutu left the stuffy cabin for a long walk in the chilling night air. He realized that there were many things which he had to settle within his own heart and mind. Yet, he felt helpless and guilt-ridden where Alisha was concerned. He had set a plan into motion which had cost two lives so far, nearly costing both his and Alisha's too. If only he could be certain that he was right . . .

While he was out walking and thinking, Alisha came to for the second time. Once again she was temporarily confused by her weakened condition and the unfamiliar surroundings. Before Joe even realized that she was awake, she had fully come to her senses. Her soft weeping alerted him to her wakefulness. He went to her side to comfort her. He tenderly stroked her mussed hair and spoke quietly to her, trying to lighten her dismal spirits.

"Why, Joe?" she cried in anguish. Still a little feverish, she rambled, "Why did it all happen? Hatred is such a destructive emotion. I've lost everything, and I do not understand why. How can I comprehend a situation that makes no sense? One day the world is a beautiful place, and I am free and happy; the next day, it is ugly and cruel, and I am the captive of another person. Can you imagine what it is like to be the slave of another person, one who hates you deeply, one who has complete control over your life in every way? Why me, Joe? What did I do to warrant this vile destiny? How could he hate me so much? How, Joe?"

There was no explanation he could give her. "I'm sorry, Alisha. Who can explain hatred or violence? I surely can't. I have always known Gray Eagle hated the whites, but with some just causes, I must admit. But there is no excuse for what he has done to you. I cannot even come up with a good reason for why he captured you in the first place. It just isn't like the man I kn—I've heard about. From what I've learned about him, he's a man who rewards courage and generosity. It seems strange for him to harm someone who's saved his life. He is a smart man; how could he not know what you've done for him?"

She was staring at him wide-eyed and open-mouthed. "You know about us? Powchutu told you . . . everything?" Her lovely face flushed with humiliation, feeling naked to his gaze. Tears sprang into her lucid eyes. "He had no right to tell you or anyone such personal things about me. I can imagine what you must think about me now."

"Powchutu loves you, Alisha. He's been worried sick about you. He blames himself for all of this. He's hardly been able to eat or sleep since you've been here," he stated softly, feeling compelled to defend the scout's confessions to him. "He only wants what's best for you. I told him you and I are old friends, so he felt it was all right to explain those matters to me."

Remorse filled her. "I know . . . If it wasn't for him, I don't know what would have become of me. In truth, Joe, he's the only friend I've had since our fortress was destroyed."

"He wants to marry you when you two get to St. Louis. He seems like a good, honest, strong man, Alisha," he offered, hoping that she might shed some light on this unexplainable feeling of suspicion which gnawed at his heart. He was also hoping to learn of her feelings toward Powchutu. He would not interfere if she loved him and wanted to marry him; but if not, then the door was still open for his own pursuit . . .

"You and Powchutu are the only friends I have left, Joe. I can't even begin to tell you all he's done for me. If not for him, I would be dead right now. Did he tell you . . . how he found me?" she stammered, not knowing just how much Powchutu had related to him.

"Yes, he did. I've never thought of Gray Eagle as a vile coward, but that is certainly a coward's way out. Powchutu says he did it for revenge." Joe paused, then asked, "What do you think, Alisha?"

There was such naked pain in her green eyes that Joe instantly wished that he had not asked such a tormenting question. She swallowed with great difficulty, bravely forcing back unbidden tears. Emerald eyes met sky blue ones.

"He's partly right," she painfully agreed. "But there was more to it. When he looked at me, all he ever saw was white skin. He saw his avowed enemy, someone to be killed or tormented. He never permitted himself to look at me as Alisha, or even as a woman. As to his real motives, I cannot venture a truthful guess. All I know is that he wanted me dead. Do you know how much hatred it takes to want someone dead, Joe? Do you know how it feels to have someone actually want you dead, want it enough to do it himself? He had so much hatred bottled up inside of him. For some reason it kept pouring out on me. It just kept coming and coming and there was no end to it."

Staring off into space, the words spilled forth as Alisha tried to purge herself of her grief. "Do you know what it's like to love someone more than life itself? To believe this same person loves you too, only to discover it was all some cruel and spiteful joke? He has paid a great price for this honor he prizes above all else: the life of his first-born son. I will never forgive him for this evil deed. To vent his hatred for the whites upon me is one thing; to pay the life of our child is another."

"Powchutu said Gray Eagle married you. Is that true?" he inquired softly, not wanting to further upset her.

"Married?" she repeated the word, as if she did not understand the meaning of that word. She closed her eyes and mentally envisioned the night of their joining. His image was as clear in her mind as if he were standing before her that very minute. She could almost feel his strong arms around her; she could almost smell the manly odor of his powerful body. She could picture his captivating smile; she could hear his deep laughter. Her mind's eye saw the stygian eyes which could lock with hers and hold them prisoner at will. Her beautiful daydream ended abruptly when the smile in his eyes and upon his full, sensual mouth turned into a jeering smirk.

She finally answered him, "I suppose you could say we are married. There was a ceremony in Black Cloud's village which joined Gray Eagle with the Blackfoot princess Shalee. But since I am not Shalee, I guess we are not truly married. I didn't know what was said during that ceremony until later. Gray Eagle told me that morning he caught up with me in the wilderness. He claimed we had pledged our hearts and lives as one. He told me he loved me. He said he wanted me for his wife, no matter who I was. My acceptance as this Shalee seemed to give him the excuse to openly claim me as his wife and love, but it was all a lie. Every word he spoke that day was a lie."

"If you didn't understand the joining ceremony, then how did you understand his explanation? Do you speak Oglala that good?" Joe curiously inquired in confusion.

Without thinking or caring anymore, Alisha unwittingly replied, "Not really. He speaks English. Of course that was the first time he had ever spoken to me in English, but he did it very well and very easily. All those months I had been his captive, he never once talked to me in my tongue. From that very first day we met, he knew every word I had spoken and never let on that he could. He waited until he knew I could not ever reveal his dark secret, then told me. He wanted to make certain I suffered as much as possible before I died. He wanted me to know what it was like to taste his love and acceptance. God, how he lied and betrayed me! I must be the most gullible, naive person in the world! I truly believed him. I trusted him completely until he left me in the desert and never came back. Two whole days and nights I waited for him and worried about him. I was a stupid, blind fool, Joe. I didn't have any food or water, and not horse or weapon either. He didn't even care enough to allow me a quick and easy death. He said, 'I love you, Alisha,' and then rode away forever. I believed him; I trusted him. . . ."

Her eyelids gradually closed. Soon, she was asleep with glistening teardrops still wet upon her ashen cheeks. Joe studied her face for a long time. He finally stood up and turned to move away from the bunk. His gaze alighted on the scout standing in the open doorway, a tormented expression etched on his face. Their eyes met and fused, each seeking some secret knowledge that the other might possess. Powchutu was the first to glance away. Joe continued his intense scrutiny.

Powchutu walked over to Alisha's side. He gently caressed her tear-stained cheek with the back of his hand. For the first time in his life, tears came to his own eyes; they unknowingly eased down his tanned cheeks and slowly dropped to her right arm. In a voice filled with sorrow and remorse, he murmured, "What have I done to you, my love? Even in all that danger, would you have been better off with him? If only we had known about his child . . ."

Seeing the highly emotional state that Powchutu was in, Joe quietly left the cabin. He himself now felt in need of some fresh, mind-clearing air. He was angered and baffled by all the facts which were being thrown at him so unexpectedly. He wanted to understand how the man whose life he, too, had once saved could be the same man who had tormented Alisha for months, finally trying to kill her. It just didn't add up to him. Either Gray Eagle had drastically changed in the past year, or there was more to this mysterious situation between him and Alisha than anyone but Gray Eagle knew.

If only Powchutu had attested to this cowardly Gray Eagle, Joe would challenge him. But Alisha agreed with the scout. Far worse, she had added even more vile charges against Gray Eagle. She stated he spoke English, and spoke it well. She would have no reason to lie about

129

such a matter. Yet, why had Gray Eagle never spoken to Joe, his friend, in English? They had always conversed in Sioux, for Joe had an excellent command of many Indian tongues.

There was nothing he could do at the present but accept Alisha's version of the truth. But the next time his path crossed with Gray Eagle's, he would demand the absolute truth of this matter concerning Alisha. He would not rest until he heard Gray Eagle's explanation of their relationship. In fact, he would head up that way next summer and check out this disturbing matter. If he did not have some good reason for her brutal treatment, then he would be forced to make him pay for it.

He reluctantly returned to his cabin. He found the scout sitting at the table, obviously in very deep thought. "Powchutu," he called out, not wanting to startle him with his sudden return.

He did anyway. Powchutu jumped up and knocked over his chair. Both men instantly glanced over at the sleeping Alisha to see if the loud crash had disturbed her. It had not. In her state of near exhaustion, she slept on. Powchutu leaned over to upright the chair, placing it back near the table. He sat down and motioned for Joe to come and to join him.

First, Joe went to look for something in his small pantry. He came back shortly with two tin cups in one hand and a bottle of Irish whiskey in the other. He sat down and poured out two half-cups. He handed one to Powchutu and placed the other one before himself.

Grinning jovially, he declared, "I think we both need a stiff drink, Powchutu. This has been one helluva week. To better days ahead," he toasted, clinking his cup with Powchutu's. Both men promptly emptied their cups as if they had only been filled with cold spring water. Joe hastily refilled them. "Been saving this for a long time," he murmured.

About five cups later, both men found it easier to get to sleep. They had been sleeping on bedrolls in the middle of the cabin floor. It was but minutes later when both were sound asleep, lost in much-needed slumber.

Alisha was the first one to awaken the following morning. She observed the two men sleeping peacefully upon the floor, like two brave cavaliers guarding a queen. It warmed her heart to realize how much they were doing for her. Recalling the power of the hunter's sixth sense that both men possessed, she remained very still and quiet. She did not want to interrupt their rest. No doubt they were both exhausted after taking care of her night and day for a week. She lay back against the feather pillow and let her mind roam at will.

She knew that she could not hide from the painful truth for much longer. It was past time to face it and deal with it. She could not go on mourning a lost love for the rest of her life. The sooner she came to grips with reality, the sooner her heart could mend, and the sooner she could begin a new life without Gray Eagle.

She added up the facts: she still loved him; their child was gone; she was on her way to freedom; he did not love or want her; she had two valuable friends who really cared about her; she had lost everything, but was still alive; surely she could survive this new tragedy as she had done others; and the last fact was that she could change none of these other facts.

It had become clear to her that crying would not help matters. In fact, she had already cried too much in the past months. Weeping had gained her nothing. She came to the conclusion that hatred was a two-edged sword which could hurt her far more than it could ever hurt

131

him. She recognized the terrible pain and emptiness within her heart; yet, she determined to not allow it to destroy her.

From now on, she thought fiercely to herself, you will not be used by any man. You will not permit Wanmdi Hota to ever hurt you again. If it takes the rest of your life, you will forget him.

Even as she vowed forgetfulness, she feared it might take the rest of her life. Still, she would honestly try with every fiber of her being to get over him. She could only pray that his vivid memory would fade with the passage of time and distance. Those two elements were her life-savers: time and separation. Surely it was impossible to love someone that you never saw again or to love someone forever without any reciprocation.

As her gaze passed over the two sleeping men, she also determined that she would not give them any more trouble. She had been far too much trouble as it was. She would show them her appreciation by being a good patient and a fast healer. As her misty gaze settled on Powchutu's proud features, she hoped that one day she could love him as much as he now loved her, more than she now loved Gray Eagle.

She could not deny that he would be good to her. But it was too soon to think of such things. The lacerations upon her tender heart were still fresh. But who could say what time would bring? She feared the facets of Powchutu which were so similar to Gray Eagle's: his looks, his behavior, his personality. More so, she feared this might be the major attraction which he held for her. Powchutu was frequently like a mixture of both men: himself and Gray Eagle, and only the very best of Gray Eagle. This concerned her deeply, for she knew that in all fairness she could not use him as a substitute. Yet, he might not be willing to settle for a platonic relationship.

Alisha unthinkingly rolled to her side, instantly moaning from the discomfort in her left shoulder. Both men were immediately on their feet and at her side, faces mirroring their love and concern.

She surprised them when she smiled cheerfully and stated, "Just a little tender, that's all. I didn't mean to awaken you two."

Simultaneously they asked, "How do you feel this morning?"

She laughed merrily, her eyes showing the first signs of renewed life since her accident. "I must admit I've had better days. Worse, too," she added with a twinkle in her green eyes. "With all this attention, I just might stay ill for months."

Joe got the first question out, "Do you need anything? Flapjacks? Coffee? Potage?"

She mischievously replied, "Hot tea and scones, please. Oh, yes, plenty of fresh butter too."

"The closest I can come to that is pandowdy and coffee. Will that suffice you, Miss Williams?" Joe teased her lightly, just as in their old days along the trail.

She pouted her lips and sighed. "If I must, then I guess I must." Afterwards, she giggled contentedly and replied, "Anything is fine, Joe. Surprise me."

"Coming right up," he stated, giving her a low sweeping bow. They both laughed at his gay animation. It had always been easy for her to be natural, saucy, and playful with him.

Fingers of jealousy clawed at Powchutu's mind as he observed them. He reminded himself that these two were old and close friends. He chided his envy as he suddenly realized that Joe was surely in his late thirties or early forties, much too old for Alisha. No doubt theirs was a brotherly or fatherly relationship. Pleased with this new assessment of a would-be rival, he relaxed and joined in on their merriment.

Both men were delighted to see how hard Alisha was trying to cope with her new situation and with her old set of troubles. Not once did anyone mention the miscarriage or the trappers. It was as if there was a silent agreement among them that those two topics were taboo.

As Joe prepared their breakfast while humming cheerfully, Powchutu came over to check her more closely. Noticing the small bandage on his upper arm, Alisha cried out in alarm, "You're hurt!"

He chuckled to alleviate her concern. "Just a small scratch. Joe fixed it up for me. I don't hurt easily, remember?" he proudly announced, puffing out his chest like a vain peacock.

She laughed with him. Powchutu settled himself on the edge of the bunk and set in to relating his past tales of great courage and daring to entertain her. Joe observed the easy way they spoke together, revealing their closeness. Joe could read the admiration and trust in Alisha's eyes from clear across the room. He couldn't decide if he was jealous, suspicious, or pleased with their closeness. It didn't take a smart man to surmise that Powchutu stood a better chance of winning her hand than a man who was almost twenty years older than she. Yet, many twenty-year-old girls married forty-year-old men . . . especially when they were still in top physical condition and were not bad to look upon, he admitted without conceit.

They ate breakfast at the table which Powchutu had pulled over to the bed. Since she was still very weak, they did not linger over it very long. Afterwards, the two men went outside while Alisha tended to her private business.

Joe had been thoughtful enough to slip the dress from the wagon onto her frail body while she was still unconscious. He had known how embarrassed she would be to find herself naked before two men, whether they were friends or not. He had been correct. Had she guessed about the medical treatments which she had received or her state of undress for most of the time, she would have been mortified. Alisha simply assumed that one of them had changed her dress sometime during her long illness. She refused to think about what had occurred while she was delirious.

While she bathed and dressed, she silently prayed for the child which she had lost . . .

The next two weeks were spent in concentrating upon getting stronger. Alisha did everything they gently ordered her to do. She received plenty of rest, extra sleep, constant attention, and delicious food. She gradually regained the weight she had lost due to her illness and their long, arduous travels. Her color and her mood steadily improved with time and rest.

On warm days she would sit outside in the sunlight and watch the two men work on Joe's traps and gear. Other days she would watch them chopping firewood for the long winter or salting down meat to hang in the narrow pantry inside the cabin. It was clear that Powchutu was adequately repaying Joe for his kindness.

It did not take Alisha long to realize that one man remained at the cabin at all times with her. She was grateful for their protection and concern. Still, she was occasionally plagued with fears that Gray Eagle might soon discover her escape and come after her. Each day she prayed for more strength and courage, hoping she and Powchutu could soon be on their way to St. Louis again. She hated to leave the comfort and security of Joe's cabin, but she wanted to get away from the forests and Indian territory. She wondered how Joe could stand being here all alone for the entire winter. But as much as she loved Joe as a dear friend, she could not force herself to agree to spend the coming winter here with him.

At last she was able to help out in the small kitchen area of his cabin. She cooked for the two working men, then washed the dishes. Afterwards, they would both insist that she rest. They would not permit her to wash clothes or to do any heavy chores. Her easily fatigued body told her that she was still healing. Sometimes her weakness was greater than on other days. But all in all, she was getting better and stronger each passing day.

She watched the weather as closely as Powchutu did. They would burst into shared laughter when they spotted each other doing the same thing, each knowing the reason for their mutual concern. If Joe noticed their preoccupation with the coming winter, he did not let on.

At night they would sit around the table, eating and talking. Joe informed them of the news from back East which sluggishly came to him by way of travellers and trappers. Most of the news was old, yet still disheartening and frightening. Alisha feared that the war back East between England and the Colonies would interfere with her planned return to her homeland. How she dreamed of seeing the cliffs of Dover rising up before her as she sailed by them!

One particular night the talk came around to the war. Carried away with his narrative, Joe innocently forgot that she was English. It wasn't until much later that he recalled her parents had come to these Colonies only to be killed soon after their arrival in a carriage accident. Her uncle, being a peace-loving and intelligent man, had realized that war between his adopted country and his mother land would soon be inevitable. Thad had been one of the leaders for their tragic journey to the Dakota Territory, a land where he had hoped to find peace and safety.

Joe leaned back in his home-built, wooden chair and began to talk. Alisha was all ears, wanting to learn if it would be possible for them to continue down the Missouri River to the mighty Mississippi. It was there where they could rent a flatboat to take them down to New Orleans—a town settled in 1718 by the French, but ceded to England back in 1763. It was rumored that New Orleans was now a rapidly growing seaport, one where ships to other countries could dock and trade. Alisha's goal was to reach New Orleans first; then, return to England by ship. She focused her attention upon Joe's ramblings.

"For the life of me I can't figure out why all these countries keep passing around this area out here. First it belonged to the French, now to the Spanish. The smart thing for those Colonists to do is set their claim on it. Wouldn't do to have your sometime enemies right at your back. One day those Colonists are going to heavily settle all of this area; you mark my words. This area is a gold mine; it has everything from wood and food to furs and gold. Could be mighty important in the future. 'Sides, it's beautiful and peaceful out here."

Alisha was the first to show her skepticism and anger, "Everyone keeps forgetting this land belongs to the Indians. It's very clear to me they do not intend to give it up or even to sell it. How many more lives will it take for both sides to learn this truth?"

"You're partly right, Alisha," Joe agreed. "But as sure as there's a sunrise every morning, more and more will come here. I see it every few weeks now. People are tired of wars and poverty. It's like having the stars within your reach and knowing they're magic; this land is a dream-come-true to them."

"I say it's more like a bloody nightmare! Besides, wishing upon stars is for children. These are adults we're talking about, supposedly intelligent people. To challenge the invincible Sioux for their territory shows anything but intelligence or courage," she argued.

"In a way, Alisha, they are like little children," Joe commented in a softer tone. "They're poor; they're hounded by laws which are strict and unjust. They're unhappy; they're persecuted for their religious beliefs. They want freedom, Alisha; they want a new beginning. Even if it is wrong or dangerous to come here, they see hope and promise in this new land. Not too long ago, you could also see both sides of this battle," he gently reminded her.

Her eyes flew up to glare angrily at him. Her chin trembled with the force of controlling the flood of stinging words which she wanted to virulently shout at him. She waited until her heart stopped racing wildly and her breathing slowed to normal before she dared to speak.

"That was before I knew how true my people's words were. I was too naive and too stupid to accept their claims against the Indians. I just couldn't believe that such horrors and brutalities existed. I couldn't even comprehend such fierce hatred and unreasonable violence. After surviving it, I can vow it does exist; it exists in the hearts and minds of both sides." Abruptly she declared, "I should have allowed them to kill him that day!" But her eyes belied her statement.

Powchutu reached out to grasp her quivering hand. He gently squeezed it to comfort her. His voice tenderly implored, "Don't do this to yourself, Alisha. It's over now. You did what you had to do. You can't blame yourself for man's hatred and brutality."

"Can't I?" she nearly screamed back at him. "In a way, I'm responsible for all of my people's deaths. If I had not interfered with Gray Eagle's beating that day, they would have killed him. He could not have led that massacre against our fortress after his escape; my people would still be alive. The same is true of the fort. If the soldiers had not raided his camp to free me, then he would not have attacked there and killed all of them. Then, I almost cost Brave Bear his life. If Gray Eagle could have proven I was not Shalee before he challenged Brave Bear for my hand in marriage, he could be dead now; I could be dead now. Look at the times I've placed your life in danger. Every one of those incidents revolved around me. If you hadn't found me where he left me to die . . . don't you see, Powchutu? It's always me, or his hatred for me. How can anyone hate that much?"

With tears streaming down her cheeks, she rushed outside for privacy and fresh air. Until then, she had been successful in keeping her emotions and thoughts under strict control. Once the anger, bitterness, and pain began to filter through the tiny cracks in her guard-wall, it lost its strength and stability; it finally gave way to a flood of uncontrollable tears.

Joe halted Powchutu from going after her, "Leave her be for a while. Maybe it's good for her to release some of that pent-up anger and bitterness. She's been trying hard these past days. Let her get it out in the open and deal with it. Better here with us than later with strangers. She's been through a lot, Powchutu, too much for a girl like her. I don't see how she's held up this long. Alisha's stronger and wiser than she knows. It'll be hard going for a while, but she'll make it. I'd stake my life on it. Damn!"

he abruptly swore under his breath. "I sure as hell wished I knew why he did those things to her. You might think I'm crazy, Powchutu, but you know what I think? It almost sounds like he loved her, but wouldn't admit it even to himself, and surely not to anyone else. Could that be possible, Powchutu? Maybe it was his forbidden love for Alisha that he was trying to punish or to destroy, not her. For damn sure, it's clear he was hell-bent on having her for some reason! A man don't go to such lengths and dangers to recover his white slave and to keep her alive and well. Then, there's this desertion matter. Just doesn't sound like the great, fierce warrior to me," Joe muttered in pensive thought. "Mighty strange to me . . ."

To conceal his guilt and alarm, Powchutu fired back in an icy tone, "Like him or not, I saw him do just that! He doesn't need excuses for his actions. He's a savage!" He snatched up his cup of coffee, spilling most of it onto the table.

Joe got up and poured himself and Powchutu another cup of coffee, then sat down once more. Trying to find some other topic to discuss which would ease the tension in the small cabin, he seized upon their coming trip. "It's a good thing you're heading downriver toward Orleans. Few years back old Chief Pontiac of the Ottawa wiped out every British fort west of Fort Niagara, except for the one at Detroit. It wouldn't do to go passing through his territory during the winter, not alone. Course those British have rebuilt at Cahokia, Kaskaskia, and Vincennes. One thing about heading south is better weather too. If you don't care to spend the winter here or in St. Louis, there's another settlement at Ste. Genevieve which is a few weeks further south; it's about thirty years older than St. Louis, just not as populated. Mostly farmers and trappers in that area."

Powchutu joined in on his attempt to restore peace and to make light talk, "How far down the Mississippi is this Orleans?"

Joe pondered his question for a few moments, then remarked, "I'd say about fifteen to twenty days' travel by boat, if the river isn't too rough or too icy. It would be best for Alisha if you waited until spring to head there. Travel is bad enough in good weather, but terrible during the dead of winter," he warned.

Before he could reply to Joe's comments, Alisha opened the door and came inside. She was rubbing her bare arms to ward off the night chill. Without speaking, Joe got up and wrapped a light blanket around her shoulders to help warm her. She flashed him a warm smile of thanks, one with hints of apology and shame.

He naturally returned it. "I've always found it best to clear out such feelings in the cold night air. Feeling better?" he solicitously inquired.

"Much. I'm sorry, both of you. I didn't mean to attack you like that. It was rude and shameful. I suppose I'm just tense. It isn't easy to be a pampered patient."

"Yep!" Joe readily agreed. "Much easier to be the doctor, except when your patient's very ill and much loved. It's good to see some of that old spunk and energy returning. Means you're getting better." Laugh lines deepened around his eyes and mouth as he flashed her a wide, engaging grin.

She joined his laughter. "Good news at last. Now, how about a cup of that horrid coffee to warm my freezing bones?"

Joe eyed her merrily and retorted, "If I had tea, I bet you'd be wanting coffee. Women! Just can't please 'em."

Alisha sat down at the table, hoping neither man would

realize how much she was trembling from weakness. Yet, both alertly noticed this, but said nothing. Soon they were all settled back around the table, discussing the war. Alisha leaned forward and propped her elbows on the edge of the table, then lightly rested her chin upon her cupped hands.

"What happened back East after we left there, Joe?"

"Like your uncle and the others feared, war soon broke out. In fact, right after we left Harrisburg in the spring of '75, fighting began in the Massachusetts Colony. The way I heard it, some British general named Gage attacked their secret munitions supply at Concord. The Colonists sent a fellow called Nat Greene to do battle with him. Seems the Americans, as they're now calling themselves, appointed George Washington as their commander of the American Army. It appears they'll follow him anywhere and anytime. Lots of guts and stamina, they say." He lifted his cup and took several swallows of coffee before continuing.

"You said there was lots of fighting back there?" Powchutu injected during his break.

"One trapper told me two Americans—Allen and Arnold, I believe—captured Fort Ticonderoga up Canada way. Course it's only good for protecting their hind section or for granting those boys some claim to fame. It's battles like that one which give other men the courage and daring for future battles. From the last reports I got, those British and Americans are mighty busy with this war."

"But that was last year, Joe. What's the latest news? Surely they cannot continue to fight forever." Alisha listened closely to Joe's vivid recounts, praying she would not hear the names of any of her friends among them.

142

"Some Colonist named Montgomery was killed up Canada way earlier this year. Heard tell of a series of battles back in June of last year around a place either called Breed's Hill or Bunker Hill. Heard several different versions on it. Don't rightly know who won, not with both sides claiming the victory. The British gained the major victory, but those Americans received the most encouragement from the showing they put on there. Guess it really don't matter who won to all those boys who died there. That war's gonna be costly afore it's over."

"Is that the very latest news you've had?" she anxiously probed.

"Nope. About March of this year, a British general called Howe fought with Washington in Massachusetts. They claim he turned tail and headed off for some place called Nova Scocia, or something like that. Appears the Continental Congress is going to push for total independence from England. There's a Thomas Jefferson from Virginia Colony and a Ben Franklin from Massachusetts Colony stirring up quite a ruckus with their war statements. You'd think with over twenty-five newspapers back there that someone would bring me at least one copy to read. Might explain those 'Tolerable Acts' of '74 which are causing so much fuss. If we're gonna fight the mother country, I'd sure like to know the whole truth on it."

Alisha smiled, but did not correct his error. She did not want to alter his line of thought with a discussion on the "Intolerable Acts" and other charges the Americans had leveled against England. "This General Howe, would his first name be Sir William?"

"Don't rightly know, but that sounds familiar. Know him?" he curiously speculated, brows raised inquisitively.

"Only socially, and a very long time ago. I've also met this Thomas Jefferson. He came to England years back to explain the Colonists' positions and problems to King George. As you can see, it did not make any difference to him. From what my father told me, the king is determined to subjugate these colonies at any price. Uncle Thad said it wouldn't have been so bad if the king had stopped placing all those impossible acts and regulations upon the people here. The king thought the grumblings were all poppycock and wouldn't amount to great trouble. Evidently he was mistaken. It still seems to me that they could work out these difficulties if they truly wanted to. Why do they always resort to wars and killing to settle matters?"

Joe quickly moved on to another topic. "This Howe does have a brother, an admiral in the British navy. Jacques Dufoe, that's an old friend of mine who travels back and forth pretty regularly, says the American spies report this other Howe is planning to blockade most of the seaports here. By now, it might already be done. Seems to me like a long strip of coast to bottle up for very long."

A startled Alisha exclaimed, "Are you certain, Joe? Admiral Richard Howe is going to blockade all the seaports? That means I won't be able to catch a ship home until this war's over! Unless . . ." Her eyes widened with renewed excitement. "Perhaps I could find some way to get a message to him! He and my father were close friends. He used my father's shipping business many times. I'm positive Admiral Howe could find me a safe passage back to Liverpool."

Joe was shaking his head. "I hate to quash your optimism, Alisha, but getting a message to this Howe would be near impossible. Dangerous, too," he added.

"What do you mean, dangerous?"

"If that message were intercepted by some American spy or if it reached the attention of the new government, they just might view you as a traitor," he warned her.

"Traitor!" she shrieked in astonishment. "How can I be a traitor when I'm English? I'm afraid you've forgotten whose side I'm on," she meekly refreshed his memory.

It was Joe's turn to be shocked. "Surely you don't agree with what England's doing here! They're practically enslaving a whole new country. Ain't right or just, Alisha."

She shook her head in mild exasperation. "Of course not, but I am British, Joe. No matter, it looks as if I'm stuck here until this war is settled one way or the other. In a way, I fully agree with your quarrel with England. But what I think or feel doesn't count."

Joe faced Powchutu and stated, "I'm not so certain I would head for Orleans at this time. Now that I think about it, might not be safe there. Since she's a seaport, the British and the Colonists could be fighting it out there right now. Have you ever seen what those big cannons can do to a town at a close range?"

"You mean bombard the town? That's murder, Joe! It's simply barbaric. There are women and children living there. No doubt many of those people are friends and relatives of some of those seamen. Surely Admiral Howe would not permit such an outrage, such a travesty of justice."

Powchutu was the one who replied to her naive comments, "In war, Alisha, victory is won at any price or in any way necessary. Never underestimate what any man is capable of doing when pushed into a corner. Desperation often breeds panic. Clear heads usually come after the battle, not in the heat of one."

"But that means I can't get a ship home, Powchutu. I'm stuck here in this savage land? We can't even return to their civilization back East? I won't believe that! Some way, I will get back to England. I will not remain here. I won't!" she vowed fiercely, angered by this new obstacle.

"Don't worry about that now. By the time we get to this New Orleans, I'm sure this war will be long over," Powchutu said to encourage her.

"There hasn't been any more news since this battle between Washington and Howe back in March? But this is December, Joe. Surely something has happened by now," she said in a somber tone.

"The last group which came near here left the Colonies in the spring, Alisha. You remember how long it takes to get this far out. It'll be the first of the year before I get more current news. Winter travel, as you must recall, is something to avoid. Unless some foolhardy group headed out during the summer, that's all I can tell you right now." He could read her disappointment and dejection.

"Surely they will have more news down in St. Louis. We stopped there for a long rest on our way here. Perhaps some later group has gotten stranded there," she hopefully reasoned. "If so, they can tell us when we arrive there soon."

"Could be," Joe agreed just to please her, not really believing her suggestion. He stretched and yawned lazily, hinting at the late hour. "I'd say it's pretty late. Best we all turn in for some sleep, especially you, Miss Williams. Those pale cheeks tell me you're pressing yourself."

With that suggestion, they all went to bed, each having much different thoughts and dreams.

Chapter Eight

Another week passed. Alisha's strength was increasing every day. She presented a vivacious front to her two friends. More and more she assumed the lighter indoor chores of cooking, dishes, cleaning, and sewing. But the men were adamant about her rest and her care. They constantly checked up on her to make certain that she was not over-extending her growing energy. She felt loved and protected, and she flourished in this warm atmosphere.

Since game and fish were still in abundance, most days they had fresh stews or roasts. She would often prepare spoon bread, dried beans which had been bought from the Omaha, or nourishing potage. The men enjoyed her cooking and her company at the table. It did not take long for her old wit and charm to return to full bloom. Once the reality of her freedom and her self-confidence returned, she gradually became the girl whom Joe had first met and known. To Joe, it was like watching the legendary Phoenix return to life.

Powchutu eagerly observed this new woman unfolding before his very senses. He had not believed it possible for her to become more desirable or more beautiful, but she did. With each passing day and with increasing strength, Alisha began to radiate that same warmth and charm which had attracted Gray Eagle to her. Her moods were sunny and vivacious. Her smile was subtly provocative, yet artlessly innocent. She could be witty and playful or serious and tranquil. She could be herself.

With fear, torment, and doubt gone from her daily life, she slowly transformed into more than the woman of either man's dreams. At first glance, she appeared totally untouched by her recent experiences. Joe had known her this way before; he was ecstatic to see that former girl return and take over. Powchutu finally saw what Gray Eagle must have seen in her that first time they had met; now he could easily understand how that fierce warrior could have loved and wanted this particular white girl. The very thought accused him.

Powchutu had met Alisha long after Gray Eagle's imprint had been put upon her heart. For the first time, he was actually viewing and meeting the real Alisha Williams, not the ex-captive of a legendary warrior. As never before, the full reality of what Gray Eagle's feelings for her must have been came to life. As if struck by a blinding light, everything about Alisha and the brave made complete sense: their love must have been real. This unexpected conclusion alarmed and distressed him. His guilty conscience demanded that he ignore the truth. Gray Eagle could blame no one for his ultimate downfall except himself, Powchutu reasoned defensively. His past actions had forced Powchutu's hand, for he had not revealed his love.

When Alisha would find him staring at her in brooding silence, she would playfully coax and tease him out of his dark gloom. She assumed that he was only fretting about their long delay in reaching St. Louis. Perhaps his somber thoughts were upon the war back East which was affecting their future plans. Still, she was slightly perplexed by his cool attitude toward her since her accident and recovery. Not once had he attempted to be more than amicable and polite with her. He had not mentioned marriage or love to her again. She could not help but wonder if her pregnancy by Gray Eagle had somehow changed his feelings about her. If so, then perhaps it was for the best, for her love still remained in Gray Eagle's tepee.

As she repaired Joe's clothing, Alisha would find herself thinking about Gray Eagle and their past life together. The pain of his betrayal had lessened with the time she had spent with her friends. Still, she could not stop thinking about her Indian husband, and about the raging passion they had shared. Something deep within her soul refused to accede to the tormenting truth of his hatred. Even if she never learned the whole truth, she would always believe there was more to his actions than she knew, something which had prevented his return to her side.

Yet even as she reminisced about their times of joy, anguish intruded on her happy thoughts.

"Was it so hard to love me? Or was it only impossible to accept your one-time enemy as your new lover and wife? If only I knew why, Wanmdi Hota, if only I knew why . . ." she murmured sadly.

Dreams and wishes changed nothing, a cruel fact which she had learned all too well in the recent past. Even she came to realize how much she had changed in these past weeks at Joe's. She could sense the vitality and the very essence of life returning to her. She became conscious of how often she smiled, how wonderful and carefree she felt, and how easily she laughed these days— things which had been missing for many months. It almost seemed strange, even frightening, not having Gray Eagle responsible for her very life. The realization of how deeply she had been bound to him thundered through her awakening mind.

149

It was as if she had been totally immersed within his being, as if she had temporarily existed only through him. For a time Alisha Williams had ceased to exist. She had been ordered about from sunup to sundown. She had never made a decision on her own during her captivity. Her life had consisted of listening and obeying, or of being punished for not complying with his wishes. But her love for Gray Eagle had made her endure.

It was apparent that freedom in itself did not bring joy or happiness. Never had she been as happy as when she had shared a tepee with Gray Eagle, despite her enslavement to him. Alisha knew that if she could live it all over again, she would certainly be obedient from the start. She would never force Gray Eagle to punish her for mistakes which she intentionally made. She would not innocently or purposely humiliate him before his warriors; that had caused many problems in the past. She was forced to admit that her own pride had cost them as much as his had. But once the events had taken place, there had been no way to alter them. Perhaps she had even forced him to hate and abuse her . . .

"So very tragic and costly, my love," Alisha spoke to Gray Eagle in her heart. "Our child is dead, and we have been separated for all time. Such needless waste, such futile sacrifices. Did you ever love me, Wanmdi Hota? 'What price my honor demands of me; the world demands, but cannot see; for I alone must pay its fee; to be wildly tossed on life's stormy sea.' Such bitter truth in those famous words, my love. If only the fee had not been the life of our child."

During the second week of December there was a light snowfall. She stood at the small window for a long time until the cold draft forced her to close it. She went to sit at the table, her thoughts in a wintry maelstrom: the coldest season was upon them and they were still far from their goal. She suddenly jumped up and began to nervously pace the small confines of Joe's cabin.

Joe was secretly watching her from beneath lowered lids as he worked on several of his traps. To him, she seemed like a trapped badger who was furious and restless. He put aside his work and made some fresh coffee. He decided that this was a very good time to bring up the news of the money back in St. Louis. He assumed such news would certainly enliven her dismal spirits.

"Alisha, come over here and sit down. I have something to tell you which is mighty important," he stated mysteriously, a broad grin on his face, a devilish twinkle in his blue eyes.

As she came forward, Powchutu was instantly alert. Without trying to appear over-anxious, he also came to sit at the table with them. Joe passed around cups of coffee, then settled into his own chair. His keen gaze studied the scout's fathomless face. That gut instinct which warned that he could, yet could not, trust this particular man returned to annoy and to confuse Joe. He vainly tried to shake off his groundless suspicions.

His gaze shifted to Alisha's lovely face, and he smiled warmly as their eyes met. "Good news, Alisha. First, don't be angry with me because I've waited so long to tell you about it. I've had my reasons, mainly that you wouldn't sit still long enough to heal properly. Before I tell you, promise me one thing: remain here at least another week or two. By that time, I'm sure all your strength will be returned and you'll be completely well. Travel in winter is very bad, as you well know. I had to make sure you were all right before we had this talk. Understand?"

He waited for her agreement, unaware of where her

thoughts would run to. "What are you talking about, Joe? What news could be this import—" She halted in mid-sentence and blanched white. She fearfully whispered, "Surely you haven't heard that he's coming after me?"

Joe wondered if he had read excitement in her expression just prior to fear. "Heavens, no!" He quickly settled her rising suspicions and panicked heart. Once again there was that curious mixture of emotions within her eyes: relief and disappointment.

"It's about something your Uncle Thad did when we passed through St. Louis. Do you recall the man who ran the mercantile store, Hiram Bigsley?" He waited for her to refresh her memory and to nod her head yes.

"You see, Alisha, Thad feared a robbery or wagon accident along the trail. In such a case, a man could lose everything he owned. Thad thought it wise to place a small nest egg, as he called it, in Mr. Bigsley's keeping. You might recall Bigsley's a sort of banker for people around here, including for me. He was told to keep this money for five years. In the event Thad never returned for it, he was told to give it to someone in need of help. Bigsley's a cunning and tight-fisted man, but an honest one. I've had lots of dealings with him in the past. Now that your Uncle Thad is dead, the money belongs to you: one thousand pounds in English currency." He patiently awaited her reaction to this lifesaving news.

Alisha was temporarily stunned speechless. She could hardly trust her ears. Countless thoughts raced through her mind at the same time, but one in particular kept returning: money meant all of her troubles were solved. No longer would she be destitute and vulnerable. She would now have the means to support both herself and Powchutu; she could now repay him for many of the things which he had done for her. There would also be plenty of money for ship passage back to her beloved homeland. Tears of happiness filled her eyes. She suddenly cried in unsuppressed glee. She jumped up and pirouetted merrily around the small room. She laughed, she giggled, she wept, feeling that at long last the Fates were on her side.

She pulled Joe to his feet and hugged him tightly in joyful gratitude. "This is the happiest day of my life, Joe. For the first time in ages, I'm truly free of the past. No more am I poor, defenseless Alisha. I'm free, Joe, free!" But even as she said it, he could still read the lingering pain in her emerald eyes.

He chuckled as he witnessed the effect of his unexpected news upon her. "I hope you can see why I didn't dare tell you this sooner. Why you would have shot out of here like a spooked quail from the brush. Now you can relax. There's nothing to worry that pretty head about except getting well. Agreed?" he pressed, tugging playfully on a stray curl.

She lovingly cuffed his strong chin with her small fist and laughed. "Yes sir," she joked with a mocking salute. "Whatever you say is just dandy with me. Everything is fine with me now." She began to dance around, hugging herself in this new elation of freedom.

"In that case, this calls for a celebration. That last trapper who came by traded me a small keg of applejack for some staples. I'm afraid Powchutu and I finished off my only flagon of Irish whiskey while you were so ill," he discreetly confessed, then chuckled with great zest.

"What, pray tell, is applejack?" she asked amidst her girlish giggles.

"Just a fancy name for apple brandy. Not excellent quality, but pretty good on a cold night," he whispered, suppressed chuckles ready to erupt from his grinning mouth at any moment.

"As good as Irish whiskey from a French flagon?" she jested impishly, standing arms akimbo and feet apart, feigning an old shrew about to reprimand his daring suggestion that she actually join them in a cup of strong, manly spirits.

He rubbed his forehead as if trying to recall something vital, then shrugged his powerful shoulders in mock distress. "Hum-m-m. Can't rightly remember, ma'am. That night's still a little fuzzy. You might say I got slightly soused. I believe it had to do with worrying about somebody pretty special who was powerfully ill," he confessed, flashing her a rueful look.

"Just as I suspected. Two drunk doctors caring for an unsuspecting female patient. For shame! No wonder it took me so long to get well," she charged, struggling to control her mirth.

At that accusation, Joe feigned a serious expression and gingerly walked around her several times, looking her up and down. "What are you doing, Joe?" she inquired.

"Making certain there's no permanent damage from our rash incompetence, of course. Can't say that I've ever seen you looking any better or prettier," he voiced his final opinion.

She casually laid her right hand over her still tender shoulder injury. She sighed and challenged, "With the haphazard job you did on my shoulder, I shall never be able to wear those provocative, low-cut French gowns. But since I never did anyway, I suppose I won't miss them," she sighed.

She and Joe burst into genial laughter. "You might not miss them, but all the fellows will. It's probably a good thing you were too young for such dresses when you left that England. With everything else you got to offer, it's a good thing you won't be allowed to take such unfair advantage of ignorant men."

"Why, Joe Kenny, how dare you imply such a dishonest thing! A woman needs all the help she can manage when it comes to bedazzling the right man. Now I shall have no soft, white shoulders to entice him with."

Powchutu had been silently watching the jovial exchange between Joe and Alisha. Unaware they had always teased each other in a similar manner, jealousy flooded him anew. He feared that Joe was making his position as romantic rival known to her. He envied their closeness; feelings of resentment and discontent stormed his troubled mind. He yearned for her to be that carefree and affectionate with him, but she was not. He fretted about his mixed bloods, reasoning that had something to do with her feelings for him. He angrily concluded that Gray Eagle was an Indian and that Joe was . . . was what? he wondered. With momentary contempt, he decided that Joe was one of those new Americans; he was a white man. When compared with those two, dominant men, Powchutu feared that he was nothing, nothing important to her.

Alisha tugged at his shirt with persistence. "Powchutu! Wake up," she joked lightly, calling him from his destructive brooding. "I was asking your opinion about a crucial matter."

"What opinion, Alisha?" he asked in a solemn tone.

She knelt before him and gazed up into his unreadable face. "Is something wrong? You seem so pensive." A radiant smile lit up her lovely face and entrancing eyes. "Didn't you hear what Joe said? We're rich! You and I. Uncle Thad left plenty of money on deposit with Mr.

Bigsley in St. Louis. We have nothing to worry about now. There's money for clothes and food and lodging, even passage back to England," she rambled on and on in her state of glee, eyes aglow with renewed life.

"You have money, Alisha. Now you can return to this land you speak about. You don't need me anymore," he sadly informed her.

To Alisha, they had been through so much together that it only seemed natural for them to remain together. Her bright smile and buoyant mood faded instantly. She stared at him in astonishment. "You . . . don't want to come with me? But you said we were a family. You said we would leave here together. I don't understand. My money is yours, too. I couldn't make it without you. Why this sudden change?"

Without regard for Joe's presence, he took her lovely face between his hands and stared down into her anxious eyes. "Do you honestly want me to come with you?"

"Of course I do! You're all the family I have left, except for Joe." Without thinking, she vowed with sincerity, "You're like a brother to me; I love you and need you."

His sudden, sharp intake of air and the look of pain which filled his eyes warned her of her slip. She had not wanted him to learn the truth this way. She had wanted to gently prepare him for this disappointing news. Seeing his hurt and embarrassment, she entreated, "I'm sorry, Powchutu. I didn't mean for it to come out like that. I was only . . ."

He hastily released her face as if her touch had suddenly burned his hands. He quickly stood up, his feelings obvious to both Alisha and Joe. Yet, his tightly clenched fists were noticed only by the alert and confused Joe. She hurriedly tried to explain her words and feelings to him, but he silenced her attempts.

"Don't say anything else, Alisha. Please. By now I can see how you feel about me. I'm a grown man, remember? You've already proven love doesn't kill a person. I think I'll get some fresh air." He was trying hard to hide his tormented emotions from both of them, but was unsuccessful. Humiliated by her rejection of him in front of another man, he left the cabin.

His doleful mood clutched at her tender, aching heart. Alisha stared at the closed door. "That was a very cruel and thoughtless thing for me to do, Joe. If not for him, I would be dead right now. He was the only friend I had at Fort Pierre. He protected me and helped me. I cannot even name all of the things he's done for me. He's even risked his life for me. But he wants what I cannot give to any man, not yet anyway. It's still too soon after Gray Eagle. I wish he could understand."

Joe gathered her into his arms and comforted her. In many ways Joe was also like a dearly loved and respected brother. The main difference between him and Powchutu was that Joe accepted his brotherly role, despite his wish to be more than a brother. Powchutu could not. Joe spoke to her as if she were a child. She lay her tear-stained face against his leather jerkin and listened to his encouraging words.

"He loves you, Alisha. He hopes to marry you one day. He has done all those things for you because of these feelings. But, they cannot alter your feelings for Gray Eagle. You love Powchutu like a brother; he loves you as a woman. You want a sibling relationship; he wants marriage. Don't marry him out of gratitude or pity. It would be tragic for both of you. Perhaps in time you can come to love him in that same special way you loved Gray Eagle."

He felt her stiffen within his embrace at the mere

mention of his name. "I know you still love him, Alisha. But you can get over him in time. One day you'll find some lucky young man who will steal your heart away. You'll marry him and have lots of fat, healthy babies." He instantly realized his wrong choice of arguments. She violently erupted with fierce denials.

"Never! I won't ever marry anyone else. I won't ever love anyone either. Love only brings pain and suffering. I trusted him; I loved him! He betrayed me and deceived me! I wish he had killed me. At least I wouldn't have learned of his full measure of treachery and hatred. I wouldn't have lost our child!"

For the first time in weeks, she began to weep softly. She had managed to seal off that section of her heart and of her memory until Joe had accidentally re-opened them by mistake. All of the old, restrained emotions came rushing through the ruptured barrier. Joe could have bitten off his traitorous tongue. He sought to find some way to repair his damage.

"Listen to me, Alisha. You can't blame yourself for Gray Eagle's actions. You've done nothing wrong, nothing to be ashamed of. My God, you loved him! There's no crime in loving a man, even if he doesn't return it. If you hadn't saved his life that day, you wouldn't be the woman you are now. Your actions had nothing to do with this. Without a doubt, both of those raids would have taken place whether you were there or not. You're not responsible for this bloody hatred and warfare. It existed long before you came here; it'll go on long after you leave. The child is gone, Alisha, but there can be others. Don't kill all your feelings of love because of what he put you through. Someday you'll meet another man, one who'll deserve your love, one who'll return it. Wait for that man, Alisha. Don't embitter your heart against life or other men," he earnestly pleaded with her. "He's done enough damage to you. Don't permit any more."

She lifted her tear-filled eyes to gaze at him. "But it still hurts so much, Joe. When will the pain and emptiness go away? When will I stop remembering what it was like in his arms? Why did he tell me he loved me if he didn't mean it? Why didn't he just stick his knife into my heart; that couldn't have hurt any more. I was so trusting and so dumb. I believed that the infamous, dauntless warrior fell in love with his English captive," she cried bitterly.

"Perhaps he did, Alisha," came Joe's startling conclusion. "But perhaps he could not accept what his love for you might cost him. In time he'll recognize his mistake and great loss. He'll hunger for the return of his woman to his tepee. How could he not love you and want you, unless he's a blind, stupid fool? Somehow that description doesn't seem to fit the indomitable Wanmdi Hota."

She was gaping at him in utter disbelief and astonishment. "But why would he want to kill me? Why not send me away?"

"I think you already know that answer. If he couldn't have you, then no man would. He's a proud and possessive man from what I hear. How could he turn the woman he loved and wanted over to another warrior to enjoy? Yet, as much as he desired you and as much as he refused to allow another man to have you, evidently he couldn't murder you in cold blood. From what I know about him and from what you two have told me, I am positive he did want you. But such forbidden love was doomed from the beginning, Alisha. You're white, an enemy in the middle of a war. He's a Sioux warrior, a future chief. Neither of you can change these facts. He must have realized you would never be happy in continued captivity, just as he could never admit to loving a white girl."

"You're saying he could kill me, but not love me? Oh that damned pride of his! Just how valuable is this kind of pride, Joe? Pride . . . something I haven't known in a long time, but I will regain it. I'll never allow anyone to ever take it from me again."

She hesitantly continued, "Part of what you said is true, but for his loving me. When you love someone, nothing and no one matters. Love isn't selfish or destructive. It doesn't demand your soul or your life. Love is something he will never understand or feel. His heart is too full of hatred to allow any love to enter it. Escape was definitely not in his plans for me. I wonder if he ever went back to see if I was dead . . ."

"Perhaps it was his plan, Alisha," Joe said, stroking her hair. "That could explain why he left you alive. Could be he thought it would be a sign from the Great Spirit if you somehow survived. Indians are very superstitious people. Who can say what he was thinking?"

"I can: revenge and death to his sworn enemy," Alisha said adamantly. "I can promise you one thing, Joe: he has taken the last thing from me. I am free of his hold. If you're right, then I will also be free of him in every way. Once I return to England, this will all seem like some ghastly nightmare during a violent thunderstorm. Funny, but every passing day it seems more and more unreal. If I didn't carry these scars upon my back and shoulder, I could almost convince myself that it never really happened."

The hour grew late, and the scout did not return. Joe and Alisha were finally forced to turn in for a restless, tense night of very little sleep.

Powchutu did not come back to the cabin until the

following afternoon. Alisha lived with the growing fear that he had left her with Joe and had gone on his way alone. As he was entering the small clearing which surrounded the cabin, she sighted his fatigued frame coming toward her. She shouted his name in relief and ran to greet him. She hugged him fiercely and related her fears about his safety.

"Why did you run off like that? I've been worried about you all night and half the day." The blue smudges beneath her green eyes attested to her lack of sleep; her eyes and voice revealed the depth of her concern and affection. "Please don't be upset with me, not now. Things are going so well for us for a change. Don't spoil them, Powchutu. Please," she implored him with misty eyes and quavering voice.

She lowered her head in shame and continued, "I know how much I hurt you last night. But I honestly did not mean to. Can you forgive me? Can you try to understand my feelings? You said we are a family. Are you sorry you saved my life and helped me escape?" she asked him coyly, striving to win his empathy and to inspire remorse.

It worked. He lifted her chin with his hand and stared into her bewitching eyes. "Why would you even think such a thing? Your life and safety are the most important things to me. Of course, I'm not sorry. I'd do it all again if need be. I just needed some time to work out a few things. I understand what you were trying to tell me. It doesn't hurt any less, but I will try to accept it. Besides, who can say what the future holds for us? As long as we're together, I can still hope, can't I?"

She smiled and hugged him again. "Yes. We can both hope for a better future. I do love you, Powchutu. Not in the same way you love me, or in the way I should love you before marrying you. Perhaps I will some day. In all honesty, I cannot think of any man more deserving of my love and loyalty than you. But I cannot force such feelings to suddenly enter my heart, even if I want them to come."

Either her words or his soul-searching during his absence conquered Powchutu's pride. He readily agreed with her decisions. "Then you will come with me? You won't leave me alone? We'll be a real family," she sweetly said.

"I'll never leave your side until you ask me to," he promised, grinning broadly at her.

"I would never do that. For as long as I live and breathe, we are family: this I swear to you."

He pulled her into his warm embrace and held her tightly for a few moments, desperately wanting to cover her mouth with his, yet not daring to do so. Knowing Powchutu needed this small comfort from her, Alisha did not pull away or stiffen. She relaxed against his hard chest and linked her hands behind his back. He closed his eyes, savoring the feel of her tantalizing body pressed close to his. It was a struggle to control the turbulent emotions which inflamed his passions.

In a husky voice he stressed, "Just as long as you know I love you, that I'm here for you when you need me. That's all that matters for now," he vowed, hoping he could keep these pledges to her. A distressing thought shoved its way into his tranquility: you have her now; yet, you do not have her at all. He could not decide which was worse, to half possess her or not to possess any of her.

His senses dulled by his inner turmoil, Powchutu did not take note of Joe's nearby presence. This moving scene between them vividly registered in Joe's keenly perceptive mind. He surmised that the scout was craftily manipulating the unsuspecting, artless Alisha into total dependence on him out of Alisha's sense of gratitude to him. It was clear to Joe that the scout actually did love her deeply and strongly. Yet, it was also just as clear to Joe that she did not return this kind of love. Joe could perceive her loyalty and devotion to Powchutu. He could only hope that the scout would not exploit her emotions.

"Damn you, Wanmdi Hota!" Joe cursed mutely, too softly to be overheard. "You have no idea what you've lost, my koda. How could you reject a woman like Alisha? There isn't an Indian maiden anywhere who is better suited to you. She loved you, man. Why?" he angrily wondered, just as Alisha had so many times.

Joe was quick to note a superficial change in the scout. After his return that afternoon, Powchutu professed acceptance of his role as pseudo-brother. Yet, Joe would frequently observe the covert way in which Powchutu studied Alisha while she was busy. There was not any one thing Joe could discern as the problem. What really worried the wary Joe was that he could not guess what the scout was waiting for.

The next few days, things returned to the way they were. The men worked harder to prepare Joe for the swiftly approaching winter. Alisha mirrored health in body and spirit as she fluttered around the cabin carrying out her own chores. Everything was moving along fine until the day when Powchutu suggested that he and Alisha head out for St. Louis. He and Joe had argued and reasoned for hours. In the end, the decision was placed in her lap.

She paced back and forth as she considered the arguments from both men. As much as she enjoyed the warmth and safety of Joe's cabin, if they did not leave soon, they would be stranded there for the duration of the winter. Powchutu had ingeniously reminded her of their precarious location. The thought of being confined in that small cabin which was within a few weeks' travel of the Sioux village was terrifying to her. If they pressed on to St. Louis, she would be further away from this tormenting place with its bittersweet memories and lingering dangers. Powchutu presented her with bald facts; Joe merely offered wise suggestions. Her choice seemed obvious.

Joe was her dear friend, and he had helped her during a terrible crisis. But her loyalties and considerations lay with Powchutu and her own freedom. Distance and new surroundings could inspire forgetfulness: something she desperately needed. She hated to leave Joe all alone for the winter, but he was accustomed to this solitude, though she enjoyed his company and hated to disappoint him by leaving.

She finally rejoined the two waiting men. To voice her decision was unnecessary; it was evident in her determined expression. She politely attempted to explain her motives to Joe. He graciously accepted her judgment, but did not agree with it. He kindly offered her his help and hospitality any time she might need them in the future. He even promised to look them up in St. Louis in the spring if they were still there. He could tell how relieved and grateful she was by his not fighting her choice.

As for Powchutu, he behaved like a child at Christmas. Her decision meant victory for him. He grinned from ear to ear. He could hardly contain his exuberance long enough to make their coming plans. He promptly suggested that they get things ready and leave within a week.

Although this seemed too short a time for Alisha, she obediently agreed.

Joe thought it best not to interfere with their plans, for it might prevent her trust in him. He wanted Alisha to feel that she could turn to him in any crisis. He also wanted to make certain that she understood that he would never judge her. To attack Powchutu's intentions on the basis of his instinct would force Alisha to defend her friend. If this Powchutu was up to something, Joe would be alerted to it by spring. He informed her of the best and quickest way to reach him in case of emergency. Then he told her that she could expect him to arrive in St. Louis by April.

Chapter Nine

During that following week, Powchutu was a bundle of energy and excitement. He checked and rechecked all of their supplies. He examined the canoe for any damage; finding none, he announced it was adequate to finish their journey. With the swift currents in the Missouri River, he deduced that they would arrive in St. Louis within two weeks. He then busied himself with helping Joe complete his supply of firewood for the winter.

The day before they were to depart, Powchutu went hunting for rabbits or some fowl which could be roasted and carried on their journey. Alisha made johnnycakes and wrapped them in a clean cloth. The cold weather would help to preserve their rations for many days, expediting their trip. Joe was also busy with last-minute tasks. Each seemed occupied with his own assignments and thoughts.

Shortly after Powchutu had left to hunt, Joe headed to his cabin to speak privately with Alisha for one last time until spring. He entered so quietly that she did not hear him. Joe could see that she had been folding her scant possessions and packing them in the leather parfleche he had given to her the day before.

Her distant, dreamy-eyed stare had halted his entrance just inside the doorway. He curiously studied her strange mood for a few moments, hesitating to intrude on her deep reverie. Alisha was sitting on the edge of his bunk, slightly turned in the other direction, presenting him with her profile.

She was holding a creamy white leather dress clutched protectively against her bosom with her right hand. In her left hand she held a white, artistically beaded headband. She was gently blowing on the single white feather attached to it. As it would quiver in the draft which she created, she would smile secretly and pensively.

Time and time again she repeated this curious act. As soon as the fluffy feather ceased to waver, she would purse her soft lips and leisurely exhale upon it once more. Abruptly she halted her ritual. She angrily crushed the little plume inside her tight fist, as if it had suddenly offended her in some mysterious way.

"Damn you!" she cried out in unleashed anguish, startling Joe with the vehemence and grief in her voice.

Before Joe could make his presence known, she forcefully threw the headband across the room. It struck the wall and fell to the floor. Almost hysterically she began to yank and to tear at the beautiful white dress, bent upon its destruction. She was crying and cursing Gray Eagle between ragged gasps for air.

Joe rushed forward and seized her by the forearms. He called her name as he gently shook her to her senses. Her frenzied eyes came up to lock with his alarmed blue ones.

"It's mine!" she screamed at him. "I can destroy it if I wish and you can't stop me."

"What's the matter with you, Alisha? You're beside yourself. Calm down and talk to me," he commanded in a concerned tone.

"The dress, I hate it! I want it destroyed!" she vowed, barely in control of her emotions and words.

"Why? It's lovely. An albino hide is rare and valuable."

She glared at him, then sneered contemptuously,

167

"Just as rare as a white girl marrying a chief's son!"

Enlightenment filled his robust frame. He mellowed and softly stated, "I see. Your wedding heyake?"

"My death's shroud," she acidly countered. "I was safer as his slave than as his wife."

"Want to talk about it? Might help to resolve some of that bitterness and anger." He offered his friendly ear, more so to hear her story than from idle curiosity.

"Talk changes nothing. Besides, Brave Bear is the one who gave it to me; it was made for our joining. After Gray Eagle won his challenge for me, I was forced to wear it for him instead."

"How did you feel about this Brave Bear? He's Chief Black Cloud's adopted son, isn't he?"

"Yes. He was very kind to me. But why shouldn't he have been? They all believed I was this missing daughter of Black Cloud's. In all fairness, he was a brave and respected warrior. He was very kind and gentle with me. I suppose I really liked him. He was strong and virile, handsome too. I guess I was just too scared and confused to think very much about him at the time. All I knew was that I was in his control and I didn't understand why. I was under the impression Gray Eagle had sold me to him."

"Now I'm confused. How did they come to the conclusion you're Shalee?"

She sighed heavily, giving Joe the idea that she was not going to discuss this matter any further. But she said, "There was this old woman who lived in the Sioux camp. The way I understand it, she had been banished from the Blackfoot camp a long time ago. She was selected as my . . . mentor, you could say. In the beginning she was very mean and spiteful to me. Later I learned it was because I was a near replica of a captive who had once belonged to Chief Black Cloud. White, no less. Irish, I believe. Strange as it sounds, Black Cloud loved her. Her name was Jenny, and she gave him a girl child about twenty years ago. When Shalee—their daughter—was about two years old, she was stolen from his camp during a raid by some whites. Matu, the old woman, was banished for not protecting his daughter during that raid, since Jenny was killed. After Gray Eagle had tricked the cavalry at Fort Pierre into returning me to him, Matu went to Black Cloud and told him I was his Shalee. He came to the Sioux camp and demanded my return to him. Since Gray Eagle couldn't disprove his claim, I had to go with him. At that time, I believed he had sold me to Black Cloud or Brave Bear. I couldn't understand their kindness to me. I was also baffled by Gray Eagle's fury that day. No one takes anything from him! About a week or so later, he came charging into the Blackfoot camp demanding to marry me."

She swallowed several times to moisten her dry throat, then fetched a cup of water. After a few sips, she continued with her incredible narrative. She spoke as if she were talking about another girl.

"Black Cloud refused. Brave Bear refused. They informed me I was to wed Brave Bear. After that massacre at Fort Pierre, Powchutu had gone to live with another tribe. He told me Gray Eagle himself had spared his life. Anyway, Gray Eagle went after him and brought him along to explain all these ridiculous things to me. Why, I don't know. I suppose he didn't want anyone alive to know he can speak English. No doubt he would have eventually killed Powchutu also." She shuddered at this dreadful thought.

"I didn't learn his dark secret until that last day I saw him. To go on, Powchutu was ordered to tell me who I

169

was and why I was there. You can imagine my reaction. I was both confused and elated. I hadn't been sold to another warrior, and I was reputed to be a chief's daughter. Then I knew why I was being given the grand treatment. Gray Eagle's fury surely made sense by then. If he could keep me as his lowly white slave, then he certainly deserved to keep me as a chief's daughter. Now that I was a worthy prize, he couldn't stand for someone else to claim it. Perhaps he figured it might damage his image if I chose another warrior over him, a symbolic slap in the face."

She drank more water before going on. "You must see the great shock I received when Powchutu explained their ideas to me. I honestly tried to convince them it was a trick. They refused to listen to me. In the end, I had no choice but to agree to becoming Princess Shalee. I was so weary of all the fear and trouble. It seemed the only solution to happiness and peace, so I relented."

Her eyes fluttered as she recalled her frustration and terror. "That was when the trouble really began. Gray Eagle would not be bested by anyone in any way. There was an uproar in the camp. I quickly learned he had challenged Brave Bear to possess me: 'Ki-ci-e-conape' was what they called it, duel to the death. It had something to do with tribal custom and his prior possession. I was helpless to prevent it or to refuse to join with the winner. Naturally Gray Eagle won. I seriously doubt any man alive could conquer him."

When she halted and lapsed into pensive silence, Joe impulsively pressed, "Then what happened?"

She shrugged her shoulders and replied, "We were joined the following night. He did learn the truth about Matu's trick before the joining ceremony, but not before his reckless challenge. He must have overheard a talk between me and Powchutu in Matu's tepee. We figured out how the deception was carried out, and we faced her with our accusations. The three of us were trying to decide how to handle Matu's treachery and my predicament."

"Matu's treachery? What do you mean?" he echoed in rising confusion. "How did she convince him of your identity?"

"Have you ever heard of the Blackfoot custom of tattooing their family members with the same symbol, 'akitos' they're called?" When Joe nodded his knowledge of this fact, she went on, "I was unconscious after my lashing for trying to escape. Matu was left to tend me. She accidentally found a scar shaped like a crescent moon in just the right area of my body. The combination of my similarity to this Jenny and my scar gave her the bold idea of passing me off as Shalee. That way, she could return home with a heroine's welcome. She cunningly added two small stars to make it match Black Cloud's akito. She wanted to return home to her people before she died, and I became her ticket."

"But tribal law prohibits such things! It means instant death, perhaps even torture," Joe exclaimed in disbelief.

"She was very old. What did she care? With my likeness to Jenny and with the akito as proof, Gray Eagle could not dispute Black Cloud's claim on me. But when he learned it was only a ruse . . . well, you already know how he took that humiliating news: he left me to die. Now, he's playing the grieving husband back in his village. Poor Black Cloud, he was really very kind and gentle. He will think he has lost his child for a second time." Alisha experienced sincere sympathy for the old man who had proclaimed her as his daughter.

Joe reflected upon all this new information, then questioned, "If he never spoke English to you before that last day, how did you know he had learned your secret?"

She walked over to the wall, leaned over, and picked up the headband which she had so angrily discarded. "This told me," she stated simply.

"I don't follow you. What could that headband reveal to him? Its markings and color say you're a chief's daughter."

"Shortly before the ceremony, two events warned me of Gray Eagle's coming betrayal. First, he came into Black Cloud's tepee. He picked up this headband and smiled, that secretive kind that tells you something is going on inside his head. He started to toy with the feather, blowing on it and making it quiver as with fear. He then took out the white feather and put one of his yellow ones in its place. I suppose he was reiterating his claim of ownership and power over me. I snatched it out and replaced the white one. After several such rounds, he was finally satisfied to leave both feathers in the headband. Definitely some kind of warning," she concluded.

"Is that what you were thinking about when I came in, that feather incident?"

"That and the wedding," she confessed dispiritedly. "At least it was very impressive and beautiful. It took place at night under a starry sky. Everyone was all dressed up in colorful outfits. There was a big celebration afterwards. I was wearing this dress. I don't think I've ever looked better in my life than I did that night, though I was scared stiff. And Gray Eagle," she sighed, "he was dressed in a long robe made from all kinds of feathers. There was soft drumming in the background. Or maybe it was just my heart thumping. I've never seen any man look so hand . . ."

She caught herself before completing her wistful

memories. She flushed a deep red, crimson reaching down her neck. She modestly lowered her lashes.

"Don't be embarrassed, Alisha. His good looks and prowess are well-known facts. There isn't a woman around who could resist his magnetism. From what I hear, even Apollo and Adonis would be envious of him."

"You're teasing me, Joe. Please don't."

"I wasn't. You of all females must know I speak the truth. Can you deny he's the best specimen of manhood you've ever seen?" he challenged her.

She opened her mouth to accept his annoying dare, but could not disclaim his remarks. "I suppose you're right," she reluctantly agreed.

"What was the second thing?" he quizzed her.

"Second thing?"

"You said he warned you in two ways, remember? If that feather incident was the first clue, what was the second one?"

She promptly presented him with her slender back. But not before he caught a glimpse of the crimson guilt which overtook her lovely face once more. "Nothing. Just forget it," she murmured in embarrassment and modesty.

He pulled her back around to face him. Her features were hidden from his probing eyes. He lifted her chin and pushed her long curls out of her face. Her long, thick lashes were still lowered to conceal some secret which might be written there.

"Look at me, Alisha," he commanded in an authoritative tone.

Conditioned by Gray Eagle to instantly obey such orders, she looked up at him. "What did he do or say to make you run like a frightened rabbit? I think you're as much afraid of yourself as you are of him."

173

Her involuntary reaction told him that he had struck a nerve. "It's very personal, Joe. I don't want to discuss it with anyone, not even you."

"Did he try to force himself on you before the joining? Did something else happen in Black Cloud's tepee that afternoon?" he ventured his only logical conclusion.

"No," she replied quickly.

"If he didn't say or do anything to you, then how could he make you feel so threatened?" His jaw was set in grim determination to have the whole truth, as if it somehow affected him personally. His blue eyes probed her green ones, trying to compel some new evidence to surface there.

"Don't do that!" she abruptly shrieked at a startled Joe.

"Do what?" His brow lifted in doubtful question.

"Try to see into my very soul. He was always doing that. It makes me uncomfortable," she admitted.

Joe stunned her with his next question. "Were you hoping for him to make some romantic move toward you after the challenge, and he didn't? Perhaps court his newly won bride-to-be?" he jested to lighten her spirits.

"Why should he? He owned me lock, stock, and barrel, as they say. Why should he consider my trivial feelings?" She carelessly opened a previously closed door, dropping a clue.

"Is that it? He ignored you, so you thought he didn't want you? Alisha! He had just risked his life to marry you! He had just risked his honor to win you. Didn't that prove something to you? It tells me he wanted you and wouldn't give you up, no matter what the cost to him."

"Wanted me!" she shouted scornfully. "A lot you know! When I acquiesced to the dashing champion, he threw me aside like some . . . as if I were worthless, a mere nuisance to be endured. He spoke English; he knew how I felt about him. He knew how confused and frightened I was. I was dumb enough to say it and to show him! He wanted me so much that he pushed me away," she said breathlessly, mentally blocking out the reason for his temporary rejection of her.

This apparent contradiction flabbergasted Joe. "You went to him of your own free will, and he rejected you! He fought for you, then discarded you! Is that what you're saying?" He shook his head in disbelief. "That's absurd! There must be a reason!"

Feeling dishonest, Alisha reluctantly explained, "We were alone after the challenge. It was the first time since I had been forcefully taken from his tepee that morning. We had parted in anger and silence. Before he captured me, he was supposed to marry another girl. The night before Black Cloud's arrival to claim me, she had tried to kill me. I could understand her hatred and desperation. Yet tender-hearted Alisha tried to prevent her punishment. Take it from me, open defiance from a white slave was a terrible mistake. He was so furious with me, he didn't even return to our tepee after Chela's punishment. I didn't see him again until that following morning when Black Cloud came to stake his claim on me. By the time the challenge was over, I was already one lesson and punishment behind."

She modestly lowered her lashes. As she continued, her partially obscured face grew pinker and pinker. "When we were finally left alone, he seemed different somehow: calm, gentle, pleased, and even loving. It had been a long time since we . . . had been together. He was a very skilled, persuasive man when it came to . . . romance. Joe, he was irresistable. As you can guess, things were quickly out of hand. White Arrow, his best friend, came looking for us because it was almost time for the celebration.''

Her following words were spoken as if she were painfully bringing them from the very depths of her inner soul. "Without any warning, he suddenly became very cold, forbidding, and stern. He seized my hand and practically dragged me back to the camp. He was almost as angry as he had been that morning when Black Cloud took me away from him. He practically forced me to respond to him, then attacked me for doing so! Knowing English, he could have explained what was wrong or why he was so furious. He didn't say a word. If that isn't rejection, then what is?"

Aware of how a proud man might react to being caught in a passionate and compromising position, Joe could easily understand Gray Eagle's defensive reaction, but not his calloused way of handling the situation. Why hadn't he explained his feelings to her? "My naïve Alisha, he was no doubt embarrassed by his loss of control over himself. Evidently he became overly defensive at his bad timing."

She stared at him wide-eyed and gaped. Joe had just unwittingly given her the same explanation that Gray Eagle had that last morning on the plains. "What would you have done in that same situation?"

"Probably killed the so-called friend whose timing was so humiliating," he replied devilishly.

"Why?" she innocently questioned, eyes filled with curiosity and ignorance.

Joe chuckled, slightly timid about replying. "Under such heated conditions, to be denied fulfillment is most painful to both your manly pride and your . . . your private parts, shall I say?"

She flushed again as enlightenment was shed on her naïve mind. She had also experienced that same kind of frustrated anguish at being denied his love. She wondered if he had wanted her so much that he had suffered physically and mentally from White Arrow's innocent intrusion. "Served him right for leading me on!"

Joe could not control his mirthful laughter at her peeved expression. She beat upon his chest with her two, small fists. "That isn't funny. How should I know such things?" she stormed at him, half in anger and half in embarrassment.

"You do now. Remember that in the future. Men are hot-blooded creatures, Alisha. They have many secrets and peculiarities. Passion can often be an uncontrollable wildfire. Sex is hard enough to control with a woman you know, but nearly impossible with one you love and desire. Take a lesson from him, don't ever lead any man on with kisses and promises of more to come if you don't intend to finish what you both started. Men don't take kindly to teasers. Desire is like a smoldering fire: with the fuel of encouragement, it can burst into flames. I can almost assure you that wasn't any rejection from him. If anything, he suffered more than you." Joe almost visibly winced, as he empathized with Gray Eagle at that unfortunate moment.

"I still say it served him right for getting me all . . . Besides," she hastily changed the subject, "you're forgetting why I'm here. Gray Eagle pretended to be drugged so I could escape. He only wanted me out of the Blackfoot village so he could secretly dispose of me," she accused, annoyed by Joe's sympathy for Gray Eagle.

"Or perhaps for privacy to settle all these secrets and problems between you two?" he boldly challenged.

"You think just like he does!" she hotly charged. She had meant it as an insult, but Joe took it as a compliment.

He grinned roguishly. Alisha continued, "You're giving all the same arguments he did. But, he also told me he loved me and wanted me. Yet, he rode off for supplies and water and never came back. We were going to camp there for a week or so. Some honeymoon!" she snapped.

"Are you certain he betrayed you? Absolutely positive, Alisha?"

"I've already told you!" she shouted in rising irritation. "I waited for two grueling days without food and water. He never came back. He never sent anyone to get me."

"What if he had an accident, was injured?"

"Damn you, Joe!" she nearly shrieked, her exasperation showing vividly in her flushed cheeks and stormy eyes. "Powchutu was at his village with White Arrow when he returned. He told them I was dead and buried, killed by some renegade braves. He played the grieving widower. He lied! He betrayed me! He left me to die! Why all these questions? It's over! I have to forget him and what happened back there. What difference does it make if he did have justifiable motives? I still won't die for his bloody love!"

Joe wondered if it was truly over. If Gray Eagle had always refused to let her leave him, then would he do so now? If he discovered her survival, would he come after her? Could he possibly track her after all this time and distance? Everything hinged upon Powchutu's honesty. If he had lied to Alisha, then why hadn't Gray Eagle come after them? Powchutu wouldn't hold a candle to Gray Eagle's tracking skills, and determination. Knowing both men, Joe still could not determine the truth. Then, too, Alisha's feelings and thoughts were colored by this unproven betrayal by her husband. It just didn't make sense for him to ride off and leave her there. Pride and possessiveness should have prevented such an outrage. This curious, disturbing situation would certainly bear more thought and exploration . . .

"You're right, Alisha. I'm sorry I was so curious and persistent. It's just that I'm so fond of you, and I worry about you. You've had it hard since you came here. I just don't want to see you hurt again. We've been through a lot together. It'll take some time for those old wounds to heal, but they will. I hope you'll consider staying in St. Louis until spring. I'd sure like to see you again, just to be sure you're all right."

"I can't promise you that, Joe, but I will try. Powchutu is going to pretend to be my brother. So when you come looking for us, ask for Paul or Alisha Williams," she informed him.

She giggled at her own ingenuity and remarked, "I selected Paul just in case I forget and already have the 'Pa' out."

"Good choice," he agreed, then chuckled.

As she turned to complete her packing, he picked up the headband and dress. "What about these, Alisha?"

"Keep them or burn them. If I'm to have a clean break from him, then it's best to leave all reminders of our life together behind. The only thing I'll carry with me are the scars on my back, and those I can't leave behind, can I? When I leave here, it will be a total and last farewell."

"If you don't mind, I think I'll keep 'em for a while. Might get married myself one day. Could make use of 'em," he joked.

"Those are Indian clothes, Joe. You told me such unions were doomed and forbidden, remember?" she gently reminded him.

"So I did." He smiled secretly and thoughtfully. She sighed in fake exasperation, then smiled cheerfully. She

179

returned to her chore at hand.

Joe carefully folded the dress with the headband inside, then put it away. "See you at supper," he called over his right shoulder as he left the cabin and closed the door behind him.

She watched him go, bewildered by his strange mood and secretive smile. "I pray you do find yourself a good and loving wife, Joe. She'll be a very lucky woman to get you. If my heart were not elsewhere, I would take that protective position myself. God help us to both find happiness and love," she fervently prayed.

Mid-December finally arrived. They were packed and ready to leave Joe's cabin to continue their ill-fated journey. Joe made certain they had plenty of food, weapons, blankets, some medicine, and information. Realizing their safety lay in convincing everyone they were white settlers who were returning home, Joe gave Powchutu a set of trapper's buckskins and a red cotton shirt. He thanked Joe for his generosity and precaution.

Not being one for long and sad farewells, Joe promptly said his goodbyes. He firmly shook the scout's hand and reminded him to take good care of Alisha. He embraced Alisha, then wiped away her tears. They chatted for a few minutes before Powchutu said they needed to be on their way. They lovingly embraced once more.

Joe placed Alisha in one end of the bark canoe, then stepped back to watch their departure. Powchutu leaped into the other end with light and graceful agility. Joe untied the line and gingerly tossed it to Powchutu. He shoved the canoe into the swiftly flowing current of the mighty Missouri River. He raised his arm and waved farewell to Alisha. She smiled and returned his gesture. She quickly gripped the sides of the canoe to steady herself.

Joe's gaze went to the other end of the canoe. The

paddle rested across Powchutu's lap and the sides of the canoe. He was sitting erect and proud, his profile to Joe. It was that precise moment when Joe recognized what had been gnawing at his subconscious mind: Powchutu favored Gray Eagle closely enough to be his brother! Joe stared in utter disbelief as this startling revelation settled in. He could not understand how he had failed to notice this astonishing resemblance before. It had been right before his eyes all the time: the same stance, that same fierce pride and arrogance, the similarity in looks and personality, and the same cunning and daring. From a distance, it was like viewing that indomitable warrior himself, dressed as a white man.

Unable to call them back or to alter their plans, he could only shake his head in anger and frustration. He knew that Powchutu was a half-breed. He wondered if it was somehow possible those two men were related. He wondered if that was the reason why Gray Eagle had spared Powchutu's life following the massacre at Fort Pierre. It seemed ironical to think perhaps neither man knew his enemy could be his half-brother. Thinking his ideas a little farfetched, Joe dismissed them.

His concern focused on Alisha. He speculated on her knowledge of the fact which had just revealed itself to him. He dreaded to think this similarity was the basis for her attraction and attachment to the scout: a substitute for Gray Eagle, one who loved and accepted her. No matter now, he decided, it would be spring before he could check out his rising suspicions.

For ten days they travelled the snaking Missouri River. Wanting to arrive there as quickly as possible, they took turns resting and rowing. Of course Alisha's shift was very short and less strenuous; it only prevented them from stopping or from drifting into the bank while Powchutu rested for a while. Their luck held out; there was no bad weather or trouble along the way.

The day before their scheduled arrival in St. Louis, they halted to rest and to prepare themselves for their grand entry into civilization. Powchutu found a secluded alcove and beached their canoe. He rigged up a blind with several blankets so that Alisha could bathe and change clothes. She did not want to arrive dressed as an Indian, nor did he. Such attire would alert the people there to matters which they wanted kept secret.

Before departing from Joe's cabin, Alisha had washed her long, auburn tresses. She had also trimmed Powchutu's hair to collar length. Dressed in white man's clothing, he could easily pass for one. For anyone who might take a second glance, he would simply appear a ruggedly handsome man, perhaps of Spanish decent.

When they were both bathed, rested, and dressed in the proper attire to make a good first impression, they headed for the last leg of their long journey. Powchutu paddled slowly, not wanting to overtire himself this close to their destination or in case of trouble. Their excitement and apprehension mounted with each passing mile that went by. They began to laugh and to chat with gay abandonment. Closer to the settlement, they began to meet other boats and canoes upon the large river.

Powchutu was on guard for any signs of danger or suspicion. Without any further delay, they rowed into St. Louis and docked just before sundown. The man in charge of the shipping area told them where to find suitable lodgings and warm food. Thinking they were a white brother and sister travelling East together, he was polite and friendly.

With Powchutu's looks and command of the English language, he had no trouble passing everyone's close inspection. He was quickly aware of the natural curiosity and harmless suspicions of the people in this busy settlement. Alisha was the one who drew the stares and interest: admiring ones from the men, and envious ones from several women. Seeing there was no competition from a brother, several men openly flirted with her. Possessive jealousy flared within Powchutu.

She softly warned him to watch his reactions toward such things. "Remember, you're my big brother. They'll become suspicious if you behave like a jealous lover. Paul Williams, remember? I'll tell Mr. Bigsley you came to search for me after our parents' deaths. Like Joe said, tell him Joe helped you to find me and bring me back here. We'll let them know we only plan to remain for the winter, then head toward New Orleans. Joe said it was best not to tell them about England. As agreed, we'll say Uncle Thad died of a fever, so I wanted to return home with you. No one is to guess the truth. We must be careful, Po . . . Paul. We don't want to go through the same thing as before."

He relaxed, smiled, and nodded. "Hard as it will be, Alisha, I'll play the loving, but protective, big brother."

Music suddenly reached her ears. She halted and listened. "Christmas! It's Christmas eve," she squealed in surprise, childlike wonder flickering in her bright eyes.

"Christmas . . . I'd completely forgotten in all the rush and tension. Can we go and listen to the music after we find a place to lodge?" she sweetly entreated.

As they stood on the wharf listening to the muted music from the nearby settlement, an unforgettable and familiar voice spoke to her from behind. She whirled and

183

faced him, staring at him as if he were a ghost. Words failed her as her mind was spinning in confusion and utter disbelief.

Instinctively her startled gaze scanned the man's entire appearance. He was immaculately dressed in expensive, well-cut, flattering clothes. His black boots reflected the sparkling river. His silky, blond hair was well-trimmed. His clean-shaven, lordly face wore a taunting, cynical leer. The arrogant glitter in his crystal blue eyes warned her of danger—and retribution. He patiently awaited her close scrutiny, savoring this unforeseen opportunity.

"Jeffery? Jeffery Gordon?" She finally managed to control her shock and to get his name out.

He made a low, mocking bow, then resumed his intrepid stance. "One and the same, Miss Williams. I must admit you certainly show up at the strangest places at the most unexpected times. This must be my lucky day," he noted in a voice laced with venom. Licentious lights danced boldly in his eyes.

Dread filled Alisha. "How did you escape from Fort Pierre? I thought everyone there had been killed."

"Suffice it to say that I found a way. Certainly not the same one either you or this bloody bastard used," he snarled, referring to Powchutu for the first time. If he found it strange that they had just arrived there together after all this time, he did not let on. The fierce hatred and contempt which he had always felt toward Powchutu was as clear as a mountain stream. Alisha trembled visibly at the force of that hatred.

After a pretty, young female came over to join them, Jeffery graciously introduced Alisha as an old and dear friend of his. In turn, Alisha politely introduced Powchutu as her older brother Paul Williams. Jeffery chuckled wickedly, then fused his eyes to her panicked ones in open challenge.

Icy fingers of fear clawed at her racing heart. If he so chose, Jeffery could ruin everything for them by simply revealing who they were. He could maliciously alert everyone to their recent past, especially hers. Memories of her hellish past at Fort Pierre returned to terrify her. All Jeffery had to do was suggest that she was the cause of the fateful massacre of both her fortress and of Fort Pierre to inspire universal contempt and hatred of her. Fate had interfered with her freedom once more; she was stranded here just as she had once been there. All Jeffery had to say to these Indian haters was, "She's the ex-captive of the notorious Gray Eagle. He destroyed two forts to get her back. This here scout is really a contemptible half-breed." Those statements would be deadly and destructive for them.

For once, where Lieutenant Jeffery Gordon was concerned, Powchutu wisely and cautiously held his tongue and his temper. Although he wished he could draw out his hunting knife and slit Jeffery's throat, he knew that act was impossible right now before Alisha and the people on the wharf. For the time being, he would have to accept Jeffery's insults and threats. Later . . .

Jeffery flashed his companion Celeste an engaging grin, then sent the scout a warning glare before stating, "If you two don't mind, I'd like to have a few words with Alisha, in private. It's been a long time since we've seen each other, and we have a few old matters to discuss," he calmly announced in a deceptively mellow tone.

Alisha was torn between the urge to flee as quickly as possible and the urge to humbly capitulate to this man who could easily dash her new-found freedom and pride. She could read the triumphant smile which lit up his handsome features, but glittered ominously in his cold blue eyes. Unable to control himself, Powchutu immediately protested this insult. He began stiffly, "Mr. Gordon, our trip was arduous—"

Gordon cut him off and said imperiously, "Ah, but I have not seen Miss Williams for so long. Alisha?"

•Alisha warily weighed her choices, despising all of them. She knew how dangerous it was to cross Jeffery. She had learned that all too well in the past. She shifted uneasily beneath the stares of all three people. Her tone was low and resentful as she informed Powchutu of her decision to speak with Jeffery for a few minutes.

As she was talking to Powchutu, a new plan was rapidly formulating in Jeffery's mind. He discounted the surly, withering glare from Powchutu. He chuckled in open amusement, nearly bringing a physical reaction from the angry scout. Alisha gently clutched Powchutu's arm and silently warned him to a truce. A baffled Celeste remained silent and watchful, wondering why these two seemed so intimidated by Jeffery; yet, knowing Jeffery as she did, she was positive there was some reason for them to fear and to obey him.

With a quiver of uncertainty nagging at her troubled mind, Alisha permitted Jeffery to take her arm and to lead her to the end of the long deserted pier. Both remained silent for the entire walk. At the end of the dock, Jeffery halted and turned to face her. To her astonishment, his black scowl had been replaced by a pleased smirk. She shot him a look of suspicion and dread. His roguish grin broadened. Devilish lights played mischievously in his eyes. She waited with bated breath to learn of his intentions.

His first question stunned her. "What the hell are you doing here with that blasted half-breed? These people would tear you both apart if they guessed who you are. Shall I tell them, Alisha, or shall I keep silent? Tell me something, is Gray Eagle with you, or will he be along later? Surely you didn't cast him aside for that red bastard over there?" he taunted, nodding in Powchutu's direction.

Her quavering voice inquired, "What do you want from me, Jeffery?"

Jeffery's burst of harsh laughter chilled her very soul . . .

Chapter Ten

Alisha stared up into Jeffery's truculent gaze, realizing that his near-brush with death had not changed him at all. As she faced her old enemy, her own eyes grew hard and cold. It was too easy to recall his past treatment of her, treatment which had been degrading and intimidating. Previously at Fort Pierre, it had not taken long for his satanic personality to overshadow his dashing, debonair facade. It angered her for him to have the gall and rudeness to address her in such a brash, crude manner. Yet, it also terrified her to comprehend that Jeffery possessed information that could destroy their lives. She wisely sought to temper her outrage with caution.

"Your vision is still clouded with spite and animosity, Jeffery. If you recall, I did not elope with that infamous warrior; I was practically sacrificed to him in order to save the inhabitants of Fort Pierre! If memory serves me correctly, you were one of the officers who insisted upon my speedy return to him. You cannot hold me responsible for his cunning deceit; I did warn you not to accept his wily truce. As for Powchutu, you seem to forget we have always been friends. He was the only person at that fort who gave a fig about me, who didn't try to take advantage of my precarious position, who didn't judge me soiled for life, who didn't try to make me feel unwanted and unworthy! As you well know, I cannot say such things about you," she tersely stated.

She then heatedly charged, "There was only one thing you wanted from me, and it was not friendship or affection. You didn't care how I felt, or what I thought. You didn't even consider my emotional or physical condition. All you ever saw in me was something you wanted. Powchutu was the only one who offered me real kindness and respect. As soon as you withdrew your orders for my protection because I wouldn't become your mistress, the other men quickly revealed their true natures. The Indians have displayed more honor, understanding, and generosity than any of you did. I wasn't to blame for being taken captive, and I refuse to allow you to make me feel sullied or intimidated ever again!"

Fury and insolence glimmered dangerously in Jeffery's blue eyes. His lips grew taut and pale in a wintry sneer. The muscle in his jawline quivered in unsuppressed anger. His caustic tone informed her, "I remember everything where you are concerned, my dear Alisha. I'll never forget that day you threw my generous offer into the dirt and chose that blasted half-breed over me!"

"That's a lie, and you know it, Jeffery Clayton Gordon! Powchutu is only a friend, nothing more! Do you comprehend, nothing more! He risked his life to help me escape from the Sioux camp. He brought me here to St. Louis to catch a boat to New Orleans. I'm going home to England just as soon as I can get ship passage following this war. I can hardly wait to get away from this horrid, cruel land of yours. You see, Jeffery, there is one major difference between you and him: his generosity and friendship do not carry an impossible price; yours did. As for your 'generous offer,' exchanging one life of slavery and degradation for another is about the lowest proposal a man could make to a woman!"

Disregarding her denials and accusations, he sneered

presumptuously, "Just how close are you two? And don't hand me that brother-sister malarky!"

"You wouldn't believe the truth if it bit you on the leg! There is nothing but friendship between us; I swear it," she stated earnestly with futile hopes of halting any further reprisal upon them. It failed miserably.

"Then why didn't he just drop you off here? Why is he still hanging around you like a little, moon-eyed puppy?" He closely scrutinized her expressions and words as she spoke with him. He was resolved to have the entire truth about the scout and Gray Eagle. He had never met any woman who so captivated, infuriated, and pleased him to such great lengths. Despite Alisha's humiliating rejection of him at Fort Pierre, he was still determined to have her in some way. The only thing left to decide was, in what capacity did he want Alisha Williams to serve him?

"I don't owe you any explanation for my behavior. If it had been left up to you and those other soldiers, I might be dead right now. You're the last person who has any right to question me about anything!" Her beautiful face was flushed with the heated emotions of anger, shame, and anxiety.

"You're still afraid of me, aren't you? Why?" His keen gaze was piercing and demanding. It was obvious he was immensely enjoying her disquieting predicament.

She sharply retorted, "Don't I have good reason to be? Do you think I don't know who was responsible for my vile treatment at the fort those last few days? Do you think I didn't realize you were trying to force me to beg you to restore your protection? But I also knew what that proffered safeguard would cost me; you made that clear on several occasions."

"I wasn't asking or expecting any more than you paid Gray Eagle or Powchutu for their protection," he acidly declared.

Alisha's eyes grew wide and her mouth dropped in amazement. For a moment he thought she was going to slap him, but she did not. Perhaps she was too stunned by his scathing remark to move.

She finally managed, "How dare you! I was his prisoner! My strength was nothing compared to his! There was nothing I could have denied him. As for Powchutu, he has never touched me in such an intimate manner. He is a hundred times the gentleman you claim to be! Besides, you are the one who made matters between us impossible. Powchutu had nothing to do with my rejection of you. You wouldn't give me time to get over all the terrible ordeals I had been through; you kept forcing yourself on me. We both know the only thing you wanted from me was sex! You didn't care about me as a person. Never once did you consider my feelings. Jeffery's needs were all that mattered."

She was breathing rapidly and shallowly. She quickly continued before he could interrupt her tirade, "Just like now! All you want is revenge for some imagined wrong which we've supposedly done to you. All I want is to be left in peace, to return home to England. My God, haven't I suffered enough here in this savage land of yours? What is it you truly want from me, Jeffery?" Tears welled in the corners of her jade eyes; her chin trembled noticeably.

Like quicksilver, Jeffery altered his strategy. He flashed her a rueful, wistful grin. His tone became soft. "The only thing I've ever wanted is you, Alisha. That first time I saw you, I thought you were the most beautiful creature alive. All I could think about was having you for my wife. We were perfectly suited to each other. We would have been good together."

Alisha doubted she was hearing him accurately. She stared at him in skepticism and scorn. "You certainly have a strange way of revealing such noble intentions and loving affections. Besides, you never asked for marriage, never even hinted at it; your only proposal was to make me your paramour."

Alisha's chest heaved with indignation, and Jeffery had his chance to interrupt. "Only because you didn't give me a chance to reveal how I truly felt about you. You kept placing that red bastard in my rightful position! You knew how much I despised him. I'll never play second fiddle to any man, but especially not that damn infuriating scout! Ever since the first day I came out here, he has battled me in some fashion or another. He was constantly searching for some way to discredit me before my troops. He was always trying to make me look incompetent. Many times he cost me the respect and obedience of my own men. The only reason he got away with his despicable treachery was because his scouting services were so valuable. General Galt didn't have the courage or sense to dismiss the troublemaker. And everybody knows half-breeds are just as bad as Indians, maybe worse."

"Your private war with Powchutu had nothing to do with me or with my relationship with him," Alisha retorted. "He could no more help being a half-breed than I could help being a captive of the Sioux. If you had tried to get along with him, there might not have been any conflict between you two. You've never permitted him the chance to show his true personality; none of you did. That was a terrible injustice. No matter what you believe, Jeffery, you were the one who forced a choice between your friendship or his, not me. I tried to make you see reason; you refused."

"Hogwash, Alisha!" he snarled, placing his hands

upon her narrow waist, insolently daring her to continue.

She slapped away his hands and audaciously picked up where she had left off. "I'm not finished yet! Powchutu never put pressures on me like you did; he never threatened or intimidated me. You claimed I was not good enough for you after my sojourn with Gray Eagle; you said no man would marry his leavings. You were spiteful and cruel when I refused to share your quarters. You even went so far as to have your men harass me. You allowed their obscene insults and vicious taunts, perhaps even suggested them. I'll never forget those awful things you said to me that afternoon. Now, you calmly inform me of some secret affection and previous marital intent. Pardon me if I cannot accept such implausible news," she sarcastically sneered.

"Don't press your luck, Alisha love," he ominously warned. "If you think that life at Fort Pierre was bad, I hate to tell you that it won't hold a candle to the torment I can cause you here. The devil comes out in me when I'm crossed, especially for the second time by one person."

Alisha flinched at the truculence in his eyes and voice. "Are you threatening me, Jeffery Gordon? Are you saying you'll tell everyone about . . . my past if I refuse you?"

"Not unless you force my hand," he replied with deceptive sweetness. Without further delay, he dropped his first clue to his future scheme. "Or I should say, not unless you refuse to give me another chance with you." His eyes gleamed malevolently.

"Chance with me? Exactly what does that mean?" she inquired with dread storming her senses. She vainly struggled to conceal the petrifying effect which he had upon her. To Alisha, he possessed no sense of mercy to which she could appeal.

Jeffery chuckled in candid amusement and satisfaction. He playfully caressed her flushed cheek, then replaced a stray curl which had blown into her face. His naked gaze devoured her flawless beauty with frightening deliberation and undisguised pleasure. At last his leering gaze returned to settle on her bewitching, watchful eyes. He smiled at his own dark secret.

"Do not fear, ma petite. Surely I deserve an opportunity to make up for all the unpleasantness and misunderstandings between us? Things are very different here in St. Louis. I fully intend to change your mind and your icy feelings about me. I only hope you won't force me to use threats or pressures to gain that opportunity. But, I might as well be totally honest with you from the start, Alisha; you will grant me my chance, or you will most assuredly regret coming here and reminding me of losing you."

"How can one lose what one has never possessed? What do you hope to accomplish with these veiled threats, Jeffery? Are you trying to force me to become your mistress as you did before? Your silence in exchange for my . . . services as paramour, is that what you're hinting at?" she questioned in a shaky voice, yet knowing she had to fully comprehend what new ordeal she faced.

"On the contrary, my lovely Alisha. I fully intend to persuade you to marry me. If not with your genial agreement, then with some gentle coercion." He wickedly intimated his determination to have his own way, whatever that might be . . .

Alisha was momentarily stunned by his implications. "Surely you jest! Marry me? That's utterly ridiculous! We don't respect each other, much less like each other! Why would you want to marry me? You're not making any sense, Jeffery."

His broad chest rumbled with laughter—that sardonic, taunting, blood-chilling laugh. "Why indeed, my beautiful and ravishing delight? I think marriage makes perfect sense. Furthermore, you don't have to agree with my logic; just comply with my reasonable request." His impious lingering over the word "request" informed her his command would be anything but a polite request.

"But marriage, Jeffery? You never alluded to wedlock at Fort Pierre. Why now? Somehow I do not think wedded bliss is what you have in mind," she said suspiciously.

"Had you rather I demand you become my whore? I could, and you wouldn't be able to refuse me. Just imagine your future position here if I merely dropped the news you were an ex-squaw to the ignoble Gray Eagle. Just consider how the townfolk would view a girl who turned down a proposal from me because she preferred the memory of her demon lover to a respectable marriage. Men would be hanging around you like a she-dog in heat. How many of them could you fend off? How many could that scout pull off of you before they beat him senseless? There's no respect or kindness toward an Indian's ex-whore. You see, Alisha, you're too beautiful and delectable for your own safety. I can promise you, marriage of any kind to me will be better than what you'll face here if you refuse me. Tragically, there isn't a man or woman here who would give you a second thought if I let the truth out. I don't want that, Alisha; I would rather have you."

"You're actually serious?" Alisha protested. "But I don't want to marry anyone. I just want to return home to England. Please, Jeffery, let me go in peace this time. There couldn't be any happiness for us. You only want

195

me in your power, under your sadistic control. You know a wife is nothing more than a legal slave to her husband! Tell me what you're truly after, Jeffery. Revenge? Do you simply want me at your mercy so you can torment me? Pay me back for refusing your attentions?"

"Think about all I've said, Alisha," he advised, ignoring her questions. He was clearly not going to explain his plan to her. "I'll give you one week to make up your mind. If I were you, I wouldn't put any heroic ideas into that scout's head. He's vastly outnumbered here; it could be very dangerous for him to cause me any inconvenience. Get the drift of my warning? Another thing, make certain you two have separate rooms at Horne's; that's where you'll be staying as my guests. I seriously doubt either of you have any money, and I won't have you camping out near town. I also wouldn't advise your trying to leave here. If you managed to get past my guards, there are nasty river pirates to worry about. Sad to picture what they might do with a splendid female like you. Just so you understand, a few of them are slightly acquainted with me and delight in assisting me with problems. Before I'll permit that scout to win you over a second time, I'll see to it you spend the winter as Frenchy's guest."

She whitened and shuddered, because she had heard that name before. "Frenchy?" she repeated in unsuppressed fear.

"I see you've already heard of him. Excellent! Then there is no need to repeat my warning, is there? Just make sure Powchutu steers clear of you in private, and don't dare leave here. Savvy, Alisha?"

She dumbly nodded in comprehension. "Shall we say dinner in one week to hear your decision? Or should I say to make plans for our wedding?" he teased, assuming her answer.

Alisha remained silent and still for a few moments, trying to gather her remaining wits. She meekly entreated, "Can we keep this between us until then? Promise me you won't antagonize Powchutu into defending me. In return, I promise he won't come near me except in public. As far as anyone else is concerned, he is my older brother. All right? He won't be harmed or harassed. Agreed, Jeffery?" she insisted.

"As you wish, my blushing bride-to-be," he drawled in a mellow tone which only heightened her anxiety.

"I doubt if he'll believe me, but I'll tell him we . . . we might renew our friendship. I'm not certain I can make him accept this sudden change of heart where you're concerned. He'll be hurt and disappointed with me," she sadly murmured.

At Jeffery's sarcastic clucking, she vowed angrily, "I'm warning you, Jeffery Gordon; I won't permit you to hurt him. More than once he's saved my life. Whether or not you believe this or even understand it, I do love him like a real brother. I'll give you your answer in one week. Until then, stay away from both of us. If you must have me guarded, then fine. Just be sure Powchutu doesn't get wind of your intentions; he would kill you. I don't want that because he would be caught and hanged. One week . . ." she fearfully agreed, feeling she was facing a death sentence.

He grinned triumphantly. "Until then," he acquiesced politely, giving her a sweeping bow. He possessively seized her hand and returned her to the scout's side.

"See, Paul, just as I promised; I returned her safe and sound. I've already told Alisha I insist you two be my guests at the Horne House, and she has kindly consented to accept my hospitality. I'll send someone to see to your lodgings before Celeste and I go on to dinner and a party. Christmas, remember? If you require any help here, ask for Tommy Hardy. Tell him I said to treat you as he would me. If you need anything else, don't hesitate to call on me. Ask anyone where to find me. Good to see you again, Paul," he stated to the still speechless Powchutu, then gave his hand an amicable shake.

To Alisha, he smiled roguishly and chivalrously kissed her cold, quivering hand. "Until we meet again, Alisha," he softly murmured, gently squeezing her hand. She could only manage a civil farewell without giving away her agitated state of mind.

Jeffery caught Celeste's elbow and politely led her away, heading for a large house ringing with peals of merriment. Before entering, Jeffery called a robust man over to him. They talked for several minutes, nodded frequently in agreement, glanced in Alisha and Powchutu's direction a couple of times, then separated to go in different directions. The husky man hurried off down the semi-dark street as Jeffery ushered Celeste inside.

Powchutu watched Jeffery's nonchalant retreat with mounting suspicion. He glanced toward Alisha to find her glaring at the man's disappearing form. There was a strange expression upon her closed face, one he could not pierce.

"Alisha? What did he want?" he inquired as soon as Jeffery and Celeste were out of hearing. When she did not appear to have heard his question, he repeated it in a firmer tone.

Her stormy gaze came up to lock with his curious one. "To apologize for his treatment at Fort Pierre. He blamed it on anger and jealousy aimed at you. He offered his friendship and assistance while we're here. I thought it wise to cordially accept both," she woodenly informed him.

"You can't be serious!" he exclaimed irascibly.

"I can, and I am," she replied.

"At what price, Alisha?" he angrily retorted.

Not wishing to create a problem between them on this special night, she wearily replied, "I'm certain he will let us know before too much time has passed. I could be mistaken, but he seemed quite serious. No matter which, we cannot afford to offend him until we learn how he intends to treat us. Please don't fight or argue with him. Just stay away from him, and hopefully he will stay away from you. Can't we wait to see if it's to be truce or war?"

"If I know Lieutenant Gordon, there will be a high price for his favors. From what I saw and heard, Fort Pierre was totally demolished. How did he get away from there alive?"

"He didn't say. I asked, but he chose not to answer me. Who knows, maybe Fate stepped in as it did with us," she absently muttered, her thoughts whirling in confusion.

"What did he say about our coming here together? I bet that jerked a knot in his tail!"

"Just what you would imagine, but I set him straight. I told him you helped me to escape from the Sioux camp and get here. I explained our friendship, and I told him you are pretending to be my brother. He agreed to remain silent about us. That's about all. I didn't want to tell him anything, but he would have gotten angry if I hadn't offered some kind of explanation to him."

"But why be so friendly to us? I don't trust him, Alisha." Powchutu's eyes glittered with distrust. "He's up to something."

"As soon as I told him we are only friends, he seemed satisfied. However, he did insist upon separate rooms while we're here. He wants to be sure I told him the truth about us. I couldn't find any reasonable excuse to refuse his generous offer without angering him unduly. Besides, we do require a warm and safe place to stay, and we don't have much money. No doubt our rooms will be several doors apart!" she jested to lighten his black mood.

"Jeffery seems to feel I chose you over him at Fort Pierre," Alisha continued. "He was embarrassed by my so-called stinging rejection. I enlightened him on all those matters. He claims he's done a lot of soul-searching since my departure. He claims he's changed his mind about many things. He agrees he was mean and unfair to me back there. He says he's truly sorry, says he wants to make it up to me. You should know by now that arguing with Jeffery is like hitting your head against a tree. For the time being, I said I believed him. I agreed to give him the chance to prove his friendship and sincerity," she meekly stated.

"You what!" he shouted in a suppressed voice. "Surely I didn't hear you right. You can't let him near you again. He's lying, Alisha. It's some kind of trick. Even a blind fool could see through him!" Powchutu growled like a treed bobcat.

"Then I must be a fool, Paul! From what I could tell, he was being open and honest with me. Besides, we have no choice but to step lightly where he's concerned. Are you forgetting what he could do to our new freedom? We must bide our time until he reveals what his intentions are—if any," she cunningly added in doubt.

"I say we get out of here tonight! We could head downriver to the next settlement. He means trouble, Alisha. The glory-seeking, insolent rogue! The man's a damn fool, Alisha; he proved his stupidity and recklessness when he raided Gray Eagle's camp. It's a shame Wanmdi Hota didn't find him and kill him."

Alisha's mind was working rapidly to come up with some reasonable excuse for not leaving. Hating to lie to him and feeling guilty for doing so, she toughened her heart to do what must be done to protect his life and their safety. There was just enough validity and sincerity in her statements to convince him of her words. "We can't leave, Paul. I'm not as strong as I thought. I cannot travel another mile. If you need to head out to avoid him, then I will join you as soon as I've rested and visited the doctor here. Too, I need to see Mr. Bigsley about my uncle's money. Without that money, we have nearly nothing to survive on this winter." Seeking any and every plausible reason, she anxiously added, "What about those river pirates Joe mentioned? It would be dangerous to head out at night or alone. We've made it this far; I think we should stick it out here for the winter. If Jeffery is dangerous or insincere, then we can deal with him later. Please . . ."

"Don't be ridiculous!" Powchutu seethed. "I wouldn't leave you here alone to face him. 'Sides, you're right about the money. As for river pirates, Joe didn't mention them to me. What is a river pirate?"

"They are like renegade braves, except they're mostly white men. They hide near the shallows in the river, then prey on unsuspecting boats as they pass by. It isn't safe to travel at night or when the river is so deserted. Mainly, I'm just too weary to move on. I'm sorry to be such a weakling and hindrance. But it cannot be helped."

"Don't fret, love," he comforted her, assuming she was upset by her fragile condition. He said with growing humor, "If our friend Jeffery wants to pay for our lodgings, then I think we should politely oblige him. We'll rest here for a few days, then see this Bigsley. If it looks like Jeffery is up to no good, then I'll hire some men to take us downriver. Does that plan suit you, sister dear?" he jested cheerfully.

Alisha smiled in relief and nodded her agreement. Powchutu felt so confident that he actually called upon Tommy Hardy to help them get moved to the Horne House. He was mildly surprised to discover that Jeffery had ordered their rooms next door to each other, but they were not adjoining. No doubt Gordon reasoned she might profit from Powchutu's closeness and protection. Yet, noting the sneaky way the proprietor kept watching them, he readily concluded Jeffery was having them observed. He could not help but wonder what reason Jeffery had given for this furtive study.

While Powchutu was registering their false identities and chatting guardedly with the innkeeper, Alisha was scanning her new surroundings with little zest. The Horne House was not exactly a roadhouse or a public house, but neither did it qualify as a proper inn. It appeared a hodgepodge of all of those types of lodgings. Alisha finally decided this was because of its purpose and location. Many people were forced to survive for many months at a time in St. Louis for varying reasons; many became stranded by weather, illness, or poverty. This particular inn catered to those unfortunate transients who had somehow met with disaster. Its purpose was simply to provide food and shelter to those passing through.

Not that Alisha considered it dirty or unsound, it was just so garish and gloomy. The walls were painted dark brown; the furniture was covered in a drab coffee shade. Even the floor was stained a muted brown, giving the place a somber and depressing air. The proprietor's attempts to brighten this dismal place with some color failed miserably, for his selection was comprised of gaudy orange sofa cushions and matching curtains. Alisha judged the only advantage to this bleak color scheme to be its ability to disguise or conceal the numerous spots and advancing age upon its surfaces.

The innkeeper did not have to inform them of the dining area situated to their left behind huge closed doors; the fragrant aroma of food and the audible clinking of dishes attested to its presence. Alisha was momentarily tempted to ask Powchutu if she could eat right that minute. Her empty stomach made its condition known to her as it perceived those delectable odors. But upon hearing gay laughter and muted voices coming from the other side of those doors, she decided to freshen up before making her first appearance in public in months.

Alisha became annoyed by the seemingly intentional delay in giving them their room keys. Although the proprietor, Jamie O'Hara, was talking and laughing genially, Alisha perceived his subtle attempts at calculated procrastination. She fumed over why he would deliberately obstruct their schedule. Each time he halted to take care of some other task, she knew he was covertly stalling them. She began to pace the confines of the lobby, hoping he would detect her obvious frustration and fatigue.

Finally she approached the long wooden counter and propped against it. She tapped her nails on its scratched surface to reveal her mounting displeasure. O'Hara glanced up at her and smiled indulgently. He lowered his head once again as he pretended to study the information listed by Powchutu.

"Might I inquire as to how much longer this business will take, Mr. O'Hara? I am totally exhausted and hungry. Surely registration cannot claim so much time," Alisha haughtily stated.

Jamie O'Hara's face became rosy at her bold impudence and her shameless insinuation that he was a sluggish incompetent. Seeing the difficult time he was having with concealing his guilt and anger, Alisha knew she was accurate. Before she could ask him why he was behaving so discourteously, he supplied her with an acceptable lie. She had begun to fear that Jeffery had paid him to harass them until it was too late to seek other lodgings.

"I must apologize for the delay in welcoming you here, but it could not be helped. The rooms not in use had to be cleaned and prepared before I could send you upstairs," he caustically informed Alisha without a friendly smile.

"Why didn't you say something earlier? We could have been enjoying a hot meal while we waited," she stated coldly, annoyed further by his inconsideration and overbearing attitude.

"We get very few guests this time of year. I see no need to constantly clean rooms not in service. Upon Mr. Gordon's request, I had two rooms aired, cleaned, and prepared for you. Such tasks take time this late at night and during the supper hour. I have only two servants available this late." He did not tell Alisha that the real hold-up was the preparation of her room, preparation done on the orders of Jeffery Gordon.

Within minutes, a young girl came down the steps and nodded to the proprietor. He sighed in relief, knowing the room was ready and Gordon's men had departed down the back steps. Now he could get rid of this uppity female who had unforgivably insulted him. He called the young girl to come forward. He instructed her to show Alisha and Powchutu to their rooms. She was introduced as his niece Mary, the main serving girl.

She smiled timidly at Alisha, then rushed up the staircase as she motioned for them to follow her. They came

to Powchutu's room first. She halted and pointed to him,
then to his room. She handed him a key, then signalled
for Alisha to follow her to the next door. But this time,
she unlocked the door and went inside. It was obvious to
both Powchutu and Alisha that she was mute. After
telling Alisha he would meet her downstairs in fifteen
minutes, Powchutu entered his room and locked the
door.

Alisha slowly walked inside the room which Jeffery
had personally ordered for her—without her knowledge.
She was pleasantly surprised to discover the unexpected
beauty of this room. It boasted whitewashed walls; the
floor was covered with a blue floral rug which concealed
most of the drab wood surface. The curtains were made of
a heavy, ivory-colored material with varied shades of
blue playing subtly across its woven texture.

A small settee was positioned slightly to her left before
a fireplace whose colorful, warm flames were inviting and
comforting. Alisha momentarily fretted over the closeness of the settee and curtains to that stone hearth. She
quickly determined to make certain she never went to
bed or went outside with a brisk fire going inside it.

The smooth texture of the settee covering was a lovely
hue of French blue. Beside it sat a round table which
contained a vase of silk flowers, sewn in the pattern of the
delicate pasqueflower. Her eager gaze travelled onward to
her left and slightly to her rear. She strolled forward and
ran her hand across the glossy surface of the rich pine
dressing table. She could hardly trust her new luck; there
was an oval mirror suspended above it. On either side of
the mirror hung an oil lantern which was mounted to the
wall, insuring any female of the proper light to complete
her toilette.

Noting the girl's disappearance for the first time,

Alisha closed her door and slid the bolt into place. She continued her leisurely scrutiny of her lovely, soothing room. To her right there was a closet, for a wardrobe which she did not possess. She was almost ashamed to hang her meager garments in it, but vowed to immediately purchase some decent clothing for their spring trip. She lightly caressed the portiere which matched the window curtains, then absently dropped it back into place.

Alisha walked over to the bed. She could not even recall the last time when she had lain upon a real, feather mattress. She impulsively tossed the French blue coverlet aside. With a suppressed squeal of glee, she flung herself upon the luxurious bed and snuggled down into its softness. She turned over and stretched out upon it. She sighed heavily as her weary body relaxed and drew comfort from its plush surface. She dared not close her eyes for fear of instantly falling asleep.

Alisha's distressed mind flashed back to her shocking confrontation with Jeffery Gordon. She speculated upon Jeffery's absurd and terrifying proposal of marriage. Surely he couldn't be serious! What black mischief was he formulating in his evil heart and satanic mind? With his knowledge of her and Powchutu's past, she was now in a deadly situation which she had never imagined.

Marriage to Jeffery? It was unthinkable, revolting. As far as she was concerned, she was already married. What did it truly matter if the ceremony had been in Sioux and under a starry sky? How did her husband's tormenting betrayal change her own feelings? They did not. Even now, her traitorous heart and body loved and wanted only Gray Eagle.

She closed her eyes and called his image to mind. He was such a handsome, virile man. He was the pinnacle of power and pride. Her heart fluttered wildly and painfully as she envisioned him with his bronzed body which could drive her mindless with desire, with his arrogant and confident stance which could strike fear into the heart of an enemy, with his sensual lips which could shatter her will, with his stygian eyes which could pierce her very soul with their power and intensity.

His hatred of the white man and his excessive pride in his powerful rank as legendary warrior had prevented his acceptance of her and her love. Now that his final betrayal was complete, did he ever think about her, Alisha wondered, about what they could have shared. Did memories of their endless nights and days of love-making never haunt him as they haunted her? Did he regret his brutal actions?

"How I wish my memory was as alive in your mind as yours is in mine," she murmured. "Will you ever realize what you have traded for that honor you prize so highly? After all we shared, Wanmdi Hota, how could you wish me dead? I will never love another man as I still love you. Never again will I know those raging fires which only you ignited within me. Why, my beloved? Why did you destroy our love?"

She tossed restlessly upon the comfortable bed. To even imagine Jeffery Gordon making love to her as Gray Eagle had countless times sent shudders of disgust through her. No man could ever replace Gray Eagle for her; he was peerless; he was her heart and soul. She would never share that same intimacy with Jeffery Gordon! Jeffery was only playing spiteful games with her; he would never force her to marry him! Still, Alisha swore, she would overcome any vengeful plans he had in mind for her . . .

Suddenly aware of how much time must have passed,

Alisha hurriedly jumped up and went to the vanity. She lifted the ewer from the dresser and poured some water into the matching basin. Picking up the washcloth to sponge off her face, she was amazed to find the water was warm. Evidently the young girl had placed it there when she was readying her room. The water was fresh; vibrant silk flowers graced the room; and a cheery fire dismissed the chill from her fatigued body. Adding all these facts together, she was suddenly ashamed of the brusque and suspicious way in which she had treated Mr. O'Hara. It was clear he had taken great pains to present her with a splendid, immaculate room. No wonder he had been so taken aback and angered by her sassy manner. She definitely owed him an apology!

A knock at her door startled her from her deep reverie. She lay the washcloth aside and went to answer it. She cautiously called out, "Who is it?"

"It's Po . . . Paul, Alisha. What's keeping you so long? I thought you were starving," came his anxious inquiry.

Forgetting her promise to Jeffery, she slid the bolt aside and opened the door. She greeted him with a vivacious, captivating smile. "This room is so inviting and beautiful that I was carried away with checking it over. I can see why it took so long to get it ready. I'll only be a moment longer. Let me smooth my hair into place."

As she went to the mirror to adjust her mussed hair, Powchutu's eyes strayed to the rumpled bed and exquisite room. Compared to the lobby and to his gloomy room, this one was decorated for a princess. His angry jealousy soared as he realized that Jeffery had specifically ordered this room for her.

"I see Gordon has excellent taste in hotel rooms," he sullenly noted. "This is probably the best room available in this entire town and no doubt the most expensive! Who knows, maybe he even keeps this one rented all the time for his 'special' guests.''

She glanced at him following his terse remark, then slowly let her eyes roam around the attractive room. She finally decided that she didn't really care if he had chosen this particular room just to influence her in a positive manner. She had been away from civilization and elegance for a long and trying time. She was going to enjoy this room, then worry about its meaning later!

There was a suspicious, naughty note in Powchutu's voice when he questioned, ''Tried out the bed already? Certainly looks more comfortable than the one in my room. Big enough for two people. Yes sir, that Gordon sure knows how to select a cozy room.''

She focused wary eyes upon his unreadable features, disturbed by the accusatory tone in his voice. ''If I didn't know any better, big brother, I would think you were trying to subtly tell me something! Just to clear the air, I am not paying for this room in any way. I tried out the bed, alone! Understand? Any more questions?''

He was slightly shaken by her biting tone and obvious irritation. ''I didn't mean to insinuate you were paying him for it. I was only jesting with you. Don't get so upset with me. I think you must be a wee bit hungry and tired. You're a little pale, love.''

At his rueful tone and hurt look, Alisha smiled faintly and apologized for her curtness. ''I suppose I am exhausted and testy. That and nervous about seeing Jeffery alive and doing so well. I cannot imagine how he survived that raid. To come face to face with him like that was a great shock.''

She softly relented as she entreated, ''Suppose he did

select this room with some high hope of disarming me. Would I enjoy it any more if I had selected it myself? It's marvelous, Powchutu; I mean, Paul. I must learn to call you Paul all the time, lest I slip in public. Don't be angry or upset because I have this room. Do you know how long it's been since I've seen anything this lovely? If it would make you feel better, I'll pay for it myself just as soon as we see Mr. Bigsley and collect my uncle's money. The sight of this room makes me feel as if I'm finally pulling free of that savage wilderness."

Her decision to pay for the room seemed to settle the disquieting matter between them. "I know this past year has been hard on you, Alisha, but I do think that's best," Powchutu advised. "You don't want to be in his debt. Another thing, make sure you keep this door locked at all times. Don't ever allow him inside this room when you're alone," he needlessly warned her.

She lowered the flame on one lantern and doused the lights in the other two. She cautiously checked the fire to see if the flames were under control. Noting the soft glow of the coals, Alisha felt it was safe to leave the fire unattended. She picked up her key and announced she was ready to have dinner. Powchutu led the way out of her room, then hesitated while she locked her door. He happened to glance down the hallway to find the young girl observing them in an intense and curious manner. Catching Powchutu's keen stare, the proprietor's niece scurried away like a frightened fawn.

Powchutu shrugged his powerful shoulders as he dismissed the girl's interest. He simply reasoned she was only curious about a beautiful lady like his Alisha. He failed to mention this weird incident to Alisha. Instead, he gently took her by the arm and led her downstairs to the large dining hall.

It being Christmas Eve, the small crowd was genial and merry. They chatted and joked in several small groups. Near the far end of the long narrow room was a high-backed piano. On its bench sat a wizened old man. His bristled, gray hair was chaotic and dirty. His scraggly beard desperately needed clipping and shaping. His attire was rumpled and soiled. Yet, he possessed the warmest, brightest, slate blue eyes Alisha had ever seen.

The piano man's mellow voice surprised Alisha. She briefly halted in her tracks as she stopped to listen to his stirring rendition of her favorite Christmas song.

Seeing she was caught up in her emotions, Powchutu permitted the old man to finish his carol before taking her elbow and guiding her to the table where the young girl was waiting to serve them their dinner. He courteously seated Alisha, then sat down opposite her at the small square table. Carefully scrutinizing the dining room, they both decided it was clean and efficient. Pleased with their good fortune, they exchanged a warm and knowing smile.

Alisha turned to speak to the girl, but she was once again gone without a sound. It was but minutes before she returned, laden with two heavy plates of aromatic food and a pot of hot coffee. Alisha was astonished at the girl's ability to juggle so many hot dishes at one time. She reached out to assist her, then decided she would be more of a hindrance than of a help. It felt strange to be waited upon again after such a long time of serving someone else.

She studied the comely girl before her, busily setting down their dishes and food. She judged her to be about seventeen years old, evidently mute, but not deaf.

When spoken to, she would nod or smile meekly. Her auburn hair hung in two heavy braids down her slender back. The drab sack dress disguised her voluptuous figure, but not her agile movements. Countless freckles played across the bridge of her pug nose and pallid cheeks. Her features were clear—except for her eyes.

There, Alisha discovered a complex mystery. Mary O'Hara had what Alisha's father would have called ox-eyes: large, calm, and velvety brown. The perplexity came with their curious and confusing messages. At times they spoke of innocence and ignorance; other times, Alisha could read more knowledge and astute perception than she herself possessed at twenty years old. Mary's aura intimated shyness; yet, she radiated warmth. She looked fragile and delicate; yet, she seemed resilient and strong. In the end, Alisha was utterly puzzled by this mysterious, silent girl.

Putting aside her examination of Jamie O'Hara's comely niece, Alisha took note of the food which she had just been served: succulent steak, dried-apple cobbler, lightly browned biscuits, savory succotash from dried corn kernels and dried beans, and hot coffee. She hastily took another sip from her cup, then jerked her head up to gaze at the grinning Mary.

"It's tea! You're an absolute dear, Mary O'Hara. Wherever did you get tea way out here?" she cried in delight.

Mary smiled at Alisha's apparent pleasure at finding tea instead of coffee in her cup, thanks to Jeffery's foresight of having it sent over for her. She made a little curtsy and hurried back toward the kitchen. Alisha began to slowly and appreciatively devour the hearty meal before her. She glanced up at Powchutu's muttered curse. His eyes and expression spoke of a resentment which she did not understand.

"What's the matter, Paul? The food is wonderful," she remarked, licking her lips in delight.

"It should be," he snapped in surly annoyance. "This fare is also compliments of Lieutenant Gordon. We seem to be the only ones eating such a costly meal and drinking expensive tea."

Alisha's gaze slowly roamed the food on several other nearby plates: fried chicken, biscuits, gravy, and coffee. Her gaze came back to her own sumptuous plate. "See what I mean? I'd be willing to bet he ordered this meal just for you! Interfering ass!" he snarled.

"Do you want to send it back and ask Mary to serve us the regular fare?" she inquired just to placate him. "Honestly I don't mind. I'm so hungry that I could eat a raw snake," she teased to lighten his black temper.

Powchutu shook his head. "No need. We might as well enjoy Gordon's hospitality and foolishness," he sneered contemptuously. "Plus it might draw too much attention if we refused it."

She smiled faintly, then returned to her food. Part of the pleasure gone from their dinner, they ate in silence and listened to the old man at the piano. Not long after finishing, Powchutu escorted her back to her room. He cautiously waited until he heard the bolt pushed into place before retiring to his own room.

Without bothering to undress, he flung himself across the loud red bedspread. With his black eyes glued to the dingy ceiling, he set his mind to work on this new development. He couldn't decide what to do about Jeffery's unexpected survival, or what to think about this abrupt change in Alisha's feelings toward Gordon. It was almost

213

as if she were enjoying the lieutenant's intrusion into her life. He fretted over what was said between them on the pier, for he doubted she had given him all the details. Afterwards, her behavior had been odd and stilted. Powchutu was positive that Jeffery was up to some devious trick; but what, he could not yet surmise.

Alisha walked over to the window. She pushed aside the soft curtain and peered out into the moonlit shadows. She was totally exhausted, but her mind was still racing. For the present, she could see no way to avoid a choice between Jeffery and Powchutu. Every path her thoughts took was besieged with perils and difficulties. There appeared no safe ground. She could hurt Powchutu deeply with her submission to his formidable enemy Jeffery, or she could endanger both their lives by refusing his attentions once more. The near impossibility of a safe escape from here had been made clear to her earlier that evening on that fateful dock.

Alert to her enchanting surroundings, it was evident that Jeffery was not wasting any time or effort in forcing her positive decision. Although he was demanding marriage this time, she shuddered to think of any type of life with him. Surely he had some wicked, insidious plan in mind. She could not contemplate what it might be. For all she knew, it might encompass revenge toward all three of them: Powchutu, herself, and Gray Eagle. Perhaps he viewed a blow to her as a vicious strike on all of them.

She slipped out of her dress and lay it across the sofa. She removed her moccasins and sat them upon the floor. She went to the bed and straightened the covers. After loosely braiding her long hair to avoid tangles, she lay down upon the soft and enticing bed. She pulled the covers up and tucked them beneath her chin.

"What shall I do now?" she murmured. "Do I hurt

you deeply, Powchutu, or do I save your life? I cannot even reveal his cruel demand to you. Why does he want marriage? Why not whoredom as before?'' An idea shot into her troubled mind. Her heart lurched joyfully. "Joe . . . I must get a message to Joe. He'll know how to handle this deadly situation. Joe," she murmured, then gave herself up to restful slumber.

Chapter Eleven

Two days passed before Alisha could arrange to have her private talk with Hiram Bigsley concerning the money her uncle had left in his keeping the year before. Powchutu spent those days checking out the settlement and looking for some type of work. Other times he escorted Alisha around to view the sights. They ate all of their meals together in the large dining room, then strolled outside in the fresh, crisp air.

Alisha occupied herself with resting, observing, and planning. When she went to the mercantile store to purchase material for clothing, she was delighted to learn she could buy several dresses already made. She discovered that many women were frequently forced to trade their clothing for much-needed supplies. Using the money which Powchutu had given to her, she purchased three dresses, a pair of leather shoes, material for undergarments, a comb and brush, ribbons, and sewing supplies.

By the time two days had gone by, Alisha had the three dresses fitting her perfectly. She also made two camisoles, two long petticoats, one batiste night gown, and three pairs of bloomers. At long last, she no longer felt like an ugly duckling or appeared the pitiful orphan. Her spirits soared, and a light tranquility settled in on her previously frayed nerves. She rubbed her strained eyes, but felt ecstatic with her progress with her wardrobe.

Jeffery made certain to stay clear of both Alisha and

the scout, hoping not to panic them into fleeing. Now that he had his men alerted to his interest in Alisha, it was doubtful she could get two feet outside of St. Louis without his knowledge or permission. Besides, he had an excellent spy in little, speechless Mary O'Hara. Neither Alisha nor Powchutu could move or breathe without his knowing about it . . .

On their third day in St. Louis, Alisha was shown into Hiram Bigsley's somber, cramped office to await his arrival. She sat down in an over-large wooden chair near a grimy, sooty window. Before she could study the messy office, an immaculately dressed man came in to join her.

Greeting her, Hiram walked around his cluttered desk and seated himself. He silently shuffled several papers aside upon his massive desk, searching for her uncle's records. At last he located what he had been looking for. He carefully and intensely studied the figures and words written upon that yellowed page, as if he did not recall each one in detail.

As she patiently waited for him to begin their discussion, Alisha furtively assessed this spirited man whom she had liked that first moment she met him so long ago. He was about forty-five years old; yet, he had an ageless vitality. His one distracting feature was his hair. Although it was well-combed and neatly clipped, it was of a washed-out reddish shade. His probing brown eyes were clear and calm at the present. In fact, they almost concealed themselves beneath two bushy eyebrows. His complexion was slightly marked by smallpox scars. His body was short of stature, but solidly built.

Hiram Bigsley was a self-assured, intelligent man. He could be firm and strict, but also kind and generous. He had opened this mercantile business when he was only twenty years old. He had bravely and persistently survived bitter winters, bandits, renegade braves, and torrid summers. He had mounted the bottom rung of the success ladder, then gradually worked his way to the very top. He was easy-going and pleasant. Alisha swiftly decided she admired and respected him. Too, she enjoyed his company and honesty.

Hiram finally glanced up at the beautiful, young lady who was sitting near him. For the second time within a year or so, he concluded she was too exquisite and well-bred for this exacting territory which could extract a man's very soul. To him, she belonged in an elegant French gown sitting in a fragrant rose garden on some duke's estate in England, serving tea and scones to her wealthy guests.

"Your message said Thad died of a fever? Too bad. He was a smart and friendly man. I tried to talk him into remaining here and opening another business with me. There's a lot of opportunities for men with his know-how and willpower. Thad reminded me of myself when I came out here, bright-eyed and eager. It's a shame to see his life wasted out there," he said solemnly.

"Yes, it was a terrible waste," Alisha said with feeling. "This is a very cruel and taxing territory. I don't think I shall ever fully accept his sudden loss. If it wasn't for his insight and wisdom, I don't know what I would do right now. I never realized money and safety were so important until this past year."

Hiram glanced down at the paper in his hand once more, wondering how to break his weighty news to her. "Alisha, I know you've been through some mighty hard times since coming here and with your uncle dying so unexpectedly. Thank goodness your brother showed up when he did. This isn't a country for a fine, young lady like you. I'll feel much better knowing you're leaving here in the spring," he stated, certain she understood his sincerity and motives.

"I can hardly wait to head for real civilization, Mr. Bigsley," Alisha stated emphatically. "You're right; this is definitely not the place for me. If I ever doubted it before, I know now that I possess no frontier fever at all. I live for the day when I can go home," she confessed with a wistful glow in her emerald eyes. "With Uncle Thad's money, that will be possible. Home at last . . ." she murmured in relief.

Hiram shuffled uneasily in his chair. "I hate to burden you with more bad news. But with your brother here, that should help some."

With rising alarm, she fearfully inquired, "I don't follow you. My uncle did leave some money here with you, didn't he?" Dread knotted her stomach as she hoped this kindly man was not about to cheat her out of her survival key. Thad had trusted him; Joe trusted him. Yet, if he claimed there was no money, she could do nothing to dispute his word.

"Yes, he did, Alisha. The problem is that the money was in English currency. I'm afraid it isn't worth very much since the war broke out between us. Most people either want gold or silver, or this new American money." He tried to calmly inform her of her misfortune.

She whitened. "You mean . . . I . . . The money is worthless," she stammered in painful realization.

"Not exactly worthless, Alisha, just not as valuable as it was when Thad left it here with me," he hurriedly explained at the sight of her distress. "When I got hint of what was coming, I traded all the English pounds I had for silver and gold. I'd say you have enough to make it through the winter here, but not much more than that. Things get mighty expensive and sparse during that time.

219

I do advise you to tell your brother to find some work to earn travelling money," he remarked, still wondering why Paul Williams had not attended this vital meeting. He should be at his sister's side when such devastating news was cast upon her. Curious that he had not even known about a brother or his timely arrival . . .

"Lots of the trappers around here hire men to help them out during the trapping season. Also, some of the business folk hire helpers to hunt fresh meat for them. Maybe Jamie O'Hara will hire him to help supply meat for his Horne House. I wish I could be more encouraging, but that's how it is this time of year," he declared uneasily.

Alisha stood up and aimlessly paced around the room as this distressing announcement settled in on her. Countless ideas came to her turbulent mind, but were rapidly dismissed for one reason or another. She gradually decided it was at least a blessing they had enough money for food and shelter for the over-shadowing winter. Recalling Joe's message, she inquired as to the whereabouts of a Moses Johnson.

He eyed her oddly, then ventured, "What would you be wanting with that old skinflint?"

She smiled warmly, then discreetly replied, "We spent some time with Joe Kenny on our way here. I wanted to send a message by Moses to let him know we arrived here safely. Joe was the one who told me about Uncle Thad's money. Otherwise, I wouldn't have known it existed. I was hoping to repay him for his generosity. I do appreciate everything you've done for us, Mr. Bigsley. But I am terribly disappointed and worried. Yet, any money at all is better than none. Looks as if it will take longer to get back home than planned." She laughed optimistically, bringing a genial smile to Hiram's taut face.

"You're a wonder, Miss Alisha. Most females would be crying their eyes out over such news. I'm glad to see you're taking it in stride. Do you want me to hold the money until you need it or give it to you in small amounts along the way? Carrying around any amount of money in this settlement can be dangerous and foolish. Men get reckless and desperate when winter closes in."

Alisha sought the best way to apprise Hiram of her destitute condition. "I'm afraid I'll need all of it right now, Mr. Bigsley. You see, Paul and I ran into bad fortune on our way here. While we were out of our camp one day, two trappers raided it and stole all of our supplies, except for a small amount of money in Paul's pocket. Thankfully, Paul had insisted I accompany him while he was out hunting! Joe was kind enough to take us in and assist us. We couldn't have survived without his aid. He furnished us with almost everything we have now. Paul has been looking for a job for the past two days, but without any success so far. We'll require the money to live on this winter. Plus, we'll need clothing and other supplies immediately. Lieutenant Gordon is an old friend of ours, and he has kindly given us his hospitality until I could meet with you and work out our business." Alisha shrewdly dropped these whitewashed facts to avoid Hiram's suspicion and curiosity.

Wanting to forestall any delay, Alisha said, "Mr. Bigsley, this news is most disconcerting. If it is permissible, I'll send Paul over later for the money. As you pointed out, it would be unwise for me to carry the money with me. We certainly cannot risk losing what little we have left."

If Hiram was disturbed by her subtle demand for her money, he did not let on. He readily accepted her claim to it. He agreed to have it ready for Powchutu to retrieve later in the day. He and Alisha shared light conversation for a few more minutes before she announced she should return to the Horne House for lunch. He graciously saw her to the front door of his establishment and bid her a cordial farewell.

As Alisha leisurely walked away, Hiram was perplexed by the pensive way in which Jeffery Gordon was watching her retreat. When he finally noticed Hiram's alert eyes upon him from across the way, he flashed him an engaging grin and nodded civilly. Hiram returned the nod and then walked back into his store, acutely aware of Jeffery's more than amicable interest in her. Even through a soiled glass, his possessive look could be easily detected.

"She's very beautiful, isn't she?" Celeste noted to Jeffery as she moved to stand beside him near the window. Her hazel eyes enviously trailed Alisha's progress down the narrow, dirt street until she reached the Horne House and disappeared inside.

Her suspicious gaze returned to Jeffery's pleased, arrogant expression. "She's more than an old friend, isn't she, Jeffery?" she declared peevishly, pursing her rose-colored mouth into an unattractive, sullen pout. "She didn't seem too happy to see you the other night. She doesn't like you very much if you ask me."

Jeffery was not a man who tolerated interference with his personal affairs. His blue eyes darkened and narrowed, vividly warning Celeste she had struck a raw nerve. Before she could defensively apologize for her rash comments, he had seized her arm in a painful grasp. Slowly increasing the pressure upon it with each word he gritted out between his tightly clenched teeth, he spat, "Alisha Williams is a private matter. If you so much as mention her name to anyone, you'll rue the day you were hatched, my feather-brained Celeste."

Trying to salvage her position as his companion, she sought to use her feminine wiles to gloss over her untimely mistake. Before she had half of her excuse out of her ruby mouth, Jeffery's chest was vibrating with sardonic, taunting laughter.

"Come now, Celeste," he scathingly chided her. "You forget to whom you're speaking. I know you too well, remember? There hasn't been a female born yet who could outwit, entrap, or deceive Jeffery Gordon. Save those girlish charms and ridiculous guiles for some dolt. Fact is, you'd best be looking for some simpleton to take care of you this winter. You've exhausted my interest in your numbered charms. I find you an insult to my breeding." He calmly and callously dismissed her as if she were merely his chambermaid.

Celeste stared at him in frightened discomposure. "Surely you're teasing me, Jeffery! That's very cruel of you," she whined.

"Actually," he sneered, "you bore me to tears, Celeste."

Seeing he was serious, she exclaimed, "There's no one here who could afford to keep me like you do! Please don't send me away!"

Jeffery chuckled capriciously, enjoying his cruelty. With Alisha's arrival and unavoidable capitulation, he no longer needed to suffer Celeste's annoying company and constant demands. He had simply tolerated her company and low breeding because she had been the town's loveliest available woman. Now that Alisha was here, Celeste was like a glass bead placed next to an exquisite diamond. He no longer required Celeste's presence in order to protect his manly image and to conceal his unmentionable problem . . .

"Count yourself lucky that I have supported you for this long," he told her. "I have had my fill of your ill-bred, ignorant conduct! You possess no manners or intelligence. You're crude, boring, and cheap," he relentlessly criticized.

Celeste saucily exclaimed, "You mean compared to that prissy brat who just strutted up the street! What does that sweet snit have to offer over me?" she snapped venomously.

"See what I mean about ignorance? You don't even recognize class and quality when you see it! Alisha has breeding and refinement, things you know nothing about. She's the kind of female Jeffery Gordon deserves and demands. I can promise you she'll be at my side within a week's time," he boasted arrogantly.

"Ha! You haven't even seen her since she got here. Even you can't work such magic so soon. You said she is smart and respectable. How are you going to win her over? I doubt she'll grant you a second look from the snippy way she acted the other night!"

That evasive, confident smile which Celeste had come to know so well flickered across Jeffery's devilishly handsome features. Her heart fluttered with wild desire for him. She had done everything within her power to become his mistress, but he had steadily ignored her forward flirtations. She had let it be known that she was available for any purpose he desired, but privately, he had kept her at arm's length. In public, he behaved as if she were his property. He flashed her heated looks and caressed her in subtle ways which nearly drove her crazy with lust. Yet, she would later go to bed aching with frustration. It was a good thing Jeffery went downriver on business every few weeks, for those were the times when she would secretly entertain lusty trappers who were passing through town. If not for those frequent releases of pent-up passion, she would surely be devoured by the flames within her fiery body.

"No need to fret over my problems, Celeste. Rest assured she is mine for the taking right this very minute," he stated matter-of-factly.

Then, turning to her with a threatening scowl, he continued, "Just a word of caution: not a single word about me or my affairs! If your tongue does get reckless, you won't live to know it. Be forewarned: I always pay my debts to friends and to foes. It would be wise for you to keep your voice mute and your ears deaf where I'm concerned. A sharp hunting knife could ruin what few looks you possess. Understand?" His blue eyes burned with cold honesty. He twisted her arm behind her back to emphasize his potency.

"All right!" she cried out in great pain. "I won't say anything to anybody, Jeffery. I promise." she wept. When he did not ease up on his brutal torment, she shrieked, "You're hurting me, Jeffery! Please stop," she whimpered pitifully, drawing laughter from his black heart.

He released her so abruptly that she fell back against the wall. He instantly seized a handful of her blond hair. Yanking her head backwards, he forced her panicked eyes to meet his truculent gaze. He growled, "Just remember what I said, Celeste: one word from this sulky mouth of yours, and it will be your last. Just to make sure you behave yourself, I'll have Slim keep an eagle eye on you."

"That isn't necessary! If you wish to end our affair, then say so. You don't have to threaten me or hurt me." She lowered her wet lashes and entreated, "Could you give me some money to live on until I work something

225

out? It's winter, Jeffery! Where can I go? Hinkley won't let me stay here without payment. You can't just have him throw me out in the cold, not after how close we've been.''

He chuckled derisively. "I find your snivelling company depressing and irritating. I have already spent a small bundle on you, despite your many indiscretions with other men! I suggest you sell some of those clothes and trinkets which you so sweetly wrangled from my good-natured heart.''

Celeste's face went ashen as she realized what Jeffery implied. She stammered, "You know everything about me? You never said anything! All this time you've been spying on me!''

"Yes, my pet," Jeffery said as evil lights flickered in his eyes. "Nobody fools Jeffery Gordon. Not you—and certainly not Alisha Williams!''

Hurling her from him, Jeffery stormed from the room.

As Celeste crumbled to the floor, she recklessly vowed, "It will be a cold day in Hell before you lie next to Alisha Williams instead of me, my dashing lieutenant. Whether you know it or not, you are mine. She'll never have you while I live and breathe, never! As for that lusty brother of hers, in the throes of passion, many secrets come out. . . .''

Chapter Twelve

"So you see, Paul, we have only enough money to make it through the winter," Alisha solemnly stated, finishing her distressing report to Powchutu concerning their financial predicament. "Mr. Bigsley was very kind and helpful. At least he did have the foresight to prevent a total loss of Uncle Thad's savings."

"Don't worry about it, Alisha love," he encouraged her. "Even a small amount of money is better than none. If we hadn't stopped at Joe's, we wouldn't have known about it. Stop fretting. We'll work it out. Surely there's something around here I can do."

"You're right as usual. We should be grateful for all we have. It's just that Joe's news was so wonderful and timely. For once it seemed we were making some progress. Every time we attempt to stand up, something comes along and slaps us back to the ground. I had hoped this money would solve all our problems. Now, it's nearly worthless," she declared dispiritedly.

He smiled and caressed her cheek. "We're free, love, and we have each other. We're alive and well. That's all that counts. Everything else will work out. Mark my words: we'll make it this time."

"You're like warm sunshine on a dismal day. What would I ever do without you? You've always been there when I needed you. We do have everything that really matters. I'll try not to worry so much. It's just . . ." she halted and cautioned herself to prudence. She quickly altered her words, "It's just that you've already tried to find work for several days without success. What if neither of us can find work to see us through to New Orleans? What if we get stranded here?"

"If necessary, we can return to Joe's. He offered to let me help him with his trapping this winter, then split the profits down the middle in the spring. If worse comes to worst, we'll head back to Joe's. Satisfied, little sister?" He playfully teased a smile from her soft lips.

"I had forgotten about Joe," she lied convincingly. How could she tell him that Jeffery would never permit her to leave? "In that light, we have nothing to worry about," she stated with confidence she did not feel, hoping Powchutu could not read the doubt and anxiety in her voice and eyes.

He did, but failed to realize the meaning behind them. He simply assumed she was disappointed and apprehensive about the news which Hiram had just given to her. Knowing she had not seen Jeffery since that first afternoon of their arrival, he dismissed him as a possible cause for her worries. He announced his plans to continue his search for work that very afternoon. He suggested she get some rest while he was gone. Placing a light kiss upon her forehead, he turned and left her alone with her pensive thoughts.

Alisha prayed Powchutu would be offered a job in the nearby wilderness. She hoped he would ask her to remain where it was safe and warm. While he was away, she could work out her situation with Jeffery. If he could not be put off, she could marry Jeffery before Powchutu's return. However, the best solution was for him to head back to Joe's for the winter. She would subtly suggest this to him at the right time.

For the next two days, Powchutu did exactly as

promised. He would spend each day seeking some type of work, each day branching out further and further from the settlement in his avid search. Yet, each night he would return without success. Not wishing to overly concern Alisha, he did not relate his increasing fears to her. He refused to discuss his return to Joe's at this early stage. At night, he would joke and talk with her over a delicious dinner or during their evening stroll. He craftily managed to display confidence and optimism when in her presence. Yet, his male pride and self-assurance were taking a beating. He had already let her down once when those men attacked them; he resolved to do anything necessary to prevent her loss of faith in him.

Alisha's days varied greatly from his. She spent much of her time reading several newspapers from back East, supposedly sent to her from Hiram. The news was obsolete and distressing. Evidently the costly war with her native country was still in bloody progress. She was not surprised to learn of the Colonies' declaration of independence from her beloved England back in July of this year. She made a mental note to send this particular news on to Joe.

She studied the stories numerous times. She could not deduce the real facts from the colored ones. She failed to understand why the Americans continued to claim the victories when Admiral Howe and General Howe were creating such widespread havoc in the northern section of the country. If one sifted through the facts and figures, England seemed to have the upper hand until September. Such news was still depressing and alarming; brothers were fighting against brothers.

When she was not scanning those papers for some missed fact, Alisha would rest or would take care of her personal chores. Mary seemed only too pleased to assist her with her laundry and to spend time in her company. Although she appeared friendly, Alisha instinctively felt uneasy around her. It was not due to her muteness; it came from the furtive way the strange girl watched her. She gave Alisha the weird sensation that she could see right into her mind. Her intense scrutiny would frequently give Alisha uncontrollable shivers. When noting this disquieting effect upon Alisha, Mary would hastily glance away.

To apologize for her unkind reaction to Mary would only bring it to light and place more importance than necessary upon it; therefore, Alisha tried to suppress and to ignore it. To lighten the heavy atmosphere when they were together, Alisha would chatter freely about life back East or in England. Mary would politely listen, then smile cheerfully and thoughtfully. But no matter what she said or did, she remained uneasy around Mary O'Hara.

Several times Mary had surprised Alisha by bringing hot tea and warm muffins to her room. She would timidly hand them to Alisha, then scurry away with a bright smile upon her angelic face. When Alisha mentioned these strange awkward feelings about Mary to Powchutu, he smiled and told her not to concern herself over the girl's obvious admiration of her. Having no better argument to disprove his assumption, Alisha reluctantly accepted it for the time being.

The following morning was Sunday. Alisha informed Powchutu that she had decided to attend the religious service which was held at the far end of town in a small, wooden structure. Hiram told her about the meetings which were conducted twice monthly by a travelling minister from Ste. Genevieve. He invited them to accompany him and to meet some of the nearby townfolk.

Powchutu considered her intention for a few moments, debating whether or not he wanted to go along. Finally coming to the conclusion it would make him uncomfortable, he declined to go with her. "In heart, I am Indian. The Great Spirit holds my fate and my trust. I cannot worship him inside a closed building. I must be outside with Mother Earth. I must be surrounded by the creations of the Great Spirit. I will wait for you here. Hiram will see to your safety. Does that displease you, Alisha?"

She smiled brightly. "Certainly not. Each person must worship as he chooses. But who is to say that both Gods are not one in the same? Who is to say that Christ did not come in different forms to different peoples?" she teased him cheerfully. "Besides, I am not so certain I will gain anything from this travelling preacher. From what I gather, he isn't much better than his sinful flock. You know what, Paul, I haven't been inside a real church in almost two years . . ." Anguish filled her as she recalled that last time too well: her parents' funeral back in the Pennsylvania Colony.

Yet, another bittersweet memory returned to haunt her. Alisha closed her eyes and pictured a stirring scene which she had witnessed many times in a past existence. Each morning, Gray Eagle had faced the East and chanted to the Great Spirit in his compelling, husky voice. She had watched the handsome lines of his face and the mighty stance of his body as the warm sun had caressed him. Would his voice and image forever return to torment and inflame her? She shook her auburn head to clear it of Gray Eagle's entrancing memory.

To make this outing easier for Alisha, Powchutu ordered her early morning meal to be sent to her room. Mary seemed only too happy to comply with his request.

231

Powchutu was slightly taken back by the teenage girl's provocative smile at him before she turned and raced merrily down the staircase. And Powchutu could hardly trust his eyes: Mary boldly flirting with him! He shook his head to clear it, then returned to his room.

A soft tapping upon her door awakened Alisha early Sunday morning. She roused herself and called out, "Who's there?" No one answered. Once again the light, almost timid, tapping sounded.

Alisha threw aside the covers, immediately chilled by the cold room and her thin gown, and made her way to the door. She pressed her ear to the wood surface and listened for any suspicious noise. Once more the light, but persistent, knocking came upon her locked door. Startled, she jumped. "Who's there? I will not open this door until you answer me!"

Still no reply, just another knocking. Alisha called out in annoyance, "Answer me or be gone!"

A raspy, masculine voice called out shortly, "Miss, it's the girl Mary wanting in. She can't talk."

"Mary?" she repeated in surprise. She stepped behind the door and cautiously slid the bolt aside. Slowly she opened the door and peered around it. Her eyes settled upon the rustic, elderly piano-player from the dining room. "What is it, Zeb?" she asked.

He moved back to allow Mary to slip into her room, arms laden with wood and kindling. "Morning, Miss Williams," he stated politely, then disappeared down the dim hallway.

Alisha slowly pushed the door shut, then turned to stare at Mary in puzzlement. "What are you doing here so early, Mary?"

Mary beamed with undisguised joy. She motioned for Alisha to return to her warm bed until she had the fire going. "You come to fix a fire?" Alisha quizzed, rubbing her sleepy eyes.

Mary smiled once again and nodded agreement. "But it's so early, isn't it?" She stifled a yawn with her hand.

Mary shook her head no. She took Alisha by the arm and walked her to the window. She pulled back the curtain and pointed down the dirt street. Alisha leaned forward and followed her line of direction. Still confused, she glanced back at the grinning Mary. "What are you trying to tell me? What's down there?"

Mary giggled silently. She took the table and placed it before her. She stepped behind it and assumed a stern, serious look. She put her hands in the position of holding a book. She then began to mutely mimic a preacher giving a sermon. Afterwards, she reverently lowered her head as if in prayer. She then returned to the window and pointed down the street.

"Church?" Alisha guessed.

Mary's head bobbed up and down, her eyes filled with pleasure at Alisha's answer. "You're building me a fire so I can dress for church? That's very sweet of you. Thank you, Mary."

Enjoying her charade, Mary held up one finger and pointed to the dark fireplace. She put up two fingers and pretended to eat. She raised three fingers and imitated a tub bath in the center of the room. She immediately put up four fingers and pretended to dress. Lastly, she raised five fingers and motioned toward the door. She raced to the window and pointed down the street. She lifted questioning eyes to Alisha, silently asking if those plans suited her.

"Isn't that an awful lot of extra work for you? I don't mind eating downstairs or going to the bathcloset down the hall. It doesn't seem fair to work you this hard. Your

233

uncle might need you."

Mary nodded negatively. She stubbornly held up one finger, then two fingers, then three, then four, and then five fingers. She pointed to Alisha, then to the bed. The firm look upon her determined face convinced Alisha that she was serious.

"But I'm already awake and up. I might as well help you with the fire," Alisha gently argued with the adamant girl, who seemed insistent upon waiting upon her hand and foot.

Mary shook her head. She hugged her arms around her abdomen and shook as if cold. She pointed to Alisha and to the bed once more. "You're worried I might get cold?" she asked the persistent girl.

For her reply, Mary walked over to the bed and straightened the bedcovers. She motioned for Alisha to return there until she built a fire and had the room warm. Unable to reason with a mute and obstinate girl, Alisha sighed and obeyed her wishes.

Mary smiled sweetly at her as she smoothed the covers into place, tucking her in as if she were a child. Alisha observed her curiously as she went about her task at the hearth. Within minutes she had a cheery fire glowing there. She stacked the remaining wood near the base of the hearth and brushed the debris from her chore into the colorful blaze.

She walked over to the bedside table. She picked up the key to Alisha's room and motioned she was taking it with her while she fetched her breakfast and bathwater. Alisha nodded comprehension and permission. At the door, Mary hesitated and glanced back at the reclining Alisha. She waved her hand to claim her attention. She then pointed to herself, to her mouth, and to the door. She tapped two times rapidly, waited a second, then tapped three more times. She repeated this another time.

Alisha promptly seized her lucid message. "Two fast taps, wait, then three fast taps when it's you. You've really been a big help since my arrival. I wish I could afford to pay you extra for all your kindnesses."

Mary's eyes widened and she inhaled sharply at that suggestion. She tapped her open palm, then rapidly shook her head as if she had been insulted. She looked upset that Alisha should even mention paying for her proffered services. She hastily left the room, locking the door behind her. Alisha lay back upon her pillow, feeling distressed by the hurt in Mary's gaze. It seemed clear there was nothing she could do except allow Mary to assist her in this servile manner which appeared to make her happy.

Indeed, it did make Mary very happy. She felt there was only one person who had shown her real kindness, understanding, and affection. Many people rejected or abused this helpless, silent girl who could not reveal their cruel words or evil deeds. Many also felt that since she could not speak that she was simple-minded, perhaps even dangerous. Most people kept their distance from her; others shoved her away if she came too close to them. Several had accused her of setting the evil eye upon them when she was caught innocently staring at them. She was frequently ridiculed and tricked. She was often pinched and fondled by lustful male guests.

Tragically, she possessed the knack of making people feel uneasy or threatened. Yet, she had long since ceased crying over these cruelties; she now sadly accepted them as a natural part of her sufferings. She sought to perform her chores when the guests were out of their rooms. She struggled to keep her eyes lowered when awaiting orders from guests or while serving their dinners. When not doing chores, she huddled in her dingy room.

She had also ceased trying to communicate her fears and troubles to her uncle who ran this guest house. He had made it clear during that first week after her unexpected arrival at age thirteen that he viewed her as a burden and nuisance. It did not seem to matter if she did work from dawn to past dusk for no charge other than food and lodging. There was no love, kindness, or understanding where he was concerned. In fact, had she not worked like a slave, he would have thrown her out on her own.

Therefore, she busied herself with her appointed chores each day; then she kept to her dank and lonely room at night, except when she stole away to meet her only friend. Her hungry, empty heart craved the friendship he offered. She ravenously devoured his words and smiles. She cried over the presents he gave to her, those she carefully hid from her uncle's prying eyes and stingy hands. She sought out the solace this friend provided, this friend who never touched her in the crude and groping manner that many men stealthily attempted. Her undying gratitude and affection belonged to this friend who never asked anything of her in return for his friendship and affection . . . nothing until the beautiful Alisha Williams' arrival.

After being around Alisha for a few days, Mary could easily understand Jeffery's interest in her; she was not only the most beautiful woman Mary had ever seen, but she was also the most gentle and sweetest female she had ever met. Like her Jeffery, this female was friendly and kind. Her voice was like a rippling brook on a spring morning. Her eyes were the color of new grass. Her hair was as soft as down and the shade of a chestnut mare. Her smile was warm and honest with a natural spontaneity.

Her skin was totally flawless and appeared soft as the gentle breeze. Her features were stunning, and her figure was supple and enticing. Indeed, she was the most magnificent creature which Mary had seen.

When Jeffery had approached her about taking special care of Alisha, she had been only too pleased to follow his simple requests. She did find it strange that Jeffery did not want Alisha to know about the many wonderful things he was doing for her. He wanted her to have the very best room, had even supplied the furniture and accessories for it. He demanded she be served the best and most appetizing food, even supplying her with tea. He asked for any little extras which might make her happy and relaxed. He paid for any help she might require with her personal chores. He sent over little gifts to be placed in her room without her knowledge. It bothered Mary to receive all the credit for Jeffery's admiration and attention. She was also slightly distressed at having to deceive Alisha. But the thing which disturbed Mary the most was Jeffery's request for her constant surveillance of Alisha and the reports she gave to him. Yet, she was naïvely convinced of Jeffery's romantic attraction to Alisha and of his desire to keep his interest a secret until they were better acquainted. Bewitched by the idea of love, Mary did all he asked and more.

Jeffery had been delighted to learn that Alisha would be attending the services on Sunday morning without the company of her imposing brother. He had instructed Mary to provide a bath for her in her room. He had also suggested the early fire and the tasty breakfast. This would be their first meeting since her arrival; he wanted to make certain nothing halted her plans or dampened her spirits. His excitement could not be suppressed.

237

Mary obediently informed him of everything which went on between Alisha and her so-called brother. He was relieved to learn that Alisha had most likely told him the truth about her amicable relationship with the scout. Mary was watching them like a hawk; she would be alerted to any romantic attachment which would seem abnormal between siblings. Too, if Alisha had any plans to trick him or to flee from him, she was being very surreptitious and cautious. She would have no reason to suspect Mary's watchful eyes and ears. It was the perfect ploy.

In time Alisha would be made aware of her indebtedness to him. Meanwhile, naïve and simple Mary could do his dirty work for him, just as she had unknowingly done in the past—all for a few silly words, feigned affection, and meager presents. He had seen the value of Mary's assistance and had quickly emotionally enslaved the young and eager girl. No one could stay at the Horne House and keep any secrets from him; no one could eat and speak there without his knowing their words and plans. Mary would never know how many deaths, disasters, and thefts in which she had aided him. .

Shortly, Mary returned to Alisha's room. She brought an inviting breakfast of hot cakes, maple syrup, and hot tea—just as Jeffery had ordered. Alisha sat at the table, silently eating while Mary brought in a hip bath and filled it with warm water. After completing this tiring chore, she left Alisha alone to bathe and to dress.

Alisha remained in the water until it was nearly cold. She curiously wondered where the young girl had found the fragrant jasmine soap whose sweet scent lingered on her skin. She could not decide why Mary would so willingly share such a luxury with a near stranger. Deciding she could not analyze this unpredictable girl, Alisha dismissed her rambling thoughts about the girl.

After towelling off near the warm fire, Alisha slipped into her prettiest dress, a muted paisley of spring colors. As she slid her feet into the leather walking shoes, she pondered the identity of the woman who had sacrificed them in order to continue their trip West. She stood before the mirror and brushed her long, shiny curls until they shimmered and shone with rich color and vibrant life.

Pleased with the refined picture she presented, she smiled and hugged herself. Mary's signal drummed upon her door just as she completed her toilette. She hurried to let her inside. She smiled and pirouetted before the gaping girl.

"Well, how do I look?" she happily asked. "Do you know this is the first real dress I've had in ages?" she confessed without thinking. "Freedom, Mary . . . Do you know how very precious it is? I don't know when I've been this happy."

Mary was baffled by the joyous emotions of this captivating girl. What could she possibly know about trouble or suffering? Still, she was just the woman for Jeffery, she selflessly decided. They were so much alike. How could this girl not fall in love with him when he pursued her? No doubt she would fall into his waiting arms! In addition, it would get him away from that cheap harlot who was trying to ensnare him. This was the perfect girl for him, and she would do all within her power to help him catch her.

"Oh, my," Alisha suddenly fretted. "It's cold outside, and I don't even have a cape or shawl. I cannot go to church wrapped in a blanket or fur skin. I should have thought about this sooner before I put you to so much trouble. I'm sorry, Mary, but I cannot go like this."

Mary silenced her worries with a finger to her lips. She motioned for Alisha to wait where she was. She rushed out the door and ran to her room. She quickly recovered the exquisite, white woolen shawl which Jeffery had given to her just a few days ago. She swiftly returned to Alisha's room. She proudly placed the lovely shawl around Alisha's shoulders, then smiled.

Alisha's hand caressed the softness of the wrap. She smiled through misty eyes at the excited girl. "I promise to take very good care of it, Mary. You are the kindest, most thoughtful girl I have ever known. Thank you." She leaned forward and placed a sisterly kiss upon the startled girl's forehead.

Mary timidly sidled away from Alisha's unexpected embrace. She was unaccustomed to a physical show of affection and gratitude. The loan of the shawl would make everyone happy; besides, she could not wear it where her uncle might see it. This way, he would think it a thank you gift from Alisha. Mary opened the door and motioned for Alisha to go downstairs to where Hiram was waiting for her.

As they passed Powchutu's room, Alisha whispered to Mary, "If the service is very long, will you see to Paul's breakfast and needs? Men never know how to take care of themselves," she stated with a soft giggle.

Mary's face lit up with joy and pleasure. She rapidly nodded her head in assent. She would be delighted to assume the care of Alisha's older brother. Paul was such an attractive, compelling man. Her heart raced wildly each time he glanced at her. Besides, Jeffery had asked her to keep Paul from worrying about his sister. Now, Alisha was also encouraging Mary's attentions on Paul. Thrilled by the possibility of Paul's coming to feel the same way she did, Mary took this task very seriously.

In fact, Jeffery had encouraged Mary to pursue Alisha's magnetic, alluring brother. He had boasted that Mary was just the woman for Paul. He had given her many hints on how to gain his attention and his affection, one being the excellent care of his sister, another being her own availability for any need of his. But Mary did not comprehend Jeffery's real motives for instigating an affair between her and Paul . . .

As she neared the last step, Alisha smiled and went forward to take Hiram's out-stretched hand. Hiram had called to take her to church. They exchanged social amenities, then departed the Horne House to join Hiram's wife who was patiently awaiting them outside in their wagon.

When they reached the church, it was almost time for the service to begin. The few remaining seats available were near the back of the shadowy, oblong room. Hiram allowed Alisha to enter the pew first; then, his wife and himself followed and sat down. Several heads turned to study the newest member of the mingled congregation. Alisha not only received many warm or timid smiles, but she also noted a few sullen and envious smirks. But to each and every eye she caught, she smiled warmly and nodded cordially.

Just as the first hymn was announced, a man came in to sit beside Alisha. Her eyes widened in surprise as they fused with the entrancing ones of Jeffery Gordon. He smiled placidly as he took her elbow and helped her to her unsteady feet. He courteously found the correct page in the aged hymnal, then held it out for them to share. She was trapped between him and the squat Mrs. Bigsley.

Fearing to create a scene or to foster unwanted suspi-

241

cions, she bravely forced herself to appear poised and honored by his gentlemanly attention. After all, they were supposed to be old friends, and Jeffery was supplying them with his gracious hospitality. It would be odd for her to be hostile to him or to ignore his close proximity. To disguise her predicament, Alisha sang soft and low to conceal the uncontrollable quavering in her silvery voice.

Anxiety raced through Alisha's body as she wondered if Jeffery were making his claim to her before the other men present. There was only one more day left before his deadline. She had dared to hope he might change his mind. Evidently he had not, not from that possessive and amorous gleam in his intensely blue eyes.

Panic began to gnaw at her nerves as she sat still and rigid while the minister began his long-winded sermon. She had forbidden her mind to dwell upon Jeffery or his demands until now. She had prayed her problem would simply vanish; it had not. In fact, she was in deeper trouble now than before. There was no safe means of escape from him, nor enough money to accomplish it successfully. Somehow she would have to find a way to either discourage him or to thwart his satanic plans for her.

But how? her troubled mind raged. How can you beat a man with his influence and determination? How can you protect Powchutu from his clutches if you refuse to marry him? Far worse, how can you protect yourself if you do comply with his terrifying demand?

The temperature outside had dropped significantly since the service began. It was now slightly below forty degrees. The wind could be heard whistling around the corners of the decrepit building and into the numerous cracks around the windows and sideboards. The one potbellied stove near the front of the large room gave off very little heat, and the lanterns were burning low.

In her state of pensive contemplation, Alisha was totally ignorant of her attraction to Jeffery's warm body. It was as if her chilled flesh instinctively sought out the radiating warmth of his. Witnessing the intense look of deep meditation upon her lovely face, Jeffery realized she was totally unaware of their physical contact. He could almost imagine where her anxious thoughts must be, for surely they were not upon the minister's uninspiring words. Not wishing to alert her to their intimacy, he remained silent and immobile. In truth, if it weren't for his troubling problem, Jeffery would have been helplessly aroused by Alisha's artless nestling up to him.

In her state of reflection, she happened to glance up at the bedeviling man beside her. His blazing eyes instantly engulfed her like a powerful tidal wave. The heat of his stare brought a rosy flush to her cheeks. Managing to tear her eyes away, she was suddenly aware of how closely she had unknowingly snuggled up to his side. She pretended to shift her body's position in order to move away from his contact, but without drawing any attention to either of them. Succeeding, she sternly focused her eyes and wayward attention upon the boring man at the front of the room.

The remainder of the service went slowly and tediously. After what seemed eons to her, the last hymn was rendered by an unfeeling, impatient congregation. The people hurriedly left the icy building to return to their warm homes and their hot meals. Alisha was able to meet only a few of the townspeople and was not overly impressed with any of them. They appeared to be sadly lacking in manners in this uncivil settlement!

At the doorway, Jeffery graciously offered to see

Alisha back to the Horne House in such a convincing, helpful manner that she could hardly refuse without calling attention to some problem between them. He was on his very best behavior, displaying that genteel chivalry which he could adopt so perfectly.

Caught off guard, Alisha was trapped into polite agreement. She apprehensively watched as the Bigsleys drove away in their wagon. She cast a wary, curious glance in Jeffery's direction. He was grinning from ear to ear; mischievous lights glittered roguishly in his eyes. He took her elbow and urged her stiffened body forward. She mechanically followed his lead.

A sudden gust of wind blew the shawl away from her shoulders and sent wisps of stray hair across her face and into her eyes. She abruptly halted in her tracks to adjust the wrap and her tossed hair. Before she could, Jeffery gallantly pulled the shawl back into its place and lightly knotted it at her bosom. Without delay he tenderly brushed the stray locks out of her astonished face. He patiently awaited her gratitude.

She tartly snapped, "That isn't necessary, Jeffery! I can repair my toilette myself."

He chuckled in amusement. "I'm sure you can, Alisha love. But I preferred to do it for you. Before much longer, it just might become a welcomed privilege of your new husband," he drawled in a husky, meaningful tone.

As they continued walking back to town, Alisha's frightened gaze locked with his confident one. She stammered, "You mean you are actually serious about marriage?" She feigned disbelief and shock to learn if he were earnest, pretending she had not truly believed his previous proposal.

"Come now, Alisha," he rebuked her. "You know I never say things I do not mean. You will marry me," he vowed positively.

"But, Jeffery . . ." she began to argue with him. He pressed a finger to her cold lips to silence any protests.

"No buts, Alisha. This time, I will have you . . . on my own terms, in my own way, and on my schedule. *Comprendez-vous?*"

She whitened and trembled at the full impact of his subtle threat. Tears filled her emerald eyes. Alisha pleaded, "Please, Jeffery, you must reconsider your command. Things could never work out between us. Please don't be so wicked to me!"

A smug smile crossed his features and settled in his cerulean eyes. Anger consumed Alisha as she lost her temper. She spat, "You're enjoying this scheme, aren't you? You savor your power over people. It enlivens you to make them squirm, doesn't it? What would you know about pain? What would you know about love? I vow you have never felt any of those emotions! All you know is power, hatred, and spitefulness. I have pride and wants, too! I won't allow you to do this vile thing to me. I won't, Jeffery Gordon! I know you only want the law's consent to abuse and terrify me even more!"

"You misunderstand my pleasure, Alisha. It warms my very soul to hear a civil tongue spoken here in this godforsaken wilderness. Do you know how long it's been since I've conversed with a proper lady? You're the only person I've met anywhere near here who has any breeding. The fact you're also very beautiful, charming, and talented only adds to my great enjoyment of this situation. Reconsider my demand? I am afraid not, my dear."

"You have no soul to warm! And your heart, if you even possess one, is as black as the darkest night! If you think for one minute I will accept your words as compliments, you are sorely mistaken. You deceived me once

245

before with your silvery tongue and chivalrous actions; never again!" she breathlessly swore.

"I do know what pain and fear and denial are like, Little One. As far as relishing my wealth and power, you are perfectly right; I do. Wealth and power can get one anything he might desire; I possess both fortunately. Since I desire you as my wife, you shall be mine. It's really very simple, Alisha. If you follow my commands, there will be no reason for trouble between us. Besides, I can think of far worse fates than becoming my bride. Would you care for me to refresh your memory about your life with a certain Indian?" he taunted.

She glared at him for a long time as terrible and vivid anguish replaced all other emotions in her eyes. Without warning, she whirled and began to practically race away from him. He rapidly caught up with her. He seized her arm and halted her. He forcefully turned her around to face him. Seeing the results of reopened wounds, he instantly withheld the tirade which was poised on the tip of his tongue. He reached out his hand to brush away several teardrops which glistened like minute diamonds upon her ashen cheeks.

She slapped his intruding hand away. "I don't need your brutal reminders of my past. I lived it; I shall never forget it, nor your bloody part in it! Find someone else to torment; I have paid enough for my deeds. I am free now; and by God, I shall stay free! No man will ever hurt me or humiliate me again!" she wretchedly declared. She tried to pull away from him, but he would not release his iron grip upon her arm.

"Then don't force me to hurt you or to remind you of things best forgotten! I'll accept my part in your return to that red bastard Gray Eagle. Face facts, Alisha: there was no way Fort Pierre could have kept you from him.

Another fact, I am just as resolved to have you as he had you—maybe more so!"

A mysterious look flickered in Jeffery's unreadable eyes. "Would it favorably affect your decision if I promised you marriage in name only? If I swear to you I won't ever touch you unless you come to love me and want me in a physical way? I have a great deal of pride, Alisha. Seduction is one thing; brutal rape is quite another. I am not like that savage. I would never force my sexual attentions upon you. Of course I would expect you to feign the loving and attentive wife in public; but in private, you may have your very own room, alone and untouched if that is the only way I can have you. I need a proper wife to take home to Virginia. I have reached the point of having to settle down and take over the plantation. I've met countless females, but none of your quality and style. You are perfect for the role of Mrs. Jeffery Clayton Gordon. Role, Alisha, not reality. My father has practically demanded I marry within this year or he'll disinherit me. I've searched for the unique woman who will bear my name. You are the only choice. If I must force you to accept this role, then so be it."

Alisha was astonished at the incredible offer. "I don't believe you, Jeffery. Once before you nearly ravished me before an entire fort. Now, you vow you no longer desire me as a woman. You offer a mock marriage! Hardly! You are far too attractive, and young, and virile to be satisfied with . . ." His look warned her of her careless words. She clamped her hand over her traitorous mouth to silence her forward comments. Her face grew red with embarrassment. She could not believe what she was saying to him.

"Your compliments are greatly appreciated, my love. I can assure you a mock marriage would place no hardship

247

upon my male prowess and desires. I require a proper wife, not a beautiful mistress. I can promise to take care of my physical needs without any embarrassment to my wife or to my family. A decent wife is much harder to locate than an obliging harlot. Besides, I'm getting too old and fatigued to continue my reputation as irresistible, incomparable lover. A long rest from service would do me good."

He altered his tone to a mellow, entreating drawl, "Am I such a terrible choice for a husband? Can you find a better one? I have a lot to offer in exchange for your assistance: wealth, social position, civilization, respectability, a majestic home, elegant clothes, splendid parties, extravagant jewels, exquisite food and service, anything . . ." he tempted her.

Alisha watched him closely and keenly. She asked herself if he could possibly be serious or this desperate. "I don't trust you for an instant, Jeffery Gordon. What are you really trying to pull? I am not a fool; you are not offering treats to a simpleton. Neither am I that same trusting, gullible girl who came to this monstrous land! I have been given a harsh education this past year. Considering my upbringing and the torments of this past year, what you offer does sound tempting and marvelous. Yet, I instinctively feel it is all some malicious trick. Marriage! Why not mistress or servant? That's all you wanted from me last time," she accused.

"I have plenty of servants, both here and in Virginia. I'm tired of supporting and tolerating mistresses. If I demand sex, I'll hire some doxy for the night! I lack a respectable, flattering wife. Besides, believe it or not, I would have offered you marriage back there if you hadn't spoiled everything by clinging to that blasted scout!"

His tone became low and ominous as he warned, "If I

cannot have you, Alisha, I swear to you that no man will. I have given you until tomorrow to make your final decision. I will grant you anything you wish if you say yes. Once we're married, I won't have any reason to prove my power or control over you. As a matter of fact, my image can do without the label of a wife-beater. You will be perfectly secure in my keeping, perhaps one day even happy. There really is no other choice, Alisha. It's me or . . . nothing."

Alisha had the overwhelming feeling Jeffery was telling the truth. How could he possibly want a mock marriage—with her of all women? How could he simply dismiss all of his pent up resentment and bitterness toward her? How could he expect her to forgive him for his past cruelty? Marriage! She was troubled by the illusion of arguing with Gray Eagle through Jeffery's body and mouth. Their demands were nearly the same; the results could be the same; their feelings and motivations were the same. She shuddered at the similarities.

"Well?" he softly inquired at her continued silence.

"I need more time, Jeffery. You're talking about a lifetime commitment. Seeing you again has been a big shock; I thought you were dead. So many things have happened lately. I just can't rush into marriage with a man like you, no matter how much you threaten me. I honestly don't know if I can trust you to tell the truth or to keep your promises. Who's to say you won't change your mind once we're wed? I just can't take any more torment this soon," she painfully confessed, managing to sway him slightly.

He pondered her indecision and anxiety for a time. He concluded it would be to his eventual advantage to generously allow her two more weeks. Also, several other arrangements were still unresolved. In reality, she could not escape him. Without a doubt, his kindness would compel her to comply with his wishes. Mary could keep him informed of any possible treachery from Powchutu.

"Just to prove to you I'm not as bad as you seem to think, Alisha, I'll grant you two more weeks to make up your mind. Evidently you're under a great deal of pressure from the past. But, I'll warn you now: there will not be another delay for any reason. That should allow you the time to gently prepare our good friend Paul to accept the news of our coming marriage. We shall break the news a little at a time by seeing each other on frequent occasions. Might avoid problems if he is led to believe I am gradually sweeping you off your feet. Naturally he's going to fight like the devil to hold on to you, but slowly losing you will be the best solution for all concerned. I wouldn't want him to get hurt by interfering in my affairs again," he ominously stated.

Feeling she might better comprehend this disturbing scheme and Jeffery, she reluctantly agreed with his suggestions. As he reached up and replaced another straying lock of hair, he drawled, "Well, Miss Alisha Williams, looks as if I'll start courting you tomorrow night about seven."

While his hand was still touching her forehead and she was gazing up into his enchanting features, Powchutu stormed up and nearly attacked Jeffery right in the middle of the street. "Get your filthy hands off of her, or I'll kill you where you stand! How dare you touch her in any manner!"

Jeffery's easy stance shifted to one of defensive readiness. His blazing sky-blue eyes shouted his hatred for Powchutu. "You lousy half-breed! I could kill you without blinking an eye. Surely you don't think I was about to ravish Alisha here in the middle of the street! I

250

can assure you she is perfectly safe with me, here or anywhere!''

''As safe as she was that day at Fort Pierre when I had
to tear you away from her! You were going to take her
under that tree, and you didn't care if the whole damn
fort was watching!'' Powchutu sarcastically sneered.
''I'll tear you limb from limb if you ever come near her
again. Savvy, lieutenant?''

Realizing that Jeffery's words about spies might be
accurate, she knew how humiliating and dangerous an
open confrontation between these two men would be.
Thinking fast, she seized Powchutu's taut arm. She
sternly ordered, ''Stop it, both of you! People might be
listening and watching.''

To Powchutu she stated placidly, ''You misunder-
stood what was going on, Paul. Jeffery was not annoying
me. The wind blew a mote into my eyes, and I couldn't
see clearly. He was kindly removing it with my permission.'' She lowered her voice and continued, ''If you two
will recall, we are supposed to be old friends. A brawl in
the middle of town on a Sunday morning just might cause
suspicion and gossip. None of us wants to be the topic of
wagging tongues or curious minds. Do we?'' she
cunningly challenged them both.

At her common sense, each man quickly brought his
unbridled temper under rigid control. Yet, both men
remained on tense alert. Jeffery spoke first. ''You see,
Paul,'' he commented with great emphasis upon the false
name, ''I was being the perfect gentleman. Contrary to
your beliefs, Alisha is very special to me. I have no intention of hurting her in any way, and I have told her
just that. Frankly, I was hoping we could resolve our
past problems and become friends. I know I was a cad
back at Fort Pierre. I have already apologized for my

disgraceful conduct."

Alisha was grateful for Jeffery's attempts to smooth over the past and to lay the foundation for their future relationship. No matter how much she hated the situation he was placing her in, he was earnestly trying to make it easier for her to deal with. His diplomacy eased many of her previous worries and lessened some of her anger.

"It's getting colder, and the wind is picking up. I suggest we all return to our rooms," she entreated with a guileful smile at both men.

"I fully agree, Alisha. Good day to you, Paul." He lifted Alisha's cold hand and placed a warm kiss upon her open palm. "Adieu, ma petite," he whispered huskily. He leisurely swaggered away with his arrogant, self-assured air.

"What did he say to you?" Powchutu anxiously inquired when he was out of hearing range.

"That was French. He said, 'good day, my little one.' I must caution you to curb your temper and outbursts around him," she gently rebuked him. "Do you have any idea of the trouble he could cause us? I suggest we tread lightly around him while we're here. What harm could a little pretense of courtesy and friendship do? Please, Paul, our safety is in his control. Don't antagonize him to prove something to himself, to you, or to me. If there's one thing I've learned well, pride is very costly. Another thing, revenge exacts more from the avenger than from the avenged. We cannot afford any trouble here. Please try to be polite and tolerant around him. Agreed?"

He angrily acquiesced to her pleas. "I know you're right, Alisha, but it irritates me! He infuriates me beyond control. He's no good. He's a dangerous power seeker. Jeffery Gordon cares for no one except Jeffery. All that matters is what he wants."

"That's exactly my point!" Alisha repeated. "He can be dangerous if crossed. Strange as it sounds, he seemed honest and sincere when he apologized and offered me friendship. Who knows, maybe what happened after the massacre changed him, at least a little."

"Alisha! Men like Jeffery never change. He wants something from us, or rather from you. You can bet on that! Stay away from him, love," he anxiously cautioned her, concerned by her unexpected softening of heart. Their oblique gazes met.

"Everybody changes, Paul. Look at us. How can anyone live here and not be affected by this land? If I stay clear of him, then how can we discover his plans? It will be impossible to ignore him or to constantly avoid him for months on end. We're all here for the duration of winter. It might profit all of us if we remain calm and cordial."

"He really got to you with his sugary lies, didn't he? Have you forgotten what it was like back there because of him? If I hadn't intervened that day, he would have forced you to become his mistress. Not a soul in that fort, including gutless General Galt, would have dared to stop him and help you. That doesn't include the way he practically threw you back into Gray Eagle's clutches! How can you forgive him for such cruelties?" he stormed.

She artfully parried the accuracy in his words. "Tell me something in all honesty, Paul. Who would suffer the most from my hatred of Jeffery? What good would dreams of revenge do for me? How could I possibly hurt him or punish him? I would be a fool to attempt such an impossible chore! I cannot fill my thoughts with plans of revenge or with memories from my past. Such emotions and actions are dangerous and destructive. I have far better ways to spend my energies and hours. Yet, on the other hand, if he is telling the truth, what harm could it do to forgive him? If he is lying, how can that affect us until we allow it? Do you follow my reasoning at all?"

For a time, he pondered her words. Eventually he laughed and joked, "You're too smart and cunning for a beautiful female. You might be right. Still, I just don't trust him in the least."

She laughed merrily and tenderly caressed his tanned cheek. "Brother dear, you don't trust any man around your little sister. Time will tell us who is right and who is wrong. Let's relax and wait," she implored him.

He smiled and lovingly cuffed her chin. He took her cold hand and led her back toward the Horne House not far away. He was chatting as they covered the short distance to the door. Neither Alisha nor Powchutu was cognizant of the bewildered, doleful eyes which had been observing the curious scene in the empty street below Powchutu's window. The close proximity of the group had offered excellent sight, but eavesdropping had been impossible from her hidden position. Tears had filled the mute girl's troubled eyes, for she could easily read volatile emotions in both men.

Mary was utterly confused by the hostilities between Paul and Jeffery. Such vivid hatred and fury! For a brief moment, she had feared a bloody clash between them. It was clear that Alisha had said something to halt their argument and to bring about a reluctant truce. They all claimed to be old friends, but something was terribly wrong.

She wished she had not sighted Alisha and Jeffery earlier. She wished she had not pointed them out to Paul. She had been standing at his window looking out at the gloomy weather, wishing she could just stay with Paul. Upon sighting Alisha returning from the service with Jeffery, she had smiled and innocently motioned Paul over to look at them. She had hoped that romantic scene would inspire him to be romantic with her.

She would never forget the fury in Paul's eyes. Surely there was some logical reason for such strong and deep hatred. He had cursed violently, then rushed out to rescue his sister from Jeffery's company. She could not deduce why Paul saw Jeffery as some perilous threat to Alisha. She concluded there must be some past trouble between them. For certain, those two men were ardent enemies.

What was going on among those three people? What had gone on between them at some other time? Why had Jeffery pretended to like and to respect Paul? Why had he encouraged Mary to go after him? Had Jeffery lied to her, or had he simply denied her his private feelings? Why would Paul accept Jeffery's generosity if he despised him so much? So many questions without answers . . .

Chapter Thirteen

For Mary, this entire morning had been strange and bewitching. After she had given Alisha the shawl, she had gone to Paul's room to watch him sleep. He was such a magnetic, fascinating man. He was dark, compelling, and mysterious. He had an air of excitement and danger; he exuded courage and strength. To Mary, he was everything a man should be.

Although Jeffery was many of those same things, she had never been drawn to him in either a romantic or sexual manner. He was her hidden friend, her solace. He was fun; he was bright and charming. Yet, he had never captivated her. Paul was entirely different. Ever since his arrival, she could hardly think of anything but him.

Last night she had brought him the hot toddy laced with a sleeping potion, just as Jeffery had ordered. The lieutenant had wanted to be assured of his privacy with Alisha; he had not wanted Paul to change his mind about attending the service with her. Paul had sipped the drink while she was pretending to bank his fire for the night. He had fallen to its potency before she could leave his room. She had lovingly tucked him into bed, then blown out his lantern. On an impulse, she had taken his room key.

This morning, she had stealthily returned to his room after Alisha's departure, knowing he would still be asleep. She had stirred up the smoldering coals in the fire until it had come aglow with soft, warm light. She had walked over to his bed and gazed down at him. Irresistibly she had stretched out her hand and tenderly caressed his cheek, then traced the angle of his proud jawline. As her finger moved across his sensual lips, he had slightly roused.

His heavy eyes opened lazily and gazed up at her. His hand came up and buried itself within the fullness of her free-flowing auburn hair. She watched him attempt to clear his vision and groggy head. Unable to do so, he gradually pulled her head down to his. His mouth covered hers in a kiss which sent her senses reeling and her young heart leaping. As she hungrily responded to his ardent kiss, he pulled her willing body into his strong embrace.

In his continued dreamy state, Paul lifted the covers and pulled Mary into the warm circle of his arms. Almost instinctively, he slowly undressed her with little difficulty and without any resistance from her. He pressed his naked frame next to her slim one. She trembled with a strange, growing need and mysterious excitement. His skilled hands began to wander over her supple and eager body, bringing intoxicating pleasure to her. Soon, his hardened manhood filled her womanly recess.

Her heart cried out with great delight and increased hunger. He began to move within her responsive body. Never had it been this way for her. Those few times when she had been taken against her will, it had been painful and ugly. But with Paul, it was beautiful and passionate. Her small hands caressed his hard, smooth chest and muscled back. Her mouth refused to leave his. She moved beneath him, urging him on and on.

There was never a moment when she had wanted to stop or to turn back. Never had she felt such blissful and inviting sensations. Never had she felt so wanted or so special. Never had she been this happy or complete. Never had she experienced the giving and taking with a man. The truth was that she loved him; she wanted him without any reservations. He was her dream-come-true.

When the final moment of culmination came for both of them, she was briefly stunned as he softly whispered his sister's name! Her surprise only lasted an instant, for he skillfully claimed her full attention. However, that mystery would later return to torment her. Caught up in the blazing climax of released passion, he filled both her body and her thoughts. Afterwards, she lay within the confines of his possessive embrace.

About twenty minutes later, he began to stir and to sigh in contentment. With an entrancing smile upon his lips, he looked down at the girl whose head rested upon his powerful shoulder. His stygian eyes widened in dismay as they beheld Mary O'Hara smiling timidly at him, lights of love and satisfaction glowing in her brown eyes. He inhaled sharply at the implication of her nude body pressed against his. For in truth, he had been making love to Alisha.

"What the . . ." he began, then halted before completing his curse. "What are you doing in my bed, Mary? How'd you get in here? Your uncle will flay both of us," he declared tensely.

He was beside himself with remorse and disbelief. "I thought you . . ." He stopped his traitorous tongue. He could not say he thought she was Alisha, his supposed sister. "I thought I was only dreaming. I had no idea I was . . . I mean that we were . . ." he stammered, at a complete loss as to understand or to explain this baffling situation.

Mary just kept smiling at him, as if he could say or do no wrong. It was quickly clear to him she was not unhappy or angry with what had obviously just taken place between them. The odor of lovemaking still clung to the sheets and floated in the warm air. He glanced down at her clothes upon the floor, noting their rumpled and untorn state. He sighed in great relief.

He muttered absently, "At least I didn't rape you!" Realizing the mute girl couldn't have called out for help or her small frame couldn't have offered a powerful man like him very much resistance, "Did I?" he suddenly inquired, a look of dread upon his attractive features.

She quickly shook her head that he had not ravished her. "That's a relief! But what happened? How did we get into bed together?" he curiously quizzed the smiling girl.

Unable to gaze into his entrancing eyes and to lie to him, she mimicked her story of how she had been banking his fire the night before, of how he had fallen asleep, of how she had taken his key in order to return this morning to fix his fire, of how he had reached out to her during his sleepy state, and of how she had willingly responded to him.

"I swear I didn't mean to take advantage of you. Why didn't you wake me up, Mary? We shouldn't have made love. You're just a child! How could you allow me to do this to you? I'm terribly sorry and ashamed. What more can I say?" he exclaimed ruefully.

Mary's crestfallen expression worried him. Her troubled gaze showed her desperation to speak, knowing she could not. Tears of frustration and anguish filled her eyes. She promptly pulled away from him. Unmindful of her naked state, she threw back the covers and left his warm bed and cold heart. She hurriedly pulled on her clothes and began to run her trembling fingers through her mussed hair.

Her rush to get out of his room was obvious. She looked embarrassed, hurt, and guilty. He softly called out, "Don't go yet, Mary. I didn't mean to hurt your feelings. Of course you're not a child; you're a lovely, young woman. But what would your uncle and my sister say if they found out about this . . . morning? Are you sure I didn't hurt you?" he gently inquired, concerned by her unexpected reaction to his previous words, as if he were her lover who was cruelly abandoning her.

She glanced over at him. Her eyes roamed his bare chest and massive shoulders. Seeing the open desire and renewed passion in her warm gaze, he felt ill at ease. He defensively pulled the sheet up to his neck, like a modest virgin on her wedding night! He was stupefied by the intense emotions which he was reading in her face. He did not know how to deal with this kind of situation! If she so wished, she could claim rape or seduction. Just as serious, she could insinuate a love affair and perhaps force him to marry her.

Such thoughts alarmed him. Alisha, his precious Alisha . . . what would she think about a man who seduced a seventeen-year-old girl who was infatuated with him? What would it matter that he had no intention of doing so? He was guilty; that was all that counted. Besides, how could he deal with this strange girl who was pleased with his seduction, who clearly wanted him again this very minute? He felt trapped, a feeling that enraged him.

Noting Paul's apprehension concerning his vulnerable position and her welfare, Mary flashed him a serene smile. She slowly came over to sit upon the bed. She tenderly smoothed away the taut lines between his brows. She leaned forward and placed a kiss upon his full lips. Her forefinger drew circles in the air, indicating them and this situation, then it touched her lips to reveal her intent of secrecy.

"You won't tell anyone about this?" he asked to make sure he was comprehending her meaning correctly. She nodded no. "I didn't hurt you?" he asked once more. She nodded no. The look in her eyes told him more than that. "This is the first time you've . . . made love to a man?"

She flushed and lowered her head in shame and sadness. "The first time it was willingly done?" he inquired perceptively.

Startled eyes met his softened black ones. She nodded yes, tears glimmering brightly in her large sad eyes. Without thinking of how it would appear to her, he whispered, "I'm truly sorry, Mary. No man should ever take a woman by force. As long as I am here, no one will ever harm you again," he gallantly vowed.

She hugged him tightly, then began to spread kisses over his face. "Mary! Stop this!" he sternly commanded as soon as he realized how quickly her ardor was mounting. He had to forcefully remove her arms from around his neck. He held them imprisoned within his strong grasp as he tried to reason with the love-struck girl.

"We cannot do this again. Do you understand me? I cannot make love to you. It's wrong to take advantage of someone who cares for you. It's been so long since I've had a woman. Don't tempt me to forget myself again. You're a good girl, a kind and gentle one. But this isn't right between us. I love someone else."

His last words were like a brutal slap in Mary's face. She paled, then jumped off his bed. Confused by his mistaken change of heart, she pulled the curtain aside to gaze out as she sought to clear her muddled thoughts. That was when she saw Alisha and Jeffery standing in the street below. Alisha's back was to her, preventing any sight of her face. But from Jeffery's expression and gentle

261

touch, they seemed to be lovers whose eyes were only for each other.

Ecstatic that her friend Jeffery was making progress with his lady love, she grinned with happiness. Her own worries dimmed as she watched the way in which Jeffery was reaching out to Paul's sister. She glanced over at the silent, moody Paul. She hoped the sight of a joyous, love-possessed sister would soften his flinty heart and his cold resolve to prevent their newly discovered romance. She motioned for him to come to the window and to look out with her.

Hoping there was some action outside which might alter Mary's line of thought, he left his bed and came over to the window, the bedsheet wrapped snugly around his lower body. He followed her line of direction: Alisha was at Jeffery's mercy!

Rage filled his body. Murderous lights flickered in his eyes. He swore under his breath as he rapidly jerked on his clothes, suddenly thinking nothing about his nudity in Mary's presence. He rushed to his door, flung it open, and ran out without even closing it.

Mary hurried to the door and closed it before anyone could detect her presence in Paul's room. She could hear his boots making loud contact with only a few of the wooden stairs as he flew to his sister's side. Mary returned to the window, distressed by Paul's hasty departure and furious mood. She was confounded by his angered threat to kill Jeffery Gordon.

Powchutu raced outside just in time to see Jeffery's hand on Alisha's satiny cheek. His hatred and temper were boundless. He verbally attacked Jeffery, fully intending to beat him senseless. Alisha quickly intervened to prevent disaster.

Mary watched carefully as Alisha argued and reasoned

with both men, finally appearing to plead with them to make peace. It did not require a smart person to realize those two men were bitter enemies. It pained her tender heart to learn that the only two people she loved could feel such strong hostility toward each other.

How could she side with either of them? How could she give up either of them? She fretted over the help which she had given to Jeffery. Paul was so protective and affectionate with Alisha. Mary feared Jeffery's reaction to the news of her love for his sworn enemy. Yet, Jeffery had encouraged her to entrap Paul. Now, it was as if she was caught in a silent snare between them.

She witnessed the reluctance on both men's parts to make a truce, but had finally done so at Alisha's insistence. Mary decided that Alisha must have some sort of powerful control over both men, for they quickly consented to her wishes or to her demands. Jeffery had departed their company, leaving the two of them standing there talking. Soon, they turned and headed toward the hotel. From their expressions, all was at peace between them.

Mary abruptly leaned forward and keenly studied the look on her Paul's face. Surely she was not reading it correctly! She watched the glow in his eyes when he looked at her; she observed the way he touched her and spoke with her. Her heart gradually sank; nausea clawed mercilessly at her stomach. Without a doubt, there was love and desire written upon his magnetic features and shining in his obsidian eyes! Not sibling love, she painfully concluded, but passionate love! The love of a man for a woman!

How? her ravaged heart cried out. How could a brother be in love with his own sister? He had mistaken her for Alisha this very morning. It had been Alisha's name he had called out in the throes of unrestrained passion. He had wanted his sister, not her. But in a sexual way?

Her mind revolted from such thoughts. Surely there was some other explanation. They had separate rooms; she had observed them very closely. They had never been together long enough to . . . she could not even think such obscenities. Her mind promptly asked, why did Jeffery insist they have separate rooms? Why did he want them spied upon? Did he already know about their incestuous relationship? Was he trying to remove her from Paul's control? Was Alisha afraid of Paul? Why did they appear so nice and normal?

Recalling Alisha's panic and fear at Paul's sudden arrival in the street below, suspicion danced wickedly in her distressed mind. Did Paul have some evil control over Alisha? Did he refuse to permit her to see other men? Jeffery? Was this the basis for the animosity and contempt between the two men?

Unreasonable anger and hostility filled Mary at such lewd ideas and tormenting emotions. She decided to solve this riddle herself. She would take care of Paul, and Jeffery could have that bewitching girl. That should make everybody happy. But first, she needed more facts about all three people . . .

She walked over to the door, cautiously listening for Paul's return. She prayed he would not bring Alisha in here, then angrily changed her mind. Hearing Alisha's imploring tone, she pressed her ear to the door in alert eagerness. Only once before had she known such overwhelming happiness as she was feeling at that precise moment; both times had taken place during this same morning and in this same room. Her heart sang as she eavesdropped on the private conversation between Paul and Alisha.

"Please, Paul, listen to me," Alisha was entreating him. "I was only being cordial to Jeffery. We cannot allow anyone to learn we're not truly related. They would not understand our close friendship and innocent love for each other. They would judge us wicked and sinful for travelling together. We cannot allow them to learn we are escaping from Indian slavery. They would despise us and shun us. We're free now, Paul, free! When spring comes, we can return home. Until then, please don't give our secrets away by fighting with Jeffery."

Mary's ears perked up at the mention of her friend's name and at their connection with him. "Damnit, Alisha! How can I simply ignore the spiteful things he did to you back there? He has always hated me. He would stop at nothing to be rid of me for good. He wants you, and he knows I cannot permit his cruelty to start again here. He seeks revenge for your past rejection of him. He hates me because he thinks you chose me over him. Can't he see you only refused his advances? Can't he see you're not in love with me?" he stated, hoping she would deny his words. Fortunately, she did not.

Mary strained to hear this confusing, horrifying tale. "He was tragically mistaken, Alisha. He forced you to end your relationship with him. He shouldn't have been so demanding and intimidating. He didn't care about you; he only wanted you to be his mistress. He nearly raped you! If I hadn't been there to help you, God only knows what else he would have done to you. He made his intentions pretty clear to both of us." Mary winced at that disconcerting news.

Alisha's soft voice said, "But that was so long ago, Paul. Maybe he's changed. He did apologize for his meanness and demands. He offered us a truce. He says he won't tell anyone who we are. He knows the truth can destroy us. I know he was a cruel and malicious man; yet, we have no choice but to trust him. Please don't cause any more trouble. Spring will be here before we know it. We'll be gone from this harsh land. Lay aside your quarrel with him for at least a while. I cannot endure another Fort Pierre. Please . . ." she beseeched him. Mary literally shuddered at the agony heard in Alisha's tone of voice.

"He's up to some trick, Alisha. Don't trust him for an instant. It was his glory-seeking attack upon the Sioux camp which brought on that final massacre· at Fort Pierre. How the hell he escaped it beats me! Don't forget, he was one of the officers who sacrificed you to that red savage in order to save his own skin," he sneered in contempt.

"What choice did they have, Paul? When he demanded I be bound and sent out to him, there was no way that defenseless fort could have kept me from him. Such a waste, they were all slain anyway."

"Stop defending the cowardly bastards! You're too kind-hearted and forgiving. They could have died with honor, courage, and some dignity! To send a helpless female back to the Indian enslavement she had just escaped is unforgivable. Who cares if he claimed he wanted to humiliate the white man by forcing them to give you back for more torture! His trick wouldn't have worked if they had refused him. If Jeffery could get away with it, he would enslave you himself and kill me this very day! But he knows you would resist him to the death if he dared to do so."

"We could talk and argue all day, but it changes nothing. Neither do tears or pleas. The best thing we can do is wait and see what he has in mind. Don't call his bluff, Paul. Promise me you will avoid him. I will learn of his future intentions, if he has any . . ." There was a long, strained silence.

Then, Paul sighed heavily. "All right. But I will promise you something else, little sister, he'll never hurt you again or I'll kill him," he earnestly pledged.

"Just be patient and be careful. Control that hot temper of yours," she jested. "You're the only family and friend I have left; I could not bear to lose you or to see you hurt."

"I know, Little One. As hard as it'll be, I will try to be good. Get some rest this afternoon, and I'll see you at dinner." He escorted her to her room and saw her safely inside before returning to his own room.

Finding his door locked, he raised his brow in momentary confusion. Then, he recalled Mary's presence and this treacherous day's events. He lightly tapped upon his door, hope draining from his towering frame as it slowly eased open.

He walked inside and went to stand before the cheery fire. For a long time he stared into the colorful flames. When he could no longer postpone the inevitable, he faced the pensive, silent girl behind him. He wondered how much of their conversation she had overheard. There was only one way to find out.

"You heard?" he probed in a serious, distressed tone.

Meeting his worried gaze, she mutely nodded yes. "I see," he replied succinctly. He solemnly stated, "If you wish to betray my identity to the others, I couldn't blame you one bit. You have just cause after what I did to you this morning. But Alisha does not deserve any more torment. No woman has suffered more than she has in the past two years. Her people were massacred and she was captured by a warrior. I don't need to tell you about such an existence; I'm sure you've already heard about white squaws. Such a threat strikes terror into every white woman's heart and soul. You'd think they would be more sympathetic and understanding to girls who have endured such a life and horror."

His tone mellowed with memory. "I met Alisha when the soldiers from Fort Pierre raided his camp and rescued her. Some rescue! Those bloody soldiers treated her far worse than the Indians did! She had been beaten into unconsciousness shortly before her rescue, with a vicious whip, Mary. She was all bruised and bloody. She looked like a childish angel the first time I saw her. She was alone, afraid, and hurt. My heart went out to her that first minute. I sort of appointed myself as her guardian to protect her from all those lecherous men. As an ex-slave, she was considered a soiled dove. They hunted her and hounded her until she was afraid to leave her little room in the doctor's quarters. I was the only one she could trust."

Trying to select the words which might win him the most help, Powchutu went on. "That warrior who had first captured her came to the fort a few weeks after her arrival there. The brazen brave demanded we return her to him or he would wipe out the fort and everyone inside her walls! Do you know those cowardly soldiers tied her up and gave her back to him? You see, Mary, Alisha's brave held her responsible for the destructive raid which had saved her. Plus, he wanted to humiliate those 'brave' soldiers who had dared to ride into his camp while he was out," he scornfully snarled.

"During the ruckus of the massacre, I managed to escape the fort, dressed as an Indian. I made my way to his village and helped her to escape from him again. You know she isn't my sister, but I love her as if she were. I want to protect her from further harm and see that she gets back to her land. She's kind and gentle like you, Mary. She's a real lady, the only one I've ever met. Most of all, she was the only person who dared to befriend me or to respect a half-breed scout," he softly related his last clue to check her reaction.

He hoped and prayed with all his heart that he had not misjudged this sensitive, romantic girl. Powchutu told himself he risked lying to Mary only to protect Alisha . . .

"Will you keep these secrets, Mary? You know how whites feel about squaws and half-breeds . . ."

Mary walked over to his window and pointed outside. He came over and looked out. Seeing nothing, he curiously inquired, "What?"

She pointed to him, then toward Alisha's room, then back toward the street. "Me and Alisha outside? What about it?"

She held her hand up high, then mimicked Jeffery's stance. She made a fierce, angry expression and pointed outside again.

"You want to know about Jeffery? Why I stormed out of here that way?" She nodded yes, then sat down to listen.

"There's not much to tell, except we've always been enemies. You might say we were military rivals. We had different ideas on how we should deal with the Indian problems. Plus the fact I have some Indian blood in me. Jeffery made it clear from the start he despised any and all Indians. We were always clashing over orders. He couldn't stand for my advice to be taken over his, even if he was wrong. We fought and argued lots of times; it's a miracle we're both still alive. To Lieutenant Jeffery Gordon, I was about the lowest form of life around. He made certain everybody knew how he felt. He even went so far as to pressure the other men into treating me like he did. There's no friendship or respect where we're concerned. We could easily kill each other without a second thought," he informed her.

Staring at him with wide, searching eyes, she motioned toward Alisha's room. "Alisha?" Mary nodded.

Powchutu sighed heavily, wishing he did not have to include her in this explanation. "Jeffery led the raid on the Sioux camp where Alisha was imprisoned. There was one warrior there who was well-known for his prowess and for his daring raids on the whites and on other Indian camps. He was feared and awed by both sides. To be truthful, any man would gladly trade places with him!" he sneered enviously, instantly wishing he could retract his slip.

He hastily continued his tale, "Gordon and this notorious warrior crossed paths in battle many times. Trouble was that warrior always outsmarted him or made a complete fool of him. To defeat him became an obsession with Gordon. He dared any action which might prove victorious or challenging over that Indian. All he could think about was getting the scalp of the dauntless Wanmdi Hota. When I gave my report to General Galt about the meeting of the war council in the Blackfoot camp, he saw his one chance for successful revenge. He took his troops and raided Wanmdi Hota's camp while the warriors were gone. I don't have to explain how Wanmdi Hota took that slap in the face! He called on the entire war council to back him up in a raid on the white fort. With his reputation and power, he could dare anything, including a massacre at Fort Pierre." Powchutu was very careful not to give away Gray Eagle's name, fearing its horrifying effect upon Mary. Each time he spoke of him, he called him by his Oglala name.

270

"Wanmdi Hota was very cunning. He even talked his enemies into helping with that bloody raid with the promise it would wipe all white men out of that entire area. It did too! I never met a man as smart and crafty as he was. He cut off the fort's supply route and prevented their hunting trips. It didn't take long for the fort's food, water, and weapons to run low. One morning he rode up to the gates with a huge band of warriors and braves. Would you believe what he wanted? He boldly demanded for Alisha to be bound and returned to him as payment for Gordon's attack on his village! He promised not to attack the fort if they disgraced themselves by sacrificing her for their evil deed. Would you believe those cowards did as he commanded?"

His laughter was sarcastic and bitter as it filled the quiet room. "Trouble was he was tricking them. First he humiliated and terrified them; later, he let his warriors attack and destroy the entire fort. Gordon was one of those officers who insisted upon Alisha's return to the Indians. Gordon had been after Alisha ever since her rescue. He acted as if she owed him her life for his help. When she refused his attentions, she became his enemy too, just like me. That's how we became friends. We helped each other, comforted each other, and dreamed of freedom together. Alisha is gentle and special. She has no family except me. She had no money . . . nothing. How could I allow Wanmdi Hota or Gordon to ever hurt her again? She was the only person who treated me like a man, like a person. She became my friend; she helped me and respected me. Never once did she ask for anything in return. I owe her a great deal, Mary."

He walked over to the window and stared out at empty space. It was a short while before he continued his painful narrative. "I helped her to escape from the Sioux

271

camp; afterwards, we headed here. I am trying to help her get back to her own kind. We only pretended to be related to prevent any trouble. I didn't count on meeting up with Gordon here, or anywhere. He knows how much trouble and pain he could cause us if he reveals our secret. Without a doubt he still wants Alisha. In fact, he wants to pay us both back for what happened at Fort Pierre, just in different ways. I'm afraid he'll use that secret knowledge to get her in his clutches. How I hate to imagine what he'll do to either of us if she refuses him again! Worse, what he'll do with her if she relents . . ." he muttered to himself in apprehension.

All of this unexpected news stormed into Mary's confused mind. It was obvious that one of the men was lying and deceiving her. But which one, she wondered. It was extremely doubtful Paul would make up such an agonizing tale. Yet, Jeffery had not related any of these frightening facts to her. One truth settled in: Jeffery had lied to her about his feelings for Paul and Alisha. As tormenting as it was, Mary believed Paul was the one telling the whole truth. This conclusion led her to another one: Alisha and Paul were in great peril here.

Her tender heart went out to both Alisha and Paul, for both had suffered during the recent past. This new situation was adding up to form a tragic picture. She fretted over the implications of her naïve assistance to Jeffery. Paul was correct; Jeffery wanted Alisha, but for a much different reason than he had told her. Jeffery also hated Paul deeply and strongly. Hatred and revenge were powerful, deadly emotions which Mary feared.

She wondered how far Jeffery would go in order to gain his wishes, or how far Paul would go to thwart them. She shuddered as she came to realize that Jeffery might be as dangerous and as powerful as the many stories which she had overheard concerning him and his terrible deeds. Traitorous pain knifed at her heart as she viewed Jeffery's deception and betrayal, all for the information and assistance which she could bring to him.

She went to Paul. She lovingly and sympathetically caressed his slumped shoulders which carried such a heavy burden. He slowly turned around and met her steady, lucid gaze. "You do understand, don't you, Mary?" She nodded yes. "It's the truth, Mary; I swear it on my life and honor."

She smiled warmly and signalled her willing acceptance of his words. She pointed to herself, then lay her finger across her pink lips. He comprehended her signal for silence and secrecy. He grinned broadly, heightening his good looks. She flushed a rosy pink and timidly lowered her head. He gently grasped her chin, raised her head, and placed a brotherly peck upon her forehead. At a loss, Mary smiled and ran from his room.

She hurriedly returned to her assigned chores, knowing her uncle would soon return from his weekly hunting trip. He would be most angry if she were behind. Gaining new energy from Paul's warmth and faith, she merrily and rapidly finished the remainder of her work. Afterwards, she went to her small, dingy room to ponder the discoveries of the day.

Several days went by without any new crises and without a much needed job for Powchutu. Whenever possible, Mary spent time with Powchutu, listening to his tales about his past adventures—and falling more deeply in love with him. She cautiously and cunningly avoided any contact with Jeffery. To Alisha, she was extra nice and helpful.

Seeing such great hunger for friendship and understanding in the mute girl, Powchutu granted her his attention and kindness in exchange for her silence and her assistance to his beloved Alisha. Knowing how Mary felt about him, he wisely withheld the truth about his real feelings for Alisha from her keen perception. He also made certain the atmosphere between them remained amicable and uncomplicated. If he did appear to be misleading her emotions, he deemed it necessary in order to protect his true love. Powchutu knew unrequited love or cruel rejection could lead to trouble. If his company appeased Mary, then so be it for the time being.

On Thursday morning, Alisha received a scented note from Jeffery. It was an invitation to join him downstairs for dinner on that very same evening at seven o'clock. She nervously paced her room as she fretted over his first move toward her since last Sunday. He had granted her until Monday week to make her final decision about their future. Knowing there was no safe way which she could continue to put him off, she reluctantly sent a return note of acceptance.

The tormenting part now was to explain to Powchutu why she had agreed to see Jeffery. Eventually she convinced him this was the only way to study him and to learn of his coming intentions. He fumed and ranted, but was forced to give in to her. She spent the remainder of that afternoon preparing herself for that coming confrontation.

Mary did all she could to assist her with her grooming, but she also seemed as upset with Alisha's decision as Powchutu was. She could only reason that Mary also disliked and mistrusted Jeffery. Yet, Mary offered no explanation or advice, just cast worried glances in her direction.

In his state of turmoil, Mary persuaded Powchutu to have dinner in his room with her. He readily agreed, hoping she could keep his mind off of the circumstances and people below.

When the dinner and a moonlight stroll were over and Alisha was back in her own room, she admitted it had been a pleasant night: calm, refreshing, and entertaining. The conversation had been gay. Jeffery was indeed well-read, well-educated, and well-travelled. He was a witty, charming companion who possessed captivating savoir-faire. The dinner had been delicious. The dining room had been tranquil and their walk almost romantic.

To her surprise, the evening had passed swiftly and enjoyably once he had subtly and craftily relaxed her jumpy nerves and suspicions. She could not find fault with a single action or statement. That first moment when he had pulled out her chair to seat her at dinner, he had unexpectedly pleaded for a genuine truce and earnest attempt at compromise and friendship. Being on his most enchanting behavior, she soon found it impossible to resist his promise of a beautiful evening.

Returning to her room fairly early, Alisha thought it strange that Powchutu did not come to question her about her evening with his sworn enemy. Deciding he had rather not hear about such an annoying matter, she finished her nightly toilette and went to bed. She never guessed or suspected the reason why Powchutu could not come to her room that night.

Alisha carefully reviewed her evening with Jeffery. She shook her head as she chided herself for allowing him to disarm her. She had foolishly believed he had brightened his black soul. Jeffery hadn't changed at all; she had. For a time, she had slipped back into the civilization which she had lost after leaving England and the East. In many ways Jeffery was a great deal like she had once been. But did she truly miss the elegant gowns, the social gatherings and fancy balls, the servants, the witty banter, the carriage rides, the huge mansion, and everything else which her social rank and fortune had once given to her?

In all honesty, no. She would trade them all for a buffalo tepee, a doeskin dress, life on the open plains, rigorous chores, and her husband. No man could ever compare with Gray Eagle, especially not Jeffery Gordon!

Gray Eagle had taught her what it was to love, to be a woman, to be alive—really alive. How cruel fate was! It had given her the ultimate dream, only to brutally change it into a nightmare. How Alisha wished she could hate Gray Eagle as much as he had obviously hated her. Which was better, to have known him and lost him, or never to have known him at all? She honestly didn't know . . .

In Powchutu's highly agitated state, he had drunk too freely of the whiskey which Mary had stolen from her uncle's guarded supply. For the second time in his life, he got utterly intoxicated. He wanted to wipe out all visions of his Alisha with Jeffery, of his Alisha with Gray Eagle . . .

He was well into his cups before Jeffery and Alisha were halfway through their dinner. Reeling with dizziness and vexed with blurred vision, Mary had unbuttoned his flannel shirt to remove it and to help him into bed. She had hesitantly unbuckled his wide leather belt and unfastened his leather breeches. She slowly eased them down to his ankles, then followed them with his doeskin breechcloth. Knowing most men slept in the nude, she had done this before thinking.

As the straps gave way at her insistent tugging, her eyes instantly engulfed his slightly swollen manhood. Overwhelming desire inflamed her entire body. She gingerly pushed him down upon his bed, then pulled off his remaining garments. She eased off his high-topped moccasins and lay them beside the bed. She lifted his feet and placed them upon the lowered covers.

She inwardly knew she should leave his room immediately, but she could not force her feet to flee. She remembered their last union all too well. Her passion-filled gaze roamed over the full length of his muscular frame and his handsome features. He was a magnificent specimen of manhood, the best which she had viewed. His bronzed, firm physique demanded to be caressed and enjoyed. Desire controlled her, and she could not fight with its command.

She banked the fire for continued warmth. She lowered the lantern to give off only a soft golden glow. She removed her own garments and unbraided her auburn hair. She went to his side. Mary ran her trembling fingers through Paul's tousled hair of midnight black. She slid the palms of her hands across the enticing expanse of his chest. They leisurely travelled lower and lower, gently kneading his warm flesh as they moved past his flat, taut belly. They came to rest near his now erect and protruding member which had been aroused by her provocative teasing. Her respiration was ragged and swift, revealing her uncontrollable hunger.

The moment of decision was upon her. She knew she must either escape this tormenting situation, or she must carry out her dreams of another union with him. Her need for his love was unbearable. Throwing all modesty to the wind, Mary possessively encircled him and began to stroke. The effect of her fondling was instantly noticeable. Overpowering hunger seized her as she moaned with fervent desire and moved his hips beneath her hands.

He automatically reached up for her naked body and pulled it down to his. His mouth covered hers with heated kisses. He rolled her to her back and pressed her eager frame down into his mattress with the full weight of his body. He entered her without delay and began to grind out his craving. The tension built until he exploded within her. His whole body shuddered with the intensity of their joining, as did hers.

Mind still hazy, but clear enough to know who lay beneath him, he finally accepted the role which she was insisting upon him. If he couldn't have Alisha beneath him this way, then he would enjoy the delights of this insatiable girl's demanding body. And if this was to be the price for her continued silence, then he would comply with her charge.

Scrutinizing her closer, Powchutu readily admitted to himself Mary was a very pretty female. Most of all, she possessed a sensual, stimulating body and an eager spirit. His body tempted him to take her as his secret mistress while he was here; his mind agreed. From her previous actions, he reasoned she would come to him frequently.

He flashed her a lazy seductive smile. He felt the shivers which ran over her body as she thrilled to his mood. His dark eyes spoke of his satisfaction and of his rapidly returning hunger. "Mary, never has any woman so pleased me," he murmured the words he knew she longed to hear. "You love me as no other has. Never have I felt such pleasure. Even now I hunger for you again," he vowed as he placed her hand upon his swelling manhood.

"Your body was made for mine. See how they join in

such powerful union. I can give your body the affection it deserves, just as you have done for mine." Most of his claims were accurate, and he spoke them with an honesty and feverish emotion which Mary could not doubt. She smiled up at him as he spoke, snared by his rosy promises.

He huskily muttered, "We must keep these times between us a secret. I must find work and earn money. I need to send Alisha away from here before we can think of a life together. Guard our secret until that day. Until then, we have each other. Come to me whenever you need me or want me," he coaxed the love-struck girl, knowing instinctively that she would be willing more times than he would be.

Under the full potency of his spell, Mary quickly consented to his suggestions. He kissed her inviting mouth, closing his eyes and pretending it was Alisha's. Nibbling at her lips, he whispered, "This beautiful mouth is mine. And these are mine," he went on as he playfully nipped at her full breasts, firm with passion. He gently bit their taut nipples, licked their points, then captured one in his moist mouth.

His skilled hands and mouth began to tantalize Mary's entire body and dreamy mind. Soon, she was half-mad with flaming desire for him. She silently pleaded with him to take her. Wanting her to be in his complete control and unwilling to pleasure her demanding body this easily or quickly, he mercilessly continued his tormenting, addicting onslaught on her senses. When her supple body and frenzied mind were like putty in his masterful hands, he carried her over the edge of narcotic enslavement to him.

Totally exhausted and gratified, Mary slept deeply and peacefully within his arms. The effects of the whiskey dulled by sexual activity, Powchutu studied the girl beside him. He knew he had been mentally making love to Alisha, even sadistically punishing her for her rejection of his love. He, too, was gratified by his physical and emotional releases. He closed his eyes and slept for the next few hours, willing his keen mind to awaken in time to send Mary back to her room in order to prevent discovery.

Chapter Fourteen

Following that fiery night with Mary, Alisha noticed a subtle change in Powchutu. Although he said nothing, she sensed he was reserved and even distant. She could only assume he was sulking about her dinner with Jeffery. They still talked and laughed, but in a curiously guarded manner. They continued to take most of their meals together and strolled together each night. Yet, her feeling that something had radically changed between them persisted without explanation.

At first Alisha hoped this coolness would soon wear off—then she promptly altered her thought. She reasoned it might make her unavoidable verdict in Jeffery's favor easier for Powchutu to abide. She had learned Jeffery was the one who had been sending her the newspapers from back East and was also the one who was paying for her room service of hot tea and scones.

As the days went by, she became aware of another curious fact: Powchutu was spending a great deal of the day away from Horne House. She speculated he was still searching for work. Perhaps it was this unaccustomed leisure and feeling of helplessness which was making him moody and quiet. Another idea nagged at her own restless mind: why was he spending so much time in his room at night? He no longer lingered over dinner or suggested other diversions for them to share. Almost as soon as their meal and a rushed walk were over, he would practically fly to his room after a brief farewell. He carried on like he had some vital meeting with his own fate. Or was he only trying to avoid her and her company? . . .

Alisha struggled to conceal her hurt feelings and her rising doubts. If Powchutu was pulling away from her, then it was for the best. It was impossible for there to ever be anything serious between them. Jeffery's demand for marriage had ended any such dream he might have had. Yet, Alisha admitted she did not love or desire either of them. She knew she still loved just one man. So, she unwillingly, yet bravely accepted this mysterious, but necessary, alteration in their relationship, feeling somehow betrayed by him.

As for Mary, Alisha was at a total loss as to why she was suddenly so carefree and happy. Her velvety brown eyes radiated a new inner peace. Her movements bespoke energy and eagerness, feminine gracefulness and confidence. If Mary was not mute, she would no doubt go around humming or singing to herself, Alisha merrily concluded.

Suddenly Alisha perceived the reason for Mary's new-found tranquility and bliss: love! Feeling it an invasion of Mary's privacy, Alisha never questioned her about who the man was or how they had met. Never once did she connect Mary's new love life with Powchutu's withdrawal.

Alisha received a stunning blow on Wednesday when Jeffery asked her to have dinner with him and go for a carriage ride. When she anxiously approached Powchutu with her decision, he smiled sadly and simply nodded his assent.

After finishing their meal in strained silence, he abruptly grinned and stated softly, "How can I argue with the truth, Alisha? You do what you must. Stop worrying about me so much. In time, things will work out for the best. Just one warning, don't forget he can be dangerous and persistent. If he lays one hand on you, tell him I'll kill him," he vowed in a jesting tone which she found disturbing.

There was no need to kill Jeffery or to even upbraid him. Now he was on his best behavior. She felt stirrings of guilt because she did have such a wonderful, contented time with him. It was almost like meeting Jeffery for the first time. He used his disarming, dashing image to the hilt. She had to constantly remind herself of his goals and of his past torment. Soon finding this enforced reflection a painful and annoying chore, she allowed her mind to run along its own path at its own pace.

As for Jeffery, he was confident of his final conquest. The mere thought of controlling Alisha for life and the knowledge of how that total submission would torment Powchutu filled him with extreme joy and serenity. If courting Alisha would somehow affect her coming decision, then he would do whatever was necessary until she was enslaved to him by wedlock. If he could convince her she had nothing to fear from him, she would surely acquiesce to him. If he managed to disarm her to the point of actually falling in love with him, so much the better. What tastier revenge than to watch her squirm with unrequited love, with unsated passion, with the physical and emotional punishments which he had in mind for her!

But Jeffery also recognized two new problems to work on: Celeste and Mary. His plans for Powchutu and Alisha were going too nicely to have a brazen female mess them up for him. Mary had become totally mesmerized by that roguish half-breed. It had been a mistake to encourage her to take up with him. Jeffery had underestimated

Powchutu's charm and sexual hunger. He had mistakenly presumed that Powchutu wouldn't even glance at another female, much less begin a secret affair with her. Still, he might be able to somehow use this against him. The problem was this love was interfering with Mary's loyalty to him . . .

Mary had suddenly withdrawn from his deceitful attentions and from his service. She was clearly avoiding him. He would need to learn the extent of her relationship with Powchutu. He was not a man who dealt in suppositions. In time he would take care of foolish Mary.

Celeste . . . she was a whole different matter from dumb, trusting Mary. She could at least boast of some charm and intelligence—except where he himself was concerned. With him, Celeste was brazenly bold. If she thought for one instant she could blackmail him into taking her back under his protective wing by threatening to go to Alisha and Powchutu with the truth, she was fatally mistaken! The idea of her trying to force him into marriage was too absurd to consider.

Several plans were beginning to formulate in Jeffery's satanic mind. He was constantly working on a new plan to be rid of both Celeste and Powchutu in the same swift and deadly blow. He took his time with his plans, for plans were half the fun of any matter.

After Alisha was his legal wife and under his sole power, he would send Miss Mary O'Hara down the river to Frenchy's brothel. Soon enough he would be rid of all three and have the fourth in his possession. He chuckled sardonically. Soon, all of his problems would be solved and his high aspirations realized.

But without warning, Jeffery had to activate his plans, unformed and unsavored though they were. Powchutu paid him an unexpected visit on Thursday morning. The dauntless scout practically forced his way into Jeffery's wooden house.

Jeffery's gaze clashed furiously with the scout's matching one. "What brings you here on this fine morning, Paul?" he acidly taunted, scornfully speaking the assumed name.

"It's time we got a few things settled between us, Gordon. I won't waste time. Stay away from Alisha. I know you're up to some trick. I won't permit you to harass or frighten her again. I refuse to allow you to take her from me!" he angrily exploded, promptly coming to the point of his unanticipated visit.

"You refuse!" Jeffery sneered skeptically. "What if I also refuse? Just how do you plan to stop me from seeing her if she is so willing to forgive and forget? What about all those secrets I know about you two? How will the townfolk feel about Alisha, the ex-squaw of the infamous Gray Eagle? Or about Paul, alias half-breed scout who travels with a white girl? Or about dumb Mary O'Hara, the cheap slut who sleeps with the half-breed?" he contemptuously jeered.

The stunned, guilty look upon Powchutu's face at the mere mention of Mary and their secret affair instantly confirmed Jeffery's suspicions. Powchutu hastily blanked his eyes and expression, but too late.

Alerted to the surfaced animosity and growing danger within this man, Powchutu tensed for trouble. He remained silent as Jeffery burst into raucous laughter. He arrogantly seated himself in a plush chair, then leaned back to observe the effect of his words upon the scout marked for death. Just as Powchutu had cruelly played with Gray Eagle, Jeffery wanted to taunt, to humiliate, and to inflict countless painful wounds upon his enemy before killing him. Assuming a confident and fearless air,

Powchutu also seated himself and leaned back in his chair.

"Come now, Powchutu, surely you don't think Mary is your sole property. She's been taking care of my men for months. From what they tell me, she's completely insatiable. They say she's like a bitch in heat, never gets enough. Didn't she tell you about the show she put on for me with Tommy Hardy upstairs? Poor Tommy could hardly walk for a week afterwards."

"You filthy, lying bastard!" Powchutu shouted at him.

Jeffery only laughed maliciously. "I know personally she wasn't a virgin when you had her the first time. Tell me, were you drunk or asleep the first time she took advantage of you? You see, I do know her style. She plays the sweet, innocent female who is overcome with love and desire for you, willing to come to your room day or night."

Watching as Powchutu began to unknowingly fidget in his chair, Jeffery knew he was guessing accurately.

Pressing his advantage, Jeffery said, "If you weren't so busy next door with Mary, you might have realized your Alisha and I were just as active in the next room."

Just as Gray Eagle had let down his guard before falling prey to Powchutu, Powchutu's hunting sense was now dulled. Stunned by Jeffery's taunt that he had possessed his own Alisha, Powchutu was struck dumb, as dumb as the young servant girl.

Incapable of action, two men swiftly entered the room from curtains directly behind Powchutu's chair. Before the scout's limbs could react to his mind's command to tear the life from the sneering lieutenant, Jeffery's men seized Powchutu's hands and legs and tied them behind the back of the chair. He was utterly helpless.

Dismissing the men with a smug smile, Jeffery relished

the thought of how he would punish the arrogant half-breed.

Jeffery pulled a ladder-back chair over to face the enraged scout. He straddled it and sat down. He rested his arms on its high back, slowly sipping his crimson wine. "Now, let's get back to our Alisha. Might be helpful to hear if I knew more about her. I mean, what does she really like in bed from a man? She always does whatever I suggest, but I like to please my women too. She hasn't denied me anything. Nothing, Scout!" He mirthlessly laughed immensely enjoying his powerful position and his inevitable victory.

"I'll kill you, you son-of-a-bitch!" Powchutu swore as he strained against his bonds.

"Truth is, you've never had her; have you? You can't stand the thought of my having her when you haven't. Would you like to hear how she likes it best, Scout? Maybe hear how I make her pay for her stinging rejection at Fort Pierre? Bothers you to learn she enjoys my forcing her into my bed, sort of relieves her guilty conscience for her. Would you like me to tell you about the best things she does for me?" he asked.

That was the undoing of Jeffery's deception. Powchutu knew she would never sink that low in order to save either of their lives. He determined to expose Jeffery's trick. "Did you ask her to cut off that Injun tattoo on her right breast?" he sneered. "Knowing how you hate Injuns, no doubt the sign of one upon her body repulses you. Do you take her in the dark to avoid seeing it, or do you plan to cut off her breast to be rid of it?" he challenged.

Falling for Powchutu's ruse, Jeffery shot back, "Nope! It kinda gets me more excited to touch it. Just thinking about four or five Injun bucks holding her down while it was put there excites me."

Powchutu's taunting laughter filled the study. His smug look told Jeffery he had been duped. Without warning, Powchutu spit in his flushed face. "You'll never have Alisha Williams, you lying bastard! She'll kill you first!"

Jeffery flinched at his crude insult. He was livid with rage. He jumped up, knocking his chair over. He angrily flung the wine glass across the room, shattering it. He wiped the spittle from his hardened features. He balled his hand into a tight fist and drew it back to deliver a blow into the scout's treacherous, grinning mouth. Instead, the excruciating blow was forcefully delivered to his male privates.

Powchutu nearly retched and fainted. He stubbornly controlled his body against its torture. He knew he was going to die very soon, but he fiercely determined to do it with courage and honor. Jeffery laughed maniacally as he inflicted several more blows to that same, sensitive area. Yet, Powchutu never pleaded for his life or cried out from pain. He never called out for help, knowing it was impossible to be heard beyond this house.

As the punishment continued, Jeffery's chilling laughter increased. He breathlessly sneered. "You've had sweet Mary for the last time, and you'll never have Alisha!" With each time he struck the scout, Jeffery was fighting the fact of his degrading impotency.

Jeffery lifted a brass candlestick from his desk. He came forward and glared down at the helpless scout. Their eyes met and locked in silent battle. Annoyed by Powchutu's courageous silence, Jeffery declared, "I've waited a long time for this day, Scout. I always keep my promises, and I did warn you long ago you would get what you deserved. Rest assured I will also take similar good care of Mary and Alisha."

Powchutu's obsidian eyes glared at his killer. In the moment before his death he realized: all he had risked for Alisha's love was for naught.

Jeffery drew back his arm and forcefully slammed the heavy weapon against the scout's head. Not satisfied with only one blow, he repeated his action many times, fiendishly relishing the deadly thud of metal against flesh and bone. He then checked Powchutu's heart to make sure he was dead. Later, he called in his two men.

"Fetch that blond slut for me while I get out of these bloody clothes. Hide his body first; then clean up this mess. Make sure nobody sees Mary coming here. After you two have your fill of her, this is what I want you to do with both of them." He slowly and methodically laid out his diabolic plan for an "accident" that same afternoon.

"I'll be playing cards at the Horne House all day in plain view of many witnesses. Later, I'll have dinner with my future bride. I want the accident fixed and discovered by nightfall. Old Moses will be coming down that road about dusk; let him find their bodies and report it in town. Do everything just like I said; no mistakes, no changes, no witnesses. Until then, do what you will with Celeste. Just make sure she knows I ordered this punishment," he reminded them.

Jeffery's men, Slim and Tommy, rushed out, eager to carry out this plan. What could be better than having Celeste all day, then Mary very soon, and a large reward to boot? The plan went as scheduled. Slim secretly delivered the fake note to Celeste from Jeffery which summoned her to his house. She had been cautioned to secrecy until he could politely dismiss Alisha.

Filled with a heady sense of power over Jeffery and great happiness at being recalled to his company, Celeste did exactly as he ordered in his note. Not a soul saw her leave her shabby boarding house. Not a soul witnessed her arrival at Jeffery's. Slim opened the door and motioned her inside. He carefully looked out to make certain no one had seen her.

Over-confident, she giggled merrily and openly bragged on her stealth, unaware of the danger which she was now facing. Slim told her to go upstairs to the first bedroom on the right. He said Jeffery was dressing, but wanted to see her as soon as she arrived. Never having been in his bedroom, her eyes lit up with anticipation and excitement. She haughtily threw back her shoulders and rushed up the steps, arrogantly dismissing Slim with a vain sneer. A flip of a coin had given Tommy the first chance with her. Slim's hand quickly covered his mouth to conceal his vindictive laughter.

Celeste opened the door without even knocking first and walked into the dimly lit room. Before she could detect any danger, Tommy stunned her with a blow to her head. He leaned out the door and called Slim to join him. They hurriedly undressed her, carefully avoiding any rips in her clothing which could suggest a different story from the one planned.

After relentlessly and cruelly working their wills upon Celeste—first while she was unconscious, and then after she had come to—the men beat the young woman on the head with the same candlestick that had been the instrument of Powchutu's death. Once, twice, thrice they struck, and Celeste breathed her last.

Careful to make Celeste's death appear accidental, they cleaned off the evidence of their foul deeds. Then, wrapping Powchutu and Celeste in tarpaulins, they loaded the bodies on a wagon at the servant's entrance of the Gordon residence. Soon, their evil would be done . . .

Back at the Horne House, Mary was serving drinks to the men involved in the lengthy card game in one corner of the dining room. She wished it would soon end so she could go to her lover's room. She was worried about him. He had been gone since early morning. She hoped he had returned to his room while she was in the kitchen. She fretted over the endless game which had been going on since mid-morning. She glanced out the front window. It was nearly dusk. Soon, she would sneak up the back stairs to check on him. Jeffery's presence did nothing to ease her tensions.

The game did end at dark. The men stood around chatting, joking, and having one last drink which was compliments of the winner Jeffery. They slowly filtered out into the gathering shadows of darkness. Jeffery sent Mary upstairs with a note for Alisha which told her to come downstairs to join him for dinner. After handing Alisha the note, Mary hurried to Powchutu's room.

Expecting Jeffery's eventual summons, Alisha was dressed and waiting. Still, she let him simmer for a short time before coming down to join him. She smiled sweetly as he took her cold hand and kissed its palm. She quickly withdrew it, irritated by her unexpected reaction to such a simple action. He chuckled, then led her into the dining room. He graciously seated her. Before he took his own seat, the front door was flung open with a loud bang.

Moses Johnson dashed to the front desk. His shabby appearance did nothing to flatter his giant, husky frame. He asked in a raspy voice if the proprietor knew of a certain young man. Giving a full and colorful description of Powchutu, Jamie recognized his guest Paul Williams. Acknowledging his identity, he asked why Moses was interested in him. It wasn't necessary for Moses to give Celeste's description, for he knew her on sight.

His deep voice was difficult to ignore. For some unusual reason, the Horne House was empty tonight—except for Jeffery, Alisha, Mary, Moses, and Jamie. Mary curiously listened to the commotion from downstairs through a small crack in Powchutu's door.

Jeffery went to the front desk to check out the quality of his plan. He had shut the door to the dining room after his departure, but Alisha had quietly eased it open a crack in order to hear what the ruckus was all about.

Moses continued, "It was a foul sight. Never seen nothing like it in me entire life. You say this Paul has a sister staying here? You sure don't want her to hear about this crude thing her brother done. You should'a seen 'em, all sprawled out naked on the ground. That tree fell on 'em right whilst they was commencing to fornicate. Should say for the third or fourth time from the smell of 'em. Struck down in the very act! Never seen nothing like it," he repeated with amazement.

Jamie curiously inquired, "You mean this Paul Williams and Celeste was rutting on the ground when a tree fell on them and kilt 'em both?"

"Damn right, Jamie! I put 'em back in their wagon and brung 'em here. Didn't rightly know what else to do with 'em."

Jeffery spoke up, "Paul's younger sister is in the dining room right now. We don't want her to learn about this vile matter. Take the bodies over to Slim. Tell him I said to fix coffins for them and to seal them. We'll say they were killed in a runaway carriage accident. Say they're too broken up to look at. Miss Alisha doesn't deserve to have this thing put upon her shoulders. We'll make it sound like an accident, agreed?" he stated in his bold, authoritative tone.

Jeffery had glimpsed Mary's face as she had peered out the scout's door and down the stairs, but he did not let on he had sighted her. He subtly checked the dining room door from the corner of his eye, knowing how curious all women were. Viewing its slight movement and lighted slit, he knew both females were already advised of the scout's death and its vulgar circumstances. Seeing an opportunity to take advantage of his timely presence, he pretended to try to protect Alisha from embarrassment and emotional pain and to protect her brother from dishonor. Also knowing of Mary's alert ears and keen senses of perception, he hoped to dismiss any suspicions she might have.

"Alisha is a very sensitive and well-bred young lady. It would hurt her deeply to hear such distressing news. What could the truth serve in this matter? Are you certain they weren't robbed and murdered?" he asked for both women's benefits.

"No sign of such. Appears to me it was a vengeful act of God Almighty. I tell you, they was right in the very act! They pulled off the road a piece, stripped naked as the day they was born, then fell to the ground, and joined like animals in mating season. He seed their sinning, and He flung that tree down on 'em. Both they heads was crushed flat! Both dead as iron nails," he commented dramatically.

Mary eased from Powchutu's room and raced down the back stairs to her own room. Alisha thought she would surely be sick on that very spot. She went to the table and slowly sipped some cold water. She dampened a cloth napkin and mopped her brow. She slowly sank into the chair. She was numb with grief and shock.

Powchutu's death was difficult enough to believe, but the lewd manner of it ripped at her naïve heart. Alisha blamed herself for pushing him into the fateful arms of another woman. If she had agreed to marry him, he would still be alive. If only she hadn't made it appear she was turning away from him and turning toward Jeffery. No doubt he had been too ashamed to take a woman like Celeste into his room in fear of her discovering it.

She could not help but wonder if this relationship with Celeste was where he had been spending his days and nights. She also wondered if this was the explanation for his abrupt change of heart and his distant mood. She could only assume that Celeste and Powchutu had come together following their rejections by her and Jeffery. Now, they were both dead.

She reasoned it was possible that Powchutu had just needed a woman in a sexual way. It was rumored that men had to have sex and to have it frequently. Perhaps Powchutu had incredibly fallen in love with this other female. She would never know the truth now, for he was gone from her life. Agony and emptiness flooded her body. How could she survive without him? she cried sadly.

Jeffery opened the door and came inside the dining room. He observed her for a few minutes, smiling at his genius. He was now rid of two annoying problems. Soon, he would have his other two resolved to his great satisfaction. He came forward and knelt before her. His face assumed a look of sorrow and pity toward her.

"You heard?" he solicitously asked, a feigned look of sympathy in his blue eyes.

"Part of it," she reluctantly admitted as fresh tears

began to ease down her pale cheeks. "He's dead," she painfully stated. "You're all positive it's Po . . . Paul?"

"As much as we disagreed and fought, Alisha; I am truly sorry, for your sake. He was a good friend to you. Sure I disliked him, even hated him. But I do feel sympathy for you over his loss. Much as I hate to admit it, he was quite a man." He paused dramatically. "If you don't object, I'll see to the coffin and burial for you. Unless you'd rather I didn't . . ." He left his sentence hanging, its meaning clear.

Alisha's ravaged heart could stand no more tonight. She didn't want to think of anything, much less her friend's funeral. Jeffery was the only one who could help her shoulder this unwanted responsibility. "If you will be so kind as to do this for me, Jeffery, I will be very grateful." With tears now streaming down her cheeks, she pleaded softly, "Could you also place a marker on his grave? He never really had a name to be proud of. I should like him to be buried as my brother. Can you do that for me?"

"The marker will read, Paul Williams. Don't fret, love. I'll see to everything for you. Do you want me to send Dr. Cramer over with a sleeping potion? Or perhaps something to calm your nerves a bit?" he tenderly suggested.

"No thank you, Jeffery. I would prefer to deal with this tragedy as quickly as possible. I've known great losses before: my parents and my uncle. The longer you postpone your grief and acceptance, the harder it is for you. I just need to be alone for a while. You don't mind if I skip dinner, do you?" she implored in a trembling tone, praying he wouldn't force his attentions and control over her on this particular night.

He politely shook his head. "I'll see to the burial and everything else, love. You get some rest. If you need anything at all, just send me word through Jamie O'Hara. Understand?"

She absently nodded yes and thanked him for his assistance and understanding. He walked her to her room, suggested she call for Mary if she needed anything later, then left her at her door. She walked inside and closed the door. She leaned back against its hard, cold surface. Her heart felt in a painful vise.

"First my parents . . . then all my friends and Uncle Thad . . . My precious, unborn child . . . Powchutu . . . My husband . . . Gray Eagle, why did you do these terrible things to me? If you had loved me and kept me, none of this would have happened. You said you loved me and wanted me. Why did you lie? Why? How long will I pay for loving you? Will the pain and emptiness ever go away? Now, Powchutu is gone, too. I have no one, no one to love. Why couldn't you have killed me instead of betraying me this way?" She sank to the floor and gave herself over to uncontrollable weeping.

Yet even as she cursed Gray Eagle's betrayal, Alisha longed to have him here with her and comforting her. How she wished he could magically appear and enfold her within his strong arms, and tell her that everything would be all right. But he was many miles and a lifetime away.

She recalled another day long ago when she had been so afraid, so alone, and so tormented: that day Gray Eagle had attacked Fort Pierre and recaptured her. He had been there for her on that agonizing day. Why couldn't he be here now? Why hadn't he spared her this terrible pain and loss?

Alisha shivered. How she longed to return to that sunny autumn day! Gray Eagle had actually challenged an entire fort for her possession. Once back in his life, he had held her with love and gentleness. When Black Cloud had taken her from Gray Eagle claiming she was his daughter Shalee, Gray Eagle had fought a duel to the death to regain her. He had married her. He had vowed love for her. Where were his love and acceptance on this wicked day? She had given him everything; what did she gain in return?

"I need you, Gray Eagle. Where are you?" she sobbed in pain.

Jeffery returned to his house to meet with his men. He congratulated them on their excellent job and suggested a victory celebration: a victory which had been a long time in coming. The three men drank and talked for hours. Slim and Tommy related their amorous adventures with Celeste.

"Just like you said, Mr. Gordon, she took real good care of us. When she thought we was only going to punish her and let her go, she was eager and willing to have a good time with us. She did anything we said. Geez, but we hated to stop and git rid of her. Hope you have another female like her to punish real soon," he hinted openly.

"As a matter of fact, I do. That is, if Tommy doesn't mind sharing his reward with his best friend. If so, I'll have to find you some other wench, Slim," he suggested, intending to reward both men at the same time.

"Shucks, Mr. Gordon, I don't mind sharing with Slim at all. We work real good together. When kin we have a go at 'er?" he eagerly questioned, licking his dry lips.

"I told Miss Williams we would kindly take care of the coffins and burial for her. I say we get things ready for the funeral by tomorrow evening. Get some men to help you dig two graves. We can't have you two hurting your backs right before a big night. I'll pay a dollar to each man; hire about three or four. Of course we'll take care of the arrangements for our dear, departed friend Celeste. We'll say our sad farewells and put them in the ground on Saturday," Jeffery informed them, without a hint of remorse.

They joined in raucous laughter as he refilled their empty cups for the countless time. "No need to delay getting rid of 'em. The sooner they're planted, the better. Fix me a nice marker with his name on it. Put it at the head of his grave. That should be worth a real nice reward from his sister."

"You still planning to marry his sister?" Tommy asked, hoping he had changed his mind, increasing their chance to have her too.

"That's the reason why I got rid of her troublesome brother," Jeffery calmly stated. "As for you two, I'm going to send for Miss Mary on Sunday morning while her uncle's out hunting and everyone else is at the service. I'll spend the day with my bride-to-be, and you two can use that same room upstairs. I'll fix her up good before I leave. After four days and nights without her lover, she'll be eager to please a man."

When Friday came, Alisha refused any company all day. She could not bring herself to speak with anyone, including Jeffery or Hiram. She did not eat all day. She just sat on her small sofa, recalling their mutual past. The realization finally settled in on her that he was gone forever, that she was on her own once more. No matter what Powchutu had done, or how he had died, he would always be a very special part of her life and her memories.

Later that night, she fell across her bed and slept deeply from sheer exhaustion. Her soul-searching, weeping, and lack of food had finally taken its toll. She did not stir until early Saturday morning.

As for Mary, she concealed her torment in hard, draining work. She mindlessly went about her daily chores. She even assumed extra duties in order to force her body into forgetful fatigue. Unable to speak, she could not share her grief with anyone. Besides, how could she say anything about their love affair and future marriage? No one would understand her great loss or her endless love for him. No one would see the agony which she had endured since learning of how he had died.

Her heart pleaded there was some other explanation for the traitorous situation which Moses had so vividly described. Somehow that sluttish Celeste had tricked Powchutu into betraying Mary and their precious love. Her body hungered for his; her heart ached with loneliness and grief.

Mary could not even bring herself to visit Alisha, to learn if she was all right. Her uncle had told her that Alisha wished to be left alone with her suffering and sadness. She knew Alisha had stayed in her room since the fateful news had arrived. Yet, Mary felt her loss was greater and her pain deeper. He and Alisha were only close friends; she and Paul were lovers. How could she feel sympathy for Alisha when she needed it all for herself?

On Saturday, the funeral only lasted a few minutes. Hiram generously and kindly gave the brief service at the graveside. Afterwards, the few who politely or curiously attended Powchutu's service spoke meaningless clichés of comfort to Alisha and then hastily departed. Knowing it was best to leave her alone on this stressful day, Jeffery placed a loving kiss upon her forehead, said a few tender words, then left her with Hiram. Hiram did much the same, then walked away with his tearful wife to await Alisha in their wagon.

Alisha knelt beside the fresh grave. She stared at the ugly dark mound of black dirt which glittered with small crystals of ice. She lifted her bleary eyes skyward. Such pain, bitterness, and emptiness filled her heart and mind at his untimely death. He was so vital and young that even the elements rebelled against his premature departure from life.

The sky was shrouded in a sorrowing gray cloak. The laden clouds wanted to shed tears of chilling ice. The bitter winds wailed a mournful song. The sun declined its brilliant light and comforting warmth. The frozen earth nearly refused to be invaded for this dire purpose. Death had surely claimed this one too soon . . .

Alisha searched her heart for the words to say her last farewell to her beloved friend and loyal protector. "How does one say goodbye forever? How can I simply walk away and leave you here alone? It's so hard to know I shall never see your smile again, never hear your laughter, never speak to you from the very depths of my soul. How can I forget all you have done for me, all you are to me? I am to blame for your death. Perhaps you would still be alive if you had not bravely rescued me and brought me here. Was my freedom worth your life? I fear not, my friend. I would gladly exchange my freedom to have you back alive again. God, I feel so empty and alone now. Why, Powchutu? Why did you have to die and leave me?" She wept for a time, then gradually controlled her wracking sobs.

"You never really had a chance at freedom and happiness. You were so very special and unique. It is wrong for you to be dead! I wonder what your life would have been like if you had been born a white man or an Indian. Middle ground has no purpose. You had so much to give, and they wouldn't permit it. Damn them all! God, how I hate this vile, cruel country! I hate what they did to you, to both of us. So much hate and destruction . . . I shall pray for you each night, both to my God and to your Great Spirit. In all that truly counts, you are my brother. Never could I have loved or needed you more if we were truly kin. How I wish I could trade my life for yours. I love you, Paul Williams; I honestly love you . . ."

Alisha tightly gripped the heavy, wooden marker which proclaimed the words, "Paul Williams, Beloved Brother," and wept bitterly.

Hiram returned to check on her. Finding her sobbing as if her tender heart would surely break, he pulled her to her feet and hugged her. "You must let him go now, Alisha. He is now in the hands of the Maker. He wouldn't want you to suffer this way. Come, we'll return to the Horne House for some hot tea," he urged.

Alisha allowed herself to be taken from that dismal place. No one even noticed the mute girl standing in the nearby shadows. When everyone had departed, she slowly approached the grave. She silently wept for her lost love, thinking and feeling many of those same things which Alisha had said. She remained at the site until darkness and cold forced her to return home.

This being the Sunday for services, Mary decided it was time to face Alisha. She went to her room to see if she needed any help with dressing. Giving their pre-arranged signal, Alisha finally opened her door to permit Mary to enter. The room was dark and chilly, and Alisha was not making any effort to leave.

Mary stared into her pale, sad face with its look of

301

anguish. She noted the darkened smudges beneath her large, glassy eyes. She saw her listlessness. It was clear she had no intention of going out. Mary fervently wished there was something she could say or do for this girl who had been so special to her beloved; there was not.

Another knock came to her door. The voice of Jamie O'Hara called out to Alisha. "I'm not dressed yet, Mr. O'Hara," she stated through the closed door. "What do you want?"

"I hate to bother you at a time like this, Miss Williams, but your room and board are paid only through tomorrow morning. Do you plan to stay on here?"

Stunned by this heartless news, she replied, "I'll let you know in the morning. Is my brother's room still vacant?"

"Yes'um. You have both rooms rented until tomorrow at noon. After that, you'll have to pay or leave. I can't afford charity. I mean, I'm sorry about your brother and all, but I run a business here."

"I understand perfectly, Mr. O'Hara," she tersely stated. "Either I will pay you by noon, or I'll leave. Does that suit you?" she scoffed angrily at his cold-blooded intrusion.

"That's fine, Ma'am. See you tomorrow."

She listened to his retreating footsteps, forgetting about Mary's presence behind her. "You hateful beast! You could at least allow me a few days to get my affairs settled. No one cares about people anymore. Where did human kindness go?" she murmured sadly.

She whirled around to fetch the key to Powchutu's room and retrieve his possessions. Her gaze locked with Mary's. Alisha flushed with shame. She stammered, "I forgot you were here, Mary. I didn't mean to speak ill of your uncle; he just stunned me with his news. I guess I better go to Paul's room and get his things," she said, dreading to carry out her words.

She went to the bedside table and unwrapped the bundle left for her by Moses. There was a sheathed hunting knife, a few coins, and a room key inside the dirty cloth. Tears eased down her face. "Such a meager amount to represent a man's life, isn't it? He was a loner until we . . ." she halted just before giving away a secret which Mary already knew.

"He was a good man, Mary. He was so kind, and gentle, and helpful. I wouldn't be alive if it wasn't for him. He was the only family I had left. God, how I miss him already. Such a wonderful and loving . . . brother . . ."

She quickly threw on a dress and combed her hair. She splashed cold water upon her face and dried it off. She left her room and approached his with great reluctance and sadness. She put the key into the lock and turned it. She shoved the door open and went inside. Her eyes roamed the depressing, somber room. It had none of the color and richness which hers did. She wondered how he had endured this dismal room for so many hours. She wondered if Celeste had been a stimulating diversion from this gloom.

She cast such thoughts aside and collected his scant belongings. She would decide later what to do with them. Yet, she could not bear the thought of some cold stranger disposing of them. She searched the drawers for their money. Not finding it, she began to intently search the entire room. Mary came into the room and closed the door behind her.

She also allowed her gaze to roam this tormenting room, but for reasons vastly different from Alisha's. She had loved and emotionally died in this very room. How could she ever clean it again? How could she ever watch some other man sleep in here?

Noting Mary's appearance, Alisha frantically asked, "Mary, could you help me look for our money? Paul always kept it. I cannot find it anywhere. There was none with him except a few coins. Where could he have hidden it?"

Responding to the distress in Alisha's tone, Mary joined in on her treasure hunt. Later, the room had been thoroughly gone over from top to bottom, from side to side. There was no money. She glanced at Mary and asked, "Could he have left it with your uncle?"

Mary hurried to fetch him. He joined Alisha in Powchutu's room. She explained about their missing money. To her dismay, he informed her that he knew nothing about any money. She argued, "But I know he had it with him! He paid for the things which we bought. Perhaps it was stolen, or he was robbed," she suggested.

"Surely you aren't suggesting I had something to do with this missing money!" he shouted indignantly.

"Certainly not, Mr. O'Hara!" she replied in the same tone.

"You've had the key, Miss Williams. Nobody could come in here without it. If he left any money in this room, it would still be here. I swear to you he didn't leave any with me. A man would be a fool to trust another man with all of his money or to carry it around with him out here. Your brother didn't strike me as dumb. I bet he buried it somewhere. He was always out most of the day. I bet he hid it and took only what he needed with him. If'n that's the case, there's no telling where it is," he stated her worst of fears without a single hint of sympathy.

Before thinking, she cried out in alarm, "What shall I do without any money?"

304

"For one thing, you can't stay here free! I don't cater to unpaying guests. I'm sorry as I can be for you, but that won't put money in my pockets or food in my belly," he bluntly informed the startled Alisha.

"You would actually throw me out in the street if I cannot pay you tomorrow? You wouldn't even give me some time to work something out? Perhaps borrow some money from a friend?" Her voice was shaking with emotion and her eyes were wide with anxiety.

"It's none of my affair, but you already owe Mr. Gordon quite a huge sum of money for these past weeks he done paid for. Your brother ain't give me nothing on your bill; he seemed contented to allow Mr. Gordon to pay for it all. Paid until tomorrow noon, that is," he casually reminded her of his deadline.

Deadline! Tomorrow was also Jeffery's deadline for his demand for marriage. It was perfectly timed; both deadlines would fall upon her slender shoulders at the same time.

Jamie coldly continued, "As for borrowing money from some friend, Miss, I doubt it can be done during winter. Folks here just bearly exist themselves. They sure can't give away their own survival. It ain't even right to ask, if you ask me," he sneered.

Alisha wanted to scream at him, "Who is asking you?" But she did not. Without a doubt Powchutu had continued to permit Jeffery to pay their bills in order to hold on to their meager funds; now they were irretrievably gone.

After Powchutu's recent death, would Jeffery still insist upon her immediate capitulation to his demands? Of course, he would, Alisha realized. Powchutu was not even a friend of his. Now that she was penniless and

305

alone, she would have no excuse to put him off. What argument could she give to stall him? There was none. Clearly she would be in Jeffery's clutches by nightfall Monday!

She glared at the irascible, unfeeling man who owned this house of pain and selfishness. "You have my word, Mr. O'Hara: either the money or my departure by nightfall." She picked up the little bundle and raced past him to her own room. She loudly and emphatically slammed the door and bolted it.

Jamie went down the steps and met the waiting Jeffery in the back hallway. "You told her?" Jeffery arrogantly inquired.

Jamie nodded his head, then replied, "I told her to pay up by noon or get out of my hotel. Nicely of course. She was searching her brother's room for some money she claims he had with him. Weren't none there. Appears she don't have none. Shame for such a pretty girl to be all alone and poor." Jamie hinted with a lecherous note in his tone and sparkles in his beady eyes.

Jeffery grinned. "Not for long, O'Hara. Within a few more days, she'll be my new wife."

"You're gonna marry her! Why? You already got her at your mercy and in your debt!" he shouted in astonishment. "Why you being so mean to her if you're gonna wed her?"

"What kind of plans did you think I had for a woman like her? You underestimate her, O'Hara; she's the marrying type. With her money and brother gone, she'll willingly accept my proposal of marriage. See to it she has whatever she needs until noon Monday; after then, she gets not so much as free water and bread. Savvy?"

Jamie agreed to his relentless terms, then put the gold

coins into his grimy pocket. He walked away to return to his work. He wouldn't concern himself in other people's problems!

Jeffery turned to find Mary standing in the shadows of the storeroom. He went over to her. She quickly retreated a few steps. He grimaced in disapproval. It was past time for her to receive a justly earned lesson . . .

"You've been avoiding me lately, Mary," he said solicitously. "Why? You even act afraid of me. Have I ever harmed you in any way? No! I know you overheard my talk with your uncle. Just so you don't misunderstand, I love Alisha and want to marry her. If she doesn't have any place to go, she'll come to me sooner. She's confused and hurt right now, so I have to use trickery on her. See? I was going up to see her, but your uncle says she is real upset right now. I'll wait until tomorrow."

His tone of voice changed very noticeably as he casually said, "Paul came to see me shortly before his accident. I got the idea he was about to leave here for good. He was in a strange mood when he stopped over and left some things with me. There's a package for Alisha and one for you. I didn't know you two had become such good friends. I was waiting for Alisha to settle down before I handed her a gift from him. But if you want yours, I can send it over by Slim. Or you can come over to get it. Whatever . . ."

His false concern disarmed her. At the mention of her lost love, the fearful lights left her eyes for joyous ones to enter. Her face actually beamed with love and happiness. "I can see you want it as soon as possible. If your uncle doesn't know about Paul and you, it might be best if he doesn't see you come after that gift. It might be something real personal. He did grin when he handed it to me.

307

Wait until Jamie leaves, then sneak over to my house like you used to do.''

At the glint of suspicion in her gaze, he cunningly inquired, ''You sure you don't want me to send it over by Slim? It won't be any trouble for him. I wouldn't let Jamie see it,'' he added, winning her trust again.

She nodded no, and he smiled with deceptive geniality. ''You're a smart girl, Mary. Afraid your uncle might take the gift away from you?'' She nodded yes. ''Well, you do what you like. Do you want to come after it?'' She nodded yes. ''I can promise you a surprise and your uncle won't get any of it.'' He laughed, knowing he had the grieving girl eating out of his hand.

Mary smiled brightly. She rushed away to complete her chores. After her uncle's departure, she looked around to make certain there was nothing for her to do until morning. As was her custom, she walked out of the house and headed in the opposite direction from Jeffery's home. Once she was out of sight, she circled back in the edge of the woods. She gingerly approached the back door. She tapped lightly and waited for an answer.

Jeffery and the other two men had been eagerly watching Mary's stealthy mission. He sent them upstairs to await his call. He went to let Mary inside. He led her into his study. He handed her a glass of wine and told her to drink it to settle her nerves. He warned that she might become upset by this loving contact with her lost friend. As he pretended to retrieve the package, she quickly and unknowingly emptied the glass. Feeling dizzy almost immediately, she promptly sat down on the sofa.

''Are you all right, Mary? You look a bit pale. Here, have some more wine,'' he coaxed softly.

She nodded her reluctance, but he sweetly insisted.

"Here, just a little more," he urged.

He held the glass to her lips and tilted it up. She drank it quickly, suddenly very thirsty. "More?" he inquired politely. She nodded yes. He poured more into her glass. Knowing she was too far under to see what he was doing, he opened the small packet and dumped its chalky white contents into her next glass. He held the glass to her lips while she drained it.

"Feeling better now?" he crooned in a mellow drawl. Mary smiled and sighed in contented relaxation. She began to pull at her neckline and to lick her dry lips. "You're hot and thirsty, aren't you?" She nodded yes.

"Why don't I just remove this dress so you can cool off a wee bit?" Beyond any resistance, Mary permitted him to remove her ill-fitting dress. "Still hot?" he inquired, familiar with the lustful reaction to this drug.

She nodded yes. He handed her another glass of wine. "Drink it, Mary," he commanded in a firm tone. She gulped it as he leisurely removed the rest of her shabby garments.

"Stand up and let me have a good look at you." She obeyed the hypnotic voice which commanded her. She felt warm and tingly all over. Her body flamed and yearned to be touched. Feeling a tempting hand upon her breast, she writhed in growing need and pleasure.

"Does that feel good, Mary?" She nodded yes. "Lay down on the sofa," the crooning voice calmly ordered.

She mechanically obeyed. "That's a good girl. I want the answers to some questions. The truth, understand?"

She nodded yes to each question he asked. "Were you sleeping with Paul? Did you love him? Was it good with him? Did you go to him first?" He worked as he talked, receiving the expected answers. He picked up a cloth to wipe off his fingers.

"Come with me, Mary. Paul is waiting for you upstairs. You must please him in every way." He led her up the steps as he spoke to her, implanting these suggestions within her mind.

He opened the bedroom door. Eyes and breeches bulged as the naked girl strolled into the room. "Go to the bed and lie down, Mary. Make yourself ready for Paul."

She meekly complied.

He glanced at the wide-eyed Slim. "You won the toss?"

Slim nodded yes, unable to take his eyes off of Mary's lush body. "Then have a go at her. Paul's here, Mary. Do anything he says."

Slim licked his lips. "You gonna watch us?"

"Maybe for a little while," Jeffery replied. "I must admit, I enjoy seeing females like Mary and Celeste getting their just desserts."

At four o'clock in the morning, Slim and Tommy cleaned Mary up and put her clothes back on her. On Jeffery's orders they hauled her over to the graveyard and lay her upon Paul's grave. Slim took an opened box and placed it at her side.

By the time Mary came around, she would believe she had walked to the grave and had erotic dreams all night. She might blame it upon the wine or upon her grief, but she would not recall any clear faces or details of her night. She would see the gift which Paul had supposedly bought for her, a beautiful pink dress, and believe herself temporarily possessed by delusions.

Slim and Tommy carried out Jeffery's orders without question, knowing they would soon be sharing Mary for keeps. With any luck, Jeffery might drug her again as payment for some future service. The two men decided to look for ways to help Jeffery or to persuade him to help them.

"You were right, Tommy," Slim said, "no need to stop such rewarding work. Truth is, she makes you wanna be her slave."

Chapter Fifteen

Alisha stared at the unfamiliar girl in her mirror, the one with the ashen face and blank eyes—face and eyes which were just as devoid of joyous emotion as her aching heart was. She wondered why hideous Fate had stormed into her new life and wreaked such devastation upon it. Life for Alisha had begun as a beautiful golden thread. But each time happiness and freedom loomed foremost on her horizon, the thread would tangle and knot. More than once in these past two years she had fervently prayed for a simple end to her endless misery . . .

It was Wednesday, January 16, 1777. Here she stood before a tall, oval mirror in the bedroom of Jeffery Clayton Gordon, ex-cavalry lieutenant and native of the Virginia Colony, dressed in an exquisite wedding gown. Within the next hour, she would become his sole possession, and there was absolutely no way she could prevent this ghastly vengeful horror. She could only pray for a lessening of Jeffery's wrath—or for Joe's swift arrival in the coming spring.

Following Powchutu's death and burial, Alisha had been in a state of numbness and depression. Added to that emotional turmoil was her distressing shock at learning all of her money had been irretrievably lost. She had found herself alone, vulnerable, and penniless. But this time was different from the last; there was no Powchutu waiting in the wings to help or to protect her. She was completely alone and on her own. She shuddered in fear and dread.

Alisha caressed the silky folds of the beautiful, ivory dress which she was wearing. She smiled bitterly as she recalled Jeffery informing her that this gown had been the sole reason for her stay of execution. He told her he had confidently ordered the material from downriver the day after her arrival. He grinned haughtily as he spoke of how Mary had secured her proper measurements for him. Filled with certainty, he had hired two seamstresses to secretly design and sew the elegant gown. Jeffery seemed determined to have a grand wedding and bring his blushing bride to Williamsburg.

She had to admit this gown was exquisite and costly. It was neither daring nor modest. It was made from expensive satin and delicate lace. Jeffery had broken a string of small pearls with which to edge the neckline. The town leather-craftsman had made her a matching pair of leather slippers, which were striking and comfortable. The bride's only piece of jewelry was a single diamond which was suspended on a delicate chain, made from Jeffery's personal stickpin. She wondered if she should be honored by his unselfish sacrifice. She hastily decided no, since everything would still belong to him after the wedding.

Jeffery had managed to locate only enough lace to trim the gown. Therefore, he had purchased several long strands of white ribbon for her hair. She had secured her long tresses into one heavy braid, then attached it to her scalp in the form of a coronet. The white ribbons had been artistically interwoven in the braid with their remaining lengths left to hang down her nape. All in all, she presented a stunning bride.

As she moved to view her profile in the mirror,

Alisha's eyes caught sight of the seductive peignoir set lying on the bed behind her. Her terrified heart actually skipped a beat. If Jeffery refused to keep his promise concerning a marriage in name only, there was nothing she could do. When presenting it to her earlier, he had grinned devilishly and joked, "Don't be alarmed, my fetching bride. It's just for show. Wouldn't want those ladies to think I forgot such a necessary wedding garment. Besides, from what Mary told me, you are sadly lacking in clothes and accessories. We'll have to correct that as quickly as possible. I can't permit the wife of Jeffery Gordon to go around looking the part of a scullery maid. I've hired those same two women to help you with a proper wardrobe after we're married," he had casually informed her.

Her heart was drumming madly as the time rushed by. Soon, it would be time to go downstairs and to join their guests. It would require a miracle for her to get through this day without going to pieces. At least her orphaned state had overruled the accepted one-year mourning period. No one had given the impression this hasty wedding was improper.

The house was filled with delectable odors from the kitchen. The woman who was responsible for Jeffery's cleaning and cooking had prepared a fabulous reception to follow the wedding ceremony. It was clear to everyone that Jeffery had spared no expense to have the most notable, breathtaking, and largest wedding and party ever given in St. Louis.

Invitations had been written in fancy script and then hand-delivered to anyone who was anyone in the entire area. Only this morning had she learned that those invitations had been delivered on Sunday afternoon and on Monday morning. How outrageous and presuming, since she had agreed to go through with this fake wedding only on Monday evening!

Alisha's dazed mind went back to that fateful meeting. She had agreed to have lunch with Jeffery in her room, knowing the reason for his request for lunch and for complete privacy. During lunch they had carried on a somber conversation about the new fashions pictured in the last newspaper which he had received from back East. Later, during dessert, they had switched to the serious topic of the war between their two homelands. Jeffery had sullenly informed her of the British victories in the Long Island and White Plains areas back in August. He had told her of how it had been accomplished by the combined forces of Admiral and General Howe. He had been quick to point out the mounting offenses of the American forces under General Washington who were preparing a decisive confrontation in the New England area. He had arrogantly stated who the natural winner would be: America.

Alisha had politely accepted this information, not daring to question him about his distant observation rather than his patriotic participation. He was content to sit out the entire war in safety and in opulence here in St. Louis. He jokingly implied that he could truthfully claim he was not a traitor to England because he had not fought in the war, should America lose and England win. It was clear he would side with the winner, whoever it was.

After their pleasant—but guarded—lunch, Jeffery had broached the real purpose for their meeting. He accurately and leisurely summed up her present and past predicaments. Then he reiterated his demand for wedlock. She had been stunned to discover how much he knew about her present circumstances. She angrily decided that Jamie O'Hara must have told him everything. He was even aware of her visit to Hiram Bigsley's office to check on the possibility of his having her money!

He had ended his narration with the words, "As you can see, Alisha, you really have no other option. Surely marriage to me could not be worse than the type of existence you will soon find yourself enduring should you refuse my advantageous proposal. Just a last warning, I won't accept used goods. If you attempt to survive as some other man's mistress and do not succeed, don't come back to me. You have been given ample time to make your choice. I have been most patient and generous; you must agree. Your answer, please . . ."

Alisha had risen from the table and walked over to the window. She had gazed out for only a short time, but the moment had seemed endless. A tear escaped her eye as she realized the truth: she was trapped. She was at his mercy, if he possessed any. She felt her life-thread tighten and knot, suffocating her with hopelessness.

Many unrelated thoughts and memories flickered across her tormented mind: all gone; all destroyed. Her heart ached with the knowledge of her inevitable concession to her foe. Yet, she saw no other path to take. How could there be any choice between Jeffery or enforced whoredom? How she wished she was a man!

She closed her eyes and mentally ended her connections with the past. She bid farewell to Powchutu who had been her friend and brother. They had shared so much together. She laid her uncle and her parents to final rest, all having died too young and too tragically. She said goodbye to her trusted friend Joe who was still her only hope for the future. She suppressed the painful farewell to her unborn child who rested only God knew where. Last, she bid her most tormenting farewell to her traitorous love: Gray Eagle, without whom none of these agonizing farewells would be necessary. Gray Eagle . . .

How different this wedding day was from her first one. After dressing in an exquisite albino-skin dress and headband, she had left Black Cloud's tepee for the joining ceremony. She vividly recalled the looks of awe and envy which had greeted her, the Indian princess. Her eyes had met Gray Eagle's as he stood in the center of Indian braves. He had exuded such pride and majesty. He had looked magnificent and impressive, but also imposing and haughty. She had been powerless to look away. There had been such a strange look within his jet eyes.

Gray Eagle had looked proud as he gazed upon her beauty. His smoldering gaze had caused shivers to run up and down her spine. His image that day was still as clear as a mountain stream. He had been dressed in rich buckskins with many yellow feathers in his midnight mane to proclaim his rank. Secured around his neck and flowing to the ground had been a colorful feather cape. He had never looked so handsome or so virile.

It had seemed to take forever to cross that short distance between them. Her body had trembled and flamed with intense longings for him. She had been nearly oblivious to the beginning of that ceremony. His touch had been like fire. She had felt his being with every nerve within her body. She had been lost to all reality except him. He could have seduced her right there and then, and she would have offered no resistance. Within moments they had been wed. No wedding could have been more special . . .

"Well?" The crisp word had cut into her mourning.

She had slowly turned and looked up into Jeffery's triumphant face. "Is there any need to answer, Jeffery? As you said, I have no real choice. I can only hope you are

317

the gentleman you claim to be, that you possess the necessary honor and breeding which will prevent a deadly battle between us. For certain, I will not endure a life of constant warfare and degradation. Death is preferable to such a vile existence. If your offer is honorable and truthful, then I accept your terms." With those words, it had been settled, just as he had known from that first moment at the dock on that chilling Christmas Eve.

A tap on her door called her back to the present. She inhaled several times to still her erratic respiration and to slow her racing heart. She opened the door to face her terrible destiny. Her eyes, which appeared two lifeless emeralds set into the face of an ivory statue, locked with mirthful ones of sky blue. His eyes unavoidably passed over the enchanting, beautiful picture she painted. His pleasure and appreciation were mirrored there. An arrogant smile of satisfaction spread across his handsome face.

He chuckled in open enjoyment and mild surprise. "I didn't think it possible for you to increase your allure, Alisha. By damn, I was grossly mistaken. I've known and seen a great many women, Alisha, but none as beautiful or bewitching as you. It will be heralded that Jeffery Gordon has captured and wed a goddess herself. Just wait until Papa gets a look at you! No doubt you'll dazzle and charm the old grouch that first moment. Yes sir, this is the best deal I've ever made. Rest assured, you'll be amply rewarded for your cooperation, Mrs. Gordon. A man would be a fool to mar a rare treasure like you," he noted, thinking aloud.

He entered the room and slowly walked around her. "Beauty in life and in motion," he finally decided, his eyes possessively engulfing her from head to toe. He reached out to run his hand down her alabaster arm, pleased that her golden tan had faded since his last sight of her at Fort Pierre.

Her satiny skin was cold to his touch. She had instinctively flinched. He chuckled humorously. "Relax, Alisha. This will be a day to remember. This town has never seen a wedding such as ours will be. Enjoy it, so you can give Papa a full and colorful accounting of it."

"I'm so nervous," she declared, blaming her tension on the obvious pre-wedding jitters. Feeling compelled to do so, she graciously remarked, "The gown is absolutely exquisite, Jeffery. I cannot recall ever seeing one as beautiful. Thank you. Is Hiram here yet?" she softly inquired, trying to change the subject.

"He arrived just before I came up to check on you. He was an excellent choice to give the bride away. Would you care for a glass of brandy to calm your nerves a bit?"

"I think not. I best remain clear-headed for the service and party," she replied.

Instead, Jeffery filled the room with hearty, taunting laughter. "Come now, Alisha; you have my word I won't take unfair advantage of you tonight, or any other night. I will never sleep in that bed unless you ask me. Is that clear?" he firmly stated, pointing to the double bed which took up a great deal of the floor-space in this enchanting room.

She eyed him doubtfully, but nodded yes. "How soon before we begin?" she anxiously inquired, disturbed by the smug and possessive way in which he continued to study her. "If I pass your inspection, do you have to keep staring at me?" she asked in a crisp, shaky voice.

"Surely you can't blame me," he sweetly rebuked her in his mellow Southern drawl. "A word to the wise," he began with a mischievous leer in his remarkably blue eyes. "Since this is our wedding day, we should make an effort to convince everyone present that we're madly in love. The coldness you're displaying right now just might raise some suspicions and idle gossip. I hope you agree we don't want any of that," he suggested with a lilt to his voice.

Of course he was right. She nodded agreement.

"Excellent! Then shall we go, my love?"

Alisha tensed instantly, then forced herself to relax as much as possible. Jeffery gently took her small, icy hand in his large, warm one. He walked her to the head of the stairs to join Hiram who was just heading up to call them. Hiram beamed at the ravishing girl at the top of the staircase. She smiled faintly at him, unable to conceal her apprehensions. Hiram smiled cheerfully, assuming her state to be due to the recent loss of her brother and to bridal jitters.

Jeffery passed her hand to Hiram. "Take good care of her, Hiram. She's one in a million," he remarked, then kissed her upon her slightly pinkened lips.

Her wary gaze met his proud one. Feeling awkward in front of Hiram, she tenderly caressed his cheek and stated sweetly, "I'll be just fine, Jeffery. Surely all brides are this nervous. I promise not to faint or to fall down the stairs," she teased.

She alertly noticed the way her genial mood and romantic action eased his worries. He smiled in honest pleasure. He made his way down the steps and entered the living room, glancing around at his various guests who were appropriately attired for this momentous occasion.

Mr. Grimsley, an aspiring politician, had constructed a long and ample living room. In cases of large gatherings, a series of doors leading to a large drawing room were opened, increasing the size of the area. Jeffery quickly let his eyes roam over the people present; no one had refused his invitation.

The rooms were decorated as lovely as possible for this time of year. He made a mental note to give Mrs. Lizzy Webster a bonus for her preparations and artistic decorations. He had previously checked the sumptuous menu which she had prepared with hired help. He also made a note to reward Sara King and Martha Caldwell for their superb wedding creation which so justly suited Alisha Williams; Parisian designers could not have done better.

Alisha . . . his excited mind sparked with the thought of her. Jeffery hastily dismissed such thoughts to be savored at a better time. He made his way to where his best man Henri Jean Malraux was standing. They exchanged knowing looks, then smiled genially as they clasped hands.

"Think you can carry off your part?" he teased Henri, then winked mysteriously.

"Oui, Monsieur," he replied in his mellow, deceptive tone. "What could possibly go wrong on such a fabulous day?"

"After all the money I've put out, nothing better or some heads will roll," Jeffery jested with a hint of seriousness.

The Reverend Mister Howard Matthews approached the two men. "If you're ready to proceed, Mr. Gordon, the time is here. Shall Mrs. Smith begin on the piano?" His beady brown eyes watched the man before them.

Matthews had been surprised by Jeffery's command performance, but had not dared to refuse it. His alert, curious senses had discovered many secrets about both men. Gordon was a fool if he believed no one knew of his under-the-table connections with those unsavory cutthroats who controlled the riverbanks! But Gordon was not a foolish man. He knew no one would go against him or that weaselly Frenchman at his side. He read the contemptuous lights in both men's eyes, but smiled as if blind to them. Inwardly he seethed at the blatant, wicked offenses of these two scoundrels. With all his might he wished the Lord God Almighty would strike them down!

Matthews nodded his signal to Mrs. Smith to begin the music. Jeffery, Henri, and Matthews assumed their respective positions at the far end of the room. It was but moments before Alisha nearly floated gracefully to Jeffery's side. Hiram placed her hand in Jeffery's, then stepped back a few feet.

Alisha's eyes briefly fused with Jeffery's; their lips exchanged wary smiles. Matthews opened his large, well-worn black Bible to begin this strange ceremony in which he felt was uniting a known devil with the likeness of an angel. Matthews could not even fathom a guess as to why this lovely, delicate creature was marrying Jeffery Gordon. Her soul would surely be in jeopardy!

"My dear friends and neighbors, we are gathered here to witness the joining in lawful wedlock . . ." Matthews began, as nearly every person in the room began his own mental story. The ceremony droned on and on; Matthews outdid himself with lovely clichés.

For Alisha, the ceremony seemed endless. She had great difficulty focusing on the reverend's words or on the significance of them. When the time came for her replies, Jeffery had to nudge her back to reality. Flushed with embarrassment, she mechanically repeated her vows.

Jeffery voiced his vows and promises in a deep, resonant tone. When the correct moment arrived, he lifted Alisha's frigid left hand and slipped his ring upon her middle finger. She stared at the Gordon family crest emblazoned upon its face, feeling the satisfaction of his possession of her.

Alisha failed to hear the remainder of the ceremony or the final pronouncement of her terrifying fate. Suddenly it was all over, and Jeffery was lifting her quivering chin for his rightful kiss. His mouth was warm and gentle; yet, there was a subtle demand and smoldering fire beneath it. His hands on either side of her oval face prevented any refusal or termination without it being noticed by their guests.

The unwilling bride helplessly surrendered her mouth to his. As his lips left hers, after a very lengthy kiss, her baffled gaze met his equally puzzled one. They simply stared at each other, each trying to analyze their strange reaction to a mere kiss. Annoyed by her unexpected power over him, Jeffery was the first to recover and to end the unexplainable spell.

Alisha blamed her illogical feelings upon the beauty and magic of such an event. Then, too, there were her warring emotions to accept some of the blame for her lapse. There was no time to analyze this peculiar matter any further, for they were rapidly surrounded by well-wishers.

The party which followed was much too long and tiring for the hostage bride. She could hardly eat any of the delicious treats which Mrs. Webster had prepared. She commanded herself to be the gracious hostess and to keep her mind off her shadowy future. For the first time, she was keenly aware of the great expense and trouble which her new husband had gone to for this occasion. For the first time in a long time, Alisha smiled at the beauty surrounding her.

"Does that lovely smile mean I did a marvelous job with our wedding, Mrs. Gordon?" Jeffery's playful tone teased her.

She faced him; the flickering of an enchanting smile threatened to brighten her face if she permitted it. She did, and truthfully replied, "It's stunning! I cannot imagine how you accomplished all of this beauty in the dead of winter. I seriously doubt anyone could have done better. But of course, Jeffery Gordon is accustomed to victory and to grandeur. Believe it or not, Jeffery, but I do appreciate the gown and all of this," she stated as she motioned to their surroundings.

He flashed her a genuine smile, his eyes and features softening noticeably. "In all honesty, I couldn't be more pleased with the arrangements or with you. I was a wee bit afraid you might not comply with my wishes," he confessed with a buoyant grin which made her deeply conscious of his handsome, clean looks.

She glanced around her, then down at her ravishing gown. She laughed skeptically, then mirthfully challenged him, "Not for a single moment did you doubt your success, Jeffery Clayton Gordon. I venture you had this entire deal worked out down to the very number of petit-fours. Besides, why would any sensible female give up the chance to be the center of attention at such a grand event? As you said earlier, my reprieve was granted only because my wedding gown was not completed by your first deadline," she gently teased him.

"Does that tone and smile mean you're not sorry you agreed to marry me?" Jeffery murmured close to her ear, as several people came near to them and stole their privacy.

She assumed an expression of deep and serious thought, then laughed. "Let's just say that so far you haven't given me any reason to regret my decision," she whispered up at him. Steadily relaxing and feeling a deceptive confidence building, she added saucily, "In fact, only reasons to prove it was an extremely excellent one."

Before Jeffery could make any comment concerning her unexpected remarks, Henri came over to join them. He bowed gallantly to Alisha, then politely inquired, "Am I interrupting anything of major importance, or may I join you for a few moments?"

Henri was cordially invited into their company. Quick and easy banter was exchanged, often slipping into French. At first, Henri's brow had raised in astonishment; then, he had grinned in unsuppressed pleasure. Jeffery informed Alisha that Henri was a river merchant and was mostly responsible for getting all of his needs for him from New Orleans. She was alert to realize this was how Jeffery had secured everything for this wedding. She immediately thanked Henri for his assistance and kindness.

"It was worth all the rush and trouble, Madame Gordon. You look *magnifique*," he breathed, kissing the tips of his fingers, then casting the kiss to the wind.

"You are most kind, Monsieur Malraux."

"Henri, please," he urged.

She smiled warmly and nodded. "Henri, it is. If there is time later, will you tell me about this New Orleans which I have heard so much about? Has the war touched there yet?"

"Oui, but only in *petite* amounts. We shall discuss it in much detail when these ragamuffins have stuffed their bellies and departed."

Alisha quickly clamped her hand over her mouth to prevent her uncontrollable giggles from spilling forth into the room. "Monsieur Mal . . . Henri, you are a rare delight in this wilderness. I shall look forward to your

325

visits with eagerness."

Henri gave her another sweeping bow, then chuckled with growing cheerfulness. "You, my dear Mrs. Gordon, are the rare delight in these crude parts. How I have sorely missed such company and conversation."

"Merci," she sweetly replied, eyes bright with joy.

Jeffery had quietly witnessed this humorous exchange between Alisha and Henri. He curiously wondered what Alisha would think if she knew the truth about this particular man. He could easily predict her reaction to Henri's dealings in river piracy, trafficking in female flesh, and stooping to murder when necessary. He astutely decided that Henri was just as skilled in deception as he himself was . . .

The party continued on a lighter, more relaxed, note. There was dancing, eating, drinking, and merrymaking. It did not take long for Alisha to begin to feel the mingling effects of her tension, fatigue, and champagne. Jeffery had wisely waited until the majority of their guests had departed before ordering Mrs. Webster to bring out the case of chilled champagne, a gift from Henri.

Jeffery personally filled only two glasses, leaving the remaining chore to his housekeeper. He handed one to Alisha, then lifted the other one in his steady hand. He clinked his glass to hers, toasting, "May you always be as beautiful, happy, and treasured as you are this very minute."

After taking several swallows, he grinned slyly and boldly countered, "Your turn, Mrs. Gordon . . ."

She thought for a few moments, trying to come up with a witty and appropriate toast. Smiling playfully, she touched her glass to his and bravely met his intense gaze. In a honeyed tone she murmured, "May you always be as handsome, pleasant, and pleasing as you are this most treasured night . . ."

Flames danced brightly and meaningfully in his blue eyes. Henri chuckled and devilishly noted, "Perhaps it is time we all left you two alone?"

Jeffery grinned painfully, knowing solitude wouldn't profit him. He politely refused Henri's suggestion, "Alisha and I have all the time in the world. Tonight, we wish to share our joy and hospitality with our friends who have travelled so far in such inclement weather. Right, my lovely bride?"

She smiled at Jeffery, relieved and encouraged by his action. She calmly agreed, "Jeffery is correct, Henri. This is a night to celebrate and to enjoy to the fullest, one to be treasured and remembered forever," she stated, joining in his pretense.

"In such case, Madame Gordon, may I have this dance?" Henri entreated, holding out his hand to Alisha.

Alisha sent Jeffery a teasing, inquisitive look. "If my new husband does not object?" she replied.

Jeffery smiled at her for her cunning display of a loving bride. "By all means, my ravishing wife. Just remember where you borrowed her and return her promptly," he jested to Henri.

Henri flashed a rueful look at both of them. "*Au contrare*, if I could sneak her away from you, *mon ami*, I would be about it this very moment, you lucky devil." Both men laughed.

The dancing and drinking continued into the early morning hours. When Jeffery closed the front door behind the last guest, which was of course Henri, he turned to find Alisha poised in the center of the room. There was an anxious look written upon her face, fear in her emerald eyes.

He grinned knowingly. He swaggered over to her and

looked down into her upturned, pale face. "The party's over, Alisha. Is everything else as well?" he asked mysteriously.

She fluctuated between flushes and blanches as she searched for the proper response—which evaded her. Seeing her fearful hesitation and fatigue, he smiled and dropped any serious conversation.

"Later," he stated flippantly. "You look exhausted, but still beautiful. Off to bed with you, wife. You were perfect tonight; I was well pleased. I think I'll have another glass of champagne to toast my good fortune. Think you can find your way back to your room?" he inquired solicitously.

She nodded yes, confusion tinging her expression. "Good night, Jeffery. Everything was exceptionally lovely tonight. I shall never forget it." She turned to head up the stairs. She halted and turned as he softly called her name. She tensed very noticeably. Dread filled her eyes. She waited nervously.

"For a good night kiss, you can have the key to your bedroom door," he tempted with a roguish hint in his voice as he dangled the key before her wary eyes. "Just for practice, nothing more. You seem too skittish and reserved with me before others. With a little work and honest effort, you can become just as calm around me as I am around you," he stated.

Desperately wanting the key, but fearing it was only a cruel taunt, she hesitated just long enough to witness annoyed lights flicker in his chilling blue eyes. Dreading to inspire a savage confrontation at this early date in their new life, Alisha came forward and eased up on her tiptoes to comply with his request. In all honesty, she feared his disapproval and revenge more than she feared his touch.

As her trembling lips met his sensual ones, his strong arms went around her slender body and possessively pulled her very close to him. His skilled mouth claimed hers in an ardent kiss; his hard body pressed intimately against hers. Knowing she was his legal property and he could do whatever he pleased, she deemed it best to permit his unwanted attentions. Afraid to jerk away from him, she endured his enticing kiss and fierce embrace.

It had been such a long time since Gray Eagle had held her and kissed her in a similar way. Her senses reeled, partly from the champagne and partly from the physical need which he was awakening. As the kiss continued and deepened, she instinctively relaxed against him. She unknowingly slipped her arms around his narrow waist and helplessly returned the intoxicating kiss. Yearning and loneliness gave way to a warm response to him.

When he finally withdrew his lips from hers, Jeffery stared down at her, utterly perplexed by the meaning of her response. Witnessing the scarlet flush which stained her face and ivory bosom, he had his answer: she was not frigid or unreachable. She hastily lowered her long, thick lashes to conceal her look of shame. She fidgeted nervously at comprehending what he had just revealed to her. Frightened and confused by her actions and feelings, Alisha could not meet his steady gaze.

Realizing the folly of making an issue of her instinctive reaction to him, he lightheartedly teased, "That wasn't so difficult, was it? This pretense shows great promise. No one will guess the truth. Get some sleep, Alisha," he tenderly advised, pressing the key into her icy hand.

Her head jerked upwards; her wide eyes stared at him, hardly believing he was relenting this easily. "That's all?" she asked incredulously.

329

"Contrary to your opinion of me, I can be trusted to keep my word. That's all—for tonight. However, there will be many future practices until we get our act right and natural. By the time we return to Williamsburg, we'll be so perfect around each other that no one will guess our pretense. I know I have certain legal rights as your husband, but I will not force them upon you."

He placed a light kiss upon her forehead. "Goodnight, Alisha. Sleep well."

"Goodnight . . ." she stammered, more confused and wary than ever. She lifted the bottom of her gown to climb up the steps. Not once did she glance back at Jeffery; there was no need to tempt him to break his word by allowing him to recognize her temporary, lustful weakness.

She went to her room and closed the door behind her. She almost reluctantly locked the door, dreading to irritate Jeffery with her mistrust. She began to undress, only to find she could not unfasten the long row of seemingly countless buttons down the back of her wedding gown.

She contorted her body this way and that. It was futile. She was forced to admit she could not remove it alone. She was tempted to lie down and to sleep in it. Mrs. Webster could help her out of it when she returned in the morning to clean up after the party. At once she deduced the error of that idea. There was only one thing she could do.

She lifted the key off of her dressing table and unlocked the door. She went to the head of the stairs and called down to Jeffery. He came out of his study and looked up at her. He wondered what he could say or do if she was about to offer some compromise in their sexual relationship. No matter how she felt about him, he had forced a physical response from her. Perhaps . . .

"Jeffery, I hate to disturb you," she apologetically began, "but I cannot unbutton my gown. I thought it unwise to wait for Mrs. Webster in the morning. The gown is too exquisite to ruin with such carelessness. It would seem strange to Mrs. Webster, don't you think? There are so many buttons and I cannot reach them all," she said nervously, hating to ask Jeffery's assistance. Alisha wasn't certain if she feared his hot blood or hers. She only knew she did not want to tempt him beyond his endurance. It terrified her to think about undressing before a strange man, but especially Jeffery Gordon.

He headed up the steps toward her. He took her arm and led her back to her room. She did not notice his look of mingled relief and disappointment. The important thing was that he knew he could extract a heated, uncontrollable response from her, if he wanted to. He turned her around and began to deftly undo the numerous buttons.

Within a few moments, she felt a cool draft touch her flesh. She placed her hand on the bodice to prevent the gown from falling down. She turned and thanked him. He stared at her left shoulder. "Is something wrong?" she asked, noting his moody silence.

He touched the scar there and coldly demanded, "How did you get this scar? It was not there when I rescued you from the Sioux camp. Who dared to destroy such beauty?" Fury filled him as he imagined it to be the brutal work of his former foe Gray Eagle.

Reading the intense anger in his voice and expression, she feared not to answer honestly. "After Pau . . . Powchutu rescued me from the Sioux camp, we headed here. One day while we were stopped to eat, two white trappers attacked us. We fought with them. Powchutu

331

was shot by one, and I . . . the other one grabbed me and tried to . . . tried to . . . I'm sure you know what he tried to do!'' she snapped irrationally at him.

''Well, what happened?'' he shouted impatiently.

''We fought! Powchutu killed one man and I . . .'' She halted suddenly and went stark white. She shuddered, recalling the vivid truth for the first time since that fateful day. She had completely blocked his manner of death out of her mind.

She whirled and presented her semi-bare back to him. She hastily finished, ''I was stabbed during the fight.''

Keenly aware of her sudden anguish, Jeffery stepped in front of her. ''What else happened that day?'' he sternly demanded.

She remained silent, tugging at her lower lip with her teeth. ''Did he rape you before Powchutu could help you?''

She grimaced at what might have been the truth if she had not slain him. She trembled. She did not reply, simply shook her head in the negative. Impatient and curious, he seized her by her bare shoulders and shook her lightly. ''What happened out there, woman?''

She stubbornly held her silence. How could she tell anyone what she had done that day? He shook her roughly this time and shouted tersely, ''Damnit, Alisha! Tell me this instant!''

She glared at him for his angry insistence. ''No!''

''I won't leave this room until you do,'' he threatened, hinting at the power he held over her. He grabbed her face beween his hands and forced her to look at him. ''Tell me what happened! Something evidently did!''

There was a mixture of fear and anger in her eyes as she screamed at him, ''I killed him! Satisfied, Jeffery? I killed him, so his friend stabbed me.''

Their gazes fused and locked. Hers was filled with torment; his filled with utter disbelief. "You couldn't even squash a cicada!" he spat.

"I didn't know what I was doing. I was . . . sick and feverish. I was terrified and desperate. He said they were both going to . . ." Horror filled her eyes. "I had to do it, Jeffery. He forced me to defend myself. Don't you see? I had no choice," she pleaded for his understanding and reassurance.

He wanted to take her into his arms and to comfort her. He knew what her reaction to him might be in her emotionally drained and distressed state of mind. He cursed his impotency and raged at the warrior's arrow which had maimed him for life, making him only half a man. He dared not risk her helpless overture to him. She was in the palm of his hand, and he could do nothing about it. Trapped and embittered, he took his hands from her face and verbally comforted her.

"Of course I understand. Scum like that deserves to die! If you hadn't killed him, I would now be forced to search him out and to have him slain myself. There's no way you could ever hurt anyone without just provocation. Get some sleep. You'll feel better in the morning. It appears you've been through more than I realized. We shouldn't open old wounds. I'm sorry, love. You're right; this should be kept between us. How much does Hiram know about you?" he abruptly inquired.

She sniffled to control her tears. She accepted the handkerchief which he handed to her. She quietly blew her nose and cleared her hoarse throat. She related the explanation which she had given to Hiram upon her arrival here. She also told Jeffery about her brief stay at Joe Kenny's, but omitted the news of her miscarriage. By the time she finished her narrative, he had learned all

333

he needed to know for the present.

Later, he vowed to know every single detail about her, from the moment of her arrival in this territory to the present day. On second thought, he resolved to know everything about her from birth until this moment. If there were any damaging secrets concerning her or her lineage, he wanted to know about it before taking her back to Virginia. If he did discover some unacceptable fact, then he would return home the grieving widower: still supplied with a reason for avoiding women. Alisha was very rare and valuable, but not as much as his pride and social position.

"That's enough talking and crying for tonight, Mrs. Gordon. Off to bed with you," he tenderly ordered.

When he left her room, he was mildly mystified and pleased by the noticeable silence of an unlocked door. He returned to his study for another, much needed, drink. Much later when he did head up to bed, he walked straight to her door to test his new theory. His hand reached out for the knob; he hesitated before quietly grasping it. It turned easily and silently. He slowly pushed the door open and peered around the edge.

The room was almost dark. Rays of moonlight filtered through Alisha's window and played upon her bed. He went to stand beside it. She lay completely motionless. He gingerly lifted a heavy curl and moved it away from her face. She shifted slightly, but did not awaken. The soft moonlight glowed upon her angelic face, shadowing its angles and revealing flawless perfection. Long, dark lashes rested upon her cheeks. Her lips were slightly parted.

Twinges of unnatural remorse and tenderness pulled at his toughened conscience. He stared at what he considered to be the most beautiful, desirable, refined woman he had ever met. He raged at the fate which was denying him sole and complete possession of her. Unreasonable fury at her past rejection of him returned as he realized she had unknowingly denied him his last chance to have a woman in a sexual way. He had wanted her more than he had ever wanted any other female. Now, she was totally out of his physical reach forever. He cursed her and the Indians.

Yet, for the briefest of instants he was tempted to seek a complacent, compromising arrangement with her. But just as he reached out to run his finger across her inviting lips, she uttered the most fateful and disastrous words possible.

A single teardrop slid down her cheek as she sadly murmured, "Kokipa sni . . . waste cedake . . . waste cedake . . ."

His body grew rigid and enraged as the words of Sioux slipped from her sleeping body. He maliciously wondered where her mind was headed. He did not have to wait long, for she spoke the name which sealed her doom: "Wanmdi Hota . . ."

Unable to translate her previous words, he definitely recognized the name of his most feared and hated enemy. His heart became a lump of ice and stone. He vowed to serve her Gray Eagle's scalp upon a silver tray before heading back to Virginia. She would not have another man in her mind with which to compare him, especially not that particular man!

He hurriedly left her room. Still, Alisha did not awaken from her deep slumber or dreams of her lost love. He glanced back only once. His blue eyes flamed with bitterness and hostility. "You are as good as dead, my savage foe. She is mine alone now. Mine alone . . ."

335

Chapter Sixteen

When Alisha stirred and sat up that next morning, she was surprised to learn it was past mid-day. She had slept deeply and soundly. She answered the light tapping at her door to find Mrs. Webster holding a tray with hot tea and muffins. She smiled and moved aside to allow her entry.

"This wasn't necessary, Mrs. Webster. But it is very kind of you. I didn't mean to sleep so late. Has Jeffery already eaten?" she inquired, feeling that was the proper question for a new bride.

"Course, Ma'am. He left for town early this morning. Said he had some 'portant business to care for. Said he'd be back at dinner time," she stated in a friendly tone.

She placed the tray on a low table which was positioned before the French blue sofa. Alisha sat down to devour this fragrant temptation as the middle-aged woman began to busy herself with straightening her room. If Mrs. Webster noticed that she and her husband had not shared a bed last night, she did not let on . . .

As Alisha savored her warm, sunny bedroom, her husband was attending to business. First, he ordered a new wardrobe for his bride. Then, he headed to the Horne House, for a meeting with Henri.

At the inn, Jeffery was disappointed at not seeing Mary. He was curious about her reaction to her gift and to her mental lapse. Not wanting to create any suspicion, he did not ask about her. Later, he would order some lunch sent up to Henri's room to lure her upstairs. He was positive Frenchy would enjoy the recounts of her little adventures with his magic drugs. Hearing about such wanton abandonment and great skill might encourage Henri to arrange her mysterious disappearance. For certain, he was past ready to be rid of the little wench!

Frenchy eagerly listened to Jeffery's accounts of Mary's abilities. He pondered this news very carefully. "You're right, *mon ami*. She would make a most valuable investment. The only thing better than a hot, provocative body is a silent tongue! There's a ship docking in New Orleans in late June. There will be a man on board who will pay highly for such a rare combination of talents. I will come for her the first of June. Until such time, keep your brutes away from her. She will be of little use to me if she becomes pregnant or is injured. In return, I will not charge you for the supplies for your wedding."

They exchanged pleased, amicable smiles. "Now, on to this other problem . . ." Jeffery hesitantly began, wondering how to broach his demand without giving away too many secrets. A man such as Henri could be trusted and admired only so far.

At his halt, Henri chuckled and joked, "What problem could a new groom have when he has just wed the most beautiful and ravishing creature alive? If she is too much for the dashing lieutenant, I will gladly take her off your hands . . . free of charge. She is like a breath of spring air, a taste of aged brandy. Such charm and wit! Such beauty and breeding! You are a very lucky man, *mon ami*. She is *magnifique!*" he vowed, dramatically kissing the tips of his bunched fingers.

"Alisha isn't the problem," he quickly informed this hot-blooded Frenchman who was clearly so taken with

337

her. Jeffery had never seen his eyes light up with such overwhelming emotion before. There was a different kind of desire written in his dark eyes where Alisha was concerned. It amused Jeffery to observe a genuine concern and affection for his woman in the eyes of another man, especially an experienced and particular man like Henri.

"That deal we have for buying scalps and jewelry is very lucrative and enjoyable for both of us. Hardly a week passes now I don't get at least a few. I upped the bounty for souvenirs of chiefs and their sons since theirs is the best quality. I also added one to cover female scalps. Those fools back East won't know a woman's hair from a man's, especially Injun hair! I've come across some mighty fancy jewelry that way, some of it pretty valuable."

"Sounds fine to me," Henri agreed with his actions. "It matters not to me if they kill every one of those red savages, male or female! Just for variety, I tried several of them in one of my houses near New Orleans. Stupid, unreasonable, quarrelsome lot! Finally had to slit their miserable throats and cast them into the river. Good riddance, too! So, what's this new problem?"

Jeffery's eyes glowed with satanic pleasure. "There is this one Indian in particular I want to set a higher bounty for, a prize which will entice countless trappers and even enemy warriors to seek his scalp for me. I was thinking of sending out the word for five thousand dollars in gold." Jeffery casually dropped his startling news.

Henri's eyes enlarged, and he gasped in vivid shock. *"Mon ami!* Surely you jest! Such an amount for a mere savage's hair and necklace?" he questioned Jeffery's absurd announcement.

Jeffery chuckled wickedly. "Not just any Indian,

Henri. Besides, it will be a farce. We will simply state that large amount to interest any takers who have the courage or recklessness to search him out. Once he brings us this scalp and wanapin, I will get rid of him myself," he arrogantly asserted.

"Who is this warrior who demands such attention from my good friend? This is a personal matter, no?" Henri's eyes twinkled with growing excitement, for he relished brutal revenge.

Knowing of Henri's affection and admiration for his new wife, he gave an explanation which he new Henri would accept. "There are two reasons. First, he is the one who massacred Fort Pierre and nearly cost me my life. No one has dared to seek his life for the meager rewards we have offered for the items of chief's sons. This warrior is without fear; he is powerful, cunning, and daring. Both the whites and the Indians fear him! His scalp and wanapin will hang in my study in Williamsburg!"

"You speak of Gray Eagle, do you not? You are correct in your assumptions; who would dare to strike him dead? Would a larger bounty increase the courage of his enemies?" Henri asked skeptically, well aware of the glorious infamy of Gray Eagle.

"For five thousand dollars in gold, men would slay their own mothers and sell their own scalps! If he is attacked from many sides at the same time, he will soon fall victim to some man. I would stake my life upon the success of this deal! I will have his life before I leave here," Jeffery claimed with firmness.

"There is more to this hatred than your past rivalry with him, no?" Henri was detecting potent emotions from his business partner. He contemplated on what that warrior had done to Jeffery to cause such fierce animosity and obsession.

"Tell no one this secret, Henri. I must have your word of honor," Jeffery demanded, knowing Henri did possess a certain code of honor when he gave his solemn word.

"*Mon ami*, there is no need for such demands between friends," Henri gently rebuked him. "Yet, you have my sworn word of silence."

"You are right, Henri; there is more than rivalry here. He captured and tortured Alisha, among other things which I need not spell out to you. The man who posed as her brother was only a half-breed scout who befriended her and helped her to escape the Sioux camp. I had him slain because he was going to force her to marry him as payment for his rescue. For what Gray Eagle has done to both of us, I will see him dead before I leave this area!"

"*Sacre bleu!*" Henri angrily exploded. "He has dared to defile such innocence and beauty! He is but an animal. I shall personally send out the messages of this new offer. Within a few months, we shall have this fiendish devil! Now I understand the sadness and fear in her. You must be gentle and patient with her, *mon ami*; such tragedies are difficult to forget."

Desiring Henri's continued assistance and sympathy, he noted sadly, "To this day she cries in her sleep. She awakens and pleads for mercy from some unseen demon who still haunts her dreams. He must pay for this cruel outrage, this dishonor to her and to me! Send out the word of his bounty this very day. Soon, he will tire of running and hiding; soon, some foe will slay him. I do not wish Alisha to know you have learned her humiliating past."

"You have my word. It will remain between us. I promise you the hair of the man who has done this detestable thing."

With that agreement, they shifted their talk to other

business. Later they had a pleasant lunch as Henri was given the opportunity to study Mary. It was very late before the two men separated. Henri headed downstairs to eat dinner, while Jeffery headed home to his new bride.

Pleased with his successful double-dealing with Henri and with his other tasks, he arrived home in a merry mood. He entered to find his wife sitting in the drawing room with a book of poetry in her hand. She glanced up as he strutted into the cozy room. She timidly smiled at him, wary of her position in his home. She was greatly relieved when he smiled back.

"Would you care for a glass of sherry before dinner, my bonny bride? This has been a busy and fruitful day for me," he nonchalantly remarked, not elaborating.

"Yes, thank you," she demurely replied.

"I saw Henri this afternoon," he stated casually as he poured two glasses of golden sherry. "He sends his regards and compliments. I plan to have him to dinner before he returns home."

"Do you wish me to inform Mrs. Webster, or will you tell her?" she softly inquired, seeking to learn of her future duties here. She patiently awaited his answer.

"You may tell her we will have guests for dinner on this Saturday evening. As for your other duties," he smoothly continued as if reading her thoughts, "My dear wife, they will be as follows: hostess, companion, mistress . . . of this house, confidant, and perhaps friend one day very soon. These duties apply both here and in Williamsburg. The winters here are cold and lonely; much of the time must be spent inside. We shall enjoy the talents and company of each other. It will offer us an excellent opportunity to get better acquainted and relaxed around each other. There are many games and books here, thanks to old Mr. Grimsley. There is also a piano; do you play?" he suddenly inquired.

"I did, but it has been a long time since I have done so."

"Excellent! With a little practice, I am sure your skill will return. When the weather is permissible, we can take long, invigorating rides in the snow. I shall look forward to spending cozy, quiet evenings in pleasant and stimulating conversation with you. As for your position as mistress of 'our' home, you will assume the running of this house, as well as the one in Virginia when we return there. Mrs. Webster will assist you in any areas of doubt or difficulty until you are ready to do so."

He grinned mischievously before going on. "Of course I will ask Mrs. Webster to come here only three days a week from now on. She will continue to take care of the heavy, menial chores while you see to the lighter, more important matters. I suggest you learn all you can from her as I wish my family to be favorably impressed with my selection of a proper wife. Mrs. King will be coming over the first of next week to begin work on your new wardrobe; I cannot permit my wife to look the part of a street urchin. She has her orders; I will expect you to cooperate fully with her."

"As you wish, Jeffery," she meekly agreed.

"We will take all meals together unless I am out on business or away for a few days," he announced calmly. That unexpected news sparked her interest. She would not have to be Jeffery's captive full-time!

"Where do you go on business? Hiram says the river is unsafe during the winter."

He laughed. "My dear wife, who would dare to attack me or my boats?" was his only reply. "When I am away, you will remain in the house where it is safe and warm; understand?"

She nodded yes, her curiosity piqued, but controlled. "When we have dinner guests, I will expect you to behave as the attentive, obedient wife. To make sure you comprehend my full instructions and can efficiently carry them out, we will regularly practice our manners and warmth."

Noting the look of apprehension and suspicion which darkened her emerald eyes, he sneered disdainfully, "Do not fret, my sweet; I said practice, not perform."

He watched her face fuse a deep scarlet at his scathing rebuke. "Our deal applies only in private and only in the bedroom. I have no intention of either ravishing you or seducing you. Frankly, I do not care for dutiful or reluctant submission from my wife. I much prefer a hot-blooded, passionate female beneath me, not one soiled and terrified by some barbarian!" He revealed his continual resentment toward her and her past.

Anger outweighed Alisha's cautious fear. "I see," she icily retorted, feeling hurt by his comment for some mysterious reason. "If you are quite finished with your rules of conduct for me, I believe dinner is ready."

"Dinner is ready when I say it is, Mrs. Gordon. You will pour us another sherry, will you not?" he asked in an authoritative tone.

Jeffery was a man accustomed to giving orders and having them obeyed. Slightly cowered by his surfaced hostility, Alisha determined it best to carry out his wishes whenever possible.

She poured the two glasses of sherry and handed one to him. Misty eyes met his hard blue ones as she murmured, "Evidently I have upset you in some way. I'm sorry, Jeffery. You must agree this situation does take some getting used to. Can you honestly fault me for being afraid or suspicious of you? We're married now, just like

343

you demanded; can't we make the best of it?" she softly entreated.

Seeing she was properly subdued and punished, Jeffery saw no reason to withhold his agreement. "As you wish, Mrs. Gordon," he murmured huskily, seeming to derive some pleasure from calling her by her new name. "May I make one helpful suggestion?"

She met his steady, unreadable look. "Unless you give me reason to do so, there is no need to either fear or mistrust me in the future. In addition, I need no reminders of our shared past; it is just as clear to me as it is to you. As for your conduct, I am positive you understand my expectations of you, just as I am positive you are qualified to carry them out with great flair." With that declaration, their new life together began . . .

As the winter weeks snailishly passed by, Alisha came to the realization that Jeffery had accurately outlined their life together. Their days were a farce of love. They were neither happy nor sad, serene nor tense, good nor bad, loving nor hostile. It appeared to be a period of testing, of searching, of learning, and of waiting.

After a great deal of practice and effort, they conversed with ease and politeness. At times, they even enjoyed the other's company. When requested, Alisha would play the piano or read aloud for their mutual pleasure and relaxation. Although it was the midst of an arduous and freezing winter, they continued to share delicious meals which were mainly prepared by Mrs. Webster.

On the days when she did not come, Alisha would take over the cooking and light cleaning. Jeffery was gratified to learn of her expertise in these areas. Alisha could prepare a full meal just as efficiently and quickly as his housekeeper could. She was neat and quick with her chores. He had to concede that his house had never run more smoothly or calmly; Alisha certainly added grace and civility in this barren wasteland.

Alisha had been distressed to learn of Moses, the piano player's, departure before she could speak privately with him. She had hoped to send a message to Joe. Now, all she could do was wait until spring. By then, she would have her mind made up as to whether or not she could remain as Jeffery's spurious wife or escape to Joe's cabin with him. Her decision would hinge upon Jeffery's treatment of her between now and then. There were many things to consider.

Divorce tasted bitter in her mouth; becoming a runaway wife even more so. If matters could work out between her and her husband, she would remain at his side. She could not even think about what Jeffery would do to her and to Joe if she discarded her vows and promises to him. Besides, in all honesty, the life which Jeffery could provide for her was most tempting. To return to civilization and the kind of life which she had been born to sounded too good to be denied or cast aside. Alisha felt she was already thriving in her new and comfortable surroundings.

She could only pray that Jeffery would keep his word to her. If he did, their life could be most rewarding and comfortable. After all, Jeffery was a fascinating man. He was handsome, witty, and suave. If Jeffery could lose his evil traits, perhaps there could be more between them. After all, they were legally wed.

Alisha's most demanding times came during those seemingly endless days when a sudden blizzard would rage across the land and trap them inside for days at a span. She would glance up from her sewing, reading, or cleaning to find his intense, piercing blue eyes upon her. Being caught at this curious habit did not seem to bother him at all. After the first few times of polite inquiry into his pensive moodiness, she did not ask again; for he would simply glare at her as if she had just committed some terrible offense against him, then sullenly pass off his strange behavior with a meaningless shrug. If she had read passion or desire in his gaze, she would have been less troubled. She could even comprehend his bitterness or resentment toward her for her past rejection, or she could accept his look of triumph. Knowing his expression did not fit any of those emotions, she feared its true meaning.

The only alleged role which she did not fulfill was the one of confidant, for he remained distant and evasive in all matters which did not directly concern her. As for the role of friend, that had always been an impossible joke. Being a cautious person, Alisha did not question him concerning his business ventures. She had been told he dealt with Henri and Hiram, but he refused to enlighten her any further. When Henri did come to their home for dinner, it was always a social affair.

Those times when he came to see Jeffery strictly on business, she would be dismissed after polite banter and a single glass of imported wine, compliments of Henri. The men would either retire to Jeffery's study or to a room on the back side of the first floor, one which was always locked. As Jeffery possessed the only key, she had never gone into or seen inside that impenetrable room. It had been surprising to learn that Mrs. Webster had also never been allowed in that room.

When Jeffery did finally make one of his business trips, Alisha was delighted with her first privacy and total peace. Just to keep her busy or to keep her under a watchful eye, Jeffery ordered some new additions to her growing wardrobe.

Sadly, Mrs. King was not the kind of woman who sought out friends. In fact, Alisha found her to be austere, almost to the point of open hostility. When Alisha bravely made this observation to Jeffery with the hope of not having to work with her again, he calmly chuckled and commented, "Since when does a lady share a friendship with a lowly dressmaker? Ignore her, Mrs. Gordon; she is beneath your concern or attention."

She had softly argued, "But, Jeffery, she makes her company nearly unbearable. Surely I have enough clothes to get me to Virginia. Must she come here again?"

He had appeared to ponder her plea before deciding, "If it is necessary for her to come here again, I will make sure she treats you with the proper respect and friendliness. After all, to insult my wife is to also insult me. Besides, when does any female have enough clothes and jewels?" With that remark, their conversation had ended.

Alisha had been quick to observe the guards posted around the house, day and night, when Jeffery was away. At first she had resented his groundless suspicions and mistrust. Later, she had attributed his precaution to her protection and privacy. He had pointed out the danger of his being a wealthy man in a perilous territory. No matter his motives, she did feel safer with the guards outside. Strange, when he was home, she had never felt unsafe or threatened from outside forces . . .

Once when Jeffery was downriver for a few days, Mary O'Hara unexpectedly came by to visit with her. Alisha had the oddest feeling that the silent girl was trying to warn her. Yet, Mary seemed guarded and uncertain. Naturally, Alisha did all the talking and entertaining.

They had a light lunch together, then sat before a comforting fire and sipped a glass of sherry.

Unsettled by the girl's silent and vigilant gaze, Alisha began to play the piano to relieve her own rising inquietude. Mary smiled brightly as she watched Alisha's graceful, skilled fingers skip across the ivory keys and bring forth soul-stirring music. Her chocolate eyes became soft and warm as she listened to the enchanting, relaxing music. Seeing her interest and enjoyment, Alisha inquired, "Would you like to play, Mary?"

The girl sadly shook her auburn head, then shrugged her small shoulders in ignorance. Her eyes and faded smile spoke of her disappointment. An idea came to Alisha. "I could teach you! It's very difficult at first, but you could learn with my help."

That sunny smile filled Mary's eyes once again. She could hardly trust her ears. "Here, sit beside me." As Mary timidly obeyed her soft order, she continued, "Place your hands thus."

Mary studied the placement of Alisha's fingers and copied it. "Excellent, Mary. Now, I shall teach you the keys and the notes. If you don't understand something or if I go too fast, tap my arm." With those instructions, they began to work.

Hours passed as they sat there. Both immensely enjoyed this recreation together. Without thinking, Alisha absently remarked, "I wish we could communicate easier. If only you could talk . . ."

Instantly realizing her breach of etiquette, Alisha flushed a deep red. "I'm terribly sorry, Mary," she hastily apologized. "I didn't mean for it to sound that way. I know it must be painful to live in a world of silence."

Mary smiled warmly at her genuine concern. She

excitedly began to make motions which Alisha instantly recognized as Indian sign-language. In astonishment she exclaimed, "You know signing! I know a little. Perhaps you could teach me more signing, and I can teach you the piano," she offered her exchange in rising anticipation. At last there was some bridge of communication between them, some female companionship in this lonely land.

Mary nodded her head in eagerness and joy. If anyone could be a trustworthy friend to her, this English girl could. On a much lighter note, they returned their concentration to the piano. "Run the keys once more, beginning with A and go through G . . ."

When Mary did not comply, she glanced over at her. Mary's face was stark white, her eyes large and terror-filled. Her body was rigid. Alisha fearfully whirled to trace her line of petrified vision. Her gaze locked with her husband's visage of livid rage.

Surprised to see him home a day early and looking so ominous, she stood up and moved toward him. "Jeffery, is something wrong? Was there trouble along the way?" she solicitously asked.

Without warning, she found herself stumbling backwards from a jolting slap across her cheek. She helplessly toppled against a table and knocked it over with a loud crash. Dazed and appalled, she pushed herself up to a sitting position. She shoved her loosened curls from her face. She stared at him as blood began to ease down her chin from a small split in her lip. Unaware of her injury, it dripped upon the light blue bodice of her favorite daydress. Stunned, Alisha could not get up.

Jeffery vented his unleashed fury on the mute girl. "You dunderhead! How dare you come into my home and try to contaminate my wife with your dim-witted filth! She doesn't know about your sluttish ways; but I do!

Does she know you were sleeping with her brother every day and night? Did you tell her how you seduced him while he was drunk? Did you tell her about all the little tricks you tempted and ensnared him with? Did you tell her you were the one occupying his time, not that cheap Celeste? Did you bother to tell her about all those other men you've had?" he snarled at her. He was infuriated by her daring to show up in his home after her defiance and disloyalty.

"Jeffery!" Alisha shrieked in alarm and disgust. Finding some courage and her tongue, she shouted, "She's only a child! You're being unkind and vulgar! If you are angry with me, then punish me. Mary does not deserve this monstrous treatment. The war is between us; do not involve a helpless child. You forget your breeding and manners!" she added in a softer tone.

Alisha had made a terrible mistake in her reasoning; she had unwittingly informed Mary of the trouble and mistrust between them. And, she was openly defying him before another person. Worst of all, she was challenging his word and position!

Jeffery whirled to oppose her, venom seeming to ooze from his pores. His blue eyes were as hard as an iceberg, and his face was contorted with such volatile emotion that she fearfully retreated a few steps. His ragged respiration warned her of his impending explosion. Too horrified to move, Mary helplessly witnessed this confrontation between them. Too stricken with disbelief, Alisha awaited his attack.

"Only a child!" he said scathingly. "You think I'm lying, my precious wife? You think I'm making this up to punish you with? You of all females know the power a woman can have over a man, over many men! Desire for you destroyed an entire fort, not to mention things other

350

men have done to possess you! You believe little Mary is just a sweet, innocent child? How sadly mistaken you are, or perhaps just plain naïve. She'd been fornicating with your dear, departed brother since your arrival here; that is, until his untimely accident with that other harlot. Why do you think he was too busy to defy my claim on you? Knowing how he felt about me, why do you suppose he allowed you to go with me? I'll tell you why: he was too occupied with keeping two harlots satisfied to have time to worry about what we might be doing in private!"

"I won't listen to such crude, hateful words!" she shouted at him, believing his claims to be malicious lies. "Let me go to my room, and permit Mary to go home before you go too far, my dear husband," she warned. Angry, embarrassed lights filled her distressed eyes. A veiled threat was another mistake.

"You will hear the truth, my dear Alisha. Are you afraid I might tarnish that silver image of his? Would you like to know what he was really like? Are you afraid of the truth?" he taunted without mercy, determined to force her to view his jaundiced opinion of her dead friend.

"Your truth! That's what you mean! You hated him; why should I believe anything you have to say about him? If I didn't know any better, I would swear you killed him!" she voiced her innermost suspicions aloud, confirmed by this violent side of him.

Jeffery sneered, "Would you now! I wasn't the one who drained his life; Celeste was. Of course, Mary wanted that position of sole mistress, but Powchutu had a lusty appetite. One woman just wasn't enough for him. Always heard those Injuns were insatiable creatures. Are they, my enlightened wife?" he challenged.

Alisha's face drained of all color. Shock was rapidly replaced with bitter anger. "How dare you, you despicable animal! I've never met anyone as cruel and spiteful as you are! You're the reason I was returned to him! If I had agreed to become your mistress, you would never have turned me over to him and you know it! You'll never know how many times I've regretted that decision! No matter how hard I try to earn your forgiveness and friendship, you make it impossible! I hate you! How dare you call me names and insinuate such . . ." She was so upset that she could not continue her tirade. Alisha gasped, "I will not be a party to such . . . such vindictive trash!"

With that declaration, she headed for the drawing room door. Jeffery instantly pursued her and seized her by the shoulders. He pinned her against the wall. "You will hear the truth if I have to tie you to a chair and gag you," he ominously threatened.

"I will not listen to any more lies about Powchutu and Mary! If you don't release me this instant, I'll leave here this very night!"

He laughed. "To go where, my virginal wife?" he taunted.

"To Hiram's!" she shouted, giving the only name who might assist her in this impossible situation.

He threw back his blond head and filled the room with satanic, chilling laughter. "There isn't a soul in this settlement who would dare to befriend you if you left me. Not even good old Hiram. He knows who permits him to survive in this town. The minute he took you in, his business and home would be burned to the ground by those awful river pirates."

Her face whitened once more; her eyes grew large and lucid. "You're connected with those . . . that's how you earn your living out here! My God, Jeffery, they're murderers and robbers, and God only knows what else!

352

You cannot possibly be serious! Surely there are limits to your cruelty!"

"You grossly underestimate my power and my appetite, Alisha. You always have. Had it not been for Powchutu, you would have been mine long ago. But in the end, I always get my way. Frenchy and I control the river and . . . several other lucrative ventures. If you are foolish enough to leave me or to divulge such facts, I need not express your punishment." Jeffery felt the time for gentle persuasion was over; brute force now suited his needs.

His threat went unnoticed. "Frenchy?" she repeated the name in a quavering tone.

"I see you've already heard of him," he remarked casually, not the least disturbed by her reaction. "Good! Behave yourself as you have been doing until tonight, and I won't be tempted to sell you to him for one of his infamous houses."

"You wouldn't dare! I'm your wife," she argued in dismay.

"Yes, I would dare, Alisha. You will remain my wife only as long as you continue to please me. I have given you your duties, and I demand you carry them out to the very best of your talents."

Finding some courage at last, Mary tried to sneak past him while he was focusing on Alisha. Fearful consternation flooded her at the full revelation of Jeffery's character and of Alisha's precarious position. She desperately wanted to get out of this evil house. All in one smooth motion, Jeffery flung Alisha into a nearby chair and captured Mary's arm in a firm grip.

"Sit still and quiet, little wife, if you know what's good for you. As for you, Miss Mary O'Hara, it's time for Alisha to learn the truth about you and her brother."

"Jeffery, please," Alisha protested his rough handling of the mute, frightened girl. "I'll do whatever you say," she vowed, hoping to put a halt to this horror-filled night.

"The truth, Mary! If not, I'll ask Frenchy to teach you how to tell it. Alisha has to learn certain things. Did he tell you they weren't really brother and sister?" he stormed at her.

To Alisha's confusion and torment, Mary's guilty look answered before she could nod her head in the affirmative. Afraid not to tell the truth, she did as Jeffery commanded. How could she lie when he seemed to know everything? She was forced to tell the entire truth while Alisha helplessly listened.

"Were you two . . . for the modesty of my dear wife's delicate ears, sleeping together, shall we say?" Mary lowered her eyes and nodded yes.

"Look at her when you answer, Mary. I want her to see if you're telling the truth, not speaking out of fear. Look her in the eye! Did he call you by her name when he was ramming you?" he crudely shouted.

Alisha flamed red as Mary nodded yes. Yet, she dared not interfere again. Jeffery was beyond reason or control. All she could do was sit there and be torn apart with his revelations.

"Were you content to merely make love?" His insinuation was clear to both females. Mary nodded no; Alisha winced.

"Did he confess they weren't kin to halt your ideas of incest when he accidentally called her name in the throes of passion?" Mary thankfully nodded yes. "Did he tell you all about his beloved Alisha, about her countless nights and days in the tepee of a Sioux warrior?" Alisha grimaced in anguish as Mary reluctantly nodded yes to Powchutu's betrayal of her secret.

Alisha struggled to shut out the tormenting disclosures. As Jeffery persisted with his cross-examination, tears began to trickle down Alisha's cheeks. She listened to the confession of Powchutu's traitorous betrayal, the betrayal by the same man who had befriended her and saved her life and led her to freedom. Freedom! Some freedom, her mind screamed in agony.

"Did he tell you about those times when he sold himself for favors and revenge to the wives and daughters of certain officers, women who couldn't keep their hands and minds off of him?"

For the second time, she nodded no. Her brown eyes registered shock and disbelief of this claim. "You know how he really died, don't you? He died while copulating with a whore just like you!"

Mary began to argue with his last statements by rapidly shaking her head no. "You're saying you've never slept with any other man? Come now, Mary. We both know better."

She lowered her head in shame, unable to speak of her defilement by several other guests at the Horne House. She began to weep.

Annoyed, Jeffery made a mistake. "I suppose you want us to believe that weeping means you loved the red woods-colt!"

Her head jerked up. She hastily bobbed her head up and down in full agreement with his error. Seeing his mistake, he quickly attempted to correct it. "Then why sleep with other men?" he snarled.

She shook her head, telling Alisha she was not sleeping with other men, telling Alisha she was truly in love with Powchutu. Alisha promptly realized she had permitted Jeffery's crude language and the shock of this discovery to color her initial thoughts and feelings. The look in

355

Mary's eyes told her another truth, one more important than her past mistakes.

"You're wrong, Jeffery," she stated softly. "She did love him, still does. I can read it in her eyes. Isn't that right, Mary?" Mary looked at Alisha and nodded the truth to her conclusion.

Jeffery laughed sardonically. He would teach both of them a vivid lesson which they would never forget! "Stay here, wife, while I show Mary out. You and I have some more talking to do." .

He closed the double doors as he went out. He led Mary to the kitchen where Slim and Tommy were eating a light snack and having a hot toddy after their long journey. Jeffery roughly shoved Mary into the room and ordered Tommy to hold her while he fetched his "magic potions." Tommy and Slim exchanged knowing looks, leering at their luscious target. Unable to call out for help and unable to struggle with the brute strength of this man, Mary looked on in fearful anxiety. The men did not question their reward for their hard work. Their fatigue vanished instantly.

Jeffery returned from his private storeroom. He mixed the first potion in a glass of sherry. While Slim and Tommy held her still, Jeffery forced her mouth open by holding her nose. Slim held her face still while Jeffery poured the liquid into her mouth, then clamped his hand over her nose and mouth. Unable to prevent her automatic reaction, she swallowed the fiery juice.

It only required several minutes before she realized the strange effects of the drug. Jeffery tauntingly removed her frayed clothes. In mounting horror and shame, she watched helplessly as Jeffery smeared reddish cream onto her ample breasts, then coated his index finger with the same cream and inserted it into her most

356

private recess. He grinned satanically as he wiggled his finger around inside of her. The mute girl flamed in shame.

"Feels real good, don't it? In just a few more minutes, you're gonna beg Slim and Tommy to take you in any way they want you. There's no way you can stop the hunger you're feeling right now. Your body will demand to be fed, and fed, and fed . . . probably all night. Sweet dreams, Mary girl. Remember this lesson if you're ever tempted to trick me again. Don't ever come near my wife again."

Her head began to swim and to swirl. "Give her a sample while she can still know what's in store for her tonight."

Those lustful, fiery sensations were already at work on her control. She was reeling from the delights of Tommy's mouth sucking loudly at her breasts and from the thrill of Slim's large finger working its way inside her womanhood. Unable to fight the potency of those two drugs, she began to writhe in growing hunger and sensual delight, lost in an erotic world.

Jeffery ordered, "Take her up to the same room. Keep it quiet. Just to show my wife what a little slut she is, I'm gonna give her a look at Mary in full action. I want both of you working on her. Make sure it's clear how much she's enjoying it and helping you two. And make damn sure you pretend you don't see my wife!"

After seeing the group up the steps, he rejoined Alisha in the drawing room. As ordered, she had not moved. Her frightened gaze met his smug one as he entered the room. He walked to the side-table and poured two glasses of sherry. When she refused hers, he demanded she drink it.

"Drink it, Alisha; you need it. As much as you dislike

what I forced her to tell you, it was necessary."

Her look of hate and dread went ignored. He smiled cheerfully. He appeared totally relaxed; she feared his deadly calm. "You see, Mrs. Gordon, you have retained this golden image of Powchutu which drives me insane with jealousy. You continue to see me as the villain in our rivalry. I deeply resent that. No matter what you think or feel about me right now, what I showed you was the truth. I only hope you won't be too naïve to believe it. You're such an innocent when it comes to real life and human nature. When you resist my attempts to teach you these facts, I get overly angry and dangerously frustrated."

His voice and look became rueful. "I must apologize for striking you. But when I saw you sitting there with that slut, I lost my temper. Then, when you defended her and attacked me in front of her, I was so furious I didn't know what I was doing. My violent temper always did get me into trouble. I pride myself in its control. You'll have to agree I have been good and gentle with you since our marriage. Tonight was . . . a bad mistake. Do as I say, Alisha, and it won't happen again. I don't like hurting you or intimidating you. Forget Powchutu.

"As for Mary, I told you she was a born slut. I know that air of innocency has you fooled, but I promise you it's the truth. She quite frequently services several of my men, sometimes in pairs."

"Jeffery, please," she pleaded earnestly. "Must we continue this vulgar conversation? You have been kind and gentle to me; but I have also done my part as best I could. If you don't want me to befriend Mary, all you have to do is to say so. You didn't have to attack either of us in such a brutal manner. You frighten me when you look and behave that way. That poor girl must also be petrified," she remarked, unknowingly stepping into his waiting trap.

Staring up at him and listening to his apology, she could not forget his many criminal confessions and the vivid revelation of his stygian nature. She feared this was only another deception. Still, it would be weeks before Joe's arrival. She must somehow feign defensive obedience and forgiveness until then. She vowed to never mention Powchutu's name to him again.

"You really think so?" he teased arrogantly, instantly alerting her to some new show of power. "I'll bet Mary has already dismissed both of us from her thoughts. Let's go upstairs. I have a surprise for you in the front bedroom."

Mistrust and apprehension filled her anew. Yet, she felt compelled to carry out his charade. Defenseless and afraid, she prayed he would not demand her sexual surrender to him. She knew she would fight him to the death before she allowed him to touch her. She quietly followed his lead up the long staircase.

He motioned her to silence when she was about to ask him what the surprise was. He softly whispered into her ear, "We have a guest for the night."

She was appalled when he eased open the bedroom door without knocking first. He stepped aside and signalled for her to come forward and to look inside. She reluctantly did so, feeling this must be some test of obedience. Just as she glanced around the corner of the door, his hand covered her mouth; his wintry tone whispered her to silence.

He sneered into her ear, causing goosebumps to cover her entire body, "We don't want to embarrass or to interrupt innocent Mary's fun, do we? Just an innocent child, huh? Didn't I tell you I was right about her? Tell me,

Mrs. Gordon, is she being forced, or is she immensely enjoying herself? Be honest. Look at her face and eyes. Look at her hands and body. See the way she seductively licks her lips and rotates her bottom? Are you gonna tell me those are the movements of a novice or of a girl being raped by two men? Does she look petrified or upset by my earlier treatment? She's forgotten all about you and me. She has other things on her mind now. Two men at once, Alisha . . ."

Sickened by this sight before her, Alisha tried to pull away. But her husband would not release her. In desperation, she shut her eyes to the vile sight. "Open your eyes and stand still, or I'll send you in there to join them. No doubt you're just as horny and hot-blooded as she is. Would you like to work off some of your frustrations and loneliness in there?"

She glared at him in horror and repulsion. His look said he would send her in there if she refused to watch. His tone said he preferred observation as her punishment, but he would permit participation if she disobeyed him again. She reluctantly witnessed the obscene action before her gaze, hoping she would not become ill.

Alisha wished she could look away each time Mary would take on both men at the same time, but Jeffery would force her full attention back on the offensive scene. She prayed either Jeffery or Mary would soon tire. Alisha was vividly aware of Jeffery's eyes upon her humiliated expression. She nearly swooned with revulsion, but Jeffery shook her the very instant her eyes would slowly blink for a brief reprieve.

Alisha knew for certain she would retch if Jeffery did not let her leave. Her ashen face and continual swallowing warned him of her approaching sickness. He closed the door and led her to his room. Nauseated and distressed, she did not realize his direction.

"Sit down," he ordered. He poured her a stiff brandy and pressed it into her shaking hand. "Drink it," he commanded, pushing the glass to her colorless lips.

Unable to resist his determination in her weakened and distraught condition, she downed the brandy. She coughed as its fiery contents burned a trail down her throat. Tears stung her eyes.

"If you would trust me and accept my words, I wouldn't have to prove myself to you. Do you believe she's a harlot now? Did it look as if I forced her to put on that show in there? Even my imagination isn't that colorful! There are some females who love sex and will do anything to have it every night. Then, there are women like Mary who want it in different ways or with lots of men."

He was closely observing Alisha from the corner of his eye. He poured her another brandy, which she slowly sipped on without argument. "When I was showing her to the door, she met up with Slim and Tommy in the kitchen. The three of them started handling each other right there in front of me. I agreed to let Tommy use one of the bedrooms so you could personally witness the truth. She's a sex-hungry slut who was too tempting for Powchutu to turn down. Can you imagine any man refusing something like that, especially if he's drunk? Once he's been snared by a hot-blooded female like that, he can't refuse her. Didn't you even notice a change in him after your arrival?"

"Forget about him, Jeffery; he's dead and gone," Alisha said woodenly. "I promise not to mention his name again. You're right about everything; is that what you're waiting to hear? I'm naïve, and gullible, and stupid! Satisfied? I won't question or doubt your word again. I never want another show of proof again."

He pulled her head to rest upon his shoulder. Though Alisha detested the touch of him, she relented in fear of her life.

Perhaps, Jeffery thought, he had been too hard on her tonight. Yet, there were things she had to know in order to destroy that last shred of hope and defiance which would flicker in her eyes on certain occasions. "This is the last time we will ever discuss Powchutu. But what I said earlier was true, Alisha. He did take on the officers' wives and daughters. He used it as a way to get back at the ones who scorned him in public. He would laugh in their faces just knowing he was secretly copulating with their women. He was a smart devil, never was caught in the act. That's why so many white men hated him; he was rutting with their women and getting away with it."

He smiled as he gazed down into her sleeping features. He was momentarily tempted to try out those drugs on Alisha, driving her into his arms. He knew he could not risk losing his senses. Some day he would learn the depth of her passion, but not with the likes of Tommy or Slim. He would wait until their return to Virginia, then find a decent breeder for her. He would drug her heavily. Then, he would finally witness what Gray Eagle had discovered in her which was so overpowering that he had destroyed an entire fort to have her back again.

He carried her to her room and placed her upon her bed. He leisurely undressed her, knowing her slumber was deep. He relished the delight of viewing the luscious body which was now denied to him for all time. He examined her closely as she lay nakedly exposed to his lecherous eyes and senses. He was tempted to drug her just to taunt her with the same hunger which she had teased him with at the fort. He could have her writhing and pleading with him to satisfy her needs in any way he could imagine. Perhaps one night when he was bored or angry with her . . .

As he went to cover her chilled body with the quilts and warm blankets, his eyes landed upon the tattoo upon her left buttock. Tattoo! The scout had claimed she possessed a tattoo. How had he known about it since it was in such a private spot? Fury filled him anew. He wondered if the scout had possessed her after all. Thoughts of both Gray Eagle and Powchutu sleeping with her and enjoying the delights of her response when he never could enraged him to the danger point. He determined to have the truth from her, one way or another!

Chapter Seventeen

That following morning when Alisha came downstairs, Jeffery was waiting to confront her with his new discovery. Noting the simmering look upon his handsome features, she tensed in dread. She wondered if he was still angry about the previous night or if she had somehow committed some new offense against him. He said nothing until breakfast was out of the way and the kitchen was cleaned up. It was that moment when he told her to come to his study for a serious talk. She could hardly force her feet to walk the short distance between the two rooms, for she recalled his vivid show of power last night all too well.

"Yes?" she inquired softly when he did not look up from his work. She shifted uneasily beneath his withering glare when he did.

He laughed derisively, his brow making an inquiring arc. Irritated by his accidental finding last night, he acidly demanded, "Isn't there something you forgot to tell me about, Wife?"

With her trembling legs too weak and shaky to support her slight weight, Alisha sank into the chair behind her. She shot him a look of puzzlement, afraid to hear this new accusation. "About what, Jeffery?" she asked in earnest doubt.

His drawl was low and resentful as he stated the reason for his new vexation. "Where did you get that tattoo on your lovely derrière, and when did that scout view it?"

The tattoo! How could he know about . . . horror filled her as she vividly recalled waking up in her own bed, stark naked! She gradually refreshed her memory about passing out in his room. She must have blotted out those distressing events. A new thought came to her mind: had he drugged her? Had he . . . had they? . . .

"How do you know about the akito?" she angrily stormed at him. "What happened last night after I passed out in your room?"

He chuckled devilishly. "You don't remember?" he playfully teased, his expression suggesting something lewd and salacious.

"I'm not in the mood for your vicious games again this morning, Jeffery. I think you put me through enough last night," she softly rebuked him. "Please stop tormenting me this way."

"If you're asking me if I raped you last night while you were soused, the answer is no. Of course that doesn't mean you didn't get all heated up by Mary's performance and try to seduce me," he jested to see if she would take his bait.

She paled. "I did not!" she shouted her denial.

"Did not, or hope you did not?" he baited her again, enjoying her discomfiture. His roguish grin alarmed her.

"You seem intent on making some point. Well? Let's have it: did I or didn't I sleep with you last night?" she boldly challenged him, desperate to know the truth.

His harsh laughter filled the room. He was tempted to permit her to believe she would actually seduce him or surrender to him under the right circumstances. Yet, if she were convinced they had already slept together, she just might think it strange he did not insist upon his marital rights. He let her wait for a while.

He flashed her an engaging grin, his blue eyes

glittering with unsuppressed pleasure. "Just to ease your mind, dear wife, I did not make love to you last night."

Her loud sigh of relief caused him to add a cutting remark. "Not because you didn't invite me into your frosty bed! I practically had to fight you off! I could have taken you last night. But when I take a woman, it won't be because she's drunk and defenseless. And it certainly won't be because she's been inspired from watching other people rather than from her desire for me."

"That's insulting and vulgar, Jeffery Gordon! I was not affected by watching that . . . that . . . obscene display!" she shouted, unable to come up with an adequate word to describe what she had been forced to witness.

"You couldn't prove it by me!" he promptly shot back. "You asked me to help you undress for bed. Seeing how tipsy you were, I did. Then, you started rubbing that naked, provocative body against mine. My God, Alisha, I'm not made of stone! If you want me to keep my promise to you, by damn you'll have to help me! Be glad I didn't accept your brazen invitation, for I admit I was sorely tempted to do just that! You want to know why I didn't? Because I knew you would swear I took unfair advantage of you while you were unconscious. I am a man of honor, Alisha, and I won't have you ruining me," he said haughtily.

Alisha swallowed hard, determined to find out the whole truth. She asked, "So when did you see the akito?"

"I saw the tattoo when I was trying to get you into bed. I'm not even certain if it was me you wanted or if you only needed a man. Frankly, I had rather you didn't answer that. Now, what about the tattoo?" he tersely commanded.

Confused and defensive, she did not know what to say to him. Telling a half-truth seemed the only safe way out of this new predicament. "It is a mark of ownership. An old woman placed it there, in private. As far as Powchutu seeing . . ." She suddenly halted and asked, "What makes you think he's seen it?"

"Just a lucky guess," he cleverly drawled.

"Well, you're mistaken! He knew it was there because I told him about it. He is also well-acquainted with Indian customs. But view it? Never! In spite of your low opinion of me and my morals, I have never slept with any man other than . . ." She hesitated a moment before saying his name, then continued, "Gray Eagle. Surely you realize I had no choice in that. After what I heard and saw last night, I'm surprised to find myself even sane this morning," she said in anguish. "As for trying to seduce you last night, if I truly did, then I can assure you I did not know what I was doing. Even so, it is only natural for a wife to cling to the safety of her husband in a stressful situation. Perhaps you misread my need for comfort and reassurance," she exclaimed, still doubting that she had actually been promiscuous.

"As for last night," Jeffery smirked, "at least you know why I cannot allow you to befriend Mary. You don't want people thinking you share her appetites, do you?" he softly inquired.

Alisha became indignant. "Certainly not! I had no idea what she was like. She seemed so sweet and helpful, so very young. She came by to visit, and we started playing the piano. I offered to teach her just to have something challenging to occupy me during the snows," she commented to excuse her innocent part in last night's fiasco.

"Mary isn't much younger than you, Alisha, just extremely different. If you hadn't refused to accept my word last night, I wouldn't have taken such drastic measures to prove it. I do hope it won't be necessary again. We need a truce, Wife. You're forgiven," he remarked nonchalantly. "Am I?" he asked, catching her off guard with his lazy tone.

She stared at him. "That's very generous of you, seeing as I did nothing wrong. Neither did I set out to intentionally displease you." She stood up to leave, saying, "If that is all, I have some work to do."

He grinned, both knowing she had ignored his apology and her answer. "By all means, Mrs. Gordon. By the way, Hiram received some new materials yesterday. You might like to walk over and look at them tomorrow," he casually stated to ease the tension between them.

She forced herself to smile faintly and thanked him, praying she would never have need for those dresses which Mrs. King had already made and those ones which she was still working on for her.

She frequently halted during her chores that day to fervently pray, "Please, Joe, come soon. I cannot stand this hellish existence much longer. Soon his net will tighten and I will never break free again. March is already here. Please come in April as you promised. I cannot be his wife, not in any way . . ."

Another heavy snowstorm struck a few days later, trapping them inside once more for days on end. Yet, the relationship between them slowly returned to its previous guarded terms. That atmosphere of waiting, watching, and civilly enduring encompassed them once more. Not once had Jeffery touched her in any savage manner since that dreadful night. He seemed overly kind and considerate. He laughed easily and freely conversed with her on many subjects. He complimented her talents and her efforts; he admired her beauty and her cordial conduct. He became his charming, witty, carefree self again.

Yet, she refused to be disarmed by this polished, debonair manner which Jeffery reassumed. Suspicion and mistrust grew in her mind and heart with each passing day. To her, he was being too kind and pleasing. She could not accept his continual celibacy. There was a perceptive cruelty in his eyes and voice, a mysterious aura of wickedness in his manner; things which she had naïvely ignored in the past. Having viewed the full extent of his malevolence and evil, she could now recognize the subtle signs of them.

Fear and caution urged her to walk lightly around him. She made every attempt to persuade him of her honest and complete efforts to be the perfect wife, while furtively awaiting Joe's arrival.

Within those next two weeks, Alisha experienced several unexpected and agonizing discoveries. The first one came when she walked over to Hiram's general store one afternoon while Jeffery was downriver on business. There was a mild break in the changing seasons, and he quickly took advantage of it. Confident in her total submission to his wishes, he had not hesitated to leave for a few days.

This particular day was crisp, clear, and promising. Light touches of fresh green colored the bare trees along her pleasant stroll. The sky was an endless carpet of blue, with not a single snow cloud in sight. The air smelled clean and invigorating. Dauntless early birds twittered joyously among the tall branches of the lofty evergreens. It was clear that spring was definitely in the making.

Alisha's heart thrilled and sang to the gay notes of rebirth and of future freedom. Except for an unusual snow flurry, the bitter winter was past. Each day and night the weather warmed and cleared. She eagerly looked forward to the coming of April and of Joe. As she walked along, she hummed cheerfully to herself. She even ignored the lagging guard tagging behind her. She was alive and full of hope.

She chatted with Hiram after arriving in his store. As she leisurely studied nearly every item he had to sell, she came near to his office door. Before she could react, she found herself yanked inside, the door slammed shut and bolted. She stared at the daring face before her.

"Mary, we really have nothing to say to each other," she began, her breeding forcing her to be civil to this weird girl. "Jeffery will be furious with me if he learns of this meeting. I know I said I would teach you the piano; but under the present conditions, you know I cannot.

Mary firmly caught her forearm with both of her small hands and would not release her. She seemed determined to reveal something to the distressed Alisha. Unable to speak, she anxiously sought to find some way to communicate her distressing news. Her brown eyes darted, revealing her intense frustration and silent anguish.

Seeking to end this unpleasant and dangerous interview, Alisha decided to assist her. "If you wish to apologize for what happened a few weeks ago, there is no need. Jeffery says we should not see each other, and I must accept his dictates."

Mary rapidly shook her head, saying no to her hasty conclusion. "You do not wish to apologize?" Alisha inquired in a shocked tone and stunned look, Before she could control her tongue, she stated, "If you feel your behavior was permissible that night, we certainly have nothing further to discuss! I have never been so humiliated and shocked in my entire life when I viewed that ghastly scene between you and those men. How could you behave like that? Two men at the same time! I thought you were a nice girl, but I could see I had grossly misjudged you," Alisha uncontrollably aired her disillusions concerning the mute girl.

The look on Mary's face halted her next words. Her face had gone pale, then flushed a crimson red in humiliation. Momentarily it had blanched white in tormenting reality. She signalled to ask if Alisha had viewed this wicked sight. Embarrassed, Alisha only nodded yes. Mary covered her mouth; Alisha feared she was about to be sick, just as she herself had reacted that night. Mary was ashen; she was shaking violently.

Alisha studied her for a few minutes. It was not the look of humiliation or guilt or modesty written upon her face; it was the humiliating look of shocking reality which was being heard for the first time. Alisha was totally baffled by now. If the girl was play-acting, she was doing an excellent job! If not, then what really was the truth of that night?

Eventually she glanced up at Alisha, but could hardly meet her gaze. She used a combination of signing and mimicry to relate a horrifying tale to the startled Alisha. She nonverbally recounted how she had been drugged by Jeffery and handed over to those two men. She mimicked the effects of those two drugs. She signalled how the two men had taken her to Tommy's room over the warehouse on the dock and had kept her there all night. She motioned her fuzziness about the events of that night. She looked mortified to learn of Alisha's view of her own disgusting and uncontrollable behavior.

"You're saying Jeffery forced you to take some drugs which made you act like that?" Mary nodded yes. "But

I've never heard of such a wicked potion, one which can make a person act like that!"

Mary signalled the identity of Frenchy. "Frenchy has it? He gave it to Jeffery?" Mary nodded yes both times. "You don't recall what happened after he drugged you?" Mary lowered her head in shame. She signed, a little. Alisha winced in sympathy.

"Perhaps it's best you don't recall it. I'm sorry, Mary. I should have realized the extent of his evil and cruelty sooner. Even so, there is no way I can help you; I cannot even help myself," she solemnly admitted. "Jeffery is too powerful. The only thing I can do is pray for help from a friend or for escape one day soon. I wish there was something I could say to ease the pain for you or some secret way I could be your friend. I fear Jeffery would only find out and punish both of us. Stay clear of him and his men, Mary. They're very dangerous and wicked."

Mary signalled Powchutu's identity. "You want to tell me something about Powchutu?" Mary nodded yes. Tears filled her eyes as she kept tapping her heart with her small fist. "You truly loved him?" Mary nodded yes over and over. "You two were . . . close?" She met Alisha's steady gaze and nodded yes. Love, not guilt, filled her lucid eyes.

Recalling how it had been between her and Gray Eagle, her own eyes filled with unbidden tears of loss. "I understand, Mary. Don't be ashamed of having shared true love with him. You brought some happiness and love into his life. If anyone ever deserved it, he did. He suffered greatly for his mixed bloods. I don't care what they say about his death; he wasn't like that. He was kind and gentle; he was brave and unselfish. He was like my very own brother. God, how I miss him," she painfully confessed.

Mary seized her arm and shook it to get her attention. Her eyes were cold and angry. Adding to Alisha's distress and fear, she signalled her suspicions of Jeffery's part in that strange accident. "You think Jeffery had him murdered!"

Mary nodded yes. She signalled his dislike of Celeste and Powchutu. She mimicked how she had come to their house to pick up a gift which Powchutu was supposed to have left for her. She had come to learn the dress had been purchased by Jeffery, not Paul. She struggled to relate her other suspicions about the same day.

"You think he drugged you that day, too? You think he . . ." Alisha shook her head to clear it of some of these repulsive ideas. "Don't go near him again, Mary," she warned once more.

Mary sent waves of terror through her body and mind as she signed a warning to Alisha to be extra careful of what she drank and of what she said to him. "He wouldn't dare drug me!" she declared, knowing he would indeed do just that if it suited him.

"Listen to me carefully, Mary. We must both be on the lookout for his tricks. If he discovers I know the truth about him, there is no guessing what he might do to us. He wants me to think you are wanton. As for you, it must have been a warning as he claimed. He knows you cannot tell anyone, the vile bastard!" she angrily exploded.

Before Alisha and Mary departed company that day, the entire truth was out. They were then joined in defensive secrecy; they were united in hatred against Jeffery Gordon. Somehow they would find a way to be free of his power. Alisha called Hiram into his office. She entreated him to secrecy concerning her private visit with Mary. Confused, but not enlightened, he agreed. The looks on both females' faces told him they both feared that scoundrel Gordon, just as much as he did.

Alisha was grateful Jeffery did not return for two more days. She desperately needed that time to adjust to these new, terrible revelations about her husband. Beyond a shadow of doubt, she believed Jeffery had something to do with Powchutu's death. She searched the house for evidence of that "magic potion" which he had given to Mary. She fretted when she was unable to find it and get rid of it. She could only assume it was in that sealed room. Unable to jimmy the lock, she could not look inside.

Alisha intensely searched her own muddled memory for clues to her own behavior that night. She could not accept the thought of behavior similar to Mary's. She convinced herself he had only given her a sleeping potion. Evidently he had thought it a funny joke to strip her naked and to allow her some doubts about their mutual conduct that previous night. Thinking back, neither her sheets nor her body had bespoken any sexual contact between them. She wondered if he would dare such a revolting act upon her, knowing she would either leave him or kill herself before submitting to such a crude existence. He must have sensed her reaction, for he had backed away from his joke that morning.

The depth of his evil permeated her senses. Yet, she also felt it was slanted toward the punishment of others . . . for the time being. He might be tempted to use such tricks upon her in the future. But for now, he wouldn't risk losing his investment in her. It would require every fiber of her control to keep their pretense going. Yet, she was determined to leave him in the dark concerning her vast knowledge of him. It could be very dangerous for her if he learned about this new education of hers. Surely Joe would rescue her from this sadistic fiend. Suddenly recalling the peril of the wilds, she trembled at the thought of Joe's death and her permanent entrapment by Jeffery.

When Jeffery did return late one day, she faked a mild illness to cover her withdrawal and disgust. Knowing what symptoms to list, she even managed to fool the town doctor into deciding she had a throat infection. She listened as he spoke to her husband, "Nothing serious, Mr. Gordon. Slight fever . . . sore throat . . . little infection . . . I suggest she stay in bed for a few days. Get plenty of rest, fresh air, and hot soup. These things usually take care of themselves with a little care." To Alisha, he reiterated his instructions and wished her a speedy recovery. "If you get to feeling worse or if your fever gets any higher, send for me. Otherwise, you should be fine in a week or so."

She smiled faintly and softly thanked him. She lay back against her pillows and closed her eyes. Jeffery showed the doctor to the door, then returned to her room. He seemed genuinely concerned about her health, a fact she had difficulty accepting.

"You need anything, Alisha?" he inquired tenderly, then stroked her hot forehead she had surreptitiously warmed with a hot cloth.

"Just some rest, Jeffery. I feel so weak and tired. I'm sorry to be such trouble," she said disarmingly.

"Don't be silly. Illness isn't something to be controlled. Tomorrow, I'll ask Mrs. Webster to come in every day until you're well again."

That idea sounded marvelous: with company, he would be on his best behavior. "That's very kind and thoughtful of you. I shall take care to be well as quickly as possible."

His tone changed very noticeably as he inquired, "Any

chance the doctor's diagnosis is wrong?"

She glanced up at him. "What do you mean? You think it might be something else, something serious?" she innocently inquired, praying he had not suspected her ruse.

"No need to dally around the bushes, Alisha. Any chance you're pregnant?" he unexpectedly asked.

"Pregnant? How could I possibly be pregnant when we've never slept together? I might be naïve, Jeffery, but not that much." Suspicious lights suddenly filled her anxious gaze. "You did say we hadn't made love, didn't you? You said you refused me that night," she nervously challenged his earlier denial. By accepting some of the blame for that night, she hoped for the truth.

He grinned at her choice of words. "I was not referring to myself as the father. You were sleeping with another man a few months ago, not to mention travelling with one for weeks on end," he lightly suggested a vile answer.

Anger surfaced in her emerald eyes. "I have already told you over and over, I have never slept with Powchutu. Never! Not a single, solitary time! As for the possibility of carrying Gray Eagle's child, there is none. If I was that far along, both the doctor and myself would know. Besides, I would be plump by now. As you can see for yourself, I am not," she noted, pressing the covers tightly across her abdomen to reveal her totally flat stomach. "Any more accusations, Mr. Gordon? If so, ask your guards if I entertain while you're away!"

"Sorry, love, but I had to ask. Sleep now. I'll send for Mrs. Webster in the morning. She'll take real good care of you. You need anything before bedtime?" When she nodded no, he leaned forward and pressed a light kiss to her warm brow. He assumed her rigidness and coldness were a result of his questioning.

Alisha lay back against her pillows, unaware of another dreaded discovery in the making. She was not surprised to find that she was actually exhausted. She had not slept well in the past few nights. Her emotions had been in a turmoil. Her heart felt intense anguish for the hellish event which Jeffery had put Mary through. She wondered how he could be so cruel and evil.

Thoughts of such a powerful, lusty drug terrified her. Somehow she must find his supply and destroy it. But how? That secret room was always locked, and he possessed the only key. Yet, she had to find that drug very soon!

Then, there was the matter of Powchutu. The more she thought about his so-called accident, the more she became convinced of Jeffery's evil hand in it. Too many things pointed to Jeffery's guilt. She couldn't help but believe Jeffery was also responsible for her poverty and for her hasty eviction from the Horne House. Carefully reviewing her life in St. Louis, each small action became a pre-designed piece of a large puzzle which was gradually falling into place to form a most disgusting and horrifying picture of Jeffery's despotism.

She closed her burning eyes and rested them. Her body felt heavy, numb, and weak. She wanted to sleep, but her rambling thoughts would not halt long enough for her to slip away into empty darkness. She wanted to release her pent-up frustrations, fears, and anguish by weeping for hours; yet, the much needed tears of solace would not come. The tightness within her chest was oppressive, making her respiration slow and even.

Jeffery peeked into her room. From all appearances, she was sleeping. He quietly closed her door and went downstairs. Her unforeseen illness couldn't have come at a more opportune time for him. He grinned in relief and

377

serenity. While she was safely confined to her sickbed, he could have all of the boxes packed and removed to the dock to be sent downriver to Henri.

He pulled the key chain from one of his smaller pockets and unlocked the door to his treasure room. He strolled inside to lovingly handle his bloody souvenirs. After lighting several lanterns, he examined the lengths of the braids on several scalps. He studied the colorful headdresses from varying tribes. He lifted a few of the necklaces and headbands to inspect their intricate, artistic designs. He was pleased by the variety in his collection which was to be sold back East and in the growing South; some unusual pieces might even be sent abroad. It was amazing how much some people would pay for the souvenir of a bloodthirsty savage! As for himself, he relished this formidable business which enabled him to strike down his foes while earning large amounts of money. The savages owed him much for maiming him for life!

Jeffery checked the stacks of furs and hides which his men had stolen from trappers who were returning to civilization following their stay in the wilderness during the long winter. His band of cutthroats knew just where to hide and to attack unsuspecting trappers and traders. Their heavy fur coats and leather vests had also been stripped from their slain bodies. Such items would be packed away to be sold next winter to incoming trappers, beginning the evil cycle once more. Since Jeffery planned to leave this rigorous territory during the spring, Henri was taking over the storage of these valuable items.

Slim, Tommy, and Jake had built wooden crates in which to pack these treasures for the trip downriver or for storage until needed. The furs and pelts had been carefully graded and separated into various stacks; they had been rolled and bound into neat bundles. The winter clothing which could be sold for higher prices next season was already packed into separate crates and marked to reveal their contents. The headdresses from slain chiefs and infamous warriors were cautiously laid out in another crate. Their value could be maintained only by preserving their vivid colors.

The shields, breastplates, bows, arrows, knives, tommahawks, and lances had been gingerly packed in long and narrow crates with furs of lesser quality cushioning and protecting them. The number and identity of each item in such crates were listed on the outside in a prearranged code. The countless scalps—both male and female—had been tossed into a large crate together, then marked with the number enclosed. No thought or remorse had been given to the innumerable lives which had provided this horrible collection. And many more crates remained to be sealed and marked.

The jewelry was another matter. Jeffery had personally examined each piece. Pieces of lesser value and beauty had been packed in one crate; pieces of higher quality had been placed in another. Those rare and expensive items which boasted of unusual artistic design or of valuable stones were laid aside to be carefully wrapped and packed in still another crate. This was naturally after Jeffery had selected numerous pieces for his private collection, a collection which represented only the highest quality in value and in beauty. Nothing less than the personal possession of a chief was allowed into his collection.

As he handled his own items, he knew there were only two articles missing, two treasures which were more valuable than the entire miscellany in the large room. It had been months since he had sent out word of his extravagant bounty for the scalp and wanapin of the legendary Gray Eagle. April had shown her capricious face; yet, his hands remained empty. He would be leaving this territory in Mary or early June, but not before his greedy hands could fondle that midnight mane and snow-white eagle!

So far, no man—white or Indian—had dared to bring it to him. Still, his hopes remained high; his greed steadily increased. Perhaps the snows had prevented his success; perhaps that vital scalp was already hanging upon some man's belt, just waiting to be delivered. Yet, if he did not receive any promising word by the end of this month, he would up the tempting bounty to ten thousand dollars in gold. Surely that amount would force some man to risk his life!

He left the door standing ajar as he went into the kitchen to get something to drink. But the spring night air was so cool and inviting, he stepped outside for a few moments. He absently leaned against the porch post and gazed out into the gathered shadows before him. All he could think about was having some man lay that priceless treasure across his waiting palm.

Unable to sleep and restless with tossing, Alisha threw the covers aside and got out of bed. Perhaps something cool to drink would calm her frayed nerves and help her to get to sleep. For certain her ruse on Jeffery was not plaguing her with a guilty conscience! Her inability to come up with a plan to extricate herself from this marriage was the real problem.

She pulled on the crimson robe which Jeffery had brought to her from his last mysterious trip downriver. She slipped her small feet into the matching slippers. Quietly opening her door, she walked down the hallway to the head of the steps. She hoped she could secure a drink without his knowledge. She listened for a few moments to make certain there were no strange noises coming from the study or the drawing room.

Hearing nothing which might suggest company at this late hour, she soundlessly made her way down the steps. She looked into the drawing room and glanced into his study. Seeing no one, she assumed he must have gone out for a walk or to see someone. As she headed for the kitchen, she naturally passed the secret room. She halted instantly as her vision touched upon the unsealed door. Hearing no sound from within, she curiously shoved the door back to peer inside.

She could not believe the gruesome sight which greeted her terrified eyes. Lantern lights danced eerily over the piles of horror and sacrifice. Unable to stop herself, she walked into that den of evil. She looked down into the crates which were still standing open. Her trembling hand reached out and touched many items before her dazed vision, hoping they were not real. She noted the countless sealed crates which were stacked on top of each other on the far side of the room. Her incredulous gaze slowly and painfully swept the entire room, not wanting to venture a guess as to how many lives had been taken in order to fill it. Without a doubt, none of these articles had been taken from a person who still lived.

Terror raced through her as she heard two masculine voices coming from the kitchen. Jeffery was speaking to some man at the back door. She fearfully listened. "Course it isn't too late for a little business, Frenchy. Been expecting you all evening. Alisha's in bed ill. The doctor ordered her there for the next few days. She couldn't have chosen a better time! Before she's up and around, we can have all those crates loaded and out of here. The timing's perfect. I doubt we'll be getting too many more items before I leave here in a few weeks. Come on in. Drink?"

Alisha missed the muffled voice which accepted his offer as she cautiously eased out the door and silently moved toward the stairway. As the two men headed for that same lurid room, she feared to alert them to her perilous presence if the stairs creaked, as they frequently did while ascending or decending them. So, she merely pressed her slender body against the far wall and prayed they would not come her way. Hopefully they would close the door once inside that room, offering her an escape. She held her breath in fearful anticipation of discovery.

"Been a great winter, Frenchy," Jeffery was saying as they came down the hallway from the kitchen. "Those men we hired have certainly done a superb job for us. I've never seen so many pelts and furs of this high quality and excellent condition. Real generous of all those trappers to hand them over to us without so much as a fuss."

The two joined in sardonic laughter. Jeffery went on with his assumptions, "As for that Injun stuff we ordered, we have enough to sell for a tidy fortune back in the Colonies. Amazing what folks will pay for such souvenirs from savages and barbarians, isn't it? The bounty's still out for chiefs and notable warriors. We have enough booty just from the common redskins! Nothing but the very best from now on."

Alisha felt queasy and weak. There was so much more evil to absorb too quickly: river pirates, murders, robberies, bounties, Frenchy, drugs, defilement of innocent girls, deceit, lies, revenge, cruelty, horror and more horror. . . . Was there no end to his evil, no depth too low to sink, no deed too vile to command? What black demon resided within his body?

Her head began to spin with its futile attempts to block out these new, deadly facts. She feared she was about to faint; she struggled to retain control of her senses. What region of Gehenna had she unwittingly stepped into when she had landed on that dock—Christmas Eve of all nights?

Her torment was not over yet. Another voice forced its smooth French accent into her already battered mind. "Those magic potions you ordered, I brought you a small gallipot of each. Just out of curiosity, *mon ami*, who do you use them on?" Henri inquired with a lecherous laugh.

Henri . . . Frenchy? Many times she had unknowingly conversed, laughed, and smiled with that satanic fiend in this very house! No! her troubled mind and ravaged heart screamed in unison. No more; please, God, no more . . .

Overwhelming desperation and panic filled her. As she attempted to rush up the stairs, her loud steps were later assumed to be from her careless decension. She tripped over the fluttering tail of her trailing housecoat; she tumbled back down the few steps which she had just taken upwards. An instinctive cry of surprise was torn from her lips just prior to the moment when she lightly struck her head upon the post at the base of the steps. She was instantly rendered unconscious, but not seriously injured.

Hearing the loud commotion, Jeffery and Henri rushed to her side. They found her limp body lying at the foot of the stairs. Her gown and wrapper were tangled around her legs, offering both men an ample view of long and shapely limbs. Jeffery knelt over her and called her name. When she did not respond, he picked her up and hurriedly took her back to her own bed. As he lay her down, Henri was wetting a cloth in cool water and bringing it over to him.

Jeffery gently wiped her pale face with its colorless lips. When her eyelids finally fluttered and opened, her emerald eyes appeared cloudy and confused. Her shaky hand came up to touch the rising knot upon her forehead. She focused on the two men standing by her bed, frantic expressions still visible upon their faces, worry written in their eyes.

"What . . . hap . . . happened?" she stammered, not knowing how to react to her perilous situation.

"You fell down the steps. My God, Alisha, whatever possessed you to get up at this late hour? You know the doctor told you to remain in bed! You're weak and feverish. Why didn't you call out if you needed something? Are you hurt anywhere? Shall I send Henri for the doctor?" he inquired, genuine lines of anxiety furrowing his brow.

"I couldn't sleep. I was so thirsty and my throat was dry and scratchy. It's so raw and painful that I was afraid it would hurt to call out that loud. I didn't realize I was so weak and shaky. Halfway down the steps, my head started spinning and everything went black," she lied very convincingly.

She moved her slender body this way and that. "I don't think I'm injured, except for the lump on my head. It's so late to disturb the doctor. Couldn't we wait until morning to send for him? I'm all right, really I am. I promise I won't try to get up again. I'm sorry, Jeffery."

"If you're sure you're all right? Would you like for me to get you something to drink?" he politely offered his services.

"Would it be all right if I had some sherry or brandy? I'm so tired, but I keep tossing and waking," she meekly stated.

"I don't see why not. The doctor didn't put you on any medication. I'll get some for you."

"Stay here with Alisha, *mon ami*. I will fetch the sherry for her," Henri declared gallantly, then hurried downstairs.

Doubting that even Jeffery would drug his ailing wife, she obediently accepted the proffered glass when Henri returned with the decanter and a goblet. She hastily tossed down the first drink, then slowly sipped the second one. Rosy color began to ease back into her face and lips. She began to relax and to doze.

She smiled up at Jeffery and Henri. "Thank you both. I'm feeling much better now. Goodnight, Jeffery. I'm sorry to be such a bother. I hate being sick and helpless," she murmured.

"Forget it, Alisha. Next time you want or need something, call me," he gently scolded her. "Get some sleep, love. Mrs. Webster will be over to take care of you in the morning."

Mainly for Henri's benefit, Jeffery placed a tender kiss upon her parted lips and lightly caressed her rosy cheek. She smiled wanly and thanked him again. Jeffery tucked her in like some small child, then grinned rakishly at her. She smiled at him once more, then closed her eyes. Thanks to the sherry and to her injury, she was soon asleep.

Staring down at his sleeping wife, Jeffery inquired of his accomplice, "Think she heard anything?"

Henri stepped up beside him and studied her serene, lovely face. "I think not, *mon ami*. She is much too ill and weak to be spying upon her husband, even to be out of bed. See the dark smudges beneath her eyes? See the paleness of her skin and lips? Note the feverish flush and the chilling dampness upon her body? Those things, plus

385

the glassiness of her enchanting eyes, say she is indeed ill. Do as the doctor says. She must have rest and care. She is far too precious to lose to death. No matter how much resilience and stamina you think she possesses, she has suffered and endured much for one so delicate and young. Her body and her emotions are drained and weakened. It would be too easy for her to give up hope and to slowly waste away, especially if her beloved husband does not show her love and care."

Baffled by the concern and affection which was revealed in Henri's eyes and tone, Jeffery glanced over at him. Henri actually flushed, then flashed him a sheepish grin. "Can I be blamed for admiring and recognizing a rare gem? Were she mine, we would not be so far apart," he noted. At the look of surprised guilt upon Jeffery's face, he remarked, "You do not permit her to get close to you or to trust you, *mon ami*. I read fear and mistrust in her lovely jade eyes. There is hesitation in her smile and response, as if she fears to annoy or to anger you. Why is this so? Do you blame her for her painful past? Does she still suffer from such memories?"

Jeffery's eyes chilled and narrowed. His glacial voice remarked, "There are some matters which should not be discussed, even among the best of friends, *mon ami*. Alisha is one of those private matters. *Comprendez-vous?*" he almost sneered at Henri.

"As you wish, *mon ami* Jeffery. I was merely offering my ample knowledge of women for your own profit."

"Alisha is unlike any other female. Such vast knowledge in your area of females would be of little help where she is concerned," he growled, subtly admitting to some problem without meaning to.

"Perhaps it is none of my affair, but I should like one last answer. You do not plan to make use of the opiate on her, do you? Its addiction can be most dangerous and damaging. I can easily replace a whore who has become too adjusted to it. A ravishing wife cannot so easily be replaced."

Jeffery chuckled humorously. "Come now, Henri, surely you do not honestly think I would drug my own wife," he stated indignantly. Yet, his tone betrayed his lie.

"I should hope not, *mon ami*, for the pleasures would not outweigh the risks. She needs but patience and kindness."

"No man could be more patient or unselfish than I," he boasted arrogantly, a resentful tone in his voice. "I have waited a long time to have her; what is a few more weeks or months?"

With that, they returned to their business downstairs. Not another word was mentioned about Alisha. Many hours and drinks later, Henri left. Jeffery came upstairs. Before heading to his own room, he decided to look in on her. As he pushed the door open, she quickly closed her eyes and feigned deep slumber.

Jeffery swaggered over to her bed. Her steady respiration and stillness caused him to think her asleep. She was lying upon her stomach, her face snuggled into the softness of her feather pillow. Several curls had fallen across her face, concealing most of it from his view. The moonlight did nothing to aid his obscured vision, inspiring him to make a serious mistake with an unwitting confession.

He sighed heavily. In such deep thought, he did not even realize he was speaking aloud or that she heard every word. "Damn you, Alisha!" he swore softly. "You have no idea how much I want you even now. You have stolen my last chance to possess you as that red bastard has done countless times. Yes, my bewitching wife, you will make me the perfect wife in every way but one. But if I thought for one instant those magic creams would remove my impotency, I would smear the whole damn container on my manhood and I would ram you until you begged for mercy . . . or for more," he added with a lewd, cruel chuckle.

"Those red snakes will pay for what they did to me that day. I'll spill every drop of Injun blood I can to make up for every seed I'll never be able to spit into your lovely body. Damnit! If that blasted arrow could take away my ability to enjoy a woman, then why didn't it take away these tormenting hungers, too? I would trade anything I possess to have you just one time. You'd never give that savage another thought afterwards! It was bad enough he had you first, but he's also had you last."

He lifted a curl and watched it wind itself around his index finger. "How I wish you could wind your body around mine like that. But if you think for one instant I would permit you to learn about this humiliating condition of mine . . . never! I can hear your taunting laughter now. 'Poor Jeffery, he wants me so bad it hurts; but he will be forever frustrated,'" he mocked what he assumed her reaction would be to such news.

She was momentarily tempted to shout a fierce denial to that charge, to offer her sympathy and understanding to his bitterness and hatred. Caution prevented such an absurd, generous notion. He would only hate her all the more for her vast knowledge of his evil secrets. She was ecstatic to hear he had never touched her sexually and never could. Ecstatic until she heard his following words!

"Yes, my refined and ravishing wife, you will be the perfect wife and companion for Jeffery Clayton Gordon. For now, you can believe I am being the patient, unselfish husband. Later, I will decide how to deal with my continual celibacy. You will be deep within my power and control before you ever learn anything. Such an innocent should not possess the body of a seductress! I even convinced you of your attempt to seduce me, my naïve beauty."

Alisha could not see his wicked smile. "Once we have returned to my plantation and you have conquered that old dragon of a father, I will take good care of you. I'll find some worthy young stud who looks just like me if I have to search the entire Colony. Then, my deprived wife, I will breed you with him for an heir. If you're not hungry enough by then to cooperate with my orders, my little potions will make you plead for a thorough feeding. Your luscious body will beg for sweet relief. It will do anything I command of it. I shall observe this stimulating event, the conception of my son. You have denied me the pleasure of your body, but you cannot deny me the sight of such entertainment. I shall watch you play the wanton with my own image. How I wish those creams would have the same effect upon my dead stallion as they had upon Mary all those times. To imagine you carrying on like that with my image!"

Alisha reluctantly listened as he rambled on and on about Mary's innocent, yet uncontrollable, participation in those many obscene happenings. Alisha felt repulsed by his plans for her as he outlined them in vivid detail. The only thing she saw to be grateful for was the fact he did not intend to share her with men like Tommy and Slim. A child, his heir, seemed his only interest in forcing her to submit to another man's lovemaking. Yet, he sounded as if he would enjoy watching her perform such obscene acts with his likeness; he sounded insane and sadistic. And Alisha knew that if he did find enjoyment in such a horrible perversion, he would continue to force her to perform the unspeakable acts.

She prayed he would soon tire of his wicked confession and go away. But before he did, he revealed yet another fact. "If you thought I would permit that half-breed scout to ram you when I never could, you were both mistaken," he snarled, then revealed how he had rid himself of his two annoying foes.

Almost as if reading her terrifying thoughts, he sneered, "No man has more power than I do. If you are ever tempted to run away from me, you will pay dearly. I will slice to ribbons anyone who dares to help you. There are ways to make women suffer which an innocent like you could never imagine. And if you're ever foolish enough to attempt escape through death, I will fix it so you will suffer a living death. I will never permit you to humiliate me in any way. I wonder if you even know the powers of opium, those magic powders which can demand your soul and receive it. If you dare to flee me in any way, I will extract your very heart and soul, your very sanity, a drop at a time. Even if I cannot take your body, it is mine . . . every inch of it to do with as I so choose."

Laughing brashly, he strolled out of her room. He headed to his own room. Alisha wished she had the courage to rush to her door and to bolt it. But, he would only knock it down. After long and deep thought, she realized her only safety lay in feigned ignorance to his true nature and his future plans. She wondered if it was too late to feign love for him. She wondered if her total submission would alter his intentions. She decided it would not, for his bitterness and hatred were too strong and deep. Besides, she would never be able to carry it off.

"Please come soon, Joe. I need your help," she prayed,

then instantly realized the danger that assistance would place him in. Joe wouldn't stand a chance against Jeffery and his men. It would be fatal to draw him into her troubles. She wept silently until exhaustion claimed her.

For the next three days, Jeffery kept her confined to her room and in bed. She realized it was mainly to protect his business preparations downstairs. She did as ordered, savoring her privacy. Mrs. Webster buzzed around her like a mother hen, constantly checking on her or waiting upon her every whim. She was not allowed to do anything strenuous. She ate nourishing meals; she read in bed while she rested. She even slept soundly with the sleeping potions which were supplied to her by the doctor, for she could bear no more secrets.

On the seventh day, Jeffery came to her room to join her for lunch. He nonchalantly informed her of the barn-dance which he had planned for his men and helpers. He said he had rented Mr. Blakely's huge barn a few miles down the road. He talked about the food and drinks which he was generously supplying for this rewarding event. She assumed his actions could only mean that his business downstairs had been completed. Although curious, she did not question him.

Aware of her compliant, warm nature of late, he offered, "If you feel up to getting out for some fresh air later this evening, we could take a ride before dinner." His false front as loving husband was in top form. To him, her illness had mellowed her and taught her to cling to him.

He noted the change in Alisha's mood and in her conduct, but mistakenly guessed the reasons behind those changes. She was demure and softspoken around him. She watched him closely when he was with her; she clung to his every word as if it was of great importance to

her. She never argued with his orders or raised her voice
in anger or disagreement. She was totally compliant to
his wishes. She appeared even too eager to be cordial and
warm to him. On the whole, she appeared to be completely dependent upon him, completely cowed and
deceived. In fact, he convinced himself that she might
actually be falling in love with him.

"That sounds wonderful, Jeffery. Spring is becoming
more and more noticeable every day. Everything looks so
green and alive outside my window. The sky seems so
blue, the very color of your eyes. When Mrs. Webster
lets up my window, the air is crisp and fresh. A ride would
be most enjoyable after all these days in bed," she sweetly
accepted his suggestion, completely disarming him with
her excitement and submissiveness.

"I suppose you are weary of that bed," he teased
lightly.

"I know my illness has been troublesome for you, Jeffery, but you have been so patient and kind. I promise to
make it all up to you when I'm better. I suppose many
things have been difficult between us in the past. Perhaps
we could forget them and give our friendship an honest
try. I hope you know how grateful I am for everything. In
spite of everything, I am glad I married you. I only hope
you haven't regretted your decision," she softly murmured. If feigned sweetness and affection could deceive
him into allowing her a longer reprieve from his evil,
then she would play her role to the hilt!

Jeffery had admitted his continued desire for her. He
had wanted her enough to force her to marry him. Surely
he would be pleased and confident at the gradual appearance of love within his own wife. He had wanted to
conquer her. She would let him believe he had finally
won his battle. Still, she would have have to proceed

slowly and cautiously. A sudden and abrupt change might alert him to her trickery. Yet, his conceited opinion of himself would do most of the work for her. He wanted the perfect wife; she would cunningly present her to him!

"I have never made any decision which I have regretted, my dear," he murmured huskily.

She smiled into his smoldering, smug gaze. "I'll be ready to go whenever you say," she vowed in a silky tone.

"Excellent, Mrs. Gordon. I'll have Mrs. Webster assist you with a bath and shampoo. A female's vanity demands she look her very best when going out. Now, if you'll excuse the rush, I have some business to take care of before nightfall. Until later?" he murmured, kissing her open palm.

"Until later, Mr. Gordon," she softly replied, bringing a grin to his lips and flames to his eyes. Her own eyes and lips assumed an enchanting smile, knowing her dangerous ruse was working.

After his departure, she sighed heavily at the strain of holding such a demanding mask in place for so long. Surely it would become easier with time and with practice. At least she did appear to be having some success with him. She moved around her room, trying to stir some vitality into her listless body and lagging spirits. She would need her wits and energy for later . . .

With Mrs. Webster's assistance, she did enjoy a long and relaxing bath. She dressed in one of her prettiest and most becoming gowns. She allowed the woman to brush her long curls until they shimmered with soft, warm body when the light touched them. Pleased with her appearance, she joined Jeffery downstairs at the proper hour. When he suggested a glass of sherry before their long ride, she sweetly acquiesced with a bright smile.

Along the way, they laughed and chatted like two, obliging strangers. Yet, each was too caught up with his own play-acting and private thoughts to notice the charade of the other. When they returned home, they enjoyed the delicious meal which Mrs. Webster had prepared. After cleaning up the kitchen, she was dismissed for the night.

"It's been a busy first day out of bed for you, Mrs. Gordon. Perhaps you had better turn in early. Do you need anything before you go up?"

She nodded no, followed by a dazzling smile and a few words of gratitude for the ride and his concern.

"Need any help getting into bed?" he teased insouciantly at the sight of her fetching smile and serene mood. "I'll be in my study if you require anything. Don't travel those stairs again tonight. You're still too weak to overexert yourself. We don't want another accident."

If only he knew the truth! She was terrified at the mere thought of being alone with him. Being sent to her room was like a blessing, especially knowing he could not join her! "I think I can manage, but thank you. The ride was marvelous. I'm sure the fresh air and exercise did me good. But I am very tired. I'll see you in the morning," she added softly, praying she would not have to look at his demonic face again.

She wondered why he was subtly ordering her to her room. No matter. She slowly climbed the stairs, hoping she could continue to carry off this farce of recuperation for a little longer. She entered her room. She glanced around the beautiful prison, wishing it was a buffalo tepee instead.

That forbidden thought ripped at her heart. She unbuttoned her dress, having been wise enough to select one which would not require his assistance to remove.

She lay it across the sofa, then sat down to remove her stockings and slippers. Clad only in her pantalets and camisole, she went to stand before the window and to look out.

Her mind raced along that forbidden, never forgotten path back to her Indian lover. It travelled past all the pain, humiliation, and suffering until it came to halt before those beautiful times which seared her heart with longing and love. She smiled sadly as one image after another flickered and came to life. How she longed to be in Gray Eagle's arms and tepee again, to taste the sweetness of his kisses, to savor the feel of his cool hands upon her warm body, to know the delights which he had borne within her.

"Do you ever think of me, my love? Has time and distance lessened your hatred and inspired this same loneliness and pain? Will my heart and mind ever be free of you? God, how I love you." Gray Eagle was her past; still, she wished he was her future.

Alisha knew she must take some action very soon. She could not continue to wait for Joe's possible arrival; he might never come—or come too late. The instant she tipped her hand to Jeffery, he would strike her down. After tonight, that would be very soon. The question was, how could she fight him and escape without killing him?

Chapter Eighteen

"What will you do when you find him? Will you slay him on the ground where he stands, or will you take him prisoner to be slowly tortured for his evil deeds?" the resonant voice inquired of his best friend. His keen black eyes intensely studied the odd look which filled the stygian gaze of his long-time companion. Although he had known him since childhood and had shared moments of great danger and of joyous victory with him, he often felt there were times when he no longer knew the desires and pains which were buried deep within his friend's heart. It had been this way since his treacherous betrayal by the woman he had loved and married: a beautiful, white creature called Alisha.

Since that moment when he had regained consciousness, nearly two weeks following that day of infamy, he had somehow been different. Being a man unaccustomed to defeat, rejection, or weakness of any kind, he had deeply resented the impuissant condition and traitorous news to which he had awakened. Only his great weakness and the adamant insistance of his father and the medicine chief had kept him on his mats until his wound could heal properly. Seeing his wish for immediate revenge had been overruled, he sullenly and bitterly did as he was ordered.

He ate what was served to him; he slept when commanded; he exercised only when advised. Yet, his mind worked harder than his body would have had he been free to do as he wished: track down and punish his traitorous wife and her half-breed lover . . .

White Arrow's thoughts fled back to that incredible moment when he had glanced up to see Chula slowly entering their village with the unconscious body of Gray Eagle lying across his back. In fear and dread, he had raced toward the magnificent appaloosa bearing his close friend upon his broad back. He had carefully eased him to the ground, noting the wound near his heart. He had hastily placed his keen ear to his heart, overjoyed to hear a slow and weak heartbeat.

He had called others over to help him carry the legendary warrior into the medicine chief's tepee. Running Wolf's face had filled with worry and anguish at the thought of losing his only son. Gray Eagle's powerful frame had been placed upon a mat, then carefully examined.

"It is the wound of the white man's firestick. The magic ball has passed through his body. He has lost much blood; he is very weak. Unless it is not the will of Wakan-tanka, he will walk the ghost trail before the moon shows her face this very night," had been the initial conclusion of the medicine chief.

But he had not taken into account Gray Eagle's intense will to live and his great stamina. The ball had indeed travelled through his body and he had lost a great deal of blood; but the ball had not touched his heart or his lungs. It had miraculously passed through the narrow track between those two vital areas. It had taken two agonizing weeks to prove to the Sioux that it was not the time for Gray Eagle to meet the Great Spirit face to face. The entire village had prayed for his recovery; there had been silence in the camp and tension in all of their hearts until that moment when he had given the first signs of revival.

He had sighed deeply, as if having the breath of life returned to his body by the unseen Great Spirit. He had called the name of his wife: "Alisha." His eyes had shown determination as he struggled to come around. The news had spread quickly around the camp: Gray Eagle would live! There had been joyous singing and prayers of gratitude.

Several more days had passed before he was lucid and alert. At first he had appeared confused, but only until the full reality of his predicament came to him. He had ordered everyone except White Arrow out of the medicine lodge. He had focused jet eyes upon his blood brother. His gaze had been too full of other emotions to reveal what he was truly thinking and feeling.

"Did you find Alisha, my brother?" had been his first and most obvious question. "Does she still live?"

White Arrow recalled how he had lowered his head in shame and in torment, ignorant of the events of that deceitful day. He had painfully spoken the words which he had dreaded to tell his best friend. His own heart had been ravaged with the apparent truth, for he and Alisha had been friends and companions from the very first time when she had been taken captive. He had yearned to have better news to reveal to his injured friend. He would never forget the conversation which had followed:

"You have been unconscious for many, many moons. We feared you would not live. We begged the Great Spirit to save you. He heard our prayers and answered them. Soon, you will be as strong as ever. We will ride the plains together again, Brother."

"Where is she, White Arrow?" his curt, unmoved tone had demanded of his friend.

"I must hang my head in shame, Gray Eagle, for we could not find her. Many braves and warriors have searched for her many days; she is lost to us. The white man who shot you has captured her and taken her away from us. We searched everywhere; there was no trail to follow. I fear she is either captured or slain. I beg your forgiveness. Your wife is gone."

The mistake had instantly registered in Gray Eagle's astute mind. A look of utter astonishment had filled his eyes, quickly followed by a strange look of relief and satisfaction. White Arrow had stared at him, seeing his reaction to such sad news: a lazy, malevolent smile.

"Did you not hear me, my friend? She was stolen when you were shot! She is lost to you. We could not find her," he gingerly repeated his news to the grinning man before him.

"I hear your words, my friend and brother. There were no signs to follow?" he repeated in a strange tone which disturbed White Arrow.

"The winds and sands took them away. Even your trail back to camp was lost not far from here. We searched in all directions. She has vanished like the desert flower in winter. How did you escape our white enemy? You were almost dead when Chula brought you here."

"He thought I was dead. He rode away. Chula lay on the ground for me to slide across his back. That is all I remember until now. How many moons since my mind slept so deep?"

"Ten moons passed this way." Anticipating his next question, he softly added, "Thirteen since the joining ceremony."

"No signs at all, White Arrow? Did you search with all your senses? Did you search near the mountains where the sun goes to sleep?"

White Arrow's eyes and voice had filled with anguish as he replied, "Many of us looked. There was nothing to

399

see or to hear. I sent braves to all the nearby camps with a
message to look for her. I even sent offers of rewards to
the camps of our enemies for her safe return. No eyes
have seen her since your joining. Black Cloud's heart is
heavy with the loss of his daughter for a second time," he
finished.

"I see, my brother. Her betrayal has worked. She is
free of me at last. If you could not find her, then she has
escaped to her land far away. I was a fool to trust any
white-eyes, but more so to love and to marry one."

White Arrow had gaped at him in utter disbelief, then
great worry. "Your fever is still upon you, my friend. She
has been stolen from your side!"

"No, White Arrow, she was not stolen from me. This
secret must remain between us alone. I will not face the
dishonor of her betrayal and deceit. I have been shamed
by this careless defeat by an enemy. I will not allow her to
shame me again. I will allow her to take nothing more
from me. If ever our paths cross another day, I shall put
my knife into her heart and twist it. She will feel and
know the same pains my heart and body have known and
felt."

White Arrow had studied his wintry look and had
listened to his icy voice. "I do not understand these
strange words . . ."

"The half-breed scout who called himself her friend is
the man who shot me. They planned to lead me away
from the Blackfoot camp and murder me. They tricked
me. They have escaped together. She carries his child.
She deceived me and betrayed me. My blood is upon their
hands. But the Great Spirit has spared my life; I will one
day find them and be avenged."

"Powchutu shot you! She ran away with him? I cannot accept such words. There is some mistake," he

had argued.

"The scout followed me. He told me these things."

"Then he lies! He has captured her for his own. He feared you would slay her; he feared you did not truly love her or want her. Alisha would not do this thing. She loves you!"

Gray Eagle gradually revealed the events of that tormenting morning when he had been confronted and shot by Powchutu. When he had completed his tale, there could be no doubt as to Alisha's part in that terrible tragedy. White Arrow's anger and hatred was surpassed only by Gray Eagle's. He, too, had vowed vengeance upon the heads of his two enemies. Yet, he had known there was nothing else to be done to locate them. Their fates lay within the hands of the Great Spirit.

"Where is her headband? Did I have it with me?" he had abruptly asked.

White Arrow had handed it to him, while learning of how his friend had attained it. "Each day I will hold it and renew my vow of revenge upon them. It will remind me of her treachery and deceit. It will tear my love for her from my heart; it will take away any good thoughts and memories of her from my mind. It will leave only those of bitterness and betrayal. I took her to my heart and body. I kept her in my tepee. I protected her and loved her. I endured the taunts and laughter of other warriors just to keep her with me. I fought a challenge to the death for her. I married her. She was mine as no other woman has been. I bared my heart and soul to her. I, Gray Eagle, permitted her treachery! She will pay, my friend. Before I leave the face of Mother Earth, she will pay . . ."

"What if we cannot find them? How will you take their lives? They have disappeared."

"The Great Spirit will guide me to them. He will not

401

permit such dishonor to fall upon me without payment. No one will know this truth except the two of us. Let the others believe the story you have told to me. Swear silence to me."

"What of your father?"

"No one will know of my shame until she has paid with her blood! No one!" Gray Eagle overexerted himself, and White Arrow gently forced him back to the mat.

"You will not tell her father that she lives?" White Arrow asked.

"She lives only as long as the Great Spirit allows it."

"It will be as you say. A white enemy shot you as you tried to protect your wife, and she was captured. They will see you have recovered. They can only guess at her fate."

For many days and nights as he had lain helpless and healing, visions of Alisha plagued his heart and mind. His body had signalled its need of her when he would awaken from dreams of her. He had raged at his wayward mind each time it called her memory to life to torment him. How he had wished he could forget her completely. He had prayed for the Great Spirit to remove this relentless love and desire for her; yet, it still burned brightly and fiercely within him, no matter how angrily and frequently he denied it.

That day had been many months ago. The winter had come and was nearly gone. Gray Eagle had gradually regained his former strength and power. But now that his people had seen him vulnerable, he had been forced to rebuild his reputation of unconquerable power.

Resenting the need to prove himself like a young brave would, Gray Eagle became relentless and deadly with his enemies. In battle he was without fear and ever escaped defeat. His skill, cunning, and valor were quickly reinstated in the minds of his own warriors, enemy warriors, and all whites within his reach.

Before the rebirth of Mother Earth in the spring, the legend and prowess of Wanmdi Hota was once again feared and revered throughout the area. Not a soul entered the Dakota Territory without hearing of his numerous coups and fearless power. He was persistent in his desire to drive the whites from Indian lands and to prevent the entrance of others. No man, Indian or white, dared to challenge him without losing his life. Soon, even his enemies dreaded to confront him. As the months passed, his legend grew larger than life. The stories called him invincible, inescapable, infallible, and potent beyond measure or belief.

No one reminded him of the half-breed daughter of Chief Black Cloud who had been his wife for one day before her tragic capture by the white man. They blamed his great love for her as the reason for his dulled senses which had resulted in his one and only defeat by an enemy. Each friend wished he could locate her and return her to his side; each enemy wished he could find her and return her body to him.

It was soon clear to those who knew and loved him that he was harder, colder, and sterner than before her disappearance. Their hearts bled for his loneliness and pain; they grieved over the harsh effects of her loss upon him. They prayed he would someday forget her and find another woman to take her place. Yet, having seen her, they knew she was impossible to replace . . .

Gray Eagle had refused to take another female, even for physical release. It was as if he could not bring himself to touch one in any way. Several times he had been tempted to brutally ravish some of the white female captives as substitute punishment, but he had found it impossible to be intimate with any of them. He had not even been tempted to seek solace with one of his own kind. Alisha had remained a mental obsession, a smoldering fire within his blood, a ravaging disease within his body.

Once in a brief moment of fatigue and weakness, he had inadvertently confessed to his friend, "Even after all she has done to me, White Arrow, she is the only woman my body craves. It still burns for her like a fire which will not be put out. I could easily make love to her as I cut out her traitorous heart! She torments me in the black of night when my senses sleep. At times I hear her voice in the waterfall or in the nightbird's song. I can smell her sweetness in the flowers and wind. I can almost feel the softness of her skin against mine. I can close my eyes and she is there with me. My mind sees her smile, her hair inflamed by the sun, the green grass within her eyes. Yet, her heart is black and deadly. I shall kill her, White Arrow, for only then can I be free of her. Only when I feel and see her life drain from her body can I be truly free to live again."

Gray Eagle recalled his last day with Alisha, all the words and lovemaking which they had shared. "Lies!" his brain thundered. Then, another conversation came to mind: his confrontation with Powchutu, that treacherous half-breed whose life he had spared that day Gray Eagle had ridden against Fort Pierre.

"Somehow, someday, the Great Spirit must see it in His way to allow our paths to cross again," Gray Eagle fervently prayed. "This great emptiness and lingering pain in my heart and life demand Alisha's punishment. If only she did not remain so alive and green within my traitorous mind . . ."

He grinned in bitter amusement as he remembered how he had feigned ignorance of the scout's words. In truth, he could speak better English than that half-white scout! Yes, he remembered every single word! For once, he had wished he could not understand their tongue; his secret had been his undoing, his tormenting defeat. Alisha and her lover had savagely used it against him that day.

Now, he faced a new treachery from the whites. How he wished they would remain within their own lands, at least the women and children. Each day which passed made it seem more and more necessary for him to secretly venture into the world of the white man and to seek out his old enemy "Yellow-hair" from the devastated fort not far away.

His white enemy had offered a large reward for his scalp and wanapin. Now, he was not only sought out by foolish white men, but also by reckless enemy warriors. Much of his energy was consumed by these countless, futile attempts upon his life. With his reputation, a man had to either be a fool or a desperate hunter.

Gordon had finally pushed too far. Gray Eagle now felt it essential to seek him out and to stay these attacks upon him. He was being forced to slay too many men in order to save his own life and to protect his own honor. The challenge had been delivered; he would now accept it. Besides, Gordon was an evil man who dealt in death; he had to be stopped for all time.

He and White Arrow headed off in the last known direction of Yellow-hair's present location. They followed the instructions which had been drawn from the lips of his last two attackers. When they were within twenty miles of the most distant homestead from St. Louis, Gray Eagle and White Arrow made camp. They found a place which was unnoticeable from any nearby trails, a place which could not easily be found.

White Arrow watched as Gray Eagle changed himself into a white man. He took his sharp hunting knife and severed his raven black hair to collar length into the white man's style. He changed into the deep blue linen shirt, the sienna-colored leather vest and pants, and the black boots which he had taken from one of the men who had tried to slay him.

He strapped on the leather belt with its highly carved knife sheath, but placed his own knife inside of it. He attached the other smaller sheath to the inside of his left calf. He picked up the firestick, the white man's long rifle, and inserted it into the holder on the stolen saddle. He hung the powder pouch on the horn, just for appearances.

Pleased with Chula's easy adjustment to this white man's heavy saddle, he mounted up. Last of all, he placed the black hat on his head and cocked it forward to partially conceal his black eyes and bronzed skin. He glanced down at White Arrow and smiled in self-assurance. Going after his enemy—the one who had once stolen Alisha from his tepee—made him feel more alive and vital than he had felt in months.

He clasped White Arrow's wrist and exchanged a knowing look with him. "If I have not returned in three days, return to our people." That was all he needed to say of his possible defeat when surrounded by countless white enemies. "Farewell, my brother and friend, may this not be our last."

"May the Great Spirit guide your steps and return you safely to my side," White Arrow declared warmly. He watched as Gray Eagle rode away to face whatever fortune or disaster the Great Spirit might send into his path.

Gray Eagle assumed an easy gait toward St. Louis. It was his plan to keep his presence there unnoticeable and short. He would seek out the house which had been described to him and he would confront his past foe. They would finally end this long and deadly rivalry between them.

As he travelled along, he pondered the fierce hatred of this particular white man toward him. It was a powerful, endless obsession for Yellow-hair. They had battled many times in the past. Yet, it was clear his hostility and obsession had increased or been refreshed at mid-winter. It was almost as if he was suddenly desperate to have his wanapin and scalp, as if his very life and happiness depended upon it.

Gordon had been in the business of buying and selling Indian jewelry, weapons, and scalps since the destruction of Fort Pierre. Yet, his overwhelming desire to increase his personal collection had become a relentless pursuit in what the white man called January. Gray Eagle had heard that Gordon paid extra for "treasures," the belongings of chiefs and their sons. It had also been a known fact that Gordon would pay an even higher bounty for Gray Eagle's hair and jewelry. Yet, that higher reward had suddenly increased sharply to a stunning amount, an amount which the average white man considered a fortune. The reason for Gordon's sudden demand for his life escaped his keen mind. Fame, rivalry, and hatred were reasonable yearnings; but this present vengeful desire . . .

It was past nightfall before Gray Eagle reached the outskirts of the large white settlement. He halted to study his surroundings and to select his direction of arrival. He then headed toward the tall, white house on the near horizon. Just as he had been told, it was set away from the main settlement. He cautiously weaved his path through the edge of the forest, stopping in a heavy clump of trees and bushes.

He dismounted and dropped Chula's reins. Knowing how intelligent Chula was, he could find his way back to White Arrow if he failed to return or if someone else attempted to capture him. The disguised warrior lovingly patted the animal's nose and signalled him to silence. The massive beast obeyed his master.

Gray Eagle's alert, keen senses scanned the area around him and around the house. From all sights and sounds, the house appeared deserted this night. He cautiously made his way to it. Window by window, he checked out the interior. He smiled in open satisfaction, for he had sighted no one except his former enemy.

If there was anyone else in the darkened house, it would mean they were upstairs and hopefully asleep. He eased over to the nearest window, his intention to silently slip into the house and to suddenly confront Yellow-hair.

A much different idea came to mind . . .

Chapter Nineteen

Jeffery had his full attention and concentration upon the ledgers spread out before him. Pleasure filled his thoughts at seeing he was becoming wealthier by the day, even out here in this godforsaken wilderness. He could hardly wait for the war with England to be over so he could return home to his plantation in the Virginia Colony. He had no doubts whatsoever that the Colonies would win this little fray.

He was glad to have this quiet evening alone to work upon his books; it would soon be time to close out his business here. This dance for his workers had been a brainstorm. It would only encourage them to work harder and faster for him. He assumed they would all be reeling drunk by now. It would serve his purpose very well, for they would get rid of some of their abundant energy before the demanding chores began. How could they argue with a kind, generous master like he was? He had earned their obedience and loyalty.

As his thoughts wandered, Jeffery considered the girl upstairs. A malicious sneer crossed his once-handsome features, now marred with resentment and hatred. He settled back in his comfortable desk chair and sighed with pleasure.

He had naturally succeeded in forcing her to marry him. He could now admit that his greatest desire was to break her strong will. He was making progress with her, but he had not as yet won her total defeat . . . nor her loyalty and affection. He wanted and demanded all of these things from her. In the end, he would have them, too.

After his cunning disposal of her self-appointed guardian and constant companion, it had not required long for her to comprehend her vulnerable position. She feared the exposure of her past life as the captive and ex-whore of Gray Eagle. And now she feared a repetition of her past existence at Fort Pierre. Those fears had convinced her to obey his dictates. Too, his foresight to steal all of her money had left her penniless. Compared to a life of enforced whoredom, his proposal of marriage had seemed a blessing.

She had never known he could not consummate their marriage or share a normal sexual relationship. She did not know his reason for his ultimatum for marriage to her. In her defenseless position, she had been the perfect target for his plans. With an intelligent and well-bred female like her as his wife, he could return home with his manly pride intact. No one would ever learn of his humiliating impotency.

Once back in Virginia, he would one day find an acceptable man to breed her with to produce a proper heir to his name and his family fortune. Of course, the man would be killed as soon as she became pregnant. All of his plans for his privacy and comfort had been carefully considered. To have Alisha Williams at his mercy was an added benefit.

Alisha Williams . . . she obviously feared his power and his threats; yet, she still remained resentful and ungrateful. Did she really think she had him fooled with that passive, sugary pretense of hers? The thing to decide was her motive behind it. Was it based upon defensive fear? Had she finally capitulated to him out of fatigue?

Was she up to some deceit? She was definitely trying very hard to please him and to feign affection. Yet, he could read defiance and repulsion beneath her sweet facade.

He mumbled to himself, "No doubt the necklace and scalp of your past lover will bring some noted change in you. But what change, my lovely wife? Gratitude and pleasure? Or perhaps sadness and a final break from his damned power over you? Do you think I am a blind fool, my dear? You have never forgotten him. I do not know why you escaped from him. Surely not for the love of that damn scout. No matter why, he will also be out of your life forever, very soon . . ." he muttered bitterly, unaware of the man who was silently easing up to the window behind him.

His soldierly instincts dulled, Jeffery was not aware of the danger which was rapidly overtaking him. The study had become rather warm and stuffy. Jeffery turned around in his chair and went to the tall window behind him. He slowly pushed it up to catch the cool, evening breeze and to clear his groggy mind. After inhaling deeply several times, he went to his bar to fetch a brandy. He returned to his desk. A movement to his left caught his attention. He glanced back toward the open window.

"What the hell!" he sharply exploded in surprise and anger. Accustomed to respect and obedience, Jeffery was not immediately afraid or even aware of his position. Far worse, he had not as yet recognized the disguised man before him. "Who are you? What do you want here?" he arrogantly demanded of this bold intruder.

The ruggedly handsome, bronze-skinned man leaned his tall, muscular frame against the wall. A masterful, confident expression was written across his face. He seemed totally relaxed and utterly fearless. His cool stare and continued silence unnerved his unsteady opponent.

"Either state your business, or get the hell out of my house!" Jeffery exploded with anger and apprehension.

Jeffery did not like to be bested, as he had been just now. He was acutely aware of his lack of protection, a fact which added to his rising tension. Never before had he realized that a coward slept deep within him. He cursed his foolishness at being caught unprotected and alone. He was a wealthy man with many enemies. Yet, he had foolishly permitted every one of his men to attend that damn barn dance!

He promptly assumed this mysterious man to be a robber. Since criminals were supposed to honor each other, he calmly informed this man of his identity and powerful connections. There was no reaction from him. He then attempted to strike a deal with him. The other man arrogantly ignored his offer of money.

Gradually an amusing idea occured to the intimidating Gray Eagle as he witnessed the fear and vileness in his sworn enemy. He decided to play with him for a while. Dressed as a white man and far from the Dakota Territory, Jeffery never once imagined the identity of this aggressive man.

"It's late! If you don't want money, then what do you want from me? I have told you of my connection with Frenchy. If you harm me, you will answer to him and his men," he boldly warned, strained lines of fear tracing his tight features.

Gray Eagle concealed his humor and pleasure behind a placid expression. "Never heard of this Frenchy. But I did hear you buy Injun scalps and jewelry," he replied with the words which he had practiced time and time again before his arrival. "Got one they say is real valuable," he teased the reprehensible man before him.

"Want to buy it?"

Disarmed by what he now considered to be a rude outlaw, his smug air quickly returned. "Is that a fact?" he sneered, wondering who this defiant man was, wondering why he would dare to show his face at this time of night. "Just who says I buy such stuff?"

Gray Eagle smiled haughtily and shrugged his powerful shoulders. "If you ain't interested, just say so. Too late for nonsense," he stated. "Just heard you were willing to pay big for the hair of Gray Eagle. If not, then I done killed him for nothing."

His words had a noticeable impact upon Jeffery. Excitement and pleasure filled his eyes. He could hardly control the exuberant trembling in his voice. His blind eagerness to place those two items in Alisha's hands this very night caused him to throw all caution to the wind.

Studying the man before him, he decided if anyone could take on the mighty warrior and come out the winner, this man could. He would decide later how to get rid of him. He could hardly wait to realize his long-awaited dream. "Sounds as if we do have some dealing to do."

He quickly downed his brandy and placed the empty glass upon his desk. "Who are you? Where'd you come from?" Jeffery quizzed the man who had just claimed to have the courage and skill to defeat his formidable foe.

"I believe you wanted to see me real bad," the man stated, to Jeffery's bafflement. "You already know, don't you?" he added, further increasing his confusion.

Jeffery scanned the man from shiny black head to dusty black boot, trying to recall if he had indeed ever met this man. There was something vaguely familiar about him, but he could not quite place it. He did not appear to be a man one forgot easily.

413

Jeffery's curious gaze swept over the man's attire, seeking some clue to his statement. A brown leather sheath with a hunting knife was secured to the wide belt at his waist, his only weapon from appearances. The man was dressed in leather breeches, a dark blue shirt, leather jerkin, and black boots. The way his dark hat dipped low over one eye added an ominous air to his visage. His stubble-free face made it possible for Jeffery to note his amusing, sarcastic leer.

"I wanted to see you? About what? I don't even know you!" Jeffery countered to learn more about this perplexing man. "If it's money you're after, I keep very little cash here. I'll trade you my wife's jewels for that scalp you mentioned," he declared to learn if the man had only been taunting him with the answer to his dreams. Hoping to prevent any violence from this disturbing man, he added temptingly, "Those jewels are worth a lot of money . . ."

He laughed to ease his mounting tensions. "Course if you want cash for the scalp, you'll have to wait until morning. I can get the money from a friend of mine." If he could stall this man until morning, he would have his men take care of him.

Gray Eagle's lazy, humorous laughter filled the room, letting Jeffery know what he thought about his proposition. He smoothly replied, "Jewelry? I have no need for such things. But I do have a wanapin you want bad . . . real bad." As he was speaking, he casually tossed his eagle amulet to Jeffery.

Instinctively Jeffery caught the necklace which was thrown to him. His greedy eyes locked on the item in his sweaty hand. A broad grin settled upon his face; his blue eyes twinkled with joy. He looked up at the man before him and chuckled. "By God, you did defeat him! How?

414

Where? When?" he shouted in excitement.

"Only once has he been defeated. Never again. I have met him many times, but I did not know you valued his life so highly. Why do you seek his life at such a great price?"

"It's a private matter. You should have told me right off you only came to collect the bounty! Hell, man, you could've used the front door! You nearly scared ten years off my life coming through the window like that. Thought you were a robber; I might have shot you! You got his scalp, too? Give it to me," he ordered, eagerness evident in his eyes and trembly voice.

Seeing, the man's hands were empty, he feared his denial of that treasure. "Where's the scalp!"

Gray Eagle nonchalantly tossed his hat across the room and taunted, "Right where it always was, Yellow-hair." He grinned as he lightly tugged at it, joking lazily, "Just a little shorter."

For the first time in his entire life, Jeffery nearly passed out from shock and fright. He visibly shuddered in fear and in belated recognition. He blamed his deadly mistake on the fact he had only viewed this man from a distance that last day at the fort. Yet, he knew that face should have been emblazoned upon his memory for all time. His face gradually lost all normal color, and his deep voice trembled, "You . . ."

"How much bounty did you offer for my hair and wanapin, White Dog?" he taunted in light of Jeffery's terrified stare.

"Should I foolishly trade them for your wife's jewels?" He drew his knife from its sheath and absently fingered its shiny, sharp blade.

With that joking statement, Jeffery seized upon a desperate plan. "I'll trade you my life for my wife," he

415

shouted, almost laughing at the ridiculous rhyming of his cowardly offer.

Gray Eagle did laugh; he vividly scorned the weakling before his steady gaze. "I have no use for a woman who would marry a man such as you, Yellow-hair. Your life is what I demand. You escaped my vengeance once before; never again," he vowed icily.

Jeffery's eyes mirrored his rising fear and anxiety. "Not even if my wife is your ex-captive, the woman you destroyed Fort Pierre to regain, the woman who has twice escaped your camp," he nervously wheedled, ". . . the beautiful Alisha Williams?"

Gray Eagle's eyes narrowed and hardened at the mere mention of her name. "She is dead," he declared coldly.

"Dead? No way! She's upstairs asleep right now. She came here after she left your camp with that half-breed scout Powchutu. She married me," he informed the silent warrior.

This unexpected news was like a forceful physical blow. The dauntless warrior stiffened and straightened to his full and towering height, his facial expression fathomless. A statement he made long ago came to his warring mind: "The Great Spirit will guide me to them, or them to me." He recalled his words to White Arrow: "The Great Spirit will not permit such dishonor to fall upon me without payment. She lives only as long as the Great Spirit allows it. She will pay, my friend. Before I leave the face of Mother Earth, she will pay . . ."

Jeffery sensed his strange interest in the illusive Alisha. "She's a pain in the neck! Why you ever wanted her back, I'll never know! But you're welcome to her. For my life, that is," he added, his lagging courage given a false rise.

Gray Eagle instantly halted his hasty exultation. "If

she is here, I do not need your permission to take her. As you said, she is a great deal of trouble and annoyance. If she is your wife now, she will die this same night with her evil husband. She is nothing to me, White-eyes! Her life is not worth one single hair from my scalp. I will trade nothing for her. Your life is mine, Yellow-hair; prepare to die," he advised, shifting his knife to a threatening position in his strong hand.

With that warning, Jeffery panicked and made a wild dash for the door. Gray Eagle agilely bounded over the desk with one easy leap and reached it at the same time. There was a fierce and desperate struggle between them. Jeffery knew instantly that he was out-classed in every way. He had permitted himself to grow flabby and sluggish. On the other hand, Gray Eagle was at his peak. The fight lasted only a few moments.

Jeffery attempted to grab the knife, but found it buried in his right shoulder instead. He winced in pain as the bright red blood gushed from the jagged wound. He tried to knee Gray Eagle in the groin. His struggles were feeble and futile. Besides greater strength and skill, Gray Eagle also had greater motivation on his side. The battle was won almost too quickly and easily.

With Jeffery pinned to the floor, he sneered, "Never again will you buy the scalps and possessions of my Indian brothers! For what you once did to my people and village, Yellow-hair, you die!"

Another brief struggle ensued, followed by a knife buried deep within Jeffery's satanic heart. Gray Eagle arose and stared down at his dead foe. At last their private war was over. It had ended in the death of one of them, just as they had both known it would. He retrieved his amulet from Jeffery's desk and placed it around his neck.

Jeffery's earlier taunts came back to claim his attention. He left the study and made his way up the staircase. He checked every room as he came to it, finding each one empty. Near the end of the long hallway, he approached the very last door. At last, the truth or the deceit in Jeffery's claim would be evident in a few more moments.

Gray Eagle slowly eased open the bedroom door, making sure he made no sound which might alert its possible inhabitant. He gingerly slipped inside the spacious, dimly lit room. His keen gaze seized upon the slender, feminine figure which was poised before an open window. He curiously and apprehensively studied the incredible sight before him, not daring to make a hasty judgment.

Thick masses of auburn curls flowed down her back almost to her small waist, like water rushing down a rocky cascade. One ivory hand gently clutched a fold in the blue drapes, while the other rested lightly across her abdomen. She was scantily attired in knee-length pantalets and a snug, matching white camisole with narrow lacy straps; an outfit which did very little to conceal her shapely figure. His groin annoyingly tightened.

Her respiration appeared slow and even from the light rise and fall of her shoulders. One ankle was slightly raised from the blue floral carpet and rested lightly against her other bare foot. The balmy April breeze gently ruffled wisps of chestnut hair. She was evidently in very deep thought. She remained totally motionless, as if she were an exquisite carving from delicate white stone. Yet, there was something about her aura which said she was anything but relaxed and carefree. It seemed an eternity passed as he simply stared at the back of the white girl before him.

"Is it possible?" he asked himself. "Has Yellow-hair

spoken the truth for once? My wife? Alisha alive and here with . . ."

Rage flooded his powerful body as the dam on his control shuddered and gave way. Countless possibilities settled in on his warring emotions. He could not imagine how Gordon had escaped the massacre at Fort Pierre. He could not comprehend Alisha's marriage to this treacherous white-dog. Logic failed to give him any reasonable answers to his many questions.

That day long ago, she had escaped with Powchutu. He could not understand how she had come to be with Yellow-hair instead . . . *married to him*, the words thundered into his murderous thoughts. She had dared to marry another man, his sworn enemy!

But he had not as yet viewed her face. He suddenly wondered if Jeffery's last taunt had only been an attempt at revenge. His mind was besieged with jumbled thoughts. He had come to seek out and to destroy the enemy of his people, the enemy whose bounty had challenged him to come here. Even in his wildest dreams, he had not imagined he would find his lost wife, and definitely not as the wife of his most hated white enemy! There was only one way to learn the truth: to view the face of the woman at the window.

In many ways he had lived and yearned for this precise moment, the moment when his past betrayal could be avenged, the moment when his taunting gaze could lock with her terrified one. Yet, he hesitated for a few moments more, wondering what he would do if that girl was indeed his traitorous wife. Unable to decide her permanent fate that quickly, he soundlessly moved forward to stand behind her. He was close enough to touch her without any effort; yet, he did not.

The fragrant odor of jasmine left her body to float into

his nostrils. Without his awareness, he tensed at her innocent assault upon him. He realized the dreaded significance of the next few minutes and of his first reaction. Although he had planned this event many times before in great detail, dreamed of having her at his mercy, he was caught unprepared to face it. It had been so unexpectedly thrust upon him. Two victories of revenge in one night seemed too incredible to be true.

How should a man react to a long-anticipated moment, yet one he never dreamed to share? If this girl was not Alisha, he could do whatever he wished with her. It was entirely possible that Gordon had only chosen a woman who favored Alisha. Long ago Gordon had made his intense desire for her known. Yet, Gordon had also spoken of her escape with the scout. If this girl were Alisha . . .

Alisha never knew if it was his familiar manly odor and magnetic aura which had signalled his presence, or if it was a sudden sensing of danger which caused her to whirl around. Her forest-green eyes widened in disbelief; her noticeably sad face blanched snow white. Her respiration was instantly ragged and swift; her slim body trembled at the instant awareness of her vulnerable position.

She stared at the intoxicating man who was standing before her startled gaze, unable to absorb the full implication of his mysterious and incredible presence here in her bedroom. His name had helplessly escaped her parted lips at the first sight of him; she had used his Oglala name, not his English one. His keen, alert senses noted every one of her reactions. He cautioned himself to patience, for he recalled her disarming manner all too well.

Her wide gaze slowly swept over his entire appearance, that of a virile white man. She absently passed over his garments, but openly stared at his shortened hair. Even disguised, she would have known him anywhere. Her confused, frightened gaze locked with his stoic one.

She blurted out, "How did you find me?" She naturally assumed his arrival to mean he had relentlessly tracked her down after discovering she did not die.

He did not answer her; his fierce stare never left her face. Her frantic gaze went past him to the closed door. She knew his powerful body blocked any path of escape. He read each of her moves as if they were his own. She knew she was trapped, cornered like defenseless prey by a vicious predator. Her resigned gaze came back to fuse with his steady one.

The true meaning of her next words failed to reach his keen mind. "Have you come to correct your last mistake? You should have killed me that morning you found me in the wilderness. You should not have ridden away and left me behind." There was a look in her eyes which he could not comprehend.

His jawline grew taut at the reminder of that treacherous day. Instinctively his hand gripped his knife handle and pulled it from its sheath. The tip of the sharp blade came to rest near her pounding heart. Her eyes absorbed his hard features one last time. She closed them and waited for her coming death. Tears began to trace a narrow path down her cheeks, but she wisely accepted this long-postponed fate.

She did not plead for her life. She did not attempt to reason with him or to excuse her past action. She made no attempt to bribe him or to resist him. She did not call out for help, nor did she ask about her husband's fate.

He found these actions strange and disquieting. She seemed almost too willing to die, almost too eager to accept her justly earned punishment. Or was it that she was only trying to die quickly and painlessly? No doubt she suspected and feared vengeful torture before death. Yet, her total passivity was perplexing. It was only natural for a woman to attempt some type of feminine guile!

At his lengthy delay, she opened her eyes. She stared into his dark gaze. His black eyes were filled with obvious anger and hatred. He was in no hurry to finalize his deed; he was savoring his victory too much to end it swiftly and mercifully. Knowing of his savage nature where she was concerned, she dreaded the eventual outpouring of his violent revenge.

She mentally berated herself for ever loving or wanting him. She wondered why, after all this time, he had finally come to extract some final penalty from her. That last day in the desert following their disastrous marriage, he had bid her a last farewell. Why did he have to return and further gouge her still-festering wounds? Would he pursue her all the way to the gates of eternity?

She mentally cursed her traitorous heart and prurient body; for even now, all she wanted was to reach out and to caress his taut cheek. She wanted to be embraced in his strong arms, to feel his sensual lips upon her own, to hear him whisper those same words he had vowed in the desert that fateful day, to run her hungry hands over the length of his virile body. God help her; she wanted to fall upon the floor and make endless love to him.

At such bittersweet thoughts and tormenting emotions, more tears eased down her soft cheeks. Her lips and chin trembled as she struggled to control them. She lowered her head to conceal all of these unforgivable, warring emotions from his perceptive mind.

But in his anger and elation, he mistakenly read her expressions as those of fear and of guilt. "Your husband is dead," he stated succinctly with an ice edge to his voice.

Her head jerked up instantly. She had totally forgotten about him! "You killed Jeffery?" she stupidly inquired, as if such an act of violence was impossible for him.

His following words came through gritted teeth, "Did you expect me to let him live after all he had done to me? I allow no one to dishonor me or to escape my punishment! He kills my red brothers and sells their possessions to other evil men like himself. He dared to demand my scalp and wanapin for his bloody collection! He offered much bounty. Many came. I grew weary of guarding my life at all times. You did not tell him I was dead," he added mysteriously.

The truth hit her hard: he had come after Jeffery, not her! If Jeffery had not insisted upon his scalp, he might never have found her again. Gray Eagle was not a man to have as an enemy, nor one to so recklessly challenge. Besides being evil, Jeffery was a fool . . . a dead fool. She stared at him with a look of disbelief and shock in her eyes.

He erroneously assumed it to mean she was indeed surprised to see him alive. Another idea occured to him; she must have learned of his survival and had begged Gordon to succeed where Powchutu had failed. His scalp and wanapin had been ordered for her! This new thought increased his anger and resolve. Yet, maybe she had hidden her murderous deed from her second husband. Perhaps she was terrified by his success when she had assumed it to be impossible. No matter the truth!

"Three times you have chosen the wrong man to protect you from me! Did you think Yellow-hair could help you more than Brave Bear or that half-breed scout? He is more of a coward than the weakest brave," he sneered contemptuously. "Yellow-hair is dead now!"

"I did not kn . . ." She began to deny his accusations and her knowledge of Jeffery's bounty, then halted. She should not be forced to explain herself to her traitorous husband! Besides, two of those unfortunate protectors were now dead men: dead because of her. Remorse and sadness filled her.

She inhaled deeply and painfully. Her eyes came up to lock with his accusatory ones. "The biggest mistake I have ever made was that day when I saved your life. I should not have interfered with your unjust execution! Not a day has passed since then that I have not paid for it in one way or another. You have done nothing but torment me since that mistake! I didn't chose any of them to protect me or to help me! I should not have required any help. You have finally recovered your loss. Do as you wish. I will not stop you; I won't plead for the mercy which you have never possessed. There is nothing more you can do to me. I have no one to live for, and I have nothing left but my life. You destroyed everything else."

With that accusation, she turned her back upon him. It was too painful for her to relive those events. It was too agonizing to be near him without touching him. All she could do was wait and see what his brutal intentions were this time. She did not have to wait any longer.

His arm closed around her chest like an iron band, nearly cutting off her breath with its great strength. The gleaming blade of his knife flickered before her eyes before it came to rest at the hollow of her neck. Cold metal touched her warm flesh. She tensed as she decided he was about to slit her throat. She accepted this fate: it was just punishment for her own crimes.

He could feel the violent drumming of her terrified heart and the restricted pressure of her erratic breathing. She was now trembling uncontrollably; yet, she still did not plead for her life. The tears which dropped on his hand beneath her chin seemed to burn his flesh like sparks from an inferno.

He was irrationally filled with rage and disappointment. He craved to hear her pleas for mercy; he hungered to hear her explanation for her past betrayal of his love and trust. He wanted her to offer him some sacrificial bribe for her life. He yearned for her to feign innocence and love. He needed to intimidate and to terrorize her. He needed this reality to match his dreams.

It did not. She refused to comply. It was not that she doubted his deadly threat, for she knew he could easily slay her. She honestly didn't care if he took her miserable life.

Damn her! he fumed. Why couldn't she react as she was supposed to? Why couldn't he end this war between them? Why would she not resist him? Why was she making this so difficult for him, for it should be the easiest act in the world? What new deception was this?

Her voice was soft and shaky as it broke into his mental battle. She nearly whispered, "What are you waiting for, Wanmdi Hota? I lack the strength to stop you. Even so, I would not. Finish what you have wanted to do from the first moment we met. You've always hated me and wished me dead. Why do you hesitate now? Is there some new torture you wish to inflict upon me first? Our private war has been long and costly. End it here and now. I am a naïve fool, but I did not believe those lies you spoke to me that last day in the wilderness," she vowed, recalling too well how she had accepted every single word he had spoke as truth, knowing she would give her soul to hear them all again right this moment. She did not realize that it thrilled him to hear she had not believed his words of love that day, even though each one had been true.

To him, she was simply admitting to her final defeat and pleading for a honorable death. Yet, her next words confused him once again. "Your need for saving face is great. Else you would have betrayed my secret identity to Black Cloud that day when you learned the truth. Why didn't you tell him I was not his precious, long-lost daughter? You could not, for you had battled Brave Bear for my hand in marriage. You would go so far; yet, not far enough. Your hatred is so deep you will allow no one to slay me but yourself. You forbid me to find freedom and happiness. I see no great warrior in you; I see a man filled with childish hate and spite. Why did you have to come here? I hate you with all my heart," she lied, hoping he would not guess the tormenting truth behind her pain.

His arm tightened, forcing the air from her lungs with a loud rush. He hastily shoved his knife back into its sheath, unaware of the stunning impact of her troubling words and sad tone upon his guilty mind and aching heart. He yanked her around. They would have this war done tonight! He seized her wrists and slammed her against the wall. He forcefully pinned her there. He was panting hard. His obsidian eyes blazed like two smoldering black coals from the fires of Hades. Unleashed, his fury stormed the innocent girl.

He had ignored the thud of her head against the wall. He flung heated words of Oglala at her, so fast and furious that she did not catch any of them. Dazed, all she could comprehend was his volatile temper. His hands released her wrists and closed around her ivory throat. But before he could tighten them and force the life from her body, she collapsed against his inviting chest.

He automatically caught her limp body as it fell against him. He lifted her into his arms and lay her upon her bed.

He stared down at her for a long time once he knew she was not tricking him. His violent anger spent, he realized how close he had come to killing her. The strange thing was that he was relieved he had not, but the reason for this relief escaped him.

He studied her pale face, searching it for the answers to his many unasked questions. He wondered how he could have lost his temper and reason as he had. He had been completely without control. He knew he had to place a tight rein upon his emotions and temper; he must avoid another such violent outburst. Perhaps the Great Spirit had hoped to teach him patience with this long journey to locate Alisha. Gray Eagle became icily calm.

His hand reached out to caress her cheek. With the sudden thought that Powchutu and Jeffery had both probably done this very same thing, he quickly jerked it away. He paced the room for a few minutes, just as he had seen pumas do when deciding what course of action to take next. There was only one real choice: he could kill her now, or he could take her with him and decide upon her fate later.

He went to stand over her and to scan her from head to toe. Unwilling to settle for a hasty and irretrievable decision, he wrapped her in the bedspread and bound her into a light bundle with the drapery cords. He rapidly searched her armoire and drawers for the necessary clothing for their journey. Deciding which items to pick, he carelessly tossed them into a pile and secured them into a tight package.

He tossed her and the smaller parcel over his shoulder and casually strolled out of the room as if he were simply going for an evening walk. Once downstairs, he lay his two light burdens on the sofa. He returned to her room and lit the lantern. He looked around the place where he had first sighted her after these many tormenting months. He tossed the lantern upon her bed and watched the covers ignite.

Downstairs, he repeated this action in the study and the drawing room. He quickly retrieved Alisha's body from the sofa and headed for the front door. He glanced back only once to make certain the flames would do their job: destroy the belongings of his dead brothers. Hopefully Gordon's death would be a warning to others like him, those who earned their living by evil!

Gray Eagle quickly moved to where Chula was waiting for him. He mounted as easily as if he had ridden this confining way all of his life, even carrying the extra weight of Alisha. He lay her across his lap and held her much as he had a day very long ago, that day when he had first captured her. He instantly dismissed those unbidden memories, knowing they might lessen his mood for justice against her. He headed off toward the direction where White Arrow was camped, waiting for his solitary return.

He grinned to himself, imagining White Arrow's reaction to this light burden upon his lap. The smile faded almost immediately. He would make certain White Arrow did not befriend her this time or be innocently deceived by her false nature. He would make certain she could turn to no one for help or protection except him. Of course, that would be determined by whether or not he wanted to show her mercy or protection! She was his wife!

Wife . . . he had remembered, and yet he had forgotten, this fact. He could not very well take her back to his camp as his prisoner, not when everyone back there believed her to be the daughter of Black Cloud and his beloved wife! If he exposed her part in his attempted murder and her pretense as Black Cloud's daughter, he would be forced to put her to death instantly.

Question was: did he want her death? For certain, he would not tell her anything about his decisions. He would allow her to fear her precarious position!

Chapter Twenty

It was mid-morning before Alisha stirred in Gray Eagle's embrace. Her lids fluttered, then gradually opened. She gazed up at the truculent expression which was vividly written upon her first husband's portentous features. She struggled to come to a sitting position.

"Sit still, Woman! Or I'll be forced to tie you to the back of my saddle," he warned in a tone as crisp as the morning air.

His black mood and angry tone were as chilly as the frost of a November day. Alisha forced herself to remain still, but not silent. "Why trouble yourself to haul me back there? Why not kill me here and now? Why not last night? Unless that would deny you the pleasure of torturing me first," she taunted angrily to this forceful man who still possessed her heart and soul.

His hand came to her throat as he warned, "Silence! Or I will cut out your chattering tongue, Wasichun."

She glared at him, then braved, "Does my annoying tongue speak the annoying truth, O Brave Warrior?"

His black eyes locked onto her pale face and rosy cheeks. "Your annoying tongue has never spoken the truth. Why should it begin now?" he sneered, allowing her to accept his mysterious claim as only an insulting sting.

"Nor has yours, dear husband!" she instantly and uncontrollably flung back at him.

His hand tightened upon her soft neck, cutting off her

air. She automatically struggled to breathe. She weakened and relented first; she ceased to resist him. He bored
his obsidian eyes into her emerald ones, daring her to
speak again.

She wisely did not. She turned her head away from his
copper shoulder and manly smell. She focused upon the
swiftly changing scenery which they hurried past. Spring
was almost upon them. The trees were sprouting new
buds and tiny leaves. The grasses were growing rapidly,
shouting their green message to the blue sky. Early wild-
flowers had risen here and there to reveal their unculti-
vated beauty to the human eye.

But Alisha's thoughts travelled a much darker and
sinister road. Gray Eagle had confessed to slaying Jeffery
last night; therefore, she was a widow in one sense. She
could only assume he had some spiteful plan in mind for
her, or he would have killed her upon sight. She wondered if he had come for Jeffery alone, or perhaps both of
them. She wondered if he already knew about Powchutu's
death, for he had not mentioned him at all. No doubt that
news would please him.

Hours later, Alisha's back was aching and cramping
from this constant strained position. Unable to bear it
any longer, she stated firmly, "I cannot ride this way any
further. At least stop for a little while," she entreated.

"If you're hoping for another rescue, don't waste your
time," he acidly informed her.

She looked up at him. "I seriously doubt anyone
knows where I am or what has happened to me. You
aren't one to leave any clues behind," she sneered. "My
back hurts," she explained.

"Not as much as . . ." he halted his loosened tongue
before it told of how deeply she had hurt him, physically
and emotionally.

"Not as much as it will very soon? Another five lashes, or perhaps ten this time?" she concluded from his brief slip.

"Wait and see. I need not tell you my plans!"

"We certainly cannot begin a new tradition, can we? Let me sit up, or I'll force you to begin your punishment right now!" she issued a bold threat of her own.

He snorted in amusement as he halted Chula, then casually dropped her to the hard, stony ground. Confined in the bedcover, she helplessly tumbled over. She instantly strained to come to a kneeling position, resolved that he would not shame her this way. Her blazing, emerald eyes came up to glare at him.

He eased his right leg over the saddle horn and leisurely let it rest across his left thigh. "Then rest," he taunted with a chuckle.

"Will you please untie me?" she frostily implored.

"You cannot escape me again, Alisha. Face it! I can do what I please with you," he haughtily threatened, irresistible maleness exuding from every pore of his towering frame.

"If it does not please you to untie me for a few minutes of privacy, then your pants will soon be mighty uncomfortable," she retorted with a crimson face and trembling voice.

He burst into hearty laughter. He jumped down to the ground with natural agility and animal grace. He removed his knife to cut the drapery cords. Alisha defensively retreated a few steps. He laughed again as he reached for her and yanked her to him. He cut the constricting bonds.

Before she could head into the nearby bushes, he seized her upper arms and pulled her to within inches of his ruthless body. "If you make any attempt to trick me or to get away again, I need not tell you what I will do to you," he stated.

"My foolish, daring days are over, Wanmdi Hota. You have proven escape is impossible. I will return shortly. You have my word, for what it's worth to you," she declared in a wounded tone.

"It is worth nothing to me. But I do trust you know when you are defeated!"

Within a few minutes, she did return. She strolled around as she attempted to restore some circulation in her legs and back. She rubbed the taut, aching muscles near her waist. She longed for some water, but refused to ask for it. Long ago under similar circumstances he had refused her rest or water. Why should he grant her either of those luxuries today? She sighed heavily with unrelenting fatigue. Strange, she would gladly exchange that day for this one . . .

"Let's go!" his terse voice called out, as if he had read her thoughts.

She meekly came over to him and held out her hands to be bound. Noting the seductive allure of her state of scanty attire, he handed her the small bundle which had been taken from her room. "Put something on. If we meet up with others, I do not plan to risk my life to keep the men off of you. Besides, a near naked female might cause too much interest or suspicion."

She took the bundle and opened it. She was relieved to find some of her own clothing inside of it. She pulled out a floral cotton skirt and white blouse. He had chosen well, for nothing she had could be better for this type of travel. She headed for the bushes to change.

He halted her and ordered her to put the clothes on immediately. "You forget, Woman, I have seen far more of you than is revealed now," he said smugly. His dark eyes deliberately removed what little clothing she now wore.

She flushed, half in anger and half in modesty. She did as he commanded. Noting her bare feet, he shrugged his shoulders and remarked, "Guess I did forget something. Let's go," he called out again, his thoughts definitely somewhere else.

He mounted up and lifted her up behind him. When he headed out, she was forced to slip her arms around his narrow waist or be thrown from his horse. She was grateful for the shirt he was wearing; she did not think she could endure contact with his flesh.

They rode in total silence for hours. He wished he had two horses, for her nearness and touch were disturbing. There was no doubt in his mind as to what action he wanted to perform at the present time; yet, he fiercely controlled his desires. He would never permit her to know of her effect upon him. Coming to the secret place where White Arrow was camped, he reined in Chula. He threw his leg over the saddle and hopped down. He reached up and unceremoniously yanked her off of his horse.

White Arrow came forward. Astounded by the incredible sight which greeted his eager eyes, he stammered, "Where did you find her?"

Alisha whirled around at the sound of his familiar voice. Her face glowed with happiness and relief; her old friend was here, and she would not be alone with Gray Eagle. She shrieked his name and rushed to meet him. His withering glare and instant withdrawal warned her of his unanticipated hostility toward her.

She halted so quickly that she nearly fell forward into his arms. She fixed puzzled eyes upon his stony features. "Wanhinkpe Ska?" she softly inquired. She reached out to touch his arm.

He jerked it away before she could make any contact. He glared at the girl who had betrayed his affection and trust in her. His scathing look scanned the female who had dared to strike at his blood brother, all for the love of another man. Worse, she had pretended to love his friend. She had feigned friendship with him. She had permitted him to be her friend and protector. Such deceit and dishonor could not be accepted by either of them. She was unworthy of Gray Eagle's love and trust; she was unworthy of his own respect, friendship, and protection.

Witnessing the animosity and repulsion in White Arrow's face, her expression and tone of voice suddenly changed. It now hinted of a strange sadness and disappointment. "I see . . . no longer kodas, if we ever were." Resignation and bitterness edged their way into her silvery voice. "As you wish, White Arrow." She turned to face her other antagonist, trapped between them. "What now, Wanmdi Hota?"

"You are my captive once more. Do as I command," he tersely informed her. "We will leave here soon. Do what is needed before we ride."

They rode until sunset. After several furtive glances in White Arrow's direction, his vivid resentment prevented their eyes from meeting. She kept her face turned the other way, fiercely struggling to keep her tears in check. His behavior denied her the hope of ever seeing a friendly face again. Unable to reason out this abrupt change, Alisha merely accepted it as fact.

The only words spoken were between the two men. Catching a familiar Sioux word here and there, she knew the conversation centered upon Gray Eagle's defeat of Jeffery and his capture of her. Hearing those names so closely linked, she risked another glance at White Arrow.

If possible, greater anger and hatred were now revealed in his fiery eyes and tight grimace. She hastily glanced away from White Arrow's dark visage. If there had been the slightest doubt in her mind before, there was none now: no future hope of friendship existed.

Gray Eagle perceptively felt her odd reaction to White Arrow's obvious emotions. He contemplated and weighed the occasional quiverings in her body and the tautness in her limbs. He called to mind their past relationship and her initial reaction to White Arrow's reunion with her. It was almost as if his rejection was causing her physical pain. As it was an absurd deduction, he dismissed it.

When they made camp that night, Alisha obediently gathered the wood and refilled the water skins from the nearby river . . . just as ordered. She was angry when he casually stated they could not have a fire which might alert some nearby enemy. No doubt he was only seeking any means to antagonize her. She commanded herself to silence and calm. She could not afford to allow her husband to goad her into a dangerous outburst.

The two men ate from their pouches. Leisurely they devoured their dinner as they laughed and chatted in high spirits. Alisha waited to learn if she would be permitted any food and water. She sat on the blanket which Gray Eagle had indifferently tossed in her direction. It would not surprise her if he did refuse her such things.

Without warning, a small amount of food was casually dropped into her lap. She jumped in surprise, then slowly relaxed. She ate the food without so much as a murmured thank-you.

Later as she lay there beneath the shimmering stars and the dreamy yellow moon, she cautioned herself to give Gray Eagle time to become accustomed to finding her alive and with Jeffery Gordon. These facts must have shocked him greatly! To find her again was surprise enough, but to find her married to his sworn enemy was unforgivable. His fury at this unexpected discovery was only natural; his constant intimidation was not.

It was not her fault if his insidious plans for her death had failed. It had been many long hours since Gray Eagle's attempt on her life. At the present, he did not hint at a new death-plot. He seemed content to allow her to worry over her fate. Yet, he somehow seemed different in an imperceptible way.

Perhaps his hatred and need for fatal revenge upon her had somewhat lessened with time and distance. Perhaps he had realized how fortunate he had been in having such a servile, talented, and loving slave! Perhaps he had been unable to pleasantly replace her! No other slave, or woman, could offer him as much as she had . . . for she had given him everything!

She knew she was only teasing herself. Gray Eagle had never been aware of any value she might have. He had probably replaced her within that first week of her absence! He was such a virile, demanding male; he would not deny himself for very long . . . if at all. Irrational jealousy and anger suffused her body. Perhaps his dire reaction to her discovery was only temporary.

Yet, there was some new emotion written within his eyes and evident in his tone; it was one she did not comprehend. She thought it wise to do as he ordered. She resolved to be obedient, respectful, pleasant—and tempting. If she could subtly worm her way into his confidence, he would not need to constantly torment her. Far better, if she could somehow remind him of that last day they had spent making passionate love. Perhaps his fury might then change into affectionate desire. If she was to be forced to become his slave again, then why not inspire a complete and rewarding relationship?

The mere thought of being with him again brought flames into her blood. Her endless desire for him, which had lain dormant for months, had been rudely awakened and suddenly refreshed. The slumber of her senses had ended with the first sight of him. He had taught her fiery passion. He had given her exquisite, unforgettable pleasures upon his mats. He had taken her as an innocent girl and molded her into a woman, his woman. He had created a fierce hunger within her heart and body which only he could satisfy. Jeffery's magic drugs would not hold a candle to the narcotic effects of Gray Eagle's possession.

How could she truthfully deny her intense cravings for his touch and gentleness, things which he had unforgettably revealed to her long ago? Even if her love for him was sinful, she was too enslaved to him to pray for forgiveness. She recalled what it could be like between them. How she wished their passions were as intertwined as their destinies appeared to be. When it came to this hypnotic man, her heart foolishly overruled her head.

When morning came, Gray Eagle nudged her awake with the toe of his stolen boot. He ordered her to ride. Gazing down at her, it was a struggle to keep from throwing himself down upon her. He mentally cursed this unwanted effect, this annoying hunger which gnawed viciously at his groin.

"You're taking me back to your camp!" she said incredulously.

He glared at her, eyes like embers from hell's fiery pit lying in a frigid snowbank. "Silence, witkowin! Do as I say!" his deep voice growled.

She whitened, then fused red in anger. "How dare you call me a whore! You raped me, remember?" she shrieked at him.

"In truth, you wear that name now. Speak no more!"

"Damn you, I will speak! I demand to know what you intend to do with me! It wasn't enough that you tortured me and tried to kill me before, now you . . ."

The remainder of her sentence was halted by his hand over her mouth. "If you value your vile tongue, say no more! I will cut out the offending piece of meat!" His alert eyes said he meant every single word. He jerked his burning hand away.

She bit back her stinging reply. Her temper was gradually restored to an intelligent level. "As you wish, Master. I only wanted—"

"Silence!" he snarled, teeth bared like a ferocious beast about to attack his fragile prey. "I will hear no more of your lies!"

She gasped at his insult. Her eyes flew open wide, but she wisely held her tongue. They mounted up and rode away. The April weather was calm, clear, and invigorating. She focused her attention on Mother Nature around her. She tried to keep her mind off of things which she did not understand, such as his frequent allusions to her dishonesty.

That night, caged tempers escaped. His fierce struggle to contain his deadly mood and her fierce attempt to remain silent when her heart screamed for some explanation simmered all day. Everyone was tired and tense. When they made camp, Alisha did not make a move unless Gray Eagle verbally ordered her to.

She sat on her assigned blanket studying him. A lifelike painting which she had once viewed and admired back in England stood before her mind's eye. He reminded her of that same golden, mountain lion: deadly, cunning, powerful, and sleek. There was not an ounce of

439

fear in his heart or mind, nor an ounce of fat or doubt in his masterful body. He was agile and alert, lordly and magnificent. That same dauntless, self-assured aura exuded from him. He was a god in human form, but a demon in reality.

Alisha endeavored to fathom his mood and his purpose. If only she knew why he had wanted to kill her that day, then she could prevent that same deadly problem from arising anew. The longer she sat there, the more her need to know this fact became intensely overpowering. His back was now to her.

She recklessly approached him. "Why do you want me dead, Wanmdi Hota? Why is your hatred still so great after all these months? Why couldn't you let me go free this time? Why must you take me back and torment both of us again? Surely I have paid enough for my mistakes."

He whirled to face the woman who had dared to press him, who had dared to deceive and betray him. "One more word and you will pay far more!" he ominously informed her.

Tempers boiled over. She did not back down. "I have the right to know why you—"

He sharply cut into her argument, denying the opportunity for the truth to surface. "You have no rights but those I choose to grant you! And I grant you none, white girl. Silence!"

Alisha's tender beauty and nearness were a powerful magic. Gray Eagle was infuriated by his undeniable craving for her. Anger was born from that unbidden desire which mated with his lingering anguish. He wanted to hurt her as she had hurt him. No matter how difficult, he wanted to brutally reject her as she had rejected him.

She stared into his flinty features, then screamed at

him, "But I have to know why you—"

Before he knew what he was doing, Gray Eagle delivered a jarring slap across her cheek, a blow which sent her reeling backwards and tumbling to the rocky ground. Petrified by his violent reaction, she gaped at him in blatant fear and astonishment. She gingerly rubbed her tender, throbbing cheekbone, hoping it was not broken by his brute strength. Her trembling hand went to her mouth to touch the salty wetness there. She stared at the bright red blood upon her fingertips. Surely this was only a ghastly nightmare, she hopefully prayed.

He had always prided himself on his rigid control. Why had her simple words so easily destroyed it? He did not want her to talk to him; that was vividly clear to her now. He had drastically changed, and she fearfully respected this new image. She stared at him inscrutably, then lifted herself from the hard ground to head for the river. Neither spoke again.

Alisha knelt by the grassy bank and gently washed away the blood which was now easing down her trembling chin. She repeatedly cupped cool water in her shaking hands and splashed it against her flaming cheek. She did not know how long she remained thus.

When she came to her senses, it was dark. Yet, the full moon reflected enough light. Alisha's mind had journeyed a great distance along a perilous and tormenting path. White Arrow called to her and dropped some dried strips of meat into her lap.

She exploded like a volcano. She threw the food upon the ground. She screamed at him, "Keep your food to yourself! I am not some animal to be fed and watered when it suits you! I don't need your help or your traitorous friendship! I want nothing from you, Savage! Nothing!" she shouted.

441

Gray Eagle came from seemingly nowhere. He roughly seized her by the shoulders and shook her violently. "Do not speak to him in this way!" he thundered his warning at her.

Driven past the point of reasonable caution, she shouted back, "Then tell him to stay away from me! I don't want help from someone who claimed to be my friend! I don't want his pity either! Lies and deceit are all you know! I want nothing from either of you! You are both barbaric savages without mercy or kindness! I hate you both! I hate you all . . ." She collapsed into hysterical sobbing, emotionally and physically drained by the horrifying ordeals which she had endured these many months.

"Hiya!" he shouted at her to halt her heart-tugging weeping. She was a vulnerable, delicate creature who was deeply wounded.

"Kill me now and end this madness! You have tormented me for months and months! I cannot take any-more! I did all you asked and it was never enough! My God, Wanmdi Hota, what more could you want from me? What?" she screamed at him, tears of anguish streaming down her cheeks.

"Obey me, that is all I want from you!" he shouted back, cursing her magnetic allure and her artless power over him.

"Obedience isn't what you want! I gave you that and you still tormented me day and night! You forced me to be your slave and whore! Yet, that still did not satisfy you! My life is what you demand, just like before! You lied and betrayed me! You forced me to marry you! I want to be free, I want to be happy again! Why must you enslave me again? Why all of this?" she cried out in agony. Her accusations totally escaped his keen mind.

"You know why! You dared to leave with that half-breed!"

She stared at him through tear-soaked lashes, misunderstanding his meaning. "What did you expect me to do? Stay here and slowly die? I had to go; can't you see that? I had to be free and happy again. I needed . . ." Her outburst spent, she halted before carelessly stripping her soul naked before his vindictive gaze. "What does it matter now? There will always be war between us, for that is what you crave," she sadly accused.

She walked away from them. She went to her blanket and wearily dropped down onto it. She was so tired of this exacting battle. It seemed endless and persistent. No matter the outcome, she wanted it over. She rolled to her side. Her long curls slid over her face, covering it from view. She made no attempt to push them back.

For the next few days, she was very quiet and withdrawn. She mechanically obeyed Gray Eagle's orders. Yet, she refused to look at him or to address him again. She even refused to place her arms around his waist as they rode along. She would loop her fingers into his wide belt and hold on in that precarious way. If she fell from his horse, then so be it; but she would not endure his physical contact.

During the short nights, she would toss and turn in her light and restless slumber. She would murmur sorrowfully, but he could not decipher her inaudible words. She refused to go near White Arrow or to even acknowledge his presence. Yet, her subtle innocence and great beauty spoke loudly to both men. Her bruised cheek was a constant and irritating reminder of Gray Eagle's brutal loss of control.

Gray Eagle soon found himself watching Alisha more closely and more frequently as the long days and cool nights sped by. His body came to hunger for hers. The memory of how it had once been between them returned countless times to plague his peace of mind and enforced celibacy since her loss. Even if it had only been a deception upon her part, no woman had ever given herself to him as she had. No woman had ever given him such pleasure or such endless hunger. Even if it had only been a deception, he would gladly endure it all again! How he wished she had not betrayed him!

He was strangely troubled by her sadness and ever-increasing distance. Perhaps he had been overly cruel and demanding with her. Perhaps he had made her more aware of her enslavement to him than of her attraction to him. Yet, he could forgive her for those natural reactions. What he could not forgive was her desire for his death, her desire for Powchutu, her desire for Gordon! His heart warred with his lusty body day and night; one wanted to love her and the other wanted to painfully hurt her.

His nerves became jittery and taut. His loins raged against this unnecessary denial of his wife's body when she was within easy reach of his power and possession. He would discover himself staring at her, planning her defeat over and over. Sometimes it was a physical victory; others, an emotional one. He argued steadily with his overpowering frailty where she was concerned. How was it possible to desire an enemy who had tried to destroy you, who had tricked you, who had betrayed you, who had shared the heights of passion with you, who had clung to you in irresistible longing, who had soared to the eagle's domain with you? It was insane; it was tormenting; it was challenging!

Soon, his mounting agitation began to show. He began to look for ways to intimidate her or to tease her, anything which he could do to catch her attention. He was not a blind fool; she had found him virile and magnetic at one time. He would remind her of those heated nights and days which they had shared. Surely her body was just as hungry and weak as his was! He recalled those first few weeks of Alisha's captivity when he had trained her body to respond to his mere touch, or to his mellow voice, or to the sight of him. Her innocent mind had lacked the knowledge or the skill to deny him anything. But that was before she met that half-breed scout and that murderous Gordon! That was before she knew any man but him! That was when she naïvely thought she loved him! That was before she learned what hatred, revenge, and betrayal were! That was before she turned to another man . . . .

Gray Eagle now wanted Alisha to experience the same annoying hunger pangs which he was feeling. He wanted to take her, but dared not reveal this agonizing truth to her. He wanted to entice her to the point of her seduction of him. He teased and he taunted; he terrorized and he tempted. Nothing worked. She continued to parry each thrust. Not knowing of how deeply his wounds were cutting her, he witnessed her continued strength and resistence with rising anger.

One night when Alisha could not sleep, she walked to the nearby stream, for Gray Eagle usually camped near water. She sat down and stared at the moon's reflection upon the impenetrable black surface before her. How she longed for a merciful reprieve from his warfare. She drew her legs close to her chest and wrapped her arms around them. She propped her chin upon her raised knees.

A leather-clad leg invaded her vision. She looked up to find Gray Eagle staring down at her. Moonlight danced off her silky hair and played in her grassy eyes. She could not take her eyes from his. Smoldering flames uncontrollably leaped into a passionate wildfire.

He dropped down to one knee and studied her tempting face. Her look told him she was willing and eager to have him. He had set his trap for her; now, she appeared hopelessly ensnared in it. Seeing his victory filled him with potent desire. His breathing quickened and his groin tightened. They continued to stare into each other's eyes, captured by the magic of that moment.

His hand came out to gently caress her cheek, the one with the purplish-yellow bruise. She was artlessly seductive, yet cautiously restrained. She was soiled, yet naïvely pure. He wanted her; he needed her. She belonged to him. Not a glimmer of rejection or refusal could be read in her turbulent eyes.

His dark eyes unknowingly revealed his intense desire for her. Her own heart longed to reach out to him. For the first time since he had found her, he was gazing at her with desire and tenderness in his softened gaze. God, how she wanted him! Tears glistened in her eyes. She parted her lips to speak, but found his mouth covering hers. The battle was lost to her.

Time ceased. She melted into his arms and heatedly returned his ardent advances. They sank to the moist grass, unaware of its cool dampness. His mouth took hers time and time again. She had no will or desire to resist him. She clung to him even as he deftly removed their garments. His hands travelled her entire body with fiery fingers. She was his; he was her destiny.

As she arched to meet his entry, he boasted into her ear, "You are mine, Woman. I can take you when and where I choose. Never will you whore with another man. Never will you trick me with promises of love. You are my whore alone . . ."

Her passion chilled instantly at his stinging barb. She

shouted at him, "Get off of me, you filthy animal! I will never submit to you! I hate you! Savage! Barbarian! Beast!"

She fought and struggled, all to no avail. He took her with swift and deliberate coldness. He sought to appease his great hunger within her resisting body. He sought to salve his hurt pride with the sounds of her cries and pleas. White Arrow heard this tormenting punishment, but he did not interfere. She was already inspiring doubts and pity within his own weakening heart!

At last it was over. He had punished both of them, more deeply than he realized. He was quick to realize his release had only been a physical one, an almost painful deliverance into her helpless body. He was made aware of the great difference between rape and heated love-making, of the pleasure and satisfaction which had been denied to him, of the sacrifice of blissful contentment which normally followed their fiery unions. He was plagued by a feeling of frustration and incompleteness which he did not comprehend or accept.

Gray Eagle watched the tears of humiliating, painful defeat which eased from her closed eyes and rolled down her temples into her hair. Her whole body quivered in anguish. Moonlight bathed her ivory skin. Her tangled hair spread upon the ground around her head, exposing soft shoulders. He suddenly stiffened.

For the first time, he noticed the healed knife wound upon her left shoulder. If it had not been for her long hair, he would have seen it sooner. He gingerly touched it, checking its age and depth. Noting the extent of the repaired injury and the evidence of its drastic treatment, he surmised she was lucky to be alive. Irrational fury and relief flooded him.

"Who did this thing?" he questioned her, tapping

the scar.

She did not reply. "Who dared to place his weapon within your body? Answer me!" he shouted angrily, acutely aware of how close he had come to losing her to death, losing her before he could reclaim what was rightfully his alone.

She opened her misty eyes and glared at him. He was questioning her as if nothing had just taken place between them. He was guilty of placing the most deadly weapon within her body: his love. "What do you care?" she sneered through tight lips.

"Tell me who has dared this insult, or I will . . ." He hesitated as he pondered a logical threat.

She answered for him, "Or you will what, Great Warrior! Kill me? Lash me again? Destroy my freedom? Kill my family and friends? Burn my home? Enslave me? Rape me? There is nothing more you can do to me or take from me! Carry out your savage revenge. I do not care," she vowed in utter despair.

"Who did this thing?" he persisted, his dark eyes blazing with anger. He refused to let her up or to move from her body.

Desperate to end his contact with her, she declared coldly, "A white trapper, and I killed him for it! Just as I will kill you if you ever touch me again . . ."

"You killed him?" he repeated in astonishment.

She would tell him no more. No matter what he said or did, she remained silent and stubborn. When he appeared to halt his futile badgering, she scoffed contemptuously, "If you are quite done with my body, then get off of me!"

He slowly pulled on his clothes and returned to the campfire. From White Arrow's sheepish look, it was evident he knew what had taken place between them. Yet, Gray Eagle did not realize he was beginning to feel pangs of guilt and remorse at her excessive punishments.

Alisha silently stepped into the chilly water to remove the traces of his most humiliating and most tormenting punishment of all. Afterwards, she knelt beside the river and prayed for her abused body and tormented soul. She placed some of the blame for this new agony upon her own head, for she had encouraged his brutal ravishment. She had actually wanted his love and touch!

She slipped her garments onto her still wet body. Her long hair was damp at the edges. Beads of cool water dotted her flesh, quickly joined by chill bumps and an icy tinge. Her teeth began to chatter. Still, she did not move or weep. Agony ripped through her mind and body at this betrayal, this farewell to love.

A cozy blanket dropped around her trembling shoulders. She grabbed it and threw it back at him, violently declaring, "I want nothing from you! Nothing! Not food, nor shelter, nor protection, nor kindness . . . not even mercy! Because of you, I have nothing . . . I am nothing! I hate you! I was a blind fool to save your miserable life and to . . ."

Her tirade ceased; her line of vision returned to the dark water. Without a word, Gray Eagle dropped the blanket beside her and returned to the fire. It was very late when Alisha finally went to her sleeping mat. Yet, the entire night passed without any sleep for either of them. Her anguish prevented her sleepy solace; new pangs of guilt denied him his. White Arrow's furtive gaze went from one tormented friend to the other; yet, she had begun the emotional landslide which none of them could control. It was heart-rending to recall the beautiful mountain of love which Alisha had for some mysterious reason destroyed.

Later that second week, the eerie mood had finally gone beyond endurance for either of them. In her distant mood, she had played the role of servant to him. Yet, the tension between them mounted higher each day. White Arrow could see another explosion in the making, but was helpless to prevent it.

Returned from hunting, Gray Eagle tossed a bloody, beheaded rabbit into her hands. She instinctively caught it. He then handed her a once shiny hunting knife with blood still dripping from its long, thick blade. The scarlet fluid pooled in her palm and began to slide between her slender fingers. The suppressed horrors and fears of the recent past surfaced and thundered through her weary mind.

Her face lost its healthy glow. She stared at the blood on her hands; she watched as it began to run down her arm. She suddenly dropped the rabbit into the dirt. She slowly stood up, still clutching the accusatory weapon. She began to shudder. Her eyes glazed as she was gripped by memory.

Alisha was shaking so violently that the knife fell from her slippery grasp. Still, she continued to stare at her bloody hands, as if trapped in some state of unseen hell. She began to back away. Her head began to move from side to side, denying some hidden truth. Her hands began to tremble with such force that she could not halt them. She abruptly balled them into tight fists as one lone and agonizing word was torn from the very depths of her tormented soul: "No-o-o-o-o . . ."

She whirled and fled this unseen evil which haunted her. Unaware of direction or purpose, she simply ran and

450

ran. Gray Eagle was instantly after her. When he overtook her, she fought him like a crazed person. She babbled incoherently; she cried and laughed simultaneously in frightening hysterics.

For a time, he could not reach her. He tried everything: shouts, threats, shakings, slaps. Finally, he kissed her. At first she did not even comprehend his demanding mouth upon hers. They fell to the ground during their struggle. He captured her face between his strong hands and forcefully parted her lips with his own. His powerful frame pinned her thrashing body to the hard ground. But it was another man who was painfully kissing her lips; it was another man who had her trapped beneath him . . .

Unable to relive that agony again, she gave herself over to the threatening, merciful darkness. She went limp beneath him, never once responding to his kiss.

He lifted his head and worriedly gazed down into her ashen face. It was a long time before her breathing returned to normal, even longer before he could waken her. Disturbed by this strange behavior, he picked her up and carried her to the stream. He splashed cold water into her face. When Alisha did not come to, he fretted over her alarming condition. He fretted until she began to thrash around upon the grass and call for help, help from her treacherous liberator Powchutu.

Blind jealousy and renewed fury raced into his body. She dared to call the name of her lover rather than that of her own husband! She sat up and looked around, her panicked eyes darting in search of some chimeric danger. Still mentally confused and frantic, she moved to the edge of the stream. She began to rub her dusty hands together. She scrubbed and scrubbed.

"The blood won't come off, Powchutu! I had to kill

451

him! He deserved to die! They were going to rape me! He killed my baby! Don't you see, Powchutu; I had to kill him," she ranted from her other world.

"Who did you kill, Alisha?" he gently probed, hoping to learn some hidden secret while she was existing in limbo.

"The trapper who attacked us and killed my baby," she replied in a strange, void tone which had been brought on by her emotional and physical exhaustion.

"You killed him with my knife?" he continued softly, not wanting to alert her to her unwitting confession.

"It was his knife. I stole it from him while he was hurting me. My baby . . . the pains hurt so bad . . . I can feel my baby dying . . . I slit his filthy throat! Blood everywhere . . . wash it off, Powchutu. Shot! No . . . help me, Powchutu! So much blood and pain . . ." She went rigid; her eyes blinked.

Struggling to control his volatile hatred and jealousy, he inquired, "Where is Powchutu now?"

"Dead . . . I killed him . . ." she stated, stunning him. He stared at her.

"You killed him!" he shouted before thinking. "Why run away with him, then murder him?" he thundered.

The hypnotic spell broken by his loud voice, Alisha gazed up at him in fear and in confusion. She could not recall what had taken place or what she had confessed to him. "I must fix the rabbit," she stated in distracted turmoil, aware of her curious mental lapse.

"Why did you kill Powchutu?" he stormed at her.

She met his piercing, insistent stare. "What are you talking about? He was killed in an accident months ago. I suppose I am to blame for allowing him to help me, but I did not kill him! Why would you think I had? He was the only friend and family I had left. You destroyed everything else," she charged, without emotion.

"What happened to the child, Alisha?" he unexpectedly asked, his eyes cold and hard.

Her face paled. "How could you possibly know about the baby? I didn't . . ." She halted and stared at him as if he had just revealed some hidden clue to a vital puzzle, the missing piece which gave reason for all the others to connect. "Powchutu said you would never accept a half-breed child. Knowing about the baby, you still . . . I had not believed even you could be so bloodthirsty and savage . . . to wish the death of an innocent child, a first-born son."

"For certain, the next child will be mine," he casually informed her of his intentions.

"Next child! But if you did not want the first one, why would you try for another one?" It was his turn to be shocked, but only temporarily. He deduced her words to be a cruel taunt.

"This will be my first-born son," he vowed coldly, wondering if she would have dared to pass off another man's child as his.

She assumed his mysterious words to be some kind of joke or test. She was not up to his spiteful games. He could not possibly take her back to his camp, not after telling everyone she was dead. Somewhere between here and there, he would eliminate her.

She returned to camp and prepared the rabbit which White Arrow had cleaned during her lengthy absence. After a tasty dinner for the men, she cleared away the remains of their meal and went to lie upon her sleeping mat.

These new facts troubled her deeply. She could not

453

predict his actions or even understand him at all. What new deceit was he planning for her? Taking her home with him? Forcing her to bear his child?

Child . . . that meant . . . Alisha hastily dismissed the implication of that threat. Only time could reveal what new fate she must endure.

Chapter Twenty-One

"Are you sure about those facts, Moses?" Joe shouted in astonishment, then fearfully added, "Paul dead, and Alisha married to Gordon?"

"Yep!" Moses replied steadily, unaware of the impact of his shocking announcements upon his old friend, ignorant of Alisha's importance to Joe.

"Shame, too. I heard Gordon is tied up with them river pirates and that ornery Frenchy. Looked like a real nice gurl to me. Bloody shame about her brother being such a bad'un," he remarked, rubbing his scraggly beard.

"Take my word, Moses, neither of those two youngsters are bad. I know 'em both, friends of mine. From what I know, Alisha would never marry the likes of Jeffery Gordon. As for Paul, he couldn't do anything like you described. Somebody's up to no good down there. If I had to take bets, I'll lay my money on Gordon. I'd wager he got rid of Paul in order to get at Alisha. Can't understand why she didn't send me some word about this. I told her to send for you if she needed to get word to me."

"Could be she didn't have the chance. I left right after delivering those bodies. Been up North aways since then."

"That explains it. Poor girl. She's probably at her wit's end wondering where I am. I best get to St. Louis as fast as I can. If Gordon's harmed her, I'll kill 'im! Thanks for the news, Moses. You think you can close up here for me and bring my furs into the settlement? I'll pay you for

455

your trouble and time," he entreated.

"Aw, Joe. Course I'll take care of things for ye. Don't you worry none. I'll be right on yore tail. As fur payment, ya could buy me a nice bottle of that Irish whiskey, if you'd a mind to," he added with a chuckle.

Within an hour, they had Moses' horse loaded and ready to head out. Joe knew all of the trails in the entire area. With luck and persistence, he could make the settlement within eight or nine days of hard riding. All he could think about was Alisha alone and vulnerable, Alisha still suffering from recent ill fortune, Alisha forced into marriage with Gordon. He determined to get her away from him as quickly as possible. He could only hope that the months of marriage to Gordon had not taken a terrible toll on her. If so, he would kill Gordon with his bare hands. . . .

Powchutu dead . . . the thought kept returning to haunt him as he travelled along. No matter how suspicious he had been of the scout, one thing for certain was his love and loyalty to Alisha. The death scene which Moses had vividly described to him was utterly impossible. He dreaded to put together the pieces of this puzzle.

Joe urged his horse into a faster gait, but quickly recognized the sheer folly of such speed. If the horse came up lame, he would never arrive any time soon. He cautioned himself to patience. If Alisha had already been married to him for months, what harm could a few more days do?

The trip took longer than anticipated. Swollen streams from melted spring snows hindered several crossings, forcing him to continue up river to another ford. The trip required twelve days overland to make the outskirts of St. Louis. Upon his arrival, Joe promptly headed for Hiram Bigsley's, assuming the merchant would have the latest word concerning her health and whereabouts. Joe decided to secure the facts first, then head over to Gordon's. He dismounted before the large mercantile store and hurried inside. He was immediately shown into Hiram's private office.

He paced the floor as he waited for Hiram to return from a late lunch. Eventually he did come in. He smiled genially and grasped Joe's outstretched hand. Before he could open the conversation, Joe rushed ahead with the sole reason for his early and empty-handed arrival.

"Where's Alisha, Hiram? How is she? Moses said she married Gordon. Is that true?" he inquired, hoping there was some mistake.

Noting Joe's great agitation and fear, Hiram hesitated to answer his questions. He decided to begin slowly and painlessly. "She did marry Gordon back in mid-January. I gave her away at the wedding. Grandest thing this town's ever seen. She was absolutely breathtaking."

Ignoring Hiram's chatter about the fancy wedding and large party, Joe heatedly declared, "Heard Paul was killed. What happened, Hiram? Moses told me what they claimed, but that ain't like the Paul I know. Somebody's lying!"

Knowing both tales, Hiram gave them to Joe. Joe thought it strange to have two accounts of the same accident. Hiram told him that one was made up for Alisha's benefit, by Gordon. From what facts Hiram knew, it was evident that Jeffery had forced her to marry him. Joe felt his greatest fears were coming true.

"Start from the beginning, Hiram. Tell me everything you know," Joe demanded, wanting to have all of the facts.

Hiram began with Alisha's arrival on Christmas Eve. He listed the gossip which concerned her or Paul. When

457

he could no longer stall the inevitable truth, he met Joe's keen gaze and finished his woeful narrative.

"I'm afraid I have some bad news for you, Joe. About two weeks ago, somebody killed Gordon and burned his house to the very ground. They don't know if Alisha was in the house or not. Mrs. Webster said she was about to go to bed when she left there earlier. From what she told me, that was Alisha's first day up and out; she said Alisha'd been ill. Anyway, Alisha hasn't been seen or heard of since that fire. If she did get out alive, God only knows where she is now," he stated sadly.

"You think she might have been responsible for the fire? From what I hear, Gordon's an evil man," Joe felt forced to seek another opinion of his one hope for her survival.

Hiram seriously considered his suggestion. "I don't think so. I ruled out the river pirates being to blame; Gordon was rumored to be their boss. Weren't no strangers in town that week either. If she did set the fire and kill him, no one would have blamed her! If she got out, she would've come to me for help. I do know she was afraid of him. But kill him? Naw . . ." He went on to tell Joe about her strange meeting in his office with Mary O'Hara.

Joe sank into a nearby chair, feeling physically ill and dazed by his bad timing: two weeks too late! "She can't be dead, Hiram. She was to wait for me here. She knew I was coming soon. She wouldn't have run away. All three of them dead! Something's wrong . . . Think she might've been kidnapped by the killer?" He reached for one last ray of hope.

"There was only one set of tracks leaving the house, Joe, a man's bootprints. From the size and depth of them, a big man. There was only one horse used, too. Looks like he headed West, but we lost his trail in the thickets not far out of town."

"A big man heading West . . ." he repeated Hiram's last clue without grasping the significance of it.

"Some say it was an Injun lover. Gossip claims Gordon was dealing in their scalps and jewelry, if you get my drift. For certain, he sure sent out a lot of big crates. Heard he set big bounties on chief's and their sons. He was dying to get his hands on that Gray Eagle's scalp."

"He set a bounty on Gray Eagle!" Joe exclaimed. "The damn fool! You think somebody killed him to halt his bloody business?"

"Wouldn't surprise me none. Never could figure out why Miss Alisha would marry a man like that . . ." Hiram stated absently, as Joe's mind raced to discover Alisha's abductor. "You think it might have been some Injun dressed up like a white man?" Hiram questioned seriously, unaware of his accurate guess.

"Could have been, Hiram. You say Mary might know something about this business between Alisha and Gordon?"

Hiram grinned knowingly. "Yep. She was a big help to Miss Alisha when she was staying at the Horne House. From what I saw, Mary was always casting them big, doe eyes at that brother of hers. Could be she heard something. You know her, don't you?"

"Yep, we're good friends. I'll see her right now. If you remember anything else, I'll be over there." He quickly rushed out and headed to the Horne House.

He finally located Mary in an upstairs bedroom, staring around it in a strange manner. Not wanting to startle her, he called out softly, "Mary . . ."

She whirled to face him with tears in her large brown eyes. "Is something wrong, Miss Mary?" he politely

459

inquired at the look of such intense pain and loneliness in her expression.

She sighed lightly and brushed away her tears. She sadly shook her head, for she could not explain her feelings to anyone. Joe came over to where she was standing. He gently raised her chin and gazed into her chocolate eyes.

"You're mighty sad for such a pretty girl. What hurts you so deeply, Mary? You can trust Joe with the truth, can't you?"

She lowered her lashes and shook her head. His next words instantly raised them. "I was hoping you could help me find out what happened to Paul and Alisha Williams."

Noting her startled reaction to those two names, Joe knew she held the secret that he wanted to learn. "Hiram tells me they're both dead. We're all good friends. Paul was supposed to take care of her for me. She was going to wait here for me until spring. Soon as the trapping season was over, we were going to marry. Moses just came by and told me about Paul's death. I couldn't believe it. Something's wrong, Mary; somebody's lying! She wouldn't marry Gordon without some desperate reason. He's never been nothing but trouble for those two. She needed me, and I wasn't here for her. I gotta know what happened to her, Mary." He lied to win her trust and cooperation, hating himself for feeling compelled to do so.

"She just wouldn't marry him. And Paul, his death couldn't have been no bloody accident! I have to find out if she's alive or dead. Help me, Mary," he pleaded, adding a hint of desperation to his tone of sadness.

Mary tugged at his sleeve for his attention. She motioned to herself, then to her forehead. "You know what happened to her?" he asked excitedly.

She sadly shook her head. He reasoned for a time, then he tried, "You know what happened to Paul?"

She nodded yes, tears gathering in her eyes and flowing down her cheeks. Her look told him a great deal. He began on a less painful topic. "You know why she married Gordon?" She nodded yes. "Willingly?" he managed. She nodded no, just as he feared.

"Did he love her?" Mary's eyes revealed coldness and terror as she shook her head no. "Revenge?" He squeezed his eyes shut after she nodded yes.

"I should never have let her leave my cabin with Powchutu," he stated before thinking. "God, I thought she was safe with him."

Mary grabbed his arm and jerked him around. She signalled to her mouth, then made circular motions in mid-air. Joe knew that to mean to repeat his last words. When he hesitated, she motioned to herself and to her forehead, saying, "I know."

She and Joe had always shared the secret sign language which he had personally taught her. Communication was slow, but understandable. Adopted from the Indians, it was easy to learn but needed to be practiced more than she was allowed.

It was late by the time Joe could comprehend her incredible story. Learning that she was pregnant by Powchutu, he promptly decided to marry her. He knew what peril she faced if anyone else discovered the truth about her affair with Powchutu. It was clear to him that she loved him deeply.

Joe knew she would make him an excellent wife, something he had given a great deal of thought to since having Alisha around for those many weeks. Mary cried on his strong shoulder for a long time, then promised to make him a very good wife.

"I've no doubts you will, Mary girl. This could be the best thing for both of us. Best we start out with honesty. I lied about Alisha waiting here to marry me. I was afraid you might not tell me what you knew if I said we was only good friends. She's a lovely creature, Mary, but she didn't love me. She's had a hard time since she came here. I'm sure you know Powchutu was in love with her. But, I think you could've won his heart with a little more time. Alisha would never marry him; she's always loved someone else. From now on, it's you and me. We'll have a good life together. You know anything else about Alisha or Powchutu?"

She shook her head no. Upon further questioning, he came to learn of some facts of that fateful night of the fire which no one else knew. Discovering that Jeffery had murdered Paul and might harm Alisha, Mary had gone to Jeffery's home to kill him herself. Seeing a man dismounting a huge, spotted horse and secretly making his way through the bushes toward Jeffery's house, she had prayed that man was going there to kill him. If not, she would do it another time. She had hurried away, not wanting to be seen at the location of a possible crime. Later, she had heard about the fire.

"Large, spotted horse?" he repeated, ". . . mostly white with gray splotches?"

Her eyes grew wide with the look which said, how did you know? "Was the man about this tall? Black hair? Bronze skin? Dark eyes? Good looking? Proud features and arrogant walk? Fearless? Strong, muscular looking?" Each time she shook her head yes, he would add another fact to make certain of his growing suspicions.

"My God, Mary, he's come after her again! How the hell did he find her here? He never passed my cabin!" He paced nervously, trying to decide how to handle these new discoveries.

If it was indeed Gray Eagle, as he strongly suspected, Alisha might be dead already. Knowing that Joe had some clue to Alisha's fate, Mary tugged insistently at his shirt sleeve. She wanted to know if he suspected her survival and location. "Wait a minute, Mary. I'm thinking something through," he murmured in deep concentration and worry.

The thought hit him hard; she had not been killed at the house. Evidently Gray Eagle had carried her with him. Another idea came to mind: suppose he had come to kill Gordon, but accidently located Alisha as his wife? Suppose he had been shocked to find her there, or to even locate her at all? He had taken her with him; but how far and for what reason?

"I've got to go after her, Mary! You wait here for me. I'll tell your uncle you're gonna marry me when I get back next month. When Moses gets here, tell him I said to take good care of you for me until I return. If he's got her, there's no telling what he'll do to her this time."

Mary finally succeeded in gaining his attention. Joe clarified his thoughts to her. "I think the man who killed Gordon took her with him. From what you know, it could only be one man. Only one man would dare to ride into St. Louis and kill his enemy, a man without fear or weakness. The warrior who captured her several times before has taken her with him.

"I don't mean Gray Eagle came here to get Alisha; I think he came here to kill his old enemy Yellow-hair. I think he found Alisha there by mistake. Trouble is, what will he do with her? I have to go after her, Mary, or he might kill her."

Mary shook her head violently, silently pleading for

him to forget his dangerous idea. "I'll be safe, Mary. He wouldn't harm me. Never tell a soul this secret, but we're long-time friends. If anyone can help her, I can. Gray Eagle might listen to me. If not, he certainly won't kill me for trying to save a friend's life! I promise you he won't harm me."

She hugged him fiercely, recalling all of the years she had known him while growing up. He was a good man, an honest and hard-working one. He would make a wonderful husband and father. In turn, she would make him a good wife. Besides, Joe was still a very attractive and virile man. In time, perhaps they could share a real marriage, real love. She would pray for his safe return and for their promising future together.

Joe leaned back and gazed down into her smiling, serene face, sensing her commitment to him. He smiled and stated, "I think I'll have a talk with your uncle tonight before I turn in. I want to make sure he knows you are my future wife. I'll tell him we've been seeing each other secretly during the winter. And I'll tell him I'll kill him if he lays one finger upon you. That goes for anyone else," he added possessively. "You take care until I get back. I'll turn in early and head out in the morning."

She smiled and nodded. She hurried to prepare his room, wishing they were already married, knowing he could ease some of her loneliness and pain. She quickly dismissed her guilt about concealing the truth of Jeffery's evil treatment against her; she could not bear to tell him of such wicked things. Surely that was too much for any man to hear about his wife. It should remain her secret forever. With a boating accident which had recently claimed the lives of Tommy and Slim, that secret was safe.

Joe did as promised; he spoke to Mary's uncle about their plans for marriage. Jamie didn't seem too pleased about the idea of losing his free help, but was forced to comply with Joe's adamant demands.

Afterwards, Joe had returned to Hiram's to order his supplies for his trip. He did not tell Hiram of his fears and plans. He did, however, tell him about his future marriage to Mary. He secured a promise from Hiram to take care of her if he failed to return from this business trip. He also trusted Hiram with the news of Mary's pregnancy, but generously claimed the baby as his own. When Moses arrived, he was to be placed in charge of Mary's health and protection. Hiram was to see to it that Mary had whatever she needed from his savings. But if he failed to return, the money and property were hers.

Everything set into motion, Joe returned to the Horne House for a good night's rest. He had explained everything to Mary in full detail, setting her mind at ease, telling her that he was serious. The sunrise would see him on his way to help Alisha for one last time. He could only pray for Gray Eagle's understanding and mercy. If that ploy failed . . .

Chapter Twenty-Two

For many days Alisha, Gray Eagle, and White Arrow travelled their arduous journey in varying moods, from open resentment to reserved silence. When they finally neared the joint lands of the mighty Sioux and his red brothers, both warriors became increasingly anxious to arrive home. They quickened their demanding pace by shortening their stops for rest and sleep.

Gray Eagle's mood became lighter and calmer as he neared his home. It was impossible not to notice the energy and excitement that began to flicker in his black eyes. More noticeable was the change for the better in his mysterious, masterful aura.

His open aggression and extreme coldness toward Alisha showed a marked difference. But Alisha was wary of this clemency.

Just to prove his powerful control, many nights Gray Eagle forced Alisha to sleep upon his mat. Some nights he took her; others, he did not. He made it appear as some game in which the rules and the prizes were secrets to her. She endured this degrading show of hostility, for she refused to grant him the pleasure of her pleas or tears. She steadily remained obedient to his every whim or command. She wisely offered him no further reason to punish her for some new offense. Yet, she remained tight-lipped since that night she had nearly lost her mind.

She asked him nothing; she told him nothing. Following that day, she gradually retreated into a remote and protective shell. Outwardly, Gray Eagle seemed pleased with her passivity and obedience. Yet, he was angered by the many secrets which she continued to withhold from him. Not wanting to appear interested in her or lenient with her, he refused to converse with her. He used this damming up of his great curiosity as the building blocks for his new patience and temper control.

After travelling for nearly a month, they neared his camp. Gray Eagle sent White Arrow on ahead to prepare things for their return. Left alone with her husband, Alisha began to fidget nervously. If he was going to slay her, it would either be that night or in the morning. If not . . . if not, how would he logically explain her survival and return?

He laughed heartily as he took advantage of this last night of privacy. Several times he made love to her. Knowing she might not be alive to see the morning sun, Alisha wanted him one last time. Yet, each time she was overcome with passion or with desperate need for him, Gray Eagle would hastily withdraw until her shame and anguish had chilled her fiery blood and torrid body.

When she could no longer hide her tears of pain and her tremblings of frustration, he had stormed at her, "Do not practice your deceit upon me, Alisha. I take you; you do not take me! Do not use your body as a weapon to trick me as you did before. I will not fall for such a trick again. Be warned, woman; I want no whore beneath me!"

Although totally baffled by his words, her pride did not permit her to question him and her anguish would not allow her to argue on their last night together. Surely it was only common sense to think a woman was a whore when she willingly gave herself to a sworn enemy. Why shouldn't he believe she was trading her responsive body for his mercy? Yet, he should know that she loved him!

Her mind fiercely struggled with her ravaged heart, demanding she bid a last farewell to any remaining love and desire for him. If this was to be his tormenting plan for their future, then Alisha decided she must learn to steel herself against her traitorous body's weakness and Gray Eagle's intoxicating assault upon her senses. Surely with time and with practice, he would come to have no effect upon her. She would learn to develop a heart as cold and as empty as his. She would have fought him to the death that night if the hypnotic thought of bearing his child to fill her barren heart and life had not been more tempting than permanent escape.

That following morning, they completed the last leg of their journey. Once again she entered the Dakota Territory during a beautiful April morning, one year later . . .

Only a year? her disbelieving mind countered. Was it possible for her world to be destroyed in one short year? Was it possible to live and to die in that trying span? Was it possible to learn of such violent hate and endless love, to win her dream and then to lose it, to go from Gray Eagle's tormenting demesne and to suddenly be returned to it? Was it justice for that vicious circle to begin anew? Was it right for her to be included within his sacred-life cycle? He was Indian; she was white!

Just before they reached his camp, he reined in his steed. "Listen to my words and obey them, Wife. Only White Arrow know of your escape with the half-breed Powchutu. All others believe you were taken captive by some white enemy. When we enter my camp, you will return as Shalee, as my wife returned to me by the Great Spirit. You will show me respect and obedience. You will tell no one the truth. Do you understand? I will not be dishonored by your deceit."

Astounded, she could not trust her own ears or com-

468

prehension. "You want me to become Shalee again? I do not understand! You know I am not Black Cloud's daughter. It was only a trick, Matu's trick! Why take me back at all? Why not kill me? No one would have known that you had found me again. After all that happened, why force me to be your wife?"

"You are mine. If I kill you, I cannot punish you. You will do as I command. You are Shalee; you are the wife of Wanmdi Hota! Savvy?" he snarled the white man's slang term.

She nodded yes, but did not comprehend his meaning or motives at all.

When they rode into his camp, she was astonished by the joyous reception which she received. His people actually seemed happy and relieved to see her again! They sang and danced around his horse. He informed them of her great fatigue from her long journey and of her need for rest. He led her to his tepee and motioned her inside.

Alisha hesitantly ducked and entered the portal to her past. Her eyes burned with unshed tears as she gazed around her home of long ago. Nothing seemed changed during her absence; even her possessions were still there and in place. She slowly turned and faced him.

He removed his eagle wanapin and placed it around her neck. "Your joining necklace seems to be missing, Wife. This eagle will say who and what you are," he taunted.

Those first days after their arrival proved to be vastly different from Alisha's initial encounter with the Oglala tribe. No longer was she the lowly, white slave; she was the daughter of Chief Black Cloud and the wife of Wanmdi Hota.

Evidently he was completely serious about her pretense as Shalee. In public, he feigned the overjoyed husband whose loving wife had been miraculously returned to his side. He was gentle, attentive, and even affectionate. He exuded a relaxed, proud aura. He smiled and laughed as he spoke to her. He frequently touched her cheek or hair and stroked her hand or arm as they stood together. This loving torment took its toll upon her nerves and her stiff resistance.

Yet, in private, he remained sullen and cold. Traces of bitterness and resentment lined his handsome features. His continued hostility could be explained; he hated her for surviving his treachery. Yet, she could not fathom his inexplicable accusations; nor his hints of her deceit and wantonness. It sounded to her as if he deemed her in the wrong, as if she had been cruel and vengeful to him, instead of the other way around.

Alisha was puzzled. When Gray Eagle would permit her to speak—which was rare, except in public—she questioned him about his motives for this charade. She pleaded for a truce of acceptance and friendship between them. She relented; she cowered; she reasoned; she pleaded. Feeling a newer and deeper betrayal at hand if he relented, Gray Eagle adamantly refused to give her another chance to hurt or dishonor him.

When he made love to her, he would hastily recoil and leave his tepee if she dared to respond to him. He feared the powerful pull of her body and of her loving submissiveness. He failed to realize that his public behavior was also taking a toll upon his resistance. Yet, he could not forget this was the identical way which she had behaved while deceiving him and betraying him. To him, she had only faked love and acceptance. He had been drawn into her tender trap and snared. Never again would he reveal such a weak compliance to her.

Still, he was receiving her overt messages. Her bewitching eyes offered herself to him. Her radiant smile tugged at his cold heart. Her seductive body enticed him beyond reason or control. Her provocative moves and serene manner filled him with a growing need for her closeness and with a desire for her total submission. She sweetly pleaded for peace between them. She became the perfect wife in spite of his continued aloofness and bitter-sweet torment.

Alisha did everything within her power and imagination to melt his iciness and diminish his antagonism. Her attempts to move his granite heart and stubborn mind did nothing but cause more damage to their precarious relationship. The more she tried to reach him, the further he receded. The more she sought to thaw him, his glacial rigidity increased. The more she pleaded for truce, the more hostile he became.

It seemed hopeless. Gray Eagle seemed satisfied with their endless war, pleased with her misery and suffering. They were cruelly trapped in a vicious limbo. Alisha did not know how much longer she could keep up her endeavors or her lagging spirits or her vanishing resilience. All of her efforts of persuasion failed miserably—or so she believed.

As the days passed, she feared she could not endure his torture much longer. It was unbearable to be driven to the point of mindless surrender, then to be cast aside in quivering frustration. It was agonizing to be offered her most precious dream in public, then have it become a nightmare in private.

Seven weeks had passed since their first sexual contact when she began to experience nausea in the early mornings. At first she did not take any special notice of it. Another week went by and more symptoms were slowly added to the first. Gradually the reality of her condition settled in on her. She could not decide how he would view this news. He had hinted at a future child, but would he actually accept it?

She dreaded to tell him; yet, she feared to wait until it became obvious to everyone. Within that span of time, he could lose his temper and patience with her as he had before. If anything, his resentment heightened with each passing day. Alisha did not know what he wanted from her, and he refused to tell her. She was doing her best to make peace, but he would not permit it. And if he did over-react again, the baby could be injured.

Alisha desperately wanted this new child to fill the void in her heart and to bring some happiness to her enslaved existence. There was no decision to make; she had to find the right moment and choose the right words to inform him of their child as soon as possible. But the time came sooner than she desired. . . .

As was the Indian custom during the heat of the day, everyone was resting in their tepees during this particular mid-afternoon lull. As usual, Alisha was silently working upon the beadwork of an old dress. She forced her concentration upon her hands and upon the intricate pattern which she was steadily restoring. Yet, Gray Eagle frequently distracted her with his magnetic presence, a noisy movement, or his manly odor.

Memories of similar, but happy and relaxed, times played upon her weary senses and hungry heart. As she tried to work, tears slid down her satiny cheeks. Her position denied her husband the view of her dejected state, its voluptuousness heightened by her pregnancy. Alisha halted her task to lay her face upon her open palms. Her fingertips gently massaged her temples, soothing her strained eyes. Her slender fingers travelled down her cheeks and met at her mouth; her forefingers lightly rested upon her lips as her thumbs touched beneath her chin.

Gray Eagle curiously observed her deep quietude for a few moments. He then moved unnoticed to take in her enchanting profile. Alisha had drifted so far away that she was unaware of his eyes, of her surroundings, and of his presence. There was such intense concentration written within her pensive, sad eyes. It annoyed him to have her so close, and yet so far away. Fearing that she was joining her spirit with that of her dead lover, his jealousy mounted.

Captivated by her soft beauty and her obvious vulnerability, he resolved to make her aware of his supremacy, of his reality. "Go to the mats. I have need of your body," he stated crudely.

His laconic, cruel words reached beneath her dreamy barrier to yank her back to reality. Alisha glanced up at his towering frame; she read the look of calloused determination within his eyes. She did not know which emotion burned brighter there: antagonism or lust. She wavered on the verge of rebellion. She swallowed with great difficulty, trying to prevent a flood of nervous tears. Her eyes locked with his, mutely speaking words which he could not understand.

Gray Eagle was perplexed by the despondent expression which filled her misty eyes. He could sense her feeling of total defeat, of yawning hopelessness, of great weariness in body and spirit. He instantly recognized a drastic change in her. There was no pleading, no battling, no tempting, and no flirting. Some vital moment of decision had arrived. He wasn't sure if he was ready or willing to discover it. Yet, disturbed by the mysterious mood and obvious change, he dropped to one knee before her.

"What new trick is this, Wife?" he accused in a

tight voice.

Tears escaped and eased down her cheeks to drop upon her bosom. She looked straight into his hard, obsidian eyes and spoke so softly that he could barely make out her answer. "First, you must promise you will not harm our child. If you wish to take me, you must be gentle this time. I cannot always control my . . . hunger for you when you take me. Sometimes my body needs yours as much as yours needs mine. I know you believe that is wrong, and I know it angers you. But you taught me to respond to you and to want you. I have tried to master my weakness, but I have failed. You must teach me to withdraw as easily as you do. I do not know such things."

Alisha knew that if she must strip her heart and soul in order to protect her child, she would gladly do so. "If you take me now and I . . . respond, your rage and great strength could harm our child. I have already lost one child because of a struggle with a violent man. You must be gentle, or you must not touch me again. I beg you, Wanmdi Hota, do not permit your hatred and cruelty to destroy this child. I have honestly tried to please you, but I never seem to do the correct thing. I have tried to earn your forgiveness and trust, but you will not allow it."

Countless tears flowed from her jade eyes down her ashen cheeks. She made no attempt to brush them aside or to stop them. Too much pain and sadness demanded release. "If I resist you, you punish me. If I comply and obey, your anger and taunts are even greater. I do not know what you want from me. Tell me, and I will do as you command. Cannot your hatred be stayed for the safety of our child? You have taken everything from me; what more do I have to give or for you to take? Do not take this child from me. Is there no way for me to earn your friendship and trust? Is there to be no happiness within

474

our tepee? Will it always be this way between us?" Speechless, Gray Eagle simply stared at her.

Alisha continued. "Was it so terribly wrong to survive your hatred and revenge? Did I not deserve freedom and happiness after so much sacrifice and torment? Why did you have to continue to enslave me? Why couldn't you let me leave in peace? Was I so vile that you wished me dead? What did I do to earn this endless hatred? Is it my fault if the Great Spirit gave me white skin? Am I to blame for the war between the Indian and the white man? Why must I pay for it?

"No matter what you demand of me to insure the safety of my child, I swear to you I will do all within my power to obey you," she earnestly promised.

Gray Eagle continued to stare at her in stony silence. Was this some new trick? Was she carrying his child? Or was she hoping to teach him of how their life could be if he gentled his ways, if he permitted her to respond to him? Was she lying to earn his mercy and kindness? Was she trading for more time to trick him?

Her shoulders shuddered with the full force of her surfaced anguish. Her chin and lips quivered. His cold silence told her that he either did not believe her or was not convinced of her sincerity. She painfully accused, "Damn you for igniting this fire which I cannot extinguish . . . you should not have shown me what it was like to have . . ."

She took a deep, ragged breath as she halted her confession. She moistened her dry lips. She fused her eyes with his and asked, "How long must I continue to pay for my many mistakes? I cannot change the past or recall my actions . . . nor can you, Wanmdi Hota. All I ask is the life of my child, nothing more."

Her choice of words failed to shed any light on their

475

mutual misunderstanding. In fact, they seemed to perfectly fit Gray Eagle's preconceived ideas of her guilt. Yet, they also rang with accurate facts and with logical emotions. Perhaps . . .

Greatly distressed and moved by the effect of her words, Gray Eagle battled his overwhelming desire to relent and to fully accept her terms. But, could she be trusted this time? She had previously deceived him with this same look of innocence and sincerity. If she were pregnant, he had only her word this child was his. How could such a thing be possible in such a short time? In the past, they had slept together many months and she had not borne his child. Perhaps there was no child . . . perhaps he was not the father this time either . . . several times she had said, "My child . . ."

"Who is the child's father, Alisha?" he tersely asked.

His doubting question was like a knife in her aching heart. She drilled her eyes into his. "I have slept with no man except you. There can be no doubt the child is yours, whether you choose to accept him or not."

Confronted by the claim in her first statement, he could only assume she was lying about everything. Powchutu said she was carrying their child when they escaped together; he had found her married to another man. Now, she dared to claim purity in heart and in body! "Will you still claim the child is mine when he comes out with yellow hair and sky eyes?" he challenged coldly.

Of course! He naturally assumed she had slept with her second husband. "Jeffery never touched me! That day at the fort when you came for me and then destroyed it, he was injured in some strange way. He could not make love to any woman. Besides, I would have killed him if he had tried! That was why he set the bounty on Indian scalps. At least, that's what I overheard one night. I would die before sleeping with him!" she openly admitted, her eyes blazing in disgust at the thought of his touch.

Gray Eagle grinned wickedly at the knowledge of Jeffery's accident and Alisha's celibate life with him. At least his old enemy had not taken her. "You have a deadly way of getting rid of unwanted men. Why should I trust your words? You have betrayed me before. What if the child looks like the scout?" he asked, taking into consideration the other man in her life.

Confusion flickered noticeably in her eyes. It quickly changed to anger as she heatedly charged, "Do you wish to deny our child so badly that you would say such a vile thing? I would never sleep with a friend who is like a brother to me! That would be sinful! Of all men, only you know the secrets of my heart! For months you deceived me about your knowledge of English! You knew all I said and all I felt! I have never been a whore for any man but you!" she shouted.

"Then why were you carrying the scout's child before you left here?" he snarled, recalling his last conversation with the scout in full detail. "You speak half-truths, for you whored with him at the fort!"

"You're crazy and vile! Powchutu never touched me! No matter how much you detest the idea of having a half-breed child by me, both babies are yours! You should have thought about the possibility of a child when you raped me time and time again! Powchutu was like my brother, nothing more. He loved me and wanted to marry me. But I was already bound in marriage to you. I only considered his offer of marriage when I learned I was carrying your child. The child was in enough trouble just being half-breed; he certainly did not need to enter the world without a father's name, or as the bastard son of the notorious Gray Eagle! I did not know I was pregnant when I left here with Powchutu. If I had known about the baby, perhaps it would have changed what happened that last day. Perhaps I could have halted your . . ."

Not wanting to refresh such bitter memories or to remind him of his evil deed, she did not complete her accusation. He mistakenly finished her sentence to himself: halted your murder.

"When I wanted to return here with the news of our child," Alisha went on, "Powchutu refused to bring me back. He knew what you would do; he knew how you would feel about me and the child. He warned me you would not accept us back. He was right, wasn't he?"

He did not answer her, curious doubts plaguing him about the scout's claim.

Alisha tearfully insisted, "I swear to you on my life and the life of my child, it was your son I carried then. Just as this is your child," she added, touching her abdomen. Fearing that Gray Eagle actually suspected her of sleeping with Powchutu, she vowed, "No man has ever entered my body except you. This I swear, or may the Great Spirit strike me dead this very instant."

When Gray Eagle remained in pensive silence and studied her face intently, she added, "I should not feel joy and relief at the death of any man; but with Jeffery, I do. As impossible as it sounds, his cruelty and hatred were far greater than yours. He was an evil man; his heart and soul were ruled by the devil himself. He deserved to die. Many lives, both Indian and white, will be spared by your act of justice and courage."

"If that is true, then why did you marry him? Why did you not marry the scout?" Gray Eagle probed, knowing there were some secrets yet unrevealed. Perhaps the scout had died before they could join. Perhaps the scout had only claimed the child was his. Yet, there was some reason why Alisha believed she had to run off with Powchutu.

"Because he forced me to, much as you did long ago," she admitted honestly. Feeling the desperate need to air many things in the open while her husband was truly listening to her for the first time, she continued, "I had no money, no place to go, and no one to help me. He threatened to reveal the truth about me and you. He taunted me with another existence such as the one I endured at the fort. It was winter. There were no jobs to earn money. I had lost our child. I was tired and weak. Powchutu had been killed. I was hurt, confused, and lonely. The choice was between marrying him or becoming a whore. Since he could not touch me and wanted me only as a show-piece, I agreed."

Alisha's eyes darkened with unspeakable horrors. "It did not take long to see my terrible mistake. He was an evil and cruel man, more so than you. He was embittered by his accident. Whoredom would have been better than marriage to him." She laughed in sarcastic bitterness. "In a crazy sort of way, you rescued me from him a second time, just like long ago . . ."

Overwhelmed with her memories, Alisha felt the urgency to be alone and wanted some privacy for a time. She stated, "I need to leave for a while. If you wish, we can talk when I return. If not, then I will obey your commands." Gray Eagle made no attempt to stop her as she stood up and exited their tepee.

Gray Eagle rubbed the back of his hand across his mouth in total exasperation. Something was wrong, but what? How could a woman lie so easily and so convincingly? Why did she have to appear so sincere and tormented? There were so many contradictions in her claims and behavior. Gray Eagle was so mixed up that he could not think straight. Alisha was an enigma that fascinated and charmed him. If he only knew the truth. . . .

Had she radically changed since her last betrayal? Was she sincere and truthful this time? Or was there some other vital clue still missing in this tormenting riddle? If she spoke the truth now, the scout was lying before. If the first child was his and she . . .

The loud sound of swift, thundering hoofbeats captured his attention. A familiar voice shouted louder than the others. He quickly left his tepee to learn why his friend Joe Kenny had come to see him. As he came forward, a frantic Joe rushed to meet him. Several braves held back the desperate man. Following Gray Eagle's order for his release, Joe faced the warrior.

"Where is she, Wanmdi Hota? Have you harmed her yet?" Joe nearly screamed at him. Traces of fear and tension lined Joe's face.

Joe had spoken to him in English. Naturally Gray Eagle pretended not to understand him. "Kuwa, Koda Joe. Ia tipi," he stated calmly.

"Damnit, Wanmdi Hota! Where is Alisha? What have you done to her this time?" he shouted in rising anger and anxiety.

The warrior's eyes narrowed and darkened at Joe's brazen tone and dauntless attack. Through tight lips and gritted teeth, he asked Joe why he was shouting. How dare this man come to his village and demand the whereabouts and condition of his wife! Friend or not, this was unforgivable!

Joe recklessly sneered in rising fury when Gray Eagle continued his ignorance of English. "I know your dark secret! Friends do not lie to each other or betray a trust! She told me, but I have told no one. What have you done with her? I saw your hand in the destruction of Yellow-hair. Did you kill her along the way, or did you sell her to some other man?"

The contempt in Joe's voice and eyes alarmed and infuriated Gray Eagle. "Iyasni!" he commanded Joe to silence and to respect. "Wicaste wanzi tohni icu kte sni! Winyan de mitawa! Ia tipi. Kuwa!" he arrogantly ordered Joe to come to his tepee to talk.

Upon entering the tepee, Joe immediately attacked his previous words, "You say she is yours and no man will take her from you. If that is true, then why did you try to kill her? Why did you force her to flee for her life? Why did you send her into such danger and evil at the hands of Yellow-hair? I did not know Wanmdi Hota was a coward, a man without honor or mercy! I should kill you for all you have done to her. Set her free, or I must challenge you to the death for her return," he boldly announced in grave seriousness.

Gray Eagle quickly and unknowingly reacted to his unexpected charges. He easily slipped into English and coldly stated, "Wanmdi Hota is no coward! Mercy and honor do not belong to betrayers! I should strike you dead for these insults! She loved the scout Powchutu! She escaped to marry him! She carried his child while she joined with me! I should demand her life as payment for her treachery, but she lives," he sneered, deeply offended by Joe's insults and livid animosity.

Joe gaped at him in astonishment. "Where did you get such ridiculous ideas? She has never loved any man but you! She carried your child! Powchutu was her friend, nothing more. Show her to me. Let us speak together. Prove to me she is safe and well," he demanded.

"How do you know such things?" Gray Eagle demanded in a crisp tone. "Why have you come to find her?"

"When she left here, she came to my cabin. She had lost the child and was dying. It took me many days to save her life. There was a knife wound on her shoulder. It grew red and swollen. She became feverish. She spoke much during those days and nights. When she was well again, she told me many other things. Why did you leave her in the wilderness to die? Why did you not kill her quickly and mercifully? I had not thought you so cruel to one so weak and helpless. Without food, water, or protection, Wanmdi Hota! To just ride away and leave her there to die! I must hear this from my koda. Why did you wish her dead in this cruel manner?"

Gray Eagle was bewildered. "Your words make no sense, Koda Joe. The scout Powchutu shot me and left me for dead. Alisha left with him. When my wounds healed, their trail was lost to me forever. When I sought out my enemy Yellow-hair, she was his wife," he snarled with scorn. It was clear to him that someone had lied to his friend Joe.

Joe saw that the warrior was telling the truth. He tried to clear up this treacherous mystery. "Then why did you not return to her side? She waited where you left her for two days. She suffered without water or food. Powchutu found her and saved her life. Why would you claim he shot you? He said you had returned to your camp. He said you told your people she was dead. Powchutu told me how he searched for her after you returned to camp. He knew she was not dead! He found her right where you had left her to die! When he told Alisha you would not return for her, she wanted to come here to face you with your betrayal. Powchutu would not allow it. Why did you hurt her in this cruel way? She loved you. She even saved your life! She is too precious to destroy."

"I could not return to her side!" Gray Eagle cried in

fury. "She sent the scout to kill me! They escaped together! He said she carried his child! He revealed her lies and deceit to me! She tricked me! She betrayed me! I loved her and joined with her! She was like my own heart! She wanted the scout, not me. I have made her pay for her betrayal," he confessed, unable to curb his tongue.

"Somebody lies!" Joe insisted. "Powchutu said you left her to die. He told her you had returned to camp and would never come back for her. She was alone and unprotected for two days, with no food or water. She believes you tried to kill her. She believes you hated her and betrayed her," Joe told the troubled man before him.

Suspicion and doubt began to gnaw at both men. They stared at each other as the truth began to dawn on them.

"She told you these things?" Gray Eagle asked in disbelief.

"Powchutu told me while Alisha lay dying in my cabin. He was sad and angry. He blamed himself for her attack by those two white trappers. He spoke of his great love for her. He said he wanted to marry her. She refused him; she still felt married to you in her heart. I saw him plead with her for her love and acceptance. She could not give them to the scout, for she loved you. Many times she cried because she still loved and wanted you, even after your cruel betrayal."

Joe breathed deeply, then went on. "When she was feverish, she spoke of her love for you and of your treachery. When she was well, she told me of her days with you. Many times she wept and asked me, 'Why did he do this, Joe? Why did he hate me so much? Why did he betray my love?' She did not betray you, Wanmdi Hota. All she did was love you and accept you."

Joe witnessed the look of grief and shame which was growing within the warrior's eyes. "When she learned of the child, she wanted to return to you. She hoped the child would end your hatred and cruelty. Powchutu talked her out of coming back to you. He convinced her you would seek revenge. She wanted this child of yours because it was all she could have of you. She cried many nights because she lost both you and the child. Powchutu was only a brother to her. I saw this with my own eyes. I also saw her pain and loneliness. I listened to her tears. I held her in my arms and comforted her as she wept over your loss and betrayal."

Guilt and dread tormented Gray Eagle. If Joe's words were true . . . his piercing gaze alit on Alisha's new headband, reminding him of a missing clue. "They lied to you, Koda Joe. She sent me a parting gift to prove her hatred. The scout gave it to me before he shot me. She sent me the headband from our joining. She said she no longer needed the protection of Shalee."

Joe instantly argued, "That's impossible! She still had her wedding heyake and headband when she came to my cabin. The day before she left my cabin for the St. Louis settlement, I found her crying as she was preparing to leave. In her pain, she was trying to destroy the dress. She told me how she got it from Brave Bear. She said you fought a challenge to join with her. She told me about the joining ceremony. When she spoke of how you looked that night, her eyes and voice were filled with great love. The scout could not have given you the headband; it is at this moment in my cabin. I will bring it to you if you doubt my words." Joe went on to accurately describe Alisha's wedding dress and the headband with its fluffy white feather. He recounted her tales about the feather incidents, the ones which she had fortunately told him that last day.

Gray Eagle hurried to his parfleche and snatched out

its contents. He seized the bloodstained headband and held it up to view. For the first time ever, he examined it closely and intensely. His sudden enlightenment was agonizing. This was not the one from their joining; it was very similar, but noticeably different upon close study. But until this very day, the treacherous item had remained where he had placed it the moment after showing it to White Arrow.

At that discovery, it required very little for Gray Eagle to realize what had really happened that supposedly traitorous day. He and Joe gradually pieced together a picture which ravaged his heart and tore at his reason. Joe completed the tormenting tale with the details of Alisha's life with Powchutu and Jeffery. The riddle was solved; the puzzle complete.

Gray Eagle anxiously paced the confines of his tepee as bits of conversation echoed in his mind, this time with clarity and meaning. Now he could comprehend Alisha's honest confusion, her fearful resistance, her vivid suspicion, and her silent suffering. All of this time she had believed him to be the deceiver and the betrayer, just as he had placed the guilt and blame upon her innocent shoulders.

He could not bear to recall what he had done to her these past weeks. Even thinking him guilty of such cruelty and deceit, she had been willing to forgive him and to begin a new life. Yet, he had not offered her that same understanding and mercy. He had accused her of terrible things, called her vile names, treated her with coldness and brutality. He had refused her love and touch. He had tormented her with her need for him. The truth . . .

Alisha had truly loved him and wanted him. She had not deceived him. She had waited for him to return that fateful day. She had thought him guilty of leaving her there to die. She did not know of the scout's lies and treachery. She did not know of his own wounds. The child had been his son, just as she had vowed. She had spoken the truth, but his blind hatred and jealousy concealed it from him. No man had taken her except him. . . . She now carried another child, his child. . . . He had hurt her deeply. He had shamed her, defiled her, tormented her . . . all because she loved him. How she must surely hate him now!

"If he was not dead, Koda Joe, I would hunt him down and torture him for many moons before I cut out his traitorous heart. He has tricked us both. I have punished her for deeds she did not do," he confessed.

Joe tensed, hoping he had not arrived too late. "Where is she, Wanmdi Hota? What have you done to her? She is innocent; you must set her free. Where is she?" he asked again, afraid of the coming answer.

"You remain here. I must go to her with the truth. If she did not carry my child, I would free her if she asked. Perhaps she hates me now. Perhaps she will not forgive me. But I cannot lose them both. If she will not hear my words, you must speak with her, Koda Joe."

"Do you really love her and want her?" Joe felt compelled to ask, knowing his answer would determine his future help.

"I have always loved her and wanted her. She is my heart. She is my life and joy. She is like a part of me. I could not kill her, for I could not give her up. I believed she hated me and tricked me, but I needed her too much to avenge myself with her death. Somehow I must find the words to gain her forgiveness and trust. I must go to her now. I must tell her of the scout's treachery. Great Spirit, help me to make her understand," he prayed aloud, feeling the damage was irreparable.

Alisha knelt by the sparkling, murmuring stream. She silently prayed for peace between herself and her husband and for the safety of their unborn child. She sat upon the green grass and gazed into the clear waters, watching the circular motions of a small whirlpool which reminded her of the swirling maelstrom in her mind. She yearned to return to Gray Eagle's tepee to forge a new truce; yet, she feared to hear his renewed suspicions and hostilities.

Why did she feel there was some threatening, unknown factor which denied her his trust and love? He suspected her of sleeping with two other men. He couldn't accept the fact this child was his, nor that the other child had been his. She had told him the truth; he had no reason to mistrust her or to be jealous and resentful of those other men. Why was he so different this time? Why did he seem to be punishing her for some unknown sin? He made such strange accusations and comments which she did not comprehend. If he hated her so much for surviving his treachery, then why force her to be his wife? If he did not want her to bear his child, then why make love to her? If she lost this child, there would be no reason to live . . . no reason to continue to endure his rejection.

Gray Eagle stepped into her blurred line of vision. Her frightened gaze rushed upwards to meet his unreadable one. "I was about to return. It was so beautiful and peaceful out here, I . . ." she stammered in panic, fearing the reason for his sudden arrival.

He dropped to one knee before her. He studied her for a time, wondering how to open an old wound and to heal it properly. His hand reached out to caress away the lines of fear and sadness in her expression. She automatically flinched from his touch, terror glimmered in her wide eyes. Her breathing quickened.

"I have hurt you deeply, Little One," he whispered in a strained tone, calling her a name he had not used since that day in the desert. "I have been cold and cruel to you since I found you again. This was wrong, Alisha. I ask your forgiveness and acceptance. Return your love to me," he tenderly pleaded in a husky voice.

Astonished, suspicious lights entered her emerald eyes. She leaned away from his closeness. "What new trick is this?" she spoke his own previous doubt aloud. "I have sworn to obey you in all things. You need not trick me or lie to me. What is your command?"

"I command you to love me as I love you, to want me as I want you," he answered the stunned girl. "I do not lie or trick you, Alisha. Powchutu is the one who tricked you. I did not betray you that last day; I did not ride away and leave you there to die. I could not return to you because he came after me and shot me. The scout said you wanted me dead. He said you loved him. He said you carried his child. He said you two tricked me in Black Cloud's camp. He said it was a trap to be rid of me. He said you never loved me. He said you were escaping to marry him. He lied to me. He tricked me. I believed you guilty of betraying me that day. I believed you guilty of carrying his child while you joined with me. I believed you married to Yellow-hair. These were all lies. All tricks. I was wrong to hurt you. I did not leave you to die. Powchutu lied," he repeated, hoping his words were sinking through her confused mind.

"I do not believe you. Why do you say such things! What new torment is this vow of love and need?

Powchutu had always told me the truth. He was the only friend I had. He was the one who rescued me when you left me to die. For two days I waited for you! I stupidly feared something had happened to you! Yet, I knew nothing and no one could ever harm you. You never came back for me! When my friend Powchutu found me, he told me what you had done. O, Wanmdi Hota, why didn't you just cut out my heart with your knife! That couldn't have hurt any more! Was it such a crime to love you? I tried to win your love, to reach you with the force of mine. But your hatred of the white man consumed you. Your hunger for revenge cost the life of our child. I shall never forgive you for that! Powchutu couldn't have told you I was carrying a child; he was just as surprised as I was when I discovered the truth. We had been gone for weeks by then!"

Tears began to come again. Yet, the dam had burst and the flood waters of pent-up anguish rushed out. "Do you know how it feels to kill a man with your hands, to have his blood on you?"

Realizing the absurdity of that question to a fierce warrior, she sighed and answered it herself, "Of course, you do! Your life is full of death and killing. Mine was not, not until I met you. God, how I have paid for the mistake of loving you. You took my uncle, my friends, my home, my innocence, my child, my happiness, everything! But that wasn't enough for you! You had to torment me, humiliate me, hurt me, and then try to kill me. My God, Wanmdi Hota, let it be over! Let us find peace together. Love me or release me, even to death if necessary. I cannot live this way! I will not lose this child, I will not!" she screamed at him.

Gray Eagle held Alisha's wrists and sought out her emerald eyes. "Most of your words are true, Alisha," he

489

said sincerely. "I have sought to hurt you as I was hurt, to punish you for something you did not do. I ask for forgiveness. Upon my life and honor, I did not betray you! Powchutu lied to both of us, Little One. I love you. You are the bird of my heart. You must hear this truth."

Time crawled by as they spoke together. Whatever argument Alisha challenged him with, Gray Eagle gently and patiently parried it. He answered every single question and doubt. He silenced her long enough to relate the tale he and Joe had figured out. He forced her to recognize the treachery of her friend. He forced her to see how he had felt and why he had so cruelly tormented her since bringing her home.

He began with their last day in the desert and recounted his feelings to that very minute. At his firm insistence, Alisha did the same. He pointed out why Powchutu would attempt such treachery: obsessive love for her and mistrust of him. He related how her enforced silence had denied them the truth sooner. He pointed out how many of her statements explained his errors in judgment.

Yet, when all was said and done, neither could find the words to breach the wide and pain-filled gulf between them. At last the entire truth was out, but was it too late to matter?

Alisha stood up and walked away from Gray Eagle; her cramped legs and taut body demanded some relief. She halted near a large tree beside the riverbank. She leaned back against it. There was so much to ponder. Could she forgive all the agony which Gray Eagle had brought into her life? Could she forgive him for refusing to doubt her guilt? Could she forget his continued hostility when she had pleaded for truce? Could she still love him and want him after all of this suffering?

Her hands unknowingly cupped her womb. As she thought of the child growing there, she also thought about his father. She could envision his sensual smile, his jet eyes, his inviting embrace, and his intoxicating magnetism. Just as her heart and mind placed this tempting illusion into her mind's eye, Gray Eagle stepped before her gaze.

Their eyes met and fused. So much was said without words. She weakened at the sight of such love and desire written in his gaze. "Can you forgive me, Cinstinna? Can you love me again? I cannot bear to lose you again. Just as you thought me guilty, I thought you guilty. I should not have hurt you so deeply. I should have demanded an explanation. I should have known the scout lied. Yet, there was such skill in his words. Was there not, Little One? Did you not accept his lies as truth? Did you not question me? Did you not think me guilty? Our time together was too short; we had not learned trust and loyalty. Our love was so strong that we feared to lose it; we feared to trust it. I cannot let you go now. You carry our child. Never will I harm you again. Can we not share love and happiness?"

Alisha did not answer him. He cupped her face between his hands. His eyes pleaded as much as his voice did. "I love you, Alisha. I need you. I have taken no woman since I lost you. I have taken no woman since the first day my eyes saw you. You are a part of me. Forgive me. Love me once again."

He pulled her into his arms, hoping the heated contact with his body would sway her opinion. Alisha's arms encircled his waist. She looked up at him and softly whispered, "I will try to understand. I will try to forgive you. There has been so much pain and sadness since that day I lost you. We must learn from these mistakes and

491

hardships. We must never be torn apart again. No matter what anyone says, we must trust each other. No matter what happens or how things look, we must first listen to each other's words. If we have been given another chance to find love and happiness, we must earn it."

She smiled up at him, her eyes glowing with love and hope. "I do love you with all my heart, Wanmdi Hota. You are the only man I have ever loved. You are the only man who has taken me. No child has lived within my body except yours. These things I swear to you. All I want is to love you, for us to be happy. I grieve for the pain and suffering Powchutu has given us. I should have . . ."

Gray Eagle silenced her with a gentle finger upon her lips. "There can be no looking back, Alisha. We were both wrong. We must learn trust and acceptance. Our mistakes have cost us a great price. We must share our love and our child. These things I promise you. I cannot take back what I have done to you. I cannot recall my words or punishments. I wish with all my heart I could . . ."

Alisha silenced him with a kiss. For so long she had dreamed of a kiss with fire and love, with truth and honor, with regret and promise, with past and future. When their lips finally parted, each smiled and refused to move away from the other's touch. Their eyes spoke of newer and richer promises, of forgiveness and acceptance, of renewed trust and undying love. He pulled her to him again. His mouth closed over hers. She clung to him, returning the fiery kiss, but wanting far more.

"I take it this means you two have settled things," Joe's voice teased them. They slowly and reluctantly pulled apart; yet, now they knew they had all the time in the world to love.

"Damn if you ain't a sight for worried eyes, Miss Alisha! You had me scared plumb to death! Had to postpone my wedding to come after you. Sure was worth it though," Joe jested merrily.

"Your wedding! Who? When? How?" She shot questions at him in happy excitement.

He grinned happily. This was the first time he had ever seen such glowing lights of love and happiness within her enchanting eyes. Yep, she loved him all right! "I think you know her: Mary O'Hara. She'll make a fine wife for a man like me," he remarked. "Known each other for years. We talk through that sign language I taught her. She's the one who helped me figure out this mystery. Got her waiting for me to return."

Alisha gently disengaged herself from Gray Eagle's possessive embrace. She went to Joe and hugged him tightly and affectionately. "You couldn't have made a wiser or better choice, Joe. I hope you will both be as happy as we plan to be," she declared, sending her husband an enchanting smile, eyes burning with love and desire.

Gray Eagle returned her smile with equal warmth and meaning. "I also wish you much happiness, Koda Joe. I owe you much for bringing me such joy and peace. In time our love would have come to view, but only after much more sadness and pain. Come and bring your wife to see our child when he is born, for he will be the best from both our kinds. The blood of the Indian and the white will join in our child. My wife has spoken the truth, for not all whites are bad," he admitted with a rueful grin as he gazed at his wife and friend: both white-eyes!

Joe thought it best to conceal the news of Mary's child until next time. Powchutu and Jeffery had already caused too much suffering for everyone. This was the time for healing and for growing. This was the season for farewell to winter, to sacrifice, to separation, to suspicion, to hatred.

This was the season for new beginnings and new births. Joe had been wise to come here, for his coming had signalled the lovers' last farewell to the bittersweet past. Joe's heart sang with joy as he watched the look which passed between the English girl and the mighty Sioux warrior . . .

FASCINATING, PAGE-TURNING BLOCKBUSTERS!

BYGONES (1030, $3.75)
by Frank Wilkinson

Once the extraordinary Gwyneth set eyes on the handsome aristocrat Benjamin Whisten, she was determined to foster the illicit love affair that would shape three generations—and win a remarkable woman an unforgettable dynasty!

A TIME FOR ROSES (946, $3.50)
by Agatha Della Anastasi

A family saga of riveting power and passion! Fiery Magdalena places her marriage vows above all else—until her husband wants her to make an impossible choice. She has always loved and honored—but now she can't obey!

THE VAN ALENS (1000, $3.50)
by Samuel A. Schreiner, Jr.

The lovely, determined Van Alen women were as exciting and passionate as the century in which they lived. And through these years of America's most exciting times, they created a dynasty of love and lust!

THE CANNAWAYS (1019, $3.50)
by Graham Shelby

Vowing to rise above the poverty and squalor of her birth, Elizabeth Darle becomes a woman who would pay any price for love—and to make Brydd Cannaway's dynasty her own!

THE LION'S WAY (900, $3.75)
by Lewis Orde

An all-consuming saga that spans four generations in the life of troubled and talented David, who struggles to rise above his immigrant heritage and rise to a world of glamour, fame and success!

A WOMAN OF DESTINY (734, $3.25)
by Grandin Hammill

Rose O'Neal is passionate and determined, a woman whose spark ignites the affairs of state—as well as the affairs of men!